LITTLE DARLINGS

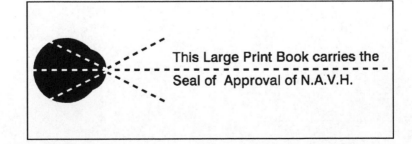

This Large Print Book carries the
Seal of Approval of N.A.V.H.

LITTLE DARLINGS

MELANIE GOLDING

WHEELER PUBLISHING
A part of Gale, a Cengage Company

x

x

x

Farmington Hills, Mich • San Francisco • New York • Waterville, Maine
Meriden, Conn • Mason, Ohio • Chicago

LP F
GOL

Copyright © 2019 by Melanie Golding.
Wheeler Publishing, a part of Gale, a Cengage Company.

ALL RIGHTS RESERVED

Wheeler Publishing Large Print Hardcover.
The text of this Large Print edition is unabridged.
Other aspects of the book may vary from the original edition.
Set in 16 pt. Plantin.

LIBRARY OF CONGRESS CIP DATA ON FILE.
CATALOGUING IN PUBLICATION FOR THIS BOOK
IS AVAILABLE FROM THE LIBRARY OF CONGRESS

ISBN-13: 978-1-4328-6904-5 (hardcover alk. paper)

Published in 2019 by arrangement with the Quick Brown Fox & Company LLC

Printed in Mexico
1 2 3 4 5 6 7 23 22 21 20 19

Dedicated to the memory of
Amber Baxter (nee Fink),
1979–2012

August 17th
Peak District, UK

DS Joanna Harper stood on the viaduct
with the other police officers. On the far
bank, across the great expanse of the reservoir, a woman paused at the water's edge,
about to go in, her twin baby boys held
tightly in her arms.

Harper turned to the DI. "How close are
the officers on that side?"

Dense woodland surrounded the scrap of
shore where the woman stood. Even at this
distance, Harper could see that her legs
were scarlet with blood from the thorns.

"Not close enough," said Thrupp. "They
can't find a way to get to her."

In a fury of thudding, the helicopter flew
over their heads, disturbing the surface of
the reservoir, bellowing its command: *Step
away from the water.* It loomed above the
tiny figure of the mother, deafening and

relentless, but the officers on board wouldn't be able to stop her. There was nowhere in the valley where the craft could make a safe landing, or get low enough to drop the winch.

Through the binoculars, Harper saw the woman collapse into a sitting position on the dried-out silt, her face turned to the sky, still clutching the babies. Perhaps she wouldn't do it, after all.

A memory surfaced then, of what the old lady had said to her:

"She'll have to put them in the water, if she wants her own babies back . . . Right under the water. Hold 'em down."

The woman wasn't sitting at the water's edge anymore; she was knee-deep, and wading further in. The DS kicked off her shoes, climbed up on the rail and prepared to dive.

CHAPTER ONE

The child is not mine as the first was,
I cannot sing it to rest,
I cannot lift it up fatherly
And bliss it upon my breast;
Yet it lies in my little one's cradle
And sits in my little one's chair,
And the light of the heaven she's gone to
Transfigures its golden hair.

From The Changeling by
James Russell Lowell

July 13th
8:10 P.M.

All she cared about was that the pain had been taken away. With it, the fear, and the certainty that she would die, all gone in the space of a few miraculous seconds. She wanted to drift off but then Patrick's worried face appeared, topped by a green hospital cap and she remembered: I'm having my babies. The spinal injection she'd

9

been given didn't just signal the end of the horrendous contractions, but the beginning of a forceps extraction procedure that could still go wrong. The first baby was stuck in the birth canal. So, instead of allowing herself to sink inside her glorious, warm cocoon of numbness and fall asleep — which she hadn't done for thirty-six hours — she tried to concentrate on what was happening.

The doctor's face appeared, near to Lauren's own, the mask pulled down revealing her mouth and most of her chin. The woman's lips were moving as if untethered to her words. It was the drugs, and the exhaustion; the world had slowed right down. Lauren frowned. The doctor was looking at her, but she seemed so far away. She's talking to me, thought Lauren, I should listen.

"Ok, Mrs Tranter, because of the spinal, you won't be able to tell when you have a contraction — so I'll tell you when to push, ok?"

Lauren's mouth formed an "o", but the doctor had already gone.

"Push."

She felt the force of the doctor pulling and her entire body slid down the bed with it. She couldn't tell if she was pushing or not. She made an effort to arrange her face in an expression of straining and tensed her neck muscles, but somewhere in her head a voice said, why bother? They won't be able to tell if I don't push, will they? Maybe I could just have a little sleep.

She shut her eyes.

"Push now."

The doctor pulled again and the dreaminess dispersed as the first one came out. Lauren opened her eyes and everything was back in focus, events running at the right speed, or perhaps slightly too quickly now. She held her breath, waiting for the sound of crying. When it finally came, that sound, thin and reedy, the weakened protest of something traumatised, she cried too. The tears seemed projectile, they were so pent-up. Patrick squeezed her hand.

"Let me see," she said, and that was when the baby was placed on his mother's chest, but on his back, arse-to-chin with Lauren so that all she could see were his folded froggy legs, and a tiny arm, flailing in the air. Patrick bent over them both, squinting at the baby, laughing, then crying and pressing his finger into one little palm.

"Can't you turn him around?" she said, but nobody did. Then she was barely aware of the doctor saying, "push," again, and another pull. The boy was whisked away and the second one placed there.

This time she could reach up and turn the baby to face her. She held him in a cradle made of her two arms and studied his face, the baby studying her at the same time, his little mouth in a trumpeter's pout, no white visible in his half-open eyes but a deep thoughtful blue. Although the babies were genetically identical, she and Patrick had expected that there would be slight differences. They're individuals. Two bonnie boys, she thought with a degree of slightly forced joviality, at the same time as, could I just go to sleep now? Would anyone notice, really?

"Riley," said Patrick, with one hand gently touching Lauren's face and one finger stroking the baby's, "Yes?"

Lauren felt pressured. She thought they might leave naming them for a few days until they got to know them properly. Such a major decision, what if they got it wrong?

"Riley?" she said, "I suppose —"

Patrick had straightened up, his phone in his hand already.

"What about the other one? Rupert?"

Rupert? That wasn't even on the list. It was like he was trying to get names past her while she was distracted, having been pumped full of drugs and laid out flat, paralysed from the chest down, vulnerable to suggestion. Not fair.

"No," she said, a little bit too loudly. "He's called Morgan."

Patrick's brow creased. He glanced in the direction of possibly-Morgan, who was being checked over by the paediatrician. "Really?" He put his phone back in his pocket.

"You can't stay long," said the nurse-midwife to Patrick, as the bed finally rolled into place. Sea-green curtains were whisked out of the way. Lauren wanted to protest: she'd hoped there would be some time to properly settle in with the babies before they threw her husband out of the ward.

The trip from theatre to the maternity ward involved hundreds of metres of corridor. Thousands of metres, maybe. Patrick had been wheeling the trolley containing one of the twins, while the nurse drove the bed containing Lauren, who was holding the other one. The small procession clanked wordlessly along the route through the yellow-lit corridors. At first Lauren thought that Patrick could have offered to swap with the nurse and take the heavier burden, but she soon became glad she hadn't mentioned it. As they approached the ward it was clear the woman knew what she was doing. This nurse, who was half Patrick's height just about, had used her entire bodyweight to counterbalance as the bed swung around a corner and into the bay, then, impressively, she'd stepped up and ridden it like a sailboard into one of the four empty cubicles, the one by the window. There was a single soft "clang" as the head of the bed gently touched the wall. Patrick would only have crashed them into something expensive.

The nurse operated the brake and gave a brisk, "here we are!" before delivering her warning to Patrick, indicating the clock on the wall opposite. "Fifteen minutes," she said.

Her shoes squeaked away up the ward. Lauren and Patrick looked at the babies.

"Which one have you got?" asked Patrick.

She turned the little name tag on the delicate wrist of the sleeping child in her arms. The words *Baby Tranter #1* were written on it in blue sharpie.

"Morgan," said Lauren.

Patrick bent over the trolley containing the other one. Later, everyone would say that the twins looked like their father, but at this moment she couldn't see a single similarity between the fully grown man and the scrunched-up bud of a baby. The boys certainly resembled each other — two peas popped from the same pod, or the same pea, twice. Riley had the same wrinkled little face as his brother, the same long fingers and uncannily perfect fingernails. They made the same expression when they yawned. Slightly irritatingly, someone in theatre had dressed them in identical white sleep suits, taken from the bag Lauren and Patrick had brought with them, though there had been other colours available. She had intended to dress one of them in yellow. Without the name tags they could easily have been mistaken for each other and how would anyone ever know? Thank goodness for the name tags, then. In her arms, Morgan moved his head from side to side and half-opened his eyes. She watched them slowly close.

They'd been given a single trolley for both babies to sleep in. Riley was lying under Patrick's gaze in the clear plastic cot-tray bolted to the top of the trolley. Underneath the baby there was a firm, tightly fitting mattress, and folded at either end of this were two blankets printed with the name of the hospital. The cot was the wrong shape for its cargo. The plastic tray and the mattress were unforgivingly flat, and the baby was a ball. A woodlouse in your palm, one that curls up when frightened. Patrick moved the trolley slightly, abruptly, and Riley's little arms and legs flew out, a five-pointed star. He curled up slowly, at the same speed as his brother's closing eyes. Back in a ball, he came to rest slightly on his side. To hold a baby, it ought to be bowl-shaped, a little nest. Why had no one thought of that before?

"Hello, Riley," said Patrick in an odd squeaky voice. He straightened up. "It sounds weird, saying that."

Lauren reached out and drew the trolley closer to her bed, carefully, trying to prevent the little ball from rolling. She used her one free hand to tuck a blanket over him and down the sides of the mattress, to hold him in place.

"Hello, Riley," she said. "Yeah, it does a bit. I think that's normal, though. We'll get used to it." She turned her face to the child in her arms. "Hello, Morgan," she said. She was still waiting for the rush of love. That one you feel, all at once the second they're born, like nothing you've ever experienced before. The rush of love that people with children always go on about. She'd been looking forward to it. It worried her that she hadn't felt it yet.

She handed Morgan to Patrick, who held

him as if he were a delicate antique pot he'd just been told was worth more than the house; desperate to put him down, unsure where, terrified something might happen. Lauren found it both funny and concerning. When the baby — who could probably sense these things — started to cry, Patrick froze, a face of nearly cartoon panic. Morgan's crying caused Riley to wake up and cry, too.

"Put him in there, next to Riley," said Lauren. The twins had been together all their lives. She wondered what that would mean for them, later on. They'd been with her, growing inside her, for nine months, the three of them together every second of every day for the whole of their existence so far. She felt relief that they were no longer in there, and guilt at feeling that relief, and a great loss that they had taken the first step away from her, the first of all the subsequent, inevitable steps away from her. Was that the love, that guilty feeling? That sense of loss? Surely not.

Patrick placed the squalling package face to face with his double, and, a miracle, the crying ceased. They both reached out, wrapping miniature arms around each other's downy heads, Morgan holding onto Riley's ear. All was calm. From above, they looked like an illusion. An impossibility. Lauren checked again, but as far as she could tell the rush of love still had not arrived.

The fierce nurse squeaked back down the ward at just after nine and began to shoo Patrick away home, which would leave Lauren, still numb in the legs and unable to move, alone to deal with every need and desire of the two newborn babies.

"You can't leave me," said Lauren.

"You can't stay," said the nurse.

"I'll be back," said Patrick, "first thing. As soon as they open the doors. Don't worry."

He kissed her head, and both babies. He walked away a little too quickly.

CHAPTER TWO

After Patrick had gone, Lauren sat, dry-eyed in the quiet, knowing there was chaos to come. For the moment, though, they slept. From the bed she observed the twin co-coons that were the babies, swaddled in white, with a disbelieving awe: did I do that?

The hospital was not silent, neither was it dark, although by now the windows were made of black mirrors. Lauren's reflection had deep shadowed holes where it should have had eyes. A vision of horror. She turned away.

The building had a hum of several different tones forming a drone, a cold chord that wouldn't resolve. Lauren put her head on her pillow and realised that one of the singers was her hospital bed, which harmonised dissonant with the slightly lower, much more powerful hum of the heating. Then there was the hum of her bedside lamp, which had a buzzy texture that she actually found quite soothing. She closed her eyes, still propped in a sitting position with the bright lamp blasting through her eyelids. She breathed deeply in and out, three, four times. Sleep was coming. She'd waited so long for this.

A whimper from one of the babies struck through her thin slumber with an urgency that felt physical. Her eyes were forced to open, but every time she blinked she could see a backdrop of red with dark streaks where a map of the veins in her eyelids had been burned onto her retinas. She batted the lamp away from her face with a clang.

Perhaps he'll go back to sleep, she thought, with a desperate optimism. Riley's whimper became a *cluck,* and then a *cluck cluck cluck waaaa,* and then she had to take action. One crying baby was enough.

She pulled the trolley as close as it would come, but found she couldn't lift him. She needed one of her hands to stop her numbed useless lower half falling out of the bed as she leaned over, but two to lift the baby, with a hand under his head and one under his body, as she had been shown. Riley's mouth was open, his eyes screwed shut, legs starting to stretch out and arms reaching, searching trembling in the air for some resistance, finding none.

Lauren thought about the womb and how it had contained them both, fed them and kept them warm. She felt bad for them, that nature had taken away their loving home and put her there in its place; that they'd been pulled from her uterus and placed in her arms, where she was the only thing standing between them and oblivion, them and failure, them and disappointment. She, who couldn't even pick up her boy and fill his little tummy, which was now, face it, her only purpose in life.

Morgan heard his brother's crying. He was shifting in his sleep, not quite awake but he would be soon. Lauren reached out and gathered up the front of Riley's sleep suit in her fist until he was curled around it tightly in a storks' bundle. She held her breath and lifted him one-handed, worrying about his head dangling backwards on his elastic neck for the second it took to transport him to her lap. But then she figured, two hours ago during the birth he'd been gripped with metal tongs and pulled by the head with great force on the confidence that that neck, seemingly so fragile and delicate, would bring the rest of him along safely.

As she struggled to feed Riley, Morgan woke up properly and cried with hunger. She listened, helpless, the sound an alarm she couldn't turn off, a scream wired directly into her body, taking up all of the space in her brain so that she could think of nothing but feeding him, of doing what was necessary to soothe the boy, to make it stop. After a few agitated minutes, she found herself sliding a little finger into the corner of Riley's mouth to unlatch him. With difficulty, she placed him back in the cot, one-handed, straining crane-like to swap him over with his hungrier brother. For a while there was only the sound of little lips smacking, one baby feeding and the other contemplating until Riley remembered he hadn't finished his meal and thought that his heart might break.

She fed one while the other demanded to be fed, and went on in this way like Sisyphus, thinking there had to be an end to it but finding that there was not. She pressed the buzzer for help, but when the midwife came she seemed so irritated and abrupt that Lauren didn't feel she could call again. The night stretched out and jumped forward as her shredded brain tried to doze, to rest and recharge after the labour, the day and night and day of not sleeping and then this night, this long night of lifting and swivelling and feeding and sitting in positions that hurt for scores of minutes too long, her back complaining and her arm muscles torn and her nipples cracking and bleeding and drying out only to be thrust into the hard, wet vice of her baby's latch. And then, as the drugs from the blessed injection wore off, there was the pain from the destruction of her pelvic floor. Where they had cut her and sewn her, where her mucus membranes had been stretched to the point at which they tore.

She lost track of whether she slept. It seemed to Lauren that she did not, yet she found herself setting one baby down gently in the cot, blinking once and noticing that most of an hour had passed.

The curtain between her bay and the next had been drawn across. The nurses must have brought in another new mum. The twins were quietly dozing, inverted commas curling towards each other, peaceful.

From the other side of the curtain she could hear a cooing, a mother talking to a baby. The voice was low, muttering, somehow unsettling. Lauren couldn't work out why it sounded odd. She listened for a while longer. Just a woman, murmuring nothings to her baby — why was it troubling her? There were baby sounds too, though this baby sounded like a bird, squawking softly, quacking, chirping to be fed. Then something else, another sound, more like a kitten. Lauren let her eyes close and drifted, dreaming of a woman with a cat and a bird, an old woman all skin and sinew, holding an animal in each hand by the scruff and feeding them worms from a bucket. Both hands full, the old woman used her long black tongue to encircle and trap each worm, pulling the wriggling thing free of the squirming tangle before trailing it into the mouths, the open beak of the bird and the gaping jaws of the kitten. The kitten's needle teeth nipped at the membrane skin of the creature and it recoiled, panicked, in a futile effort to escape before it was dropped, falling from the mother's black unfurling tongue across the beak and the jaws of the bird and the cat, each snapping at the fat wet worm until they tore it in two and turned away from each other, mouths working with smacks and gulps, sulkily satisfied with half. The old woman was telling the animals something as they fed, some urgent legacy, the details of which Lauren couldn't quite catch, whispering, pressing on them the importance that they remember everything she said to them, that their lives depended on it. In the dream, the animals listened for as long as they could, but then they cried out because they needed more food. And as they cried out, the sounds became less like a bird and a cat and more like human babies, a squawk became a cry, the kitten's meow trailed off to a soft baby whimper. In the dream, the woman held the animals and shushed them as they transformed, rocked them gently as their human forms emerged and then she laid the twin babies gently in the hospital cot.

Lauren's eyes flew open. The dream lingered — there was a smell of something animal in her nostrils and she shook her head to rid herself of the disturbing images. All was silent except the breathing of her twins and the nearly imperceptible sounds of another set of twins in the next bed. Another set of twins. The woman in the bed next to hers had twins too, she was suddenly sure of it. She listened carefully — two babies snuffling, definitely. What were the chances? The dream forgotten, Lauren was pleased — she wanted to peek around the curtain and say hi but she couldn't have reached. Besides, it was still the middle of the night. She'd have to wait until morning. Two sets of twins in one day. Maybe that was a hospital record.

Stuck in the bed, her body weakened by the spinal injection, sleep-deprived, sore and exhausted, Lauren consoled herself. At least she'd have someone to talk to now, someone who'd been through something similar. The sun was creeping into the edges of the windows, lending its peach to the white and yellow of the electric light on the ward. Behind the curtain, all fell quiet; the other mother of twins must have fallen asleep. Lauren shut her eyes again, but the moment her eyelids met she could hear the breathy swoosh of her baby's cheek rubbing up and down on the cot sheet as his little head moved left to right, searching out a nipple. She forced her eyes open, pushed her body into an upright position, braced herself for the pain in her arms as she swivelled and lifted the child to feed.

CHAPTER THREE

Come away, O, human child
To the waters and the wild
With a faery hand in hand
For the world's more full of weeping than
You can understand
      From *The Stolen Child* by W.B. Yeats

July 14th
One Day Old
9:30 A.M.
The nurse swished the curtain back against the wall, jolting Lauren awake. There was nothing behind it, only an empty space where a bed could be parked.

She had shut her eyes between feeds and the world jumped forward three hours. The sun was up and getting on with things, drowning out the electric lights and transforming the room, from a cave to an open space. From the window there was a view of the car park three floors down, and across

27

the way she could see the main entrance to the A&E department. The wide sky was a shade of bright grey but it would be hot, as it had been every day for all of July. Fresh now, clammy later. The heatwave had been going on for a week, and the forecast was more of the same. It was set to break records.

The nurse was removing a catheter bag filled with yellow fluid from below the bed. She dropped it in a bucket and reached for an empty one.

"Where's the woman who was brought in last night?" asked Lauren.

"Who — Mrs Gooch, over there?"

The bay diagonally across from Lauren was occupied. Mrs Gooch seemed to be asleep, a serene baby tucked into the bed with her. The mother had long red hair arranged artfully across the pillow and pale bare arms — the effect was akin to a Klimt painting.

"No, I don't think so. I thought there was someone next to me. I was pretty sure."

Riley was awake. His windmilling arm smacked his sleeping brother across the head and Morgan's eyes opened in shock, then screwed up shut in sorrow, his mouth a little zero of injustice. There was a pause while Morgan inhaled expansively, a comprehensive gathering of breath that would certainly be used for something loud. The long wail, when it finally came, hit Riley's face and crumpled it. Riley, in turn, inhaled at length and soon the anguish was doubled. Within a few seconds the sound built into a crescendo of indignation that interrupted their mother's thought pattern like scissors through ribbon. Lauren flapped her hands, struggling to know what to do, where to start, who to tend to. Both of them crying, and only one of her. She knew she had to be quick — she'd read so much about attachment disorder and rising cortisol levels in the brains of babies in pregnancy and early childhood. You couldn't leave children to cry. It had damaging effects and might do radical things to brain development, causing terrible long-term consequences. Already they seemed so angry.

"Please," she said to the nurse, feeling her eyes filling up, "can you help me?"

"Hey petal, no need for that." The nurse whipped three thin tissues from the box by the bed, pressed them into Lauren's hand and turned to lift baby Morgan, a furious, purple-faced wide-mouthed thing from which came forth a sound that made you want to cover your ears. "There's enough crying round here already without you joining in."

"I'm sorry," said Lauren, wiping her eyes and blowing her nose, then uncovering herself ready to feed. "I don't know what's wrong with me."

In what seemed like less than half a minute the nurse plugged Lauren firmly into the twins. She manoeuvred Lauren's body, lifting the weight of her breasts, helping her get into a position to feed both at once, a rugby ball baby under each arm with pillows holding them in place. The nurse was so efficient, so quick and practised. It made Lauren wonder how she would ever manage on her own.

"There. Snug as bugs."

She started to stride away, but Lauren stopped her.

"That woman over there," she said, "has she got twins?"

Mrs Gooch had opened her eyes. She looked as fresh and unlikely as Sleeping Beauty. Even as Lauren spoke it was obvious that there was only one child contained in the idyll — baby Gooch was with her in the bed and there was no sign of any other.

"No," said the nurse, "just the one. Yours are the only twins we've got at the moment."

Patrick brought vegetable sushi, fruit and dark chocolate. "Thanks," she said, without gratitude. She didn't fancy anything but white-bread toast.

"You need something with nutrients in," he said.

She stuck her lip out. She ought to be able to eat whatever she felt like. "All food has nutrients in. Sugar is a nutrient. So is alcohol."

"Alright, clever clogs. You need something with vitamins. Tell me what you want, I can go to the supermarket and bring you something else this afternoon at visiting time. Avocado?"

The thought of avocado made her nauseous. She wanted crisps.

Patrick took photos of Lauren holding the twins as they slept, and then turned the screen for her to see. In the images she was both gaunt and bloated, her smile weak and her hair greasy.

"Don't put that online. I look terrible."

Patrick looked up from his phone. "Oh, I, sort of already did." The phone started pinging with notifications as comments came in. He tilted the screen to show her:

Congratulations!
Glad you are all well!
Hope to see you soon!
Soooo beautiful!!!
Wow well done you guys can't wait to
meet the boys Xxx!

Later she took matching photos of him, holding the twins while he sat in the vinyl-covered armchair next to the bed. His appearance was just the same as always. Maybe he seemed a bit tired, perhaps as if he had a mild hangover, but there was no radical change. He'd lost a tiny bit of weight recently and people — friends of theirs — were saying how much better he looked for it. Where was the justice in that? They were both parents of twins now but it was her body that had been sacrificed.

Patrick put both babies back into the cot. He was handling them with less trepidation than before, putting them down as if they were fruits that bruised easily rather than explosives that needed decommissioning. He sat down but he kept one hand in the cot with them, counting fingers, self-consciously trying out nursery rhymes he could only half remember.

"Round and round the garden, like a dum de dum. Like a . . . what is it like?"

"Like a teddy bear," said Lauren.

"Is it?"

"Yes. I think so." She pictured her mother's finger, tracing circles on her palm. The anticipation of the *one step, two steps, tickle you under there.* More rhymes came to her then: Jack and Jill, Georgie Porgie, a blackbird to peck off a nose. It was like lifting the lid on a forgotten box of treasure. These gifts, not thought of for years, there in her memory all this time, waiting for her to need them, to pass them on.

"Teddy bear?" said Patrick, still sceptical. "Well, that doesn't make sense."

Lauren put her hand in the cot, too. She stroked Morgan's cheek and for a few seconds there was peace. It was such simple joy to feel the grip of a miniature hand around your thumb.

"Are they breathing?" said Patrick.

A sudden panic.

"Of course they are." Were they? They both stared hard at the boys' chests but it was difficult to tell. She tickled them in turn until they cried, voices twining together, so similar to each other, the two sounds in parallel like twisting strands of DNA.

"Yes, they're breathing."

They laughed nervously, relieved, as if they'd come close to something unspeakable but not close enough to say what it was. The ground was shifting under them. What would life look like, now?

The anaesthetist came and poked Lauren in the swollen ankles with a pointy white plastic stick. She dangled her legs so he could test her reflexes with the hammer end. She could feel it fine. It was a relief to be paraplegic no longer.

"You should be able to get up now," he said. "The nurse will come along soon to remove your catheter."

She'd miss that catheter. For months she'd been up seven or eight times in the night to empty her oppressed bladder. She quite liked not having to think about it — not being at the mercy of yet another uncontrollable bodily function.

"When can I go home?" She was sweating in the dry heat, the skin on her lower limbs stretched shiny with the swelling. Why was the heating even on in the summer? The hottest summer Sheffield had seen for forty years. Apart from anything else, what a waste of money.

The anaesthetist looked at her notes.

"Well, I can safely discharge you once you've moved your bowels."

"Moved my —"

"Bowels?" The doctor smiled indulgently at her.

She'd understood, but the term was unfamiliar. Not much mention of bowels in her former life sculpting moulds for garden ornaments. No one ever ordered bowels cast in concrete with a fountain attachment for their garden pond.

Though the talk was of catheters and bowels, she bathed in the doctor's easy confident manner and was sad when he went away again, leaving her trapped in her little family unit, her perfect four. Patrick made a little whistling sound at Lauren as she gazed moonily at the doctor's retreating back.

"What?" she said.

"I thought you went for tall men."

She laughed darkly. She was thinking of that moment again, when the needle went in and the pain went away and the anaesthetist carved a place for himself in her heart, made of gratitude and respect and a little bit of girlish adoration.

"You should have a walk around now, check that everything's working fine."

The nurse had taken out the catheter only ten minutes before and Lauren felt slightly aggrieved by the abruptness of the suggestion — one moment a bed-bound dependent, the next dragged out and forced to march around, quick smart hup-two-three. She hadn't used her legs at all in twenty hours. They needed time to think about it. No part of Lauren liked being expected to perform at short notice.

She planted her two fat bare feet onto the cool vinyl floor, feeling the many specks of grit on its surface. The nurse gestured to Patrick to take the other arm.

"Oh Jesus," said Patrick as he helped her stand up.

She twisted to see. A puddle of blood on the white sheet almost the width of the bed, a red sun. Oh, thought Lauren, it's just like the Japanese flag. And then she felt it, rivulets down the inside of her legs, pooling on the floor, red and black and hot like the fear.

After the birth, Lauren was convinced that nothing could be as awful. But towards the end, when they'd decided forceps would be needed, the worst of it had been performed behind a screen of drapery and anaesthetic. She'd not seen or felt the whole of it, not even a significant percentage of it. Where was the lovely anaesthetist now, now that she had a further stranger, a medical person (who could actually be anyone at all, some goon off the street in a costume and how would she even know) inserting a whole hand into her and squeezing her womb until it stopped bleeding? One blue-gloved hand ("Gloves, Mr Symons?" "Do you have Large?" Oh God.) on the inside, one pushing down from the top and nearly disappearing into the spongy mass of stomach flesh created by the absence of the babies.

"Just try to breathe," said the person (a doctor, she hoped). An older man this time. "This shouldn't hurt too much. Tell me if you really need me to stop."

"I really need you to stop."

The person/doctor did not stop. A nurse gave her nitrous oxide. Lauren bit down on the mouthpiece and spoke through her teeth, "Please stop."

"Just relax if you can. I need to carry on applying pressure for a few minutes longer. The bleeding has nearly stopped. Breathe slowly. Try to relax your legs." He was grunting with the effort.

"Oh," said the nurse, as a sharp pain distracted Lauren momentarily, a hot feeling of flesh unzipping around the man's forearm. "We'll have to do those stitches again."

"Please —" Her voice caught in a sob, but

37

there was no energy for crying. "Please. I can't. It really hurts." The hand inside her shifted horribly. She cried out.

"Just a minute longer."

And she kept the terrible silence for as long as she could, unable to fight or fly, a strange man's hands compressing parts of her body that she would never see or feel with her own. Not just in her but through her, further inside than felt natural, or right. She was a pulsating piece of meat full of inconvenient nerve endings and un-cauterised vessels. No intrigue here, no mystery, no power. She'd been decon-structed by nature, and then by man, then nature again, and finally by man — the two forces tossing her hand over hand, back and forth like volleyball. Where was Lauren in this maelstrom of awfulness? Where was the person she had previously thought herself to be? Intelligent, funny, in control, that Lauren. She'd been hiding as best she could, sheltering in the back of her psyche somewhere, allowing the least evolved part of her instinctive self to be the thing that was present in this trauma. Disassociation, the word like a mantra within her silence as the older man withdrew his hand with exag-gerated carefulness, the nurse took away her gas and air and inserted a needle for a drip in the back of a hand so pale she barely recognised it as her own. She was flaccid, weak, beaten. She was all shock and pain and sorrow.

Patrick was waiting, trying to comfort the screaming twins by poking his pinkie fingers in their mouths.

"You scared me for a minute there," he said, his voice only decipherable over the din because of its low register.

She couldn't think with the crying — the interference caused her mind to fill with white noise. She made an effort to form a sentence, her language processors struggling uphill in the wind against her reptilian brain.

"You were just afraid I'd leave you alone with these two."

He looked at her. His eyes were glazed in a film of tears. "Well, yeah," he said, "that too," and he kissed her.

Immediately a midwife started to arrange pillows, propping her up so she could feed the babies.

"You should feed as much as you can now," she said. "It helps your uterus to contract."

Feed as much as you can, she thought. As opposed to the meagre efforts I've been making so far.

As the midwife stuffed a tender nipple into

the mouth of one twin and then the other, Patrick turned away. He shuffled around looking for change for the vending machine and headed off to get them both a cup of tea. By the time he came back and sat down, the midwife had left. He picked up a magazine but didn't open it. His hands were shaking.

"It's six o'clock," he said.

"Right," said Lauren.

"I should go, before I get kicked out."

"I'm sure they wouldn't mind if you stayed for a while."

"OK." He breathed in loudly through his nose. She waited for what he would say next. "But I've got to get to the shops, and everything."

She wanted him to take her home and look after her. He'd done that once, early on. Only the second time Lauren had gone to his flat. In the night she'd started having terrible stomach pain, food poisoning most probably, from a bad takeaway. The next day he'd boldly insisted she stay with him until she was better. She didn't want to stay — it was early days and they were still being polite, seeking to impress each other. Neither had yet heard the other fart. For a week she vomited near-constantly and her bowels had never moved faster. If this doesn't put him off, she'd thought, and it hadn't. He set up a bed for himself on the couch and tended to her every need. He did it all without complaint, and yet even then there'd been signs that he wasn't a natural caregiver. She heard him, unable to prevent himself from gagging on the smell when he entered the bathroom after her, twice or three times that week. Also, he cooked with a certain undisguised reluctance (always did, she would discover), huffing when required to alter anything at all during the process. It didn't really matter then because she ate almost nothing that week anyway. And it meant she loved him all the more, for doing what he did, making such an effort to override his natural inclinations. It proved without question that he loved her.

The erosion of enthusiasm for self-sacrifice can happen fast in those for whom it's an effort to start with. It can be like dropping off a cliff: I care, I care, I care, I don't care; for how long exactly are you planning to be ill? Patrick must have used up all his caring that week. When she was ill in the early months of pregnancy, he'd seemed more irritated than sympathetic. She found ways of coping. She would list all his good points, in between retches.

He fidgeted in his seat for a few more seconds, then looked at his phone and got up. He kissed all three of them on the head and said he loved them, the new names sounding less strange now but still out of place somehow. "Bye-bye Riley, I love you. Bye-bye Morgan, I love you. Bye-bye Mummy, I love you." The word *Mummy* jarred. It took a moment before she realised he meant her.

Patrick walked the short distance to the corner of the bay, turned and gave a weary wave.

"See you in the morning," he said.

He earns enough so I don't have to work, she thought. My mother liked him, when she was alive. He's funny. He's got lots of friends. He's really good looking, in my opinion.

With a son on each breast she watched the tendrils of steam diminish as her tea went cold in its brown plastic cup on the bedside table. The sun sank beyond the car park but the electric lights held back the darkness. Home seemed like a different country, one to which she might never return.

CHAPTER FOUR

Night fell outside, and the babies seemed to know it: they were awake.

"Sleep when they sleep," the nurse had said, Patrick had said, her mother-in-law had said many times when she was pregnant. Sleep when they sleep: neat, and as far as unsolicited advice went, sensible enough. I would do that, she thought, if I could, but they were asleep all day in between crying and being fed. Now they were awake and she wanted to watch them discovering themselves and each other and the edges of their little world but her eyelids were heavy, her head throbbed. If she closed her eyes she knew she'd be dragged under in an instant. She felt she should be awake for them, that she was duty-bound. This and the pain helped to keep her conscious at first. Her nipples were torn and raw, and the pain in her uterus was dulled only slightly by the co-codamol she had reck-

43

lessly taken despite the implied threat of further confinement ("Are you sure? It might make you constipated, flower").

Coos and snuffles turned into cries and she fed them, both together for the first time without the midwife's help, managing to balance one while positioning the other with one hand. Riley, the smaller of the two, seemed to find it harder to get started and she had to reach around Morgan and slip her little finger between him and the nipple, repositioning him twice before he was able to feed. She wasn't watching the clock. Hours started stretching out into lifetimes when she did that. Feeding time went on and she thought it might go on all night but then they each dropped off the breast, asleep, like ripened plums from a branch, and she set them down. The moment both twins were in the cot she let her eyes shut and her brain shut down and her body melted into the bed. She entered a kind of sleep in which she was poised, a part of her remaining on high alert, jerking her out at the slightest snuffle. A meagre kind of rest, but all she could afford.

And then she woke when there was no sound: why was there no sound? Had she done something wrong, were they suffocating? Were they breathing, had they died?

She placed a hand on each baby and waited for the rise and fall, the sound of air being drawn in, a sign of life. Under the harsh light, under her two hands they breathed, they moved, they lived.

Lauren's heart slowed by degrees. She thought of all the people that would be heartbroken if she let them die. Her gran, his mother, his father and hers. Patrick's sister Ruthie and the cousins, Sonny and Daisy. The funeral, how she did not want to go through that or watch Patrick go through it. Was this the love, this fear of them dying? Perhaps it was. She lay with her eyes open, unable to stop a series of appalling ideas from flashing in her mind. Dropping them on their heads on the hospital floor. Crashing the car with them in it. A plastic nappy bag on the face, obscuring the airways in seconds while her back was turned. These things were so easy, so quick, and they actually happened, they were real. She was right to be scared. She looked at the babies, fixing them in her memory, their personalities emerging already — Riley frowning in his sleep, dissatisfied with something. Morgan, abandoned to it, relaxed and satiated. I will never forget this, she thought.

They were asleep. *Sleep when they sleep.* And she wanted to watch them to make sure they kept breathing but she clicked off like a light.

She dreamed of the bird and the cat again and awoke drenched in sweat and dread. How long had she slept? Impossible to know. The curtain between her bed and the next had been drawn across once more. This time there was no mistake: there was a woman in the next cubicle.

The lamp inside was lit; she could see a silhouette on the curtain, long thin shadows stretched out to the ceiling. A creaky voice began to sing an unfamiliar song.

As she was a-walking her father's walk
　　aye-o
As she was a-walking her father's walk,
She saw two pretty babes playing the ball
Lay me down me dilly dilly downwards
Down by the greenwood side-o

And the woman had two babies, Lauren was sure. There, the sound of two together, both cooing and grunting, as if they were singing along with the strange lullaby.

She said pretty babes if you was mine
　　aye-o
She said pretty babes if you was mine
I'd dress you up in silken fine

46

Lay me down me dilly dilly downwards
Down by the greenwood side-o

Lauren felt an urge to visit the toilet, a sudden pressure on her bladder strong enough for her to answer it with a movement a bit too fast for her body. She swung her legs out of bed. Her knees buckled as she stood, but she held herself up with both hands on the bed rails. She perched there, testing herself. She could walk; she was just a bit unsteady. There was no sunburst of blood on the sheet. The muscles in her pelvic floor, cut and torn and sewn up, held her in place for now and she took her hands from the bed, allowing her feet to take their burden back. She checked the babies, still breathing, feather breaths on her cheek. Blood rushed from her head to serve her limbs and she waited for the feeling to pass, the floor to cease shifting under her like the deck of a sea vessel.

The clock read 4.17. The windows, black
  mirrors.
She took a penknife long and sharp aye-o
She took a penknife long and sharp,
And pierced the two pretty babes to the
  heart

47

Lay me down me dilly dilly downwards
Down by the greenwood side-o

Maybe Lauren would ask her to stop. The singing might wake Mrs Gooch. Plus, it was a horrible song, the words were creepy and the tune was weird, sort of sad and angry. She'd been pleased, initially, when she'd realised there was another woman on the ward with twins but she wasn't sure she could be friends with someone who had no consideration for others.

The curtain had been pulled all the way around the cubicle, boxing it in. There was a gap of a few centimetres at one corner and Lauren widened it, peering through. The lamp was angled at her face, she was caught in the glare. She held a hand up to shield her eyes.

"Excuse me," she said. The woman did not respond, kept humming the strange old tune. She tried again, a bit louder. "Excuse me?"

There was no hospital bed. The woman was sitting in the chair, the same as the one of pale green vinyl next to her own bed, next to all the beds on the ward. The scene was too small for the cubicle — without the bed there seemed too much floor space. The distance between Lauren and the woman was wide as a river. The woman was leaning forward with her elbows on her knees and a large basket between her bare feet, feet dirty enough to stand out black against the floor. Rags from the woman's dress were long fingers trailing against those feet, against the floor, forming a fringe over the basket. The glare from the angled lamp meant that Lauren couldn't see the babies in the basket but she could hear them, ragged phlegmy breaths and two — definitely two — high-pitched voices murmuring. She took a step inside the cubicle, moving to get a better look, more from curiosity than anything else because she could see at once that this woman shouldn't be there. She must be homeless. She wore several layers of clothing, as if she were cold even though it was oven-hot in the hospital. But when Lauren stepped closer she began to shiver. She was at once aware of the thinness of her hospital gown, cold air surrounding her, whispering around her exposed legs and entering the gown from below so that she wrapped her arms across herself to stop it. There must have been an air-conditioning outlet right there above them. It was a damp cold and there was a muddy, fishy smell which must have been coming from the homeless woman. Lauren sensed that she had been

49

noticed, she knew it, but the woman hadn't moved at all, not a millimetre. She was singing again.

> She throwed the babes a long ways off
>   aye-o
> She throwed the babes a long ways off
> The more she throwed them the blood
>   dripped off
> Lay me down me dilly dilly downwards
> Down by the green-

"Listen, I don't mean to be rude but can you stop singing, please? You're going to wake everyone up."

The woman stopped singing with a sharp intake of breath. She raised her eyes from the basket. Lauren heard a high whining sound, another layer of hum but getting louder. It came from nowhere but inside her own ears. *Run,* it told her, *leave, go, now.* But her feet were rooted. Heavy as lead.

It took a long time for the woman's eyes to meet hers and when the moment finally came Lauren had to blink away cold sweat to see her. She was young, perhaps eight or ten years younger than Lauren, but her eyes seemed ancient. She had hair that had formed itself into clumps, the kind of hair, a bit like Lauren's, that would do that if you didn't constantly brush it. The woman's face was grimy, and when she opened her mouth to speak the illusion of a rather dirty youth who could even be beautiful if given a good scrubbing was destroyed. She seemed to have no teeth and a tongue that darted darkly between full but painfully cracked lips. There was something about the way the woman eyeballed her. What did she want?

"You've twin babies," said the woman.

"Yes." The word had tripped out, travelling in a cough. Lauren wanted it back.

"Ye-es," the woman drew the word out lengthily, "twin babies. Just like mine, only yours are charmed."

Lauren couldn't think what to say. She knew she was staring, openmouthed at the woman but she couldn't not.

"Mine are charmed too," said the woman, "but it's not the same. Mine have a dark charm. A curse. You are the lucky ones, you and yours. We had nothing, and even then we were stolen from."

She must have had a terrible time, this woman. And those poor little mites in the basket, what kind of life would they have? There were people who could help her, charities dealing in this kind of thing. She must be able to access something, at least get some new clothes. The long dirty hair hanging in dog's tails each side of her face was doubtless crawling with infestation. It wasn't healthy.

"I'm so sorry," said Lauren, "shall I see if I can get someone to help you?"

The woman stood up and took a few steps around the basket, towards Lauren. The muddy smell became stronger and the air, colder. It seemed to come out of this woman, the cold. There was an odour of rotting vegetation stirred up with the mud and the fish. Lauren wanted to look into the basket but the woman was standing in the way. Closer now, she lowered her voice, breathy, hissing.

"There's no one can help me. Not now. There was a time but that time passed, and now there's more than time in between me and helping."

The woman moved slightly and Lauren could see that the basket was full of rags, a nest of thick grey swaddling and she couldn't see a face, not even a hand or a foot. She hoped the woman's babies could breathe in there.

"Maybe social services could find you somewhere to stay," said Lauren. "You can't be alone with no help, it's not right."

"I've been alone. I'll be alone. What's the difference?"

"But the babies."

They both looked at the basket. The bundle was shifting, folding in the shadows. One of Lauren's boys sneezed from behind the curtain and she was unrooted.

"I'm sorry, I've got to go, my baby."

She leapt away from the woman, out of the cubicle, into the dry heat.

"Your baby," said the woman. And she lunged, crossing the space between them in an instant. A bony hand gripped Lauren's wrist and she tried to pull it free but she was jerked bodily back inside the curtain walls. They struggled, but the woman was stronger.

"Let's deal," hissed the horrible woman, bringing her face up close to Lauren. "What's fair, after all? We had everything taken, you had everything given. Let's change one for another."

"What?"

"Give me one of yours. I'll take care of it. You have one of mine, treat it like your own. One of mine at least would get a life for himself, a taste of something easy. What's fair?"

"You must be mad, why would I do that? Why would *you*?" She pulled against the woman, their arms where they were joined rising and falling like waves in a storm. Nothing could shake her off. Lauren felt her skin pulling, grazing, tearing in the woman's grasp, filthy nails scoring welts that she was certain would get infected, would likely scar. "Get off me," she said through gritted teeth. She would bite the woman's fingers to make her let go. But they were disgusting.

"Choose one," said the woman, "choose one or I'll take them both. I'll take yours and you can have mine. You'll never know the difference. I can make sure they look just the same. One's fair. Two is justice done."

The sound that came out of Lauren was from a deep place. It burst from the kernel at the centre of her, the place all her desires were kept, and all her drive. It was the vocal incarnation of her darkest heart, no thoughts between it and its forceful projection into the grimacing face of the woman. A sound of horror, and protection, a mother's instinct, and her love. The shape of the sound was *No.*

And in that moment the sound took her arm from the iron grip of the woman, her body away to the trolley where her babies lay, her feet to carry her and the sleeping twins into the hospital bathroom where she swung the handle into place to lock the door.

CHAPTER FIVE

July 15th
7:15 A.M.
Police Headquarters

Jo Harper parked her white Fiat Punto in the underground car park. The place was almost deserted, only a few civilian vehicles dotted about and a line of sleeping patrol cars against the far wall. A cool early-morning breeze flowed down the ramps from outside, shivering around her knees and elbows, and she hugged herself as she walked across to the doors. The outfit she wore was too brief for the current temperature but she knew she'd appreciate the light cotton knee-length skirt and short-sleeved shirt later on in the day when she was out and about in the full force of the sun.

She stood in the lift, nostrils full of the smell of the sun cream on her skin and the car park's oily, mechanical odour, waiting for the four-digit security code to register.

A long beep, the lift doors slammed shut and a second later she stepped into the foyer.

The uniformed desk sergeant looked up as she walked towards him. "Morning, Harper, early again I see."

"Just very, very diligent, Gregson, you should try it one day," she replied, with half a smile.

"Ha ha. I'm here too, aren't I?"

"Yes you are, mate. And where would we be without you? We'd have to get an automatic door, for a start."

Phil Gregson was probably ten or twelve years older than Harper, fifty or so, but the years had been less kind to him than they had been to her. Or perhaps he'd been less kind to himself. Either way he looked easily old enough to be her father.

"What on earth are you wearing?" He leaned over the desk to point at her feet.

She wiggled her toes. "Trainers."

"They are not trainers. They're gloves. Rubber gloves for feet. They're the weirdest things I've ever seen."

"They're good. They're for running better. Your feet are unrestricted, see?" She wiggled her toes again.

"Urg. Stop doing that. You won't get away with those if Thrupp sees them."

Harper curled her lip. She knew the five-toes trainers were a bit far out for work. She'd brought her shoes in her bag to change into before the boss arrived but she wanted to spend as much time "barefoot" as possible. It was meant to improve your technique; she was competing in a half Iron-man in a few weeks.

"You can swim in them, too, you know."

"Fascinating," said Gregson, miming a big yawn.

Though the time Jo Harper spent out-doors had added wrinkles to her face, her body was lean and strong. Whereas Gregson looked as if he was gently melting into his swivel chair. Admittedly there may have been an element of genetic advantage — she had her mother's great cheekbones and her father's naturally not-yet-grey hair. Harper had slept with men older and greyer than Gregson, back when she'd thought she only liked men, but the desk sergeant elicited nothing more than a fond daugh-terly reflex in Harper that he no doubt would have been upset to be made aware of: she wanted to get him a haircut, feed him a salad and some peppermint tea, take him on a nice long walk and make sure he got an early night. Poor old Gregson, with his slowly broadening middle section held in by the wide black police utility belt, and his car-length hair swept across the emerging scalp. Harper thought he could go up a size in shirts. Maybe two.

Harper made herself a bad coffee in a mug with a joke about dogs on it, the bottom of which got stuck to the tacky surface of the kitchenette that she shared with a hundred or more other officers, none of whom — from the evidence — knew how to work a cloth. The mug jerked as it came away, causing it to spill a little and scald her hand. She was still cursing when she reached her desk, but there was no one there to hear her; at that time in the morning the building was quiet, just the way she liked it. She took a sip of the too-hot liquid and grimaced, then fired up the system for her usual early-morning perusal of the overnight incidents. This was not technically part of her job as detective sergeant. It was a habit, a form of work-avoidance that she could just about justify because sometimes it threw up something interesting, something that hadn't been handed to her by the DI.

The list from the previous night included the usual stuff — two calls from some angry people between 2 a.m. and 3 a.m. about noisy neighbours. Three kinds of drunk people: one who called by accident, asking for a taxi; one who called on purpose, because they'd lost their mates in a nightclub and they wanted the police to help find them; and one exceptionally drunk person calling because there really was an emergency — his friend had been assaulted, then he'd collapsed and stopped breathing. This was where the skill of the operator was crucial, because it was so hard to tell the difference with drunk people. There were also several calls from stupid people (who were sometimes drunk, too, which didn't help): one calling because the cat hadn't come back, one because someone had refused to make tea when it was their turn.

Some of it was funny, but much of it was deadly serious. The list itself might have been indecipherable to a civilian at a glance, just columns of lingo dotted with police code and numerical data. But Harper could see that, hiding in the midst of the crank calls, were those entries heavy with the weight of human tragedy. The cold record of the moment a person decided they were not strong enough to deal with whatever was in front of them. These were genuine cries for help.

At the top of the last page, one of the items caught her interest. In the early hours there had been a call from a mobile phone located in the Royal Infirmary Hospital. It was marked as 4 — the lowest possible priority, judged to be a false alarm. But the description read "Attempted Child Abduction" so she clicked on it. Reading the notes, her breath quickened.

1. Time: 0429: 999 report from a mobile phone
2. Details of Person Reporting: Lauren Tranter, address (unable to obtain)
3. Detail of Incident: reported intruder in maternity ward of Royal Infirmary, reported assault, reported attempted abduction of newborn twins. Reporter is calling from inside locked cubicle, both babies inside cubicle with reporter, intruder outside door attempting to breach
4. Opening Incident Classification: 1 (URGENT)
   a. Action: hospital security alerted by telephone as first-on-scene
   b. Action: mobile patrol officers alerted by radio

```
                e.t.a. 16 minutes
    5. Time: 0444: contact by
       telephone from hospital
       security: false alarm:
       picked up by MHS
      a. Action: Mobile Patrol
         cancelled by radio
    6. Closing Incident Clas-
       sification: 4 (NO ACTION
       REQUIRED)
```

MHS stood for Mental Health Services. So, whoever had called, the mother of the twins, was seeing things. Those with mental-health issues often called the police, and it was quite often "picked up by MHS". All seemed to be in order, in this case. The dispatcher had probably been correct in ranking it 4. Harper went back to the main screen, looked at the rest of the list. Drunk people, stupid people, Road Traffic Incidents. Nothing that needed her attention. Her cursor hovered over the red button in the corner of the programme window. Better be getting on with planning that training session I'm delivering later, she thought.

But she didn't click the incident reporter shut and open PowerPoint, as she knew she ought to do. The call from the hospital was bothering her. A sliver of dread crept into her stomach, and she tried to dismiss it as ridiculous. But there it sat, black and heavy. Between the lines of text on the screen she read the mother's fear, her sure knowledge that someone wanted to take her babies away. Harper couldn't help but feel it herself, that threat of separation. Unthinkingly, she placed her hand low on her belly, where the skin had never quite tightened over the hard muscles beneath.

Perhaps she'd just make completely sure it was nothing, then she could forget about it and get on with her day. One phone call, that's all it would take. Harper dialled the security service at the hospital.

After the introductions, the guy was nervy.

"Oh, no, nothing to worry about, officer. The lady in the toilets? Maternity? She was just having a bad trip."

"She was on hallucinogenic drugs?" Harper used a stern, alarmed tone.

"No, no. No. She was, I dunno, spazzing out."

"She was . . . what?"

This *what,* delivered quietly but ripe with pointed incomprehension, implied a need for Dave, the security guy, to explain himself pretty quick and stop using such offensive out-dated language. Harper could pack a lot of meaning into one word. She was rather enjoying herself.

"Look, officer, ma'am, I dunno what happened." Dave started talking too fast, about how "your lot" had called him and said there was an intruder on the ward so he got up there sharpish. "I couldn't understand how an intruder would get in — there's a security door, and I hadn't seen nothing on the monitor. I ran there, fast as I could — it's about a mile from my office, you know. I made in it five minutes."

Five minutes. The triathlete in her couldn't help but think, not a bad time if it's true, but he wasn't about to get a medal from Harper for that. And, she didn't put much stock in the fact that Dave hadn't seen anything on his monitor. He sounded very jumpy. Very jumpy indeed. If she had to guess, she'd say he'd probably been asleep when the dispatch controller had rung him, when he should have been awake and alert for such emergencies.

When he'd got there, nothing. Just a "crazy woman in the toilet". No intruder. "So I rang your lot back. I said, nothing doing here, the psychiatric team are dealing with it. Whoever I spoke to, they said they'd tell you, that they'd cancel it. Didn't you people get the message?"

"We got the message. I'm just following

64

up on a few things, that's all," said Harper.

Harper told Dave to get together the relevant CCTV on a disk for her, and that she would be there later today to pick it up.

"Aw, man. I clock off in an hour, that's going into my own time —"

"Dave, I've asked you nicely. Please."

She had a way with pleases. Dave capitulated, sulkily.

So, Dave the security guy said it was nothing. There was no one there, trying to abduct anyone's baby. But the feeling of dread remained. If she was going to the hospital to get the disk anyway, she might as well have a chat with a few people at the same time. No hurry, of course. Maybe she'd go up at lunch time.

She glanced at the pile of notes she'd collated for the training she was supposed to be delivering, and then back at the incident on her screen. Then again, she thought, no time like the present.

Fifteen minutes after she'd first sat down she was up again, leaving her disgusting coffee to progress from undrinkably hot to undrinkably cold without her.

"You off already, Harper? Not as diligent as all that then, are we?" said Gregson as he buzzed her out of the building.

"Oh fuck off, Gregson,"

He winked at her and she mimed making herself puke, then she stood in the lift again waiting for the long beep, the slamming doors, to shoot back down to the car park.

66

CHAPTER SIX

The maternity ward doors were locked. Harper pressed the intercom. Enough time passed to make her consider pressing it again, but just as she reached for the button there was a burst of static and a flinty voice barked, "Yes?"

She gave her name and rank, and was buzzed through without another word.

A length of harshly lit corridor led to the central nurses' station, which surveyed the openings to several bays. Each was designed to hold between four and six beds, but none of them were fully occupied. New mothers were here and there, sitting in chairs, sleeping. A bleary-eyed man walked past gingerly, wearing a blank expression, holding a pink flowery wash bag.

There was the sound of crying babies and a strong smell of antiseptic. The ceilings seemed very low. Harper got a sense that there was not enough air to breathe comfortably, and the strip lights were giving her a headache. For a fleeting moment, she was cast back to her own brief time in a different maternity ward, back to another life that no longer seemed like her own.

Harper had been nearly fourteen when she'd discovered she was pregnant, and by then it was too late to think about abortion. Her parents were shocked, but they never said an unsupportive word to her. As for the baby, she was kept in the family, adopted by her parents who themselves had tried and failed for years to conceive a second child. Her "sister" Ruby was twenty-six now, and though her biological origins were not a secret, the four of them kept to the script. On the surface they were just like any other family: Mum, Dad, and two kids. It wasn't talked about, and they rubbed along fairly well. The scars didn't show. At least, Harper thought they didn't. She kept a lid on it, good and tight, and it was only in moments like these that it all came flooding back. She remembered the maternity ward, where she'd been given a private room. The pain of the labour, and the kind eyes of the nurses who cared for her. She tried to forget the boy she had loved, who had been lost to her completely from the moment he found out about the pregnancy.

His closed, childish face, his total rejection. She remembered her mother's face when she held the baby for the first time, the gratitude and the love in it. She tried to forget her instinct to snatch the baby back and run away, somewhere that she could be a mother properly, not a child, not a sister.

Harper checked herself. She allowed herself one deep breath and pushed the surfacing feelings back in the box, where they belonged.

When she reached the sweeping semicircle of desk, she flashed her warrant card at the uniformed woman behind it, and noted that the woman's name badge read: *Anthea Mallison, Midwife.*

"Yes?"

It was the same sharp "Yes" that had shot from the static at the door.

"I'm here about Lauren Tranter," said Harper.

"Bay three, bed C," said Anthea. The "Yes" had gone up at the end, a demand for information. "Bed C" went down, with a strong sense of conclusion. Anthea Mallison, Midwife was done here. Her eyes had barely left the screen.

Over at Bay three, a man in a grey shirt was leaving. He fixed his eyes on the ward exit doors and headed straight towards them, radiating busy. Harper stood in his way.

"Excuse me," said the man, meaning *get out of my way*. He wore an ID on a lanyard. Harper caught the word *psychiatrist* as he stepped sideways to go around her.

She stepped sideways with him as if in a dance, blocking him, holding up her warrant card. "Hello, I'm DS Harper. I won't keep you. And you are?"

Irritated, by the look of you, thought Harper. And tired. Very, very tired.

"Dr Gill. I'm the duty psychiatrist. And I'm afraid I've just had an emergency call, so I really must leave, I'm sorry."

There was a time, probably only ten or so years ago, when DS Harper's delicate stature and artfully messed-up blond ponytail caused people to utter that line about police officers getting younger every day. The comments trailed off as the years passed, and now they didn't seem to happen anymore, ever. She was thinking about what it might mean for her, that not only had people stopped saying she looked young for her profession but that this doctor — this fully qualified, adult doctor standing in front of her now, looked about twelve.

Dr Gill tried to side-step her once again,

but she went with him. He sighed in frustration.

Harper spoke quickly. "This won't take long," she assured him, "no need to worry. A patient, Mrs Tranter, called 999 this morning. Is there anything you can tell me about that?"

"Yes," said Dr Gill, apparently pleased to be able to provide a speedy answer, "it was a medical emergency, not a police matter. I had hoped someone would contact you about it."

"They did, but I wasn't quite clear about the circumstances."

"Well, that's standard, you wouldn't be. It's confidential. All I can tell you is that the patient in question, when she called you, was experiencing problems relating to a temporary impairment of her mental health."

"So, nothing to do with an intruder?"

A flicker of incredulity crossed the face of Dr Gill, before the curtain of professionalism dropped down. Very tired indeed.

"In my field, officer, patients often see things that are not there. And a lot of the time they call the police about it, believing what they see to be real. I'm surprised you haven't come across it before."

Harper gave the child-doctor a long look.

She wondered how old she would have to be for him not to talk down to her. But then, maybe that was it. Maybe she was already so old at thirty-nine that he saw her as a geriatric, losing the plot.

"Can I talk to her?"

As he shrugged a don't-see-why-not, something vibrated in Dr Gill's pocket and he pulled out a small device, checking its screen. "Look, I've really got to go. You go ahead though, officer. On the left, by the window. She's a bit sleepy because we gave her a mild tranquilliser to calm her down. But she'll talk to you. I'm sure you'll find there's nothing to worry the police with."

As Dr Gill strode away, Harper flipped open her notebook and wrote the words: *Dr Gill: sceptic. 8:07 a.m. Royal Infirmary Hospital.*

In some areas of the police service they had devices with note-taking apps, but nothing could beat a paper notebook. It meant that Harper could burn her notes if she needed to. The fact you could no longer erase things properly from computers or phones meant her job was easier in a way and harder in another, depending on which side of the fence one stood and whether or not one had anything to hide. She herself didn't usually have things to hide, of course.

But it was nice to have the option.

The bay had four cubicles, but only two had beds in them. In cubicle A there was a red-haired woman, her baby's hair even brighter than her own. Diagonally across, by the window, the woman in cubicle C sat in bed holding two sleeping infants, one in the crook of each arm. Brown hair, very curly, long enough to cloud around her shoulders. Late twenties, light brown skin, silver wedding band. Harper couldn't tell height and weight with any accuracy while Mrs Tranter was sitting but she seemed average, perhaps a tad taller than average. Her face was slack, motionless. The babies were paler in complexion than their mother, and both had wisps of curly blond hair. One was dressed in a green sleep suit and the other in yellow.

There was a spot of blood seeping through a bandage on Mrs Tranter's left wrist. She was dressed in a hospital gown. On the floor between the bed and the wall there was an open suitcase spilling its contents — baby clothes, nappies and what were presumably Mrs Tranter's own clothes. She'd dressed the babies, but not herself.

Something about her face reminded Harper of a photograph she had of her own mother as a young woman; the large brown eyes rimmed with sadness, gazing softly into the distance, unreachable. Harper was gentle when she spoke.

"Lauren Tranter?"

The woman turned her head towards Harper's voice. As the seconds slipped by, she gradually came to focus. It seemed a gargantuan effort. Lazily, her eyelids dropped shut and opened again, the slow blink of the drugged.

"Yes."

"My name's Jo Harper. I'm a police officer. I'm here to talk to you about last night."

"Oh."

Lauren's gaze drifted down towards the baby in yellow, and then across to the other. They were identical.

She said, "I thought they called you. I thought they told you not to come."

"They did," Harper smiled, gave a little shrug, "but I came anyway. It's my duty to investigate when there's been a report of a serious incident. You called 999 at half past four this morning, or thereabouts? The report mentioned an attempted child abduction."

Mrs Lauren Tranter's face crumpled. Tears cleaned a path to her chin. "I did call."

Harper waited for her to go on. A machine was beeping in the next bay. The sound of footsteps in the hallway, a door banging.

Awkwardly, Lauren wiped her nose with the back of a hand, getting a bit of wet on the yellow-dressed baby's arm. "But they said it wasn't real. It didn't happen. They said I imagined it. I'm so sorry."

"It must have been very frightening for you," said Harper.

"Terrifying." The word out came out on a sigh. Lauren searched Harper's face, looking for an answer to some unasked question.

"You were right to call." Harper laid a hand on the younger woman's arm, not making contact with any part of the baby she held there, but the mother flinched at the touch and the sudden movement shocked the baby, whose eyes flew open, its arms and legs briefly rigid before they slowly drew in again as Harper watched. The baby in green on the other side rubbed the back of its head on its mother's arm, side to side, yawning and rolling its tongue into a tube. The little eyes remained closed.

"Sorry," said Lauren, "I'm a bit jumpy."

"Don't worry. You've been through a lot, I get it."

"I'm really tired. I didn't get much sleep, not last night, not since I had them. I'm not complaining though. It's worth it, right?"

"Right," said Harper, "they're beautiful. When were they born?"

"Saturday night." She nodded to the one in yellow. "Morgan was born at 8:17 p.m. His little brother came out at 8.21. He's called Riley."

"Lovely," said Harper. She scrabbled for a platitude to fill the silence. "Well, you've certainly got your hands full there."

Lauren turned her eyes on Harper. "Do you have children?" she asked.

Harper didn't know why she didn't answer immediately. All her life she'd been answering immediately, giving the same almost stock response, *No, not me, I'm not the maternal type,* said in a way that made it clear she didn't want any more questions. Today was different somehow; Lauren wasn't making small talk. She wasn't implying, like some people did, that Harper's biological clock was all but ticked out. She was asking *Do you understand what just happened to me?* Standing there in front of Lauren Tranter, so devoid of artifice, not just hoping but needing the answer to be *Yes, yes I do,* the truth was on her tongue. But she swallowed it.

"No, not really," she said, immediately hearing how stupid that sounded. Not really? What did that mean? Lauren made a

76

small frown but didn't say anything more. Harper went on, "I've got a little sister. A lot younger than me. So I guess I sometimes think of her as my kid. But no, I don't have any children of my own."

Lauren's eyebrows went up and she seemed to drift away, unfocussed. Newly etched lines mapped the contours under her eyes, the topography of her recent trauma.

After a moment Harper said, "What happened to your wrist?"

The spot of blood on the bandage had grown from the size of a pea to the size of a penny in the time Harper had been standing there.

"Well, she, the woman, she . . ." Lauren seemed confused. "I don't know."

"Did someone hurt you?"

Lauren turned her head towards the window. Across the car park people were shuffling in and out of the big glass doors, needlessly high doors that dwarfed the people below. The doors were opening, shutting, opening, shutting, reflecting the morning sun as they met and flashing, leaving orange spots in Harper's eyes. Lauren kept her eyes wide open into the blinding light.

"That man, Dr Gill. He said I did it to myself."

"And what do you think, Mrs Tranter?"

"I think . . ." She looked down at the babies and up at the detective sergeant. Big, sad, frightened eyes, streaming tears. "I don't think I can trust what I think right now."

CHAPTER SEVEN

A beam of the slant west sunshine
Made the wan face almost fair
Lit the blue eyes' patient wonder
And the rings of pale gold hair
She kissed it on lip and forehead
She kissed it on cheek and chink
And she bared her snow-white bosom
To the lips so pale and thin
> From *The Changeling* by
> John Greenleaf Whittier

Ten o'clock, visiting time. From her hospital bed Lauren observed a column of fuzzy colours approaching her and tried to focus. The fuzz resolved into the familiar shape of Patrick. It felt like years had passed since she'd last seen him.

"My God," said Patrick, "what have they done to you?"

"It's fine, everything's fine," said Lauren, but all that came out were broken sobs, the

79

incoherent hupping yowls of an injured creature. Soon it subsided, trickled to whimpers. He stroked her hair.

"Shh, lovely," said Patrick, keeping his voice low. On the other side of the bay, a jubilant party of assorted family was gathering around Mrs Gooch's bed. Chairs were pulled across for older Gooches. Two smallish ginger children each possessively gripped ribbons attached to shiny silver balloons that trailed near the ceiling, announcing in bubblegum-pink lettering: *It's a Girl!* One of the balloon-bearers stared slack-jawed at Lauren so that the lolly dangling from his open mouth nearly fell out.

"Shh. I know," said Patrick, unaware of the gaping child at his back.

Another version of Lauren would have stared back until the boy looked away. This new, broken Lauren just shut her eyes.

Patrick said, "They left a message on my phone, but I didn't get it until this morning. What happened?"

Lauren couldn't respond to that immediately. She was floored by another wave of sobbing. A red-haired man — perhaps a new uncle of Mrs Gooch's baby girl — cheered loudly as he rounded the corner into the bay, holding aloft an ostentatious bunch of lilies. Mrs Gooch glanced pointedly at Lauren and the cheering man said, "What?" and "Oh," as he looked in their direction. Patrick turned and briskly pulled the curtain around, giving everyone the relief of the impression of privacy. After a time, words pushed through Lauren's swollen throat in bits.

"I don't know why I keep crying. I'm fine, I'll be fine. Nothing happened. I think I'm going mad, that's all."

She gave a mirthless laugh, holding on tightly to her husband, making dark patches of wet and snot on the shoulder of his shirt. Patrick smelled of tea tree shampoo and his own slightly smoky scent. He smelled like home.

"Lauren, my heart," said Patrick as he held Lauren's face between his hands and smiled down at her. "You were mad before."

That made her laugh for real, and the bad spell was broken. They both laughed, and then Lauren was crying again, and Patrick wiped her eyes with a wad of the cheap hospital tissues from the box by the bed. At that moment, the babies were almost as serene as Mrs Gooch's. She really didn't know why she kept crying. It didn't make sense, when she saw what she and Patrick had made.

Patrick moved towards the cot. "Morning,

boys," he said. "I hope you've been kind to your mother." He turned back to Lauren. "Did they keep you awake?"

"Of course they did. They're babies."

Her vision began to swim and sway, her eyelids felt heavy.

"I'm sorry," he said, but his voice was muffled and far away. Sorry for what, she thought.

When she opened her eyes he was on the other side of the bed. Odd, she thought, I don't remember falling asleep. A few seconds had gone, *snap,* a filmic scene change.

"I spoke to my mother this morning," he was saying. "She sends her love. She wanted me to tell you, you did really well, you know, most women would have gone straight for a C-section."

Lauren would never stop wishing that she had done just that. She couldn't go back now, nothing would change what had happened during the birth, her stupid decisions, her worthless birth plan. But the regret was heavy on her. She felt like a fool for defying the consultant, even as she blamed him for planting the doubts in her mind, about whether she was capable, whether she would succeed. Perhaps if he'd believed in her from the start, she would have been fine.

"If it was me giving birth to twins," the

consultant had said, "I'd have a C-section."

Ridiculous. He was a man. How could he know what it was like to give birth?

"Thanks," she'd said, ungratefully. "I'll think about it."

My body knows what it's doing, she thought. I'll let nature take its course. I think I can trust in myself to be able to push these babies out on my own. People have been doing this since people have existed. How hard can it really be? Everyone has to be born, right?

Idiot. She hadn't done well. She'd been washed through the birth, powerless, on a tide of modern medical intervention. *They'd* done well, the numerous, nameless nurses, midwives, doctors — without them she would have died, and the babies, too. But Lauren? She didn't feel that she'd done anything but fail.

"You're a hero, honey," said Patrick. "You deserve a medal."

I do not, thought Lauren. But she smiled, pasting it thinly over her pain.

After a moment, Patrick asked, "When are you coming out?"

"I don't know," said Lauren. "I don't know when they'll let me."

"They don't have to let you. You can discharge yourself."

The idea seemed absurd. Lauren had assumed they were in charge. "Can I?"

"Of course. It's not prison."

Home. She could go home.

"I want to go home," said Lauren.

"Let's go."

Lauren gaped at him. "Really?"

"Yeah. Why not? I brought the car seats. I'll go and get them."

"Honestly Patrick, I don't think they'll let me. What about the bleed, when they took me back into theatre —"

"Of course they will. You're OK now, aren't you?"

"Yes, I think so."

"Well then."

"And there's the other thing," she said, "the tranquilliser. I'm still a bit high, to tell the truth."

Patrick examined the size of Lauren's pupils.

"Hmm," he said. "How do you feel?"

"Better."

"The hospital didn't say what it was, in the message, only that you became very upset and needed some medication. Did something happen to you?"

Yes, thought Lauren, someone tried to take our babies. I escaped. No one else saw. But then, it wasn't true, everyone said so.

They said it was a hallucination. And yet it seemed so real.

"Lauren?"

She'd been gazing, blurry-eyed, into the middle distance. For how long? She tried to remember what Patrick had asked her.

"What did you say?"

"I said that you can tell me, whatever it is. Did something happen last night?"

A flash of cold, a blinding light. Lauren's nostrils filled with that muddy fish smell. Goosebumps, as all the hair on her arms stood up. Could it have been real?

"No," she said, "not really. I thought I saw something. I thought there was someone here who couldn't have been. Doesn't matter now."

"Of course it matters," said Patrick, leaning in, all concern. "It sounds scary, you mean like a waking dream or something?"

"Yes, I think so. I wasn't asleep though — I hadn't slept, I haven't slept properly in three days —"

"Well, that's it then, isn't it? You're not crazy, you just need some sleep."

Yes. That was it. So obvious.

Patrick went on, "No one can sleep in hospital, it's so hot and noisy. You know, I read an article about sleep deprivation, it's more important than you think, to get good rest. No-brainer, really."

Fatigue rolled over Lauren, pressing her down into the hard mattress, pulling on her eyelids, stinging her eyes.

"I feel like I'll never sleep again."

"Oh, but don't worry. It's not forever, it's only for a few weeks. Then the sleep gets better."

This seemed impossible. "Really? Only a few weeks?"

"That's what Mother said. I slept through the night at six weeks, apparently."

"You did?"

"And, if you come home, you'll have all our own bedding, our own loo. I'll be there to help."

Lauren felt the tantalising pull of normality, but she was a patient now. It was her duty to lie there and be treated. She'd been institutionalised, in two days flat.

"I want to. But I'm not sure I'm ready. I think, maybe I should stay, just for a few more days . . ."

Patrick took hold of one of Lauren's hands, where a drip needle attachment was taped in place. "Lauren, honey. It's a big deal, having a baby. Having two at the same time is huge. But. You'll be better off at home. I don't like the idea that you were here, all alone, seeing things and losing it in

86

the middle of the night. You need to be where I can make sure you're OK."

Lauren was thinking about the emergency, the bleed. If she'd been at home then she might have died. A tear dropped onto her front. They seemed to come so easily. "I think I might need to stay here," she said, thinking: near the drugs. Near the doctors.

"You hate hospitals. And, no offence but, you stink. No one's looking out for you here. Has anyone even offered to run you a bath?"

She hadn't thought about the bathroom. She couldn't go back in there. Just hearing him mention the bath caused the fear to rise again. It put her straight back to the night before, when she'd been sitting in the bathtub, rocking her two babies under the strobing strip-light as the locked door was opened from the outside and a dark figure came towards her. *No no no no get away get away from me.* She'd screamed and screamed. But it wasn't her, it wasn't the disgusting black-tongued woman, it was a nurse and behind her a man in a green uniform, then there were others, crowding into the small room, more nurses, and a doctor, but she kept screaming, searching the shadows behind and between them. *Where is she? Where's that woman, the one with the basket? Get her away from me, I'm not going back out there, I'm not, I'm not —*

"There's no one there," someone kept saying. "Look, see for yourself."

The crowd opened up, various people stepped aside so there was a clear view. She looked and looked, through the open door into the bay. Things kept happening in her peripheral vision. Near the ceiling, something was hanging from sticky feet, reaching long fingers to curl through the gaps in the air vent, but when she looked straight at it there was nothing there, only a shadow, a cobweb. A trash bin became a squatting demon when she looked away, then became a bin again when she looked back. She knew she was breathing too fast because the nurse kept saying, "Breathe slowly, Lauren," and her heart, her racing heart, she thought it might burst.

The man she later learned was Dr Gill held a white paper cup to her mouth and tipped in two blue pills, then held up another of water to wash them down.

"What did you give me?" she asked, holding the pills behind her teeth.

"They'll help you to calm down and think straight," said the doctor.

She swallowed hard, the pills sticking in her throat despite the water, a dry, bitter taste. But the panic was lifting. The woman had gone.

"You're safe, Mrs Tranter. Come out of the bath now."

She wasn't going to hand the babies over to anyone so they pulled her up as best they could and helped her step down from the bath onto the floor. Through the open bathroom door, she could see that the curtain, which had been drawn around the cubicle where she'd seen the woman, was back against the wall, exactly where it had been all day. The dawn had bloomed and bathed the room in buttercup yellow.

Everything was clean, surfaces spotless but nevertheless she thought she could detect a damp smell of mildew. Strong hands led her back to bed, past the chair where the woman had been sitting. No, where she thought she'd seen the woman sitting. As she shuffled past, with a baby son gripped in each arm, the nurse and the security guard holding her upright, she saw, she thought she saw, three silverfish spiralling out from the centre of the pale green vinyl seat in an almost synchronised wheel. She heard a clattering, a rapid tick-ticking sound of hundreds of tiny insect feet, which she surely must have imagined, and they disappeared over the edges of the chair and into its crevices.

"Lauren? Are you OK?" Patrick's voice was distant, as if heard through a wall. The ward and the people in it had dissolved slightly, back into blocks of smudged colour.

A thought occurred to her. If the woman with the basket was real, she might come back again. No one had stopped her, no one saw her. Not the nurses, not the patients. After DS Harper had left this morning, Lauren had asked Mrs Gooch, tentatively, if she'd seen anyone on the ward in the night who shouldn't have been there. The other woman had shaken her head slowly and given a long and ponderous "no", implying that even the question was insane. "I heard you, um, shouting," said Mrs Gooch. "That was what woke me up. I couldn't really see what was going on, because the curtain was pulled across, but there wasn't anyone suspicious here, I'm quite sure of that. This is a secure ward. Are you . . . OK now?"

"I'm fine," Lauren had said, hearing the tremor in her own voice, smiling to cover it up. Mrs Gooch had cleared her throat nervously, and although Lauren wanted to ask her about whether she heard the singing, she sensed that any more questions would only make Mrs Gooch more uncomfortable.

So, the creepy woman was sly. She knew how to get past security, how to make sure she wasn't seen by anyone. Therefore, Lauren should go home, where the woman would not think to look, and wouldn't be able to come after her. That was the answer.

That's if it was real. But the drugs, and the daylight, had created a distance, allowed her to look at what happened from both sides. It had *seemed* real, but really it couldn't have been, because if it were then someone else would have seen the creepy woman. The singing would have woken Mrs Gooch, before the shouting did. Security was tight on the ward — the woman would have had to get herself buzzed through the locked doors, then walk right past the nurse on the desk. So it couldn't be. But if it wasn't real then it was inside her head and it would be there inside her head no matter where she went, wouldn't it? And, at home, there were no blue pills.

Everything snapped into sharp focus. She gazed into Patrick's worried face. "What if it happens again?" said Lauren, "What if I start seeing things, or . . ."

Patrick was shaking his head, making a *shh* sound, and he said, "Take each day as it comes. You can't stay here until you're sane. You won't ever leave."

The joke was delivered deadpan, as usual, and took a moment to register. A mischievous smile played on his lips as he waited for her to laugh. But she couldn't, not this time. It was too close to the truth. Maybe they would keep her here until they thought she was sane. Perhaps she ought to leave now, while she still had the chance.

CHAPTER EIGHT

Harper sank into the swivel chair in her office and flipped her notebook open on the desk.

"Where the bloody hell have you been, Jo?"

She flipped the notebook shut again and turned to smile sweetly at Detective Inspector Thrupp, who filled the doorframe with his grey-suited form. His blue tie was askew, as usual. He tugged at it now, loosening it further — by the end of the day it was usually completely undone and flung over one shoulder like a very thin decorative scarf.

"Sorry, boss, just following up on a lead."

"Phil Gregson says you came in at seven and left again at twenty past. Now it's nine forty. I've been waiting."

"That's right, sir. There was a report overnight of an attempted child abduction at the hospital, so I went down to take a statement from the complainant."

"What child abduction?"

"Turned out to be nothing really, sir. The woman was having some kind of psychotic episode."

"Couldn't the hospital have told you that? Wasn't it marked as low priority on the system?"

"I thought it sounded odd, sir. Something a bit off, maybe. Worth a visit anyway, just to make sure."

Thrupp was frowning. "I've told you before, Jo. You need to wait for my instructions before you go off interviewing people on a whim. There's a pile of paperwork to get through, and no time to do it. Plus there's the training session later on, which I trust you will be fully prepped for. You could have sent a uniform."

He was right, of course. She should probably have sent a patrol officer to take the statement — then if anything needed to be followed up on, she could have opened an investigation. But so much was lost in the transcription. She liked to be able to look into the faces of complainants, to see the things they chose not to say. The length of pauses. The guilty glances. Lauren Tranter wasn't guilty of anything, but Harper could have filled a notebook with the things she did not say.

Giving an innocent smile, she tapped the pile of papers in her in-tray. "I'm on it now sir, don't you worry."

She swivelled to face her computer monitor, which lit up at a flick of the mouse. From the corner of her eye she observed the senior officer as he stood in the doorway, before sighing deeply, shaking his head and then walking away.

The instant he was out of sight she searched in her satchel, found the disk she'd picked up from security at the hospital and pushed it into the computer. After a few seconds, a grainy image of a hospital corridor appeared. The clock at the bottom right-hand corner of the screen read 03.38. There was the nurse's station, and there was the midwife, Anthea Mallison, in the exact same pose she'd been in when Harper had met her in person, hunched in front of the monitor. The green and white hue of the CCTV footage showed her face illuminated behind the desk by the glow from the computer screen.

She watched for a while. Nothing happened except the clock slowly marking the minutes.

Harper forwarded the video to 04.15. There. Something ran across the floor, taking the same route that Harper herself had taken earlier in the day, towards the bay where Mrs Tranter and Mrs Gooch were installed, bay three. She backed up the video and ran it again. A flash of something, rodent-like, blink and you'd miss it. The midwife kept her eyes on the screen and didn't flinch. There seemed to be a streak of them, whatever they were — more than one, anyway, flowing past the nurse's station. They'd have been right in her eye line. On the screen, Mallison made no reaction whatsoever.

Harper examined the section frame by frame, stopping it where three blurred smudges swam across the floor. The way they flickered, caught between two frames, they looked like big black fish. Shadows of fish. Maybe they *were* shadows, something flying across the light above rather than on the floor — that might also explain why Mallison didn't react. They might have been moths, or big flies or something. Harper watched it again, in real time. She shook her head, watched it once more. It could easily have been a blip; a digital anomaly, nothing at all. So why did she feel the hair rise on the back of her neck?

Mallison had said she was in the staff loo just before Lauren's crisis, which is why she didn't notice anything unusual happening

96

in the bay — Mrs Tranter would have made quite a bit of noise when she panicked and pulled the babies with her into the bathroom. Sure enough, on the tape, the midwife left her post to go to the loo at 04.21, and was still absent from the frame at 04.29, when Lauren's 999 call was made. Harper stared hard at the screen and wished she could hear what was happening, but there was no audio. The midwife did not return to her post for another six minutes, when she sat down and started typing again. One minute after that, at 04.37, Dave appeared in his security guard's uniform, using the desk to brake as if he'd been running — so he did in fact make it there in about five minutes, if you allowed him a minute or two to be on the phone with dispatch. Dave almost headbutted Mallison as the momentum carried his top half forward, and then the two of them rushed towards bay three, disappearing out of the camera's view, to get Lauren out of the bathroom where she'd locked herself before dialling for help. Harper was frustrated that the camera didn't cover the bay. If it had, she could have seen exactly what happened in there between 04.15 and 04.29. That poor woman had seemed deeply traumatised by whatever it was.

But why was she so curious about what couldn't be seen by the camera? After all, according to the nurse, Lauren's real trauma had happened in the two days before: the birth, the haemorrhage, the lack of sleep. If Harper could have seen what was happening in the bay it would have been a film of a woman losing her mind. No one needed to see that.

But those shadows. She shivered. Something about this case didn't feel right.

She took an investigative materials envelope and filled in the details on the front, before burning a copy of the CCTV footage and slipping the disk inside. She had to know what the shadows were, and Forensics would be able to tell her. Hesitating over the funding authorisation box, Harper looked over her shoulder to check no one was coming before she signed an expertly practised facsimile of DI Thrupp's signature, adding his officer number.

Turning back to her screen she opened the email from Records with the mp3 recording of the 999 call Lauren had made from inside the bathroom. Harper hadn't been able to get much out of Mrs Tranter at the hospital, and it wasn't just because the woman had been medicated up to her eyeballs. Mrs Tranter was holding back, certainly. Maybe there was something Harper could learn from hearing exactly what Lauren had said to the emergency operator. Maybe the mp3 would stop the internal detector from twitching.

She didn't like to call it a hunch. *Hunch* sounded clichéd, like something out of a bad detective novel. What she had was a keenly developed sense of intuition, one that wasn't always based on hard evidence, but that she'd learned to trust over the years. Her bosses didn't trust it, however: Harper's intuition, while it sometimes resulted in arrests, never seemed to have a warrant, or a decent evidential paper trail. DI Thrupp was particularly sore about a recent case in which some evidence had been gathered in a less than orthodox fashion.

Harper had been driving home from the office when something suspicious caught her eye. The disused warehouse could be seen from the road and she drove past it every day, but on this occasion the car parked in the usually empty lot stood out: the distinctive yellow Mercedes belonged to a suspect in a fraud case she was working. Harper had parked out of sight and approached covertly — alone and without back-up. When she got close enough, she overheard a conversation within the warehouse, which she had recorded, despite not having the correct permission to do so. Then, without shouting the standard police warning, Harper had kicked down the door, discovering two men who had just been discussing how much to pay for the huge container of counterfeit cigarettes they were standing in front of. Harper was acutely aware that the growing tobacco black market had links to organised crime and helped to fund terrorism. The people involved in it — the men she had caught — didn't care that the product was often contaminated with asbestos, rat droppings and mould, or that the smokes were frequently made in overseas factories that used forced child labour. It was easy money; often easier than smuggling drugs, as even if the lorries were stopped, the dogs at the ports weren't looking for tobacco.

One of the men, the fraud suspect, they'd been tracking for almost a year. The other one was a local businessman, very well connected, with no police record despite several extremely close calls and an intelligence file back at the station nearly an inch thick. The arrest was a huge bonus for the force, more so when they examined the truck and found that several of the cartons right at the centre of the stack didn't contain cigarettes but raw cocaine — more than ten kilos of the stuff. But. There was no previous evidence trail, no warrant. The conversation, however damning, had been recorded without the go-ahead from any senior officer.

With both men cuffed in the back of her car, Harper had rung Thrupp.

"I need verbal authorisation for a surveillance operation," she'd said.

"You'll need to speak to Hetherington. I don't have the rank for that."

"I think you might, in extreme circumstances, if a superintendent isn't available, if authorisation is needed urgently, sir."

"How urgent is it?"

"How can I put this. It's kind of . . . retrospective."

The bollocking she'd got was immense. At first, he'd outright refused to help her, was prepared to let both the case and Harper's career suffer the consequences. But eventually she'd talked him round. Hetherington would certainly have given the go-ahead, she'd said, only there hadn't been time to contact him. There were literally one or two seconds between discovering the crime and her decision to act. The authorisation issue was only a case of delayed admin, if he could just see it that way. If she'd left it any longer, the shipment would have been shipped, they'd have lost the ringleader for another six months, and maybe never have caught the other guy at all.

So, through gritted teeth, Thrupp had logged a written authorisation for the surveillance, citing that Hetherington had been temporarily uncontactable. He had tweaked the timecode in the report to make it look legit so it could be used as evidence in the court case, where both of the suspects received custodials. Harper was sure that the DI would be pleased after that. But no. He could barely look her in the eye. During the process for submitting evidence, the super had questioned the report, but had signed it off because it was Thrupp, his old pal and golf buddy. It was embarrassing, though, for both men, and Thrupp was still angry about having to ask a favour in a way that made him look unprofessional. She reckoned he planned to stay angry until the end of time. Once everyone had stopped congratulating Harper, she'd been punished, restricted to desk duties for eleven weeks, and only escaped a disciplinary by a whisker.

She wasn't sorry, though. Even after all of that, she knew she'd been right to do what she did, and what's more she knew she'd do it again, or something similar, if her intuition was strong enough.

The babies, though. The babies muddied the waters, and she knew it. So much so, that she wasn't certain she could read the signals properly. She couldn't tell if she felt so strongly about this case because a criminal needed to be apprehended, or because there were babies in potential danger.

"Jo, get your stuff." It was Thrupp.

"What's up, sir?"

"There's an incident down at Kelham Island. Uniform have been dealing with it but they need our input. You can drive."

"What's going on?" It was unusual for a DI to be summoned to an incident. It only happened when there was something high level, like a hostage situation, or something to do with organised crime, where strategic leads were required on the ground.

"Some kiddie on the roof of one of the disused factories. Reported initially as a suicide attempt. Apparently it's escalated."

"Escalated how?" said Harper.

"It's not enough to kill yourself, is it? Not when you can take out a building and a whole load of members of the public, too. Couple of police officers, maybe, for extra points. He says he's got a bomb, and he wants a bloody helicopter."

"What's the helicopter for, sir?"

"I don't know, do I? Sounds to me like he wants to blow one up. Jesus. I don't have time for this."

Harper pocketed her notebook and swung her bag over a shoulder before jumping up and heading for the door.

"Wait," said Thrupp.

"What is it?"

"Change those ridiculous bloody shoes. Now."

"Sorry, guv."

"Did you go out in those this morning?"

"Um," said Harper, slipping the rubbery five-toes trainers off and her sensible shoes on. "No?"

Thrupp shook his head almost all the way to the lift. She started to jog to keep up with him, his enormously long legs giving him an advantage when it came to striding.

As Harper and Thrupp buzzed across town, down into the valley to quell disaster and keep the peace, the computer in Harper's office blinked and went to sleep. The email from Records containing Lauren's 999 call shuffled unnoticed into the "read" section of her inbox, pressed down by the weight of the unread, soon to be consigned to the oblivion of Page Two.

CHAPTER NINE

The man lay half on the pavement, limbs twisted, head smashed. Blood pooled darkly, forming tendrils that crawled towards a drain. Harper started walking towards the body but was stopped by a uniformed officer.

"Sorry, Jo. We need to wait for bomb disposal to finish."

The jacket the dead man wore was made of black nylon, and clung to what was left of him like a second skin. However, procedures were important. It was a further fifteen minutes before the bomb squad could safely confirm what could be plainly seen: there was no explosive device in the man's jacket. There never had been. At the all-clear she stepped forward to close the staring eyes, then helped to cover the body before it was bagged and transported to the morgue.

The first journalist on the scene was also a friend, Amy Larsen, veteran of a great many of Harper's crime scenes over the last three years and chief reporter for the big local weekly, the *Sheffield Mail.* Amy, who as usual was fully made up, chic and elegant in a pencil skirt and heels, held her recording device in front of Harper's mouth. The sergeant frowned at it and tried to move away but Amy followed her.

"Tell me about the kid. What brought him to this?"

Harper said, "We don't know much about him at the moment. He's young, probably in his early twenties. That's all we've got."

"A tragic suicide? Nothing more ominous than that?" Her ironic tone implied she didn't believe that line for a second.

"We're investigating the circumstances, the identity of the victim and so on. But at this moment we don't think there's anyone else involved."

"So why did the police decide to bring in the armed response team?"

"I'm afraid I can't tell you that."

Amy rolled her eyes and huffed. "What can you tell me?"

"Only that we are treating the death as unexplained, but not suspicious."

Harper would have said more, but she was trained to minimise potentially inflammatory lines of questioning when dealing with the press. She was supposed only to release the very blandest of information. Amy knew this. It was a game they played: a gentle volley of questions and responses, the journalist trying for the topspin, the police officer stoically returning straight lobs.

"Come on, Harper. This wasn't just a suicide, was it? The police don't behave like that, shutting the roads, evacuating buildings — not for a jumper. I'm sure I saw a bomb-disposal unit. Did you think he had a bomb?"

Harper put her hand over the top of the recording device. "I can't tell you anything more about the incident. We don't even know his name yet. I'm sorry."

Amy rolled her eyes, turned off the recorder and put it in her handbag. She placed her fists on her hips.

A car drove past, the passenger staring, fishlike, at Harper and Amy. The fire service had cleared off an hour ago, and most of the patrol cars had gone too. Once the ambulances had driven away, there wasn't much to look at. Of course, the fact that

107

there was nothing to see didn't stop people's natural curiosity; they wanted the full story, with details, the juicier the better. That was where Amy came in, to dig out the facts and relay them to the public via the *Mail*. Unfortunately for her, this time Harper wouldn't be the one to tell. That alone wouldn't stop her, though: Amy was resourceful. Harper had learned that much, since the journalist had first appeared, notebook in hand, at the scene of a suspected murder up in Attercliffe, brandishing her *Mail* ID and picking through the debris-strewn back alley in a pair of unsuitable shoes. The dead woman in that case, a heroin user, turned out to have taken an accidental overdose, but the police couldn't identify her. All they found on the body was a silver heart necklace, probably left behind by whoever took her wallet and phone because of its unusual engraving, which would have made it tricky to shift on the black market. On the back of the heart was a date, and the name Holly-May.

The name didn't match any missing person's report. Accidental death, not being a crime, didn't come under police budgets for investigation, and the DI reassigned Harper the moment the coroner's verdict was reached. The dead woman might never have been identified if the frustration of being pulled from the case hadn't still been on Harper's mind the next week, when she'd bumped into Amy at a crime scene.

"They won't let me investigate, because of budgets. Ridiculous. The body will just stay in the morgue indefinitely."

"Can I see the necklace?"

Harper didn't see why not.

She'd almost forgotten about it by the time the journalist came swinging into the office in her heels, handing over the address of the dead woman's parents with a flourish.

"How did you get this?"

"Persistence," said Amy, shrugging. Then she told Harper how every day, for twenty minutes, she'd sat down with a list of jewellers and called them, one after another until she found the one who had engraved the necklace. It had taken four months. "You owe me a drink," she'd said, smiling in a way that made Harper wonder about what she meant by "drink". A drink between friends? Colleagues? Or something else? There'd been a pause, a moment, when the two women had locked eyes and something had passed between them. Harper had felt it, a low, melting sensation in her belly. She could have reached across, touched the other woman's hand, said, *Sure, let's meet up later,* and that would have been that, one way or the other. But something stopped Harper from following her usual script.

Every time they'd met since, Harper had thought about making the date. But she hadn't done it, and it hung between them, an unspoken thing that Harper thought about more often than she felt she ought to. She thought about it now. She wasn't sure what she was waiting for. She only knew that she liked Amy. Probably too much. It felt dangerous, that feeling, something she couldn't control, that got bigger even as she tried to banish it, to tell herself that these were the feelings that hurt you eventually, that destroyed lives, that needed to be ignored. She'd followed her heart once, when she was too young to know how completely a heart could be shattered. She wasn't going to do it again. Besides, they had something good going, professionally, and it would be a shame to spoil it.

Amy glanced towards the uniforms loading the van, and Harper could tell she was already checking them out, trying to discern who might be likely to fall for those charms and spill the beans.

Then Amy looked back at Harper and frowned. She stepped up closer, close enough that Harper could smell her perfume. Her eyes sharpened as she examined Harper's face. "What is it?"

"What's what?" said Harper.

"There's something the matter. Tell me."

"I've just had a bit of a shitty day, I suppose."

"Oh? You mean, apart from this?" She gestured over her shoulder at the two council workers hosing the road.

Harper nodded. She pondered how much she ought to tell Amy about the Lauren Tranter case; she didn't want her thinking it was a story she could report in the newspaper. "Can we speak as friends?" said Harper.

Amy said, "Of course."

"First thing this morning, there was this attempted abduction at the maternity ward. Identical twins."

Amy scrabbled in her bag for the recording device. "Now, this is news. Tell me everything."

Harper grabbed hold of Amy's arm. "No. I can't. I mean, it was a false alarm. There's nothing to report."

"So why are you telling me about it?"

She had a point. "I don't know."

Amy looked down at where Harper held her by the wrist. She gave a half smile,

111

raised her eyebrows. Harper let go, her cheeks flushing. Amy's skin was warm and soft, and Harper's grip had left a small pink mark that she wanted to stroke. Maybe even to kiss it better. Harper said, "I'm sorry," and searched Amy's face, wondering what was happening, if anything was happening. But the moment, seemingly, had passed.

"Come on, Joanna. You're usually so pragmatic about the job. Just now, you went right up to that poor dead guy and closed his eyes. With your bare hands. I couldn't have done that."

"I guess we all have our soft spots. Suicides, I can just about handle. But anything to do with babies being abducted, well. It gets to me."

They held each other's gaze for a moment, and Harper thought, this is it. She's going to ask me the question, right now. And I'll spill it, every bit. She'll say, why does it get to you, Joanna? You don't have any children, do you? And I'll say, I did once, but I lost her. I was too young to know what it would mean, or that I even had a choice. I let them take her, and it was like part of me had been taken: a limb, or half of my heart. After that I stopped thinking about it, because I had to, in order to survive. But sometimes I forget to not think about it, and it's like it happened yesterday. It's like I have to get her back, and the feeling won't go away until I do. Even though it's twenty-six years too late to change anything."

Behind them the van doors slammed shut. Only a couple of officers remained, and they were heading towards their vehicles, speaking into radios, off to the next thing.

Amy said, "Look, I just need to have a quick chat with one of these guys before they disappear. How about we meet up for a coffee? Tomorrow? Next week? I'll be in touch."

"Great," said Harper, watching as Amy scooted across the road after one of Harper's colleagues, already clutching the recorder. "Text me?" said Harper, but Amy was too far away to hear.

CHAPTER TEN

Those who are carried away are happy, according to some accounts, having plenty of good living and music and mirth. Others say, however, that they are continually longing for their earthly friends. Lady Wilde gives a gloomy tradition that there are two kinds of fairies — one kind merry and gentle, the other evil, and sacrificing every year a life to Satan, for which purpose they steal mortals.

W. B Yeats,
Fairy and Folk Tales of Ireland

July 19th
Six Days Old
Mid-Morning

The house was one of a thousand two-up-two-down stone terraces lined up on one of the city's eight hills, built a hundred years ago for the families of the steelworkers and the miners. Now it was all students, couples and young professionals, those with a modest budget looking to buy in a nice bit, not in the centre but not too far out.

When they moved in together, Patrick and Lauren had been lucky to bag a house in the area that didn't face another row of houses; opposite the front window was a cluster of trees and bushes, beyond which the land fell steeply away before levelling out to a small playing field, then dipping down again to a basketball enclosure. Upstairs, the main bedroom had far-reaching views of the other side of the valley, where the derelict ski village dominated the landscape. A pity, but the beauty and variety of the sky made up for it.

From her position on the low couch under the windowsill in the front room, the sky was all Lauren could see, a wild blue, fading dusty at the edges, swept with wisps of white cloud and etched with vapour trails.

The tide of visitors had ebbed away with the passing of time — a flood on the first day to a trickle yesterday, and this morning, no one. It was quiet in the house. The babies dozed lightly, side by side in their shared Moses basket placed in the middle of the carpet. Flawless, beautiful creatures; the way their lips pursed and smacked as they slept thrilled her, so that she was glow-

115

ing with pride and adoration. She felt sorry for all those other mothers she'd seen in the hospital whose babies were so average and unremarkable. They were probably jealous. It made sense, when you saw Morgan and Riley, how perfect they were, how desirable.

Exhaustion flooded her then. She allowed her mind to drift, her eyes to drop shut. Though she could have slipped easily into sleep, Lauren forced her stinging eyelids apart. There was danger in falling asleep, especially when the babies were quiet: a silent thief could seize the opportunity to sneak in, lift the basket and be away, with nothing to alert her as she slumbered, peacefully unaware. Then, when the boys opened their eyes it would be to a stranger, and when she opened her own it would be to a blank space where her heart once was. She heaved herself from the couch and up the step to the kitchen, over to the back door to check again that it was locked. For good measure, she took the key out of the lock and placed it in a cupboard. Then, she went back into the front room and checked the bolts on the front door before sitting down again. Her thoughts roamed the windows of the house. None were open downstairs. What about upstairs — was the bathroom window ajar? Could a person, should they go to the trouble of using a ladder, even fit through it? Lauren attempted to have a word with herself. You're safe now, she told herself. You can sleep. Patrick's upstairs, anyway. Just a few minutes' nap. No one can get in. She lay down on the carpet and draped an arm over the Moses basket. Her wrist throbbed where the wounds she'd got in hospital still hadn't healed, but her body settled. The throbbing receded. Her eyes closed.

Footsteps approached along the pavement outside, and Lauren sighed, knowing she'd soon be making small talk with a neighbour, or accepting gifts from one of Patrick's office buddies' wives. She didn't want to be ungrateful but she really did not feel like being sociable; maybe she'd just ignore the door this time. She stayed very still, listening to the twins breathing, not quite at the same time, in-in, out-out. The footsteps slowed and stopped, and Lauren heard the crinkling of paper. Then, whoever it was must have turned and hurried away; she heard hasty percussive heels on concrete and by the time she unbolted and opened the door there was no one to be seen. Only a gift-wrapped parcel on the step, which she picked up and brought inside.

Patrick appeared and began fussing in the

kitchen, looking for something among the mounds of detritus.

"Have you seen my phone charger?" he said, finding it a second later under a pizza box.

"Weird thing just happened," said Lauren. "Someone left a parcel but didn't knock. I heard them running away." She held up the package, with its blue dinosaur-patterned paper.

"Let's see," said Patrick, taking it and turning it over, finding a card taped to the underside. While Patrick opened the card, Lauren opened the present.

"Well," she said, examining the gift, "that's, um, different."

In her hands, there was a model that appeared at first glance to be of the kind her grandmother favoured: a supposed-to-be-quirky scene in which a family of animals dressed up like people were all sitting around a little table having tea. Taking a closer look, she recoiled, held it away from her; the surface of it was tacky with something, and gave off a faint, upsetting smell she thought might have been urine. The modelled animals were rodents, with long sinister faces: rats. The mother-rat wore a pinny with a scalloped edge while the father wore a business suit and smoked a pipe. The

118

mother was caught in the act of serving the father a slice of cake as the child-rats looked on. Matching child-rats. Twin boys. All of them were grinning with sideways eyes, as if they were planning something nasty and were very much looking forward to it. The thing was cast in resin, and the sticker on the bottom had been signed by the artist who'd hand-painted it. A limited edition of one hundred. Not limited enough, thought Lauren.

Patrick was on a chair, reaching up to add the card to the others, arranged like bunting, strung on lengths of fishing line across the far wall.

"Let me see the card," she said, and he sighed with annoyance as he got it down again. The card also had a rat motif, but this was a photograph of the inside of a nest of baby rats. They were wrinkled and downy, just opening their eyes, cupping their tiny noses with pink paws. Inside, no message, just a name.

"Who's Natasha?" said Lauren.

Patrick frowned, as he thought about it. "Oh," he said, "she's a new girl at work. Only been there a few weeks. I suppose she must think we like mice."

"Rats," said Lauren. "I think they're meant to be rats, Patrick. I think she's a big fan of rats, looking at this." Lauren laughed nervously, but Patrick didn't seem to find it very funny. "I wonder why she didn't knock, though?"

"She's shy, I guess. And sort of weird, actually."

"I can see that."

Just then, someone knocked on the door. Lauren put the model on the countertop and went to answer it, expecting to see the shy weird girl from Patrick's office, but finding instead Cindy and Rosa, two of the other mums from their antenatal class. Both Cindy and Rosa were still pregnant — hugely so. Their due dates were imminent. She invited them in for a cup of tea, and to her slight dismay, they accepted. Patrick swept away a pile of papers and washing from the couch so that they could sit. He then made tea for them all and said he was going for a lie down, "to let you ladies catch up".

"Before you do," said Cindy, "could you look outside and see if I've left the presents somewhere? I was holding a gift bag when I got out of the car but I must have put it down."

Patrick opened the front door. On the step, to the side, was a green foil gift bag.

"That's the one," said Cindy. "I'm so

forgetful these days. It's only a small thing, something for each of them. And a little thing for you, too." Patrick handed the bag to Lauren, then disappeared upstairs, firmly closing the bedroom door. Inside the bag were two wrapped gifts, and tucked in next to them, what looked like an old book, the pages edged in gold.

"You didn't have to bring a present," said Lauren. "Thanks so much."

She put her hand in the bag but Cindy said, "Don't open them now. It's really only a couple of small things. Embarrassing, really."

"Don't be silly, it's so kind of you to give anything at all. I'll open them later, when Patrick comes down."

There was much cooing over the sleeping babies, and Lauren let them tell her how very beautiful the boys were. She'd never tire of hearing it. Then, they asked about the birth.

"The birth?" she said, glancing at the straining fabric of Cindy and Rosa's maternity tops, knowing she would have to lie, worried she might be no good at it. "It wasn't too bad, really."

"What's it like, having forceps?" asked Rosa, balancing her tea on her bump.

Lauren pressed her lips together as she

considered her answer. "You can't feel it. They give you a spinal for the procedure, so it's all blocked out."

At the mention of the word "procedure" the two pregnant women appeared to lose their nerve. Cindy rushed in with, "I wonder how long these high temperatures will keep on," and Rosa was also happy to let the subject veer towards safer ground. They talked instead of the terrible heat, of feeding bras, the best models of steriliser, nappies (Rosa was thinking about investing in cloth) and baby baths. When the tea was drunk, the two women gathered their stuff. Cindy and Rosa gave Lauren big hugs on the doorstep.

"Thanks again for the gifts," said Lauren, "I can't wait for Morgan and Riley to meet your babies. Not too much longer now, girls."

"Hopefully," said Cindy, massaging her lower back, "I can't bear much more of this, to be honest."

Lauren thought she would quite like to be back where they were, happily gestating their babies. There was nowhere safer. All the danger lay out here, in the world. Make the most of it, she wanted to say, but she knew from experience that this was an extremely irritating thing to say to a pregnant woman. She knew, too, they just wanted to hold those babies in their arms, and nothing else would do. "Keep me up to date, and good luck. See you on the other side."

Rosa grinned and waved from the bottom of the steps, one hand on her protruding frontage.

Cindy gave Lauren a long look. "You do look shattered," she said. "Go and have a nap now, while they're still asleep."

"Good idea," said Rosa. "While you have the chance."

"I will," said Lauren. As long as it's safe, she thought.

After she shut the door she picked up Cindy's gift bag, intrigued by the antique book inside. The title on the front had been worn down, its gold colouring faded but still legible. *Twin Tales: Collected Twin and Infant Folklore from Around the World.* She flipped it open and scanned the contents page, and as she did, cold fear bloomed in the pit of her stomach. There in black and white, in old-fashioned serif script, someone had listed her every nightmare:

1. Lost Children
2. Orphans
3. Suspicious Deaths

4. Careless Parents
5. Twins and Curses

Lauren slammed the book shut and shoved it into the centre of a pile of presents and wrapping paper, puzzled and shocked at how Cindy could possibly think that this book was a good present for her. She tore open the other two gifts in the bag, not knowing what else they might have been given, relieved to find two very nice baby toys, a fish and an octopus that vibrated when you pulled a string.

Lauren mused that it seemed to be a day for receiving weird presents. When she wandered back into the kitchen, the rat family wasn't where she'd left it. Later, opening the trash bin to drop in a teabag, there was the underside of the model with its distinctive hand-signed label. Patrick must have put it in there before he went upstairs. Shrugging, she plopped the teabag on top of it. She let the lid fall shut.

CHAPTER ELEVEN

Harper checked her phone, again: nothing. She shoved it back in her desk drawer. It'd been four days now, since Amy had said she'd be in touch. Harper had agonised over being the one to text first, but she'd stopped herself. She knew eagerness was off-putting, and anyway, it still wasn't entirely clear what kind of thing it was with Amy. She was so hard to read. Sometimes she thought the flirting was obviously a come-on, but then Amy did that with everyone. It was probably a friendly thing, and therefore nothing really, nothing that she had to act upon, or deal with. Still, each time she saw the blank screen on her smartphone or rushed to read a notification that turned out to be from work, or spam, she considered it anew. Would it be so bad if I were to send a message? Would I really come across as desperate, or just friendly? Over friendly, maybe, which would be a disaster. And, if she pitched it wrongly, the embarrassment potential was huge. Last thing at night she couldn't stop her mind composing the perfect not-too-bothered message, a don't-worry-if-you're-busy-but. She'd even typed it into her phone once or twice before deleting it.

Thrupp knocked and entered. He placed a plastic envelope on the desk in front of Harper, and she immediately knew what it was. Feeling the waves of irritation coming from him, she glanced up but didn't meet his eye. Things she sent down to the lab were usually sent straight back to her, the investigating officer — never to the senior officer who authorised it, the signature being nothing more than a box to be ticked, an administrative matter. This one, however, had somehow ended up in Thrupp's hand with a red stamp across it spelling out the word RETURN.

"What's this?" he said.

Harper smiled at Thrupp, her face a picture of nonchalance. She lifted the bagged item, turned it over. "This? I think it's the DVD of the CCTV footage, from the hospital case last week. Did I miss out some details from the description?"

"I read the information on the form, Jo.

The problem is, I don't remember signing it."

Harper sat back in her chair, all innocence. "I'm sorry, sir. It was in with a stack of other things I asked you to sign off a few days ago. At least, I think it was — I was sure your signature was on it before I sent it. Did I accidentally send it without proper authorisation?"

"I'm not saying my signature isn't on there. I'm saying I don't remember signing it. I'm also saying, that if you had asked me to sign this off for analysis, and I had read it properly at the time, I would have said, 'No, absolutely not.' "

Well, she thought, I knew that. That's why I faked it. Harper arranged her features into an expression of concern. "Have you had memory problems in the past, sir?"

"I don't have a memory problem, Jo."

"But you did sign it, sir. Your signature is right there."

He stared hard at her for a few seconds. Then he picked up the envelope and held it close to his face, examining the signature. He frowned. "I suppose I could have been in a hurry, and not really paying attention."

"We all have our off days, sir. Actually, I believe it was sent on the same day we were called out to Kelham Island for the suspected bombing, so that would be understandable. What's the date on it?"

He peered at the form once more. "Ah, yes. Busy day, lots going on."

Thrupp narrowed his eyes and breathed through flared nostrils. He threw the envelope back on the desk. "Anyway, I've de-authorised it. They sent it back up because the disk hadn't burned properly and they wanted another copy. I came to tell you not to bother. We don't have budget for this. It's not on the live case list. What were you thinking?"

"I thought it might be significant. The victim said there'd been an intruder in the hospital. I was just being thorough."

Thrupp would not want to hear the real reasons: that she felt the case nagging at her; that she knew she wouldn't rest properly until she knew the truth; that she had a feeling there was so much more to this, if she could only get beneath the surface of it.

"I looked up the case, Jo. It's closed. It wasn't even opened. A 999 call, filed as picked up by Mental Health Services. Why are you wasting everyone's time with it?"

"When I met her, the victim was convinced it was real. I just wanted to tick all the boxes."

"That's noble of you, but you've got

enough to do without investigating crimes that everyone agrees didn't even happen. On top of all that, analysing CCTV costs money we simply don't have."

"I'm sorry, sir."

"You're very close to the line with this. If I spot anything else like it I won't let it go. It'll have to be a disciplinary."

"Sorry. I honestly didn't mean to cause you any trouble."

"Look, Jo, you're a diligent officer. But you have to operate as part of the team — you can't do whatever you want all the time. This might seem like a small thing but it affects the rest of us. Just wait until you make inspector. You'll be running around all day after your sergeants, trying to justify your use of resources, too. It's a serious business, the allocation of funds. We're talking about taxpayer's money here."

Harper nodded sagely, but thought, and that is why I won't be making inspector any time soon. Running around after other officers, thinking about funding — she felt she had quite enough tedious administrative tasks in her current role, thank you very much. The further up the ladder you climbed, the less actual hands-on policing you did. It was all stress, long hours, and shift work, which the extra money couldn't quite make up for. The previous year, Harper had aced the inspector's exam but since then, whenever a job came up she usually found some excuse not to go for it; too far away, not the department she'd hoped for. The truth was, she wasn't ready. She liked the practical side of things, and she didn't want to work any more hours if she could help it, mainly because if she did, her training would suffer.

Before he left the office, Thrupp gave her a list of all the performance reviews she needed to complete before the end of the month.

"Before you start on that, though, there are some checks I want you to make on the following case reports before they can be filed."

Duly chastened, she played humble, making a note of all the most urgent case numbers and clicking open the first file in readiness as he watched. The moment the door shut, she sat back in her chair and ran her fingers through her hair, letting it down and twisting it back up again. She binned the Forensics envelope containing the faulty DVD, took the original from the desk drawer and inserted it into the computer. Seeing those shadows on the floor of the maternity ward again was no less unsettling, especially as she was no closer to finding out if they were indeed shadows, or nothing but a fault in the recording. She copied the footage onto a USB flash drive, thinking she could at least check it again at home. Maybe something would occur to her. Harper put the flash drive in her satchel, turned back to the screen and began inputting data to the first of Thrupp's long list of supposedly urgent report forms.

CHAPTER TWELVE

How to Protect Your Child

1. Placing a key next to an infant will prevent him from being exchanged.
2. Women may never be left alone during the first six weeks following childbirth, for the devil then has more power over them.
3. During the first six weeks following childbirth, mothers may not go to sleep until someone has come to watch the child. If mothers are overcome by sleep, changelings are often laid in the cradle.

Jacob Grimm

July 20th
Seven Days Old
Early Evening

The sun was just starting to dip, taking the edge off the heat. Lauren sat on the couch, feeding both boys at the same time, one baby tucked under each arm, two perfect heads resting lightly in her hands as they suckled. She'd not located the big feeding pillow in time, so Riley was propped on top of the solid block of an unopened pack of nappies while Morgan made do with a too-small cushion, which meant she was wonky, uncomfortable. If she could just somehow push another cushion under her left arm. But she couldn't, not without dislodging one or both of them. There was no part of the couch not covered in muslin cloths, packets of wipes, baby clothes, toys, Lauren and babies. She was settled in. Stuck. Patrick was hiding upstairs somewhere. She couldn't reach the TV remote and she wanted a cup of tea. And she needed the loo, but that, all of that, would have to wait.

"Pat-rick," she hollered, making both babies open their eyes wide in surprise though they stayed latched on. "Hello you," she said to Morgan, and then to Riley, as two pairs of eyes drifted shut at the speed of soft-closing fire doors. From somewhere above her head, there was a groan.

Seconds collected themselves reluctantly into minutes, while the babies fed on and Lauren tried to think the word "contented" and not the word "bored". As time drained from the day, the shadows shifted so that the sun glared aggressively into Lauren's eyes where she was trapped under the suckling infants.

"Pat-rick," she shouted again, making the sound grow slowly so as not to shock the babies. This time there was a shuffling, a muttering, and finally two feet thudded down the stairs. Her husband appeared in the doorway, hair sticking up, shirt held together with one button matched to a wrong buttonhole, exposing the upper part of his chest, smooth skin interrupted by a small central island of honey-coloured hair.

Lauren said, "Can you shut the curtains, please?"

Patrick huffed barefoot across the room and did as she asked.

"Was that all?"

He stood, legs apart, hands on hips, looking down at her. Shards of sun cut through the gaps in the curtains, but Lauren's eyes were in blissful shade at last. Patrick was back-lit in beams of light, a halo of golden curls, a bad-tempered nativity angel.

"Would you put the kettle on, please?" she said, keeping a careful neutral tone, "I can't get up."

Patrick went back across the room and up the step into the kitchen. She heard the tap running as he filled the kettle.

"I was asleep, you know," he called, through the doorless arch between the rooms.

"Sorry."

Baby Riley unlatched himself and started crying, an engine that took a while to catch and then roared with impressive power. She had to raise her voice to make herself heard. "Can you just take him for me a minute, please?"

Patrick came back through, stepped down into the room and took the baby with a gentleness that made her ache with love for them both. He held him over a shoulder and jiggled up and down, pacing back and forth the length of the kitchen, one eye shut against the raging shrieks at the side of his head until the kettle joined in with the screaming and he flipped the whistle back and the gas off while he kept on bouncing on his heels because it seemed to be working; there were breathy silences between the wails, each longer than the last. By the time the tea was made, all was peace. Riley tongued and gummed his own fist, hiccupping while Patrick draped a muslin cloth between the boy and his own neck, to soak up the drool.

"Hey, Morgie-moo," he said. "Better now,

mister?"

"Patrick."

"What?"

"That's Riley. Green for Riley, yellow for Morgan."

"Oh," he laughed, "yeah, I knew that. Sorry, baby boy. You do look kinda similar to your brother, though. And ever since Mummy took your name tags off, I keep getting confused."

"Can't you tell the difference?"

"Well, of course, mostly. The colours help, when I don't get them mixed up, ha ha. But, I mean, come on — they are identical."

"Not to me."

He laughed again, as if she'd made a joke, then he passed her a mug of tea, one-handed, and went back to get his own. "I've been thinking."

"Oh?" said Lauren.

"I think we need to buy a bigger bed."

"Oh," she said. "OK. But the room isn't really big enough for anything larger, Patrick; didn't we talk about this before?"

"Let's do it, babe."

Still balancing the baby on one shoulder, he put his tea down on the windowsill then pushed enough items onto the floor from the couch that he could squeeze in next to Lauren. "I don't care if we have to get rid

136

of the wardrobe. Anything that might make it easier to sleep. I had a terrible night last night."

"Me too," she said. "They seem to be getting up at different times, don't they? One after the other, like a relay. I feel like I just get my head on the pillow and they're hungry again."

"Huh," said Patrick, "you did get some sleep, though. You were kicking me. You nearly pushed me out at one point."

"Did I? I don't remember."

"Well, you were asleep. Snoring away. Then the babies started crying, of course, and I had to get up and fetch them for you. I'm really struggling today. I think I probably got about three hours, in total."

He gave a pained groan as he leaned back into the cushions.

"Oh, well," said Lauren. "Sorry about that, I guess."

"If I had a bit more room in the bed it might improve things. If we both did, I mean. Space for you to stretch out — you still do that starfish thing."

"I do?"

She always woke up in a foetal position, clutching a pillow. But no one really knows what they do when they're asleep, do they? Perhaps it was as bad as he said. "I suppose, if you need to, why don't you sleep in the spare room tonight?"

"Are you sure?" he answered immediately. "That's a great idea. I think I will. Thank you."

He kissed her on the side of the head and reached over the top of her for his mug.

"So I guess I'll just call you, shall I? If I need help, changing the babies and so on."

Patrick became very still. His jaw clenched.

"What?" said Lauren.

"Oh, nothing. I was just kind of hoping for a night, just one, where I don't have to wake up at all."

"But Patrick —"

"I know, it's selfish of me."

"Well, sort of —"

"I just thought, and I know it sounds awful, but perhaps it's time for you to start learning how to handle the boys on your own. Like, a practice run — for when I really won't be around to help you."

"A what? What are you saying?"

Patrick put his tea down again and slid from the couch onto his knees in front of her. He gazed up at her through his long lashes. Riley, a frond of cuteness in his leaf-green vest, feet she could eat, wriggled and yawed and did a tiny burp. She reached out and rubbed the baby's back where he lay snuggled against his father. In her other arm, Morgan kept suckling, eyes shut, milky-dreamy.

"I'm just telling you how I feel. I've never been able to function without my sleep. You knew that about me, you've always known it."

And me, she thought, you knew the same thing about me. It's one of our things. We always laughed about it, how well matched we are, that we would both prefer to go home and sleep than stay out all night partying.

"Why should you get to sleep if I don't?" she said, her chin crumpling.

"Sweetie," said Patrick. "I know it's hard, I do. Haven't I been going through it with you? But it makes sense, if you think about it. There's no need for both of us to lose sleep, just for the sake of it. And, I'd be much more helpful in the day if I was functioning properly, wouldn't I?"

"But I need help in the night, Patrick. That's when it's worst."

"Yes, but. I know I shouldn't bring it up, but I've been stressing about work too. I mean, look at the state of me. Can you imagine if I turned up looking like this? I can barely keep my eyes open."

She shook her head. What was he talking about?

"But you're not *going* back to work for another week. You've got another five whole days of paternity leave. Plus the weekend. You can't expect me to do it all."

"I know. I'm sorry, darling. Don't cry." He shifted back onto the couch and put his arm around her. She pointed to the box of tissues and he handed it over so that she could wipe her eyes. For a few seconds he didn't speak. She thought he'd finished.

Then he said, "But you *will* be doing it all, won't you, soon?" He softened his voice, as if that alone would soften his words. "You need to get used to it, don't you, because let's face it, I won't be here after that. I'll be at work. And as much as I would love to be at home, with my sons, not actually working, one of us has to make that sacrifice."

It was the impact of what he said, the gut-punch of implications and assumptions. The desolate lonely feeling it triggered in her, as if she'd thought for all this time that she'd been married to someone else entirely, and only now — much too late — she could see his true nature. *Not actually working,* he'd said, as if looking after the boys wasn't work. He didn't care about her. He only cared about himself. Her heart sank, a

140

dinghy with a bullet hole, and the boys felt it. Perhaps they were as connected to Lauren as they thought they were, like it said in that book she'd read about newborn brain development. They *were* her, from their perspective, and maybe that meant they felt what she felt, for Morgan's mouth gaped open and he fell off the breast. Riley's back arched, his whole body tensed. They both started to scream, and Lauren and Patrick took up one twin each, jiggling them up and down, walking in circles that never met.

When the babies fell asleep, the parents followed each other upstairs and laid them top to toe in the Moses basket that stood next to the bed. The bed that, until this moment, Lauren and Patrick had always shared.

They soft-footed downstairs. Patrick seemed to feel that he hadn't said enough. The two of them stood, mirroring each other's crossed arms, on either side of the breakfast bar while they waited for their mugs of tea to heat up in the microwave.

"Please, my love. I know it's terrible of me to ask, and I wouldn't if I thought I could go on. I just need a break from it. That's all I'm saying. Just one night, and then, I don't know. See how it goes."

There was a long silence. Lauren couldn't

think how to begin. She kept returning to what he'd said: *one of us has to make that sacrifice.* What about her sacrifice? The babies were a precious gift, a blessing, of course they were. But if he couldn't see the extent of what she'd lost, what she might never get back — not just her body, but also her budding career as a sculptor, clients, friends, hobbies, practically everything — then what hope was there?

"How about this," said Patrick. "While I'm still off, I'll help as much as I can during the days, and you can do the nights. Like a sort of tag-team situation. Is that fair?"

His voice was distant, as if she'd stuffed her ears with cotton wool.

He came around and leaned on the counter next to her. "I can't do much anyway, can I? I don't have the right equipment, for a start." He chortled lightly, and touched her left breast. She withdrew as if burned.

He was so beautiful to look at. Such good stock. The sort of man who made you want to breed, because you knew your children would have a head start, looks-wise. But she'd begun to understand him properly now. Look at someone every day for long enough and you stop seeing what everyone else sees. You start to see what no one else

142

sees, what is kept hidden from most people. And she'd caught a flash of emptiness behind those lapis-blue eyes. A chasm. A vacuum. She wasn't ready to see that. Turning towards him, she searched his face and her memories for the part of him that she'd fallen in love with. She held in her mind an image of him at twenty-one, trying hard to help her, nursing her back to health that time, him knowing that it was the right thing to do, and doing it even though it didn't come naturally.

"Patrick," she said, "I can't . . ."

"Don't be silly, darling."

The image of the younger Patrick clicked off, gone. And how ridiculous, trying to invoke that Patrick, such an insubstantial version and so fleeting anyway, here for six days ten years ago and forever after talked about like an Arthurian legend: *Oh Lauren, remember that time you were sick all over my flat and I cleaned it up? Wasn't I such an uncomplaining saint? Aren't you glad you married me?*

Don't be silly, darling. Her hands formed fists on the counter.

If he saw her eyes narrowing, it didn't prevent him from continuing. "You can, of course you can. It's a confidence issue, isn't it? You shouldn't put yourself down —

you're so good at all that baby stuff. Much better than me. You're a natural. And the boys love being close to you, they just cry when I try to take them anyway."

As he went on, she started to fade him out, so that when he got to the final few words, persuasions, manipulations, he was just a slight, lilting noise. Annoying, sure, but not painful. He was using his work voice, trying to *market* motherhood, to her. She let her eyes stop focusing on him and turned slowly away. Slack-faced, she sat down on the edge of a chair that was mostly covered in used blue wrapping paper and tiny coat hangers. His voice faded to nothing, just the vague and distant repetition of her name. Her eyes followed the pattern of the floor tiles, brown and white speckles in perfect squares.

I can't stay here. I won't.

She got up and went to the shoe rack next to the back door. She reached for her runners and started putting them on. A hand encircled her wrist, but she shook it off.

"What are you doing, Lauren?"

Casting around the kitchen, she located the car keys lying splayed on the side near the toaster and grabbed them up. Patrick's face filled her field of vision and she had to step around him.

"Where are you going?"

Her ears were starting to sing with that high, piercing drone and it began to fill her head, *must get out, outside, away, anywhere, out of my way.*

"Lauren, stop," said Patrick, loud and urgent enough to break through, to make her pause, but not enough to stop her. She struggled away from him, down the step to the front room, quickly across to the door.

"Please. Please."

As she opened the front door, she turned towards her husband. Patrick looked imploringly at her, cartoon-puppy eyes covered in a film of panic. He held onto her sleeve with his thumb and forefinger. The drone in her head receded towards a silence as their eyes met. Her mouth was a thin line, where his was parted slightly as he inhaled, about to speak. Then the baby monitor vibrated with the sound of Riley's cries. She knew immediately it was Riley, not Morgan, even through the cheap speaker of the small plastic device. Even though to everyone else, apparently including Patrick, they looked and sounded exactly the same. The knowledge held her there, briefly. I am that child's mother.

And then, after stepping into the evening sun, ready to abandon her babies to the attentions of their inadequate and unwilling father, after wrenching her sleeve free and turning towards the street, ready to run, flee, get away to she didn't even know where and right then it didn't matter, she stopped. Her breath stopped in her throat.

In the scrap of woodland opposite the house, more like a clump of bushes really, four or five trees fringed by globes of stingers, a dark figure. It was her. Dog's tails for hair, on either side of her face. Eyes shadowed beneath the forehead, glimpsed in this moment but inserted, full-colour, by the power of their living image in Lauren's memory. Icy fingers of fear pressed their way up Lauren's spine as she tried to look away, couldn't, found herself staring at the woman's mouth as it curled into a cracked smile. Lauren clapped a hand over her own to stifle the scream.

She turned back to Patrick, her face changed so totally but he didn't understand. He hadn't seen . . .

"It's that woman," she breathed, "from the hospital," and she pushed him, two-handed in the chest, toppling him into the door, which banged and crunched against the wall, in her rush to get back into the house.

Patrick said, "What?" and leaned outside,

searching up and down the street.

"There," she said, pointing, but he didn't see. There in the bushes, not on the pavement, not in the street, right there across the road, in the bushes in front of the house. The woman had ducked down, but Lauren could still see the dark dome of the top of her ratty head. Crouching there, ready to pounce.

"Where?" he said. "What woman?" but he was facing the wrong way.

"Shut the fucking door, Patrick. Quickly."

She got hold of one of his arms, pulling him off balance so that he lurched backwards into the room and she slammed the door, leaned against it, breathing hard.

"What the hell is wrong with you?" He rubbed an elbow where he'd banged it on the doorframe.

She went to the window. The dark shape stood, looking right at her. Holding the basket, that basket of rags and horrors, the handle hooked over one arm.

"Look," Lauren's voice a harsh whisper, "come here and look." The woman was so close, perhaps she could even hear them through the glass. Lauren took her eyes off the woman and reached out desperately for Patrick. "She's after me. She's after the boys."

147

No sound in the room but the pounding of her heart. Riley had stopped crying. Through the monitor he gave a series of staccato sighs, asleep but still upset. Lauren retreated to the wall and pressed her back against it, behind the door, where the woman couldn't see her.

Patrick went to the window and stared outside. "I don't see her," he said. "Show me where."

"Look in the bushes. See? She might be crouching down."

"Oh, for fuck's sake."

He rushed to the door, threw it open, and was gone.

Lauren hoped he wouldn't catch the woman. She hoped he would scare her away, so that she would leave them alone, but Lauren didn't want to see her, to face her, to be forced to look at her up close again. She slipped to the carpet and hugged her knees, feeling blood pulse in the place the woman's nails had torn her skin, listening to the babies breathing through the monitor.

Something in her pocket was digging into her leg. She pulled it out — there in her hand was a business card bearing a police logo. *Detective Sergeant Joanna Harper, Greater Yorkshire Police CID.* She remembered now, that policewoman who came to the hospital, who'd been kind to her. She'd given her the card before she left that day. *Ring me anytime,* she'd said, *if anything unusual happens. Anything at all.* Lauren found her phone in her other pocket and dialled the number.

"Hello?"

"Detective Harper?"

"Speaking."

"I don't know if you remember me, but we met last week, in the hospital. I'd called the police, in the night. They told me it wasn't real, but she's come back. She's outside my house — she was staring at me. My husband's chasing her now, but if he catches her I can't have her in the house. She scares me, Harper. She wants to take my children —"

"Is that Mrs Tranter? Lauren?"

"What shall I do? Can you come? How does she even know where we live? She must be following me."

"Lauren, calm down. Give me your address. I'll be there as soon as I can, OK?"

"I'm so sorry. I didn't know who to call. You said anytime . . ."

"It's fine. Don't worry. Just tell me where you are."

Lauren told her the address and hung up.

149

Soon there was the sound of her husband walking back towards the house. His head appeared in the doorway as he reached the top of the steps and bent to inspect the sole of one foot. Blood from a cut dripped onto the doorstep.

"Did she get away?" asked Lauren.

He paused before he answered, sliding his eyes sideways, considering. "Darling," he said, "when you said it was the woman from the hospital, did you mean the one you saw in the middle of the night?"

"Yes, of course that one. The one that threatened me."

"Ah. OK. I understand now, I'm so sorry. I thought you meant a real person."

Lauren felt dizzy. "She *is* a real person. I saw her, she was right there."

Patrick was using his soft voice, the one he used with the babies. "I know, darling, I know. She seems real to you. But she's not. Remember what the doctor said? It's because of the tiredness, that your mind forms shapes from the shadows, making them seem real. There was no one there."

"No one there?"

He shook his head. "I looked in the bushes, then I went to the top of the road and down to the corner in both directions. I've only gone and cut myself. Are there any bandages?"

"I don't understand, Patrick. Where did she go?"

Patrick huffed and sighed. His patience was draining away. He prodded tentatively at his cut foot. "There was no sign of anyone, darling."

"But I saw her. She was standing there, staring at me."

"I know you think you did, Lauren. But perhaps you were just . . . could it have been a shadow, perhaps?"

She could still see the texture of the woman's skin, the dirty hair. The slow smile, and the way the sun through the branches laid a dark pattern on her face. Definitely not a shadow.

"Look at this cut. Do you think I need to go to hospital?" said Patrick.

The wound on his foot had two lips, a slashed red mouth. He eased it open and dark blood oozed out thickly, speckled with black pavement grit.

If he wasn't chasing the woman, if he couldn't find her, then maybe she was still there, hiding nearby. Lauren crept closer to the door and peered around him, searched the place where, only a minute or two ago, the woman had stood, crouched, stood again. Nothing.

151

"Is it tetanus, for this sort of thing? Have I had a booster? I can't remember."

Patrick gripped the doorframe and hopped into the room, struggled over to the couch. He took several tissues from the box and wadded them up, winced as he pressed them to the wound.

"Hey," he said to Lauren, "come here," but she didn't move. She stood in the open doorway, searching the greenery opposite.

"I must have imagined . . . I suppose I can't have really seen her . . ." What did it mean? What was wrong with her? How could her brain conjure something that seemed so real, something laden with so much horrifying detail, and yet there be nothing there at all?

The screeching drone in her head twisted its volume to piercing and painful, starting up from nothing, surging to everything like waves of feedback so high-pitched that she bent at the waist, clutched at her ears, screwed up her eyes against it. She managed to shut the door and half fell onto the couch next to Patrick, who put his arm around her. Deep breaths, she told herself. Try to stay present. Beige carpet, she thought, blue couch. Black jogging bottoms. She relaxed slightly, uncurled, and as she held onto him the drone faded away. They fitted together so perfectly, like they always had; they were just the right shape. His warmth, his skin and his smell.

"You're shaking, darling," said Patrick. "Don't worry. It's OK now. Shh. Just the way the shadows fell, made you think it was a woman out there. There's nothing to be afraid of. When the doctor explained it to me he said that if you were tired enough, your brain starts to dream even though you're awake. That's why it seems so like a nightmare; because it really is one."

"I called the police. They're on the way."

"You did what? Why?"

He really hadn't seen it. Seen her, the woman from the hospital, the woman in the bushes. But Lauren had, solid and real as the trees themselves; the eyes still glared at her when she closed her own, the image burned there like she'd looked at the sun too long. She was going mad, she must be. That or the woman was some kind of witch, some kind of demon who could disappear at will. And that was not possible, which meant she was back around at mad again. Just a shadow. Jumping at shadows. She really needed to get some sleep.

"I don't know," she said, "I thought it was the best thing to do. I'm sorry."

Patrick squeezed her tightly. "Don't worry.

We'll just wait until they arrive and tell them there's nothing to concern them. It'll be fine."

She lifted her face away from his chest. "Patrick."

"Yes, my love?"

"You have to help me."

He blew out a long sigh that held exhaustion, reluctance and resignation, but he said, "Yes, darling, I know. I will, don't worry. You're safe now, I'll keep you safe."

She slid down into the comfort of his words and pretended they could be true.

CHAPTER THIRTEEN

"I'm so sorry for wasting your time like this, Detective," said Patrick. "My wife's been under a lot of pressure, caring for the boys. Newborn babies, you know, and they're twins. She just needs some rest."

Harper was sitting opposite Lauren and Patrick in their small front room. Lauren held both babies, exactly as she'd been doing the first time they met, in the hospital, with the same protective cradle that was almost a grip. Not everything was the same: this time she was dressed in jogging bottoms and a T-shirt instead of a hospital gown. She seemed thinner, and perhaps paler than before, but the haunted expression was the same. The babies were noticeably bigger, and still colour-coded in sleeveless vests; one in yellow, one in white with green stripes.

"I can't put them down for more than a

few minutes at the moment. They just wake up."

"I know, darling. I know," said Patrick. "Don't worry, I'll make sure you get some rest tonight." Patrick stroked the head of the baby closest to him, then got up from the couch and turned on a lamp by the fireplace. Outside, the last of the daylight washed the landscape pink and orange.

When Lauren had called, Harper had been in her flat, stretching her calves after a long run. The other woman had sounded so scared. After hanging up she'd thrown on jeans and a top and raced to her car, wondering briefly if she ought to call the station to log her actions before deciding against it. One creepy woman was no match for Harper, and this situation easily passed the threshold for reasonable grounds for arrest. Traffic was sparse and she'd made it across the city to the address in less than nine minutes, already picturing the look on Thrupp's face when she brought the woman in. *Not a figment of someone's imagination after all, then. See, sir?*

It was disappointing in the extreme, therefore, to be greeted with Patrick Tranter's apologetic face, and no apparent suspect. Patrick hadn't wanted to let her in, and it had been an effort to get him to invite her inside. But she wouldn't be turned away — there was still that feeling. She needed to hear what Lauren had to say.

Harper retrieved her notebook and pen from her satchel, and turned towards Lauren. "Tell me exactly what happened."

Lauren glanced at her husband before she spoke. "I was about to go out. Patrick and I, we'd had a bit of an argument — I just wanted to get away for a few minutes, to clear my head. But when I opened the front door, that was when I saw her."

Patrick cleared his throat. Lauren glanced at him again.

"I mean, that was when I thought I saw her. In the bushes across the road. I told Patrick to look but he couldn't see anyone there. It was quite shadowy, I suppose. And it's true, I am really tired. I can't think straight most of the time, to be honest."

"It's not your fault, darl. None of this is. You can't help it." Patrick stroked his wife's shoulder. "Do you want me to take one of the boys?"

She blurted, "No," and flinched away, but immediately offered an apologetic smile. "Maybe in a minute."

The "no" had occurred in Harper, too, a stab in her gut. She wants to hold them, couldn't he see that? She needs to have them close to her. Where they're safe, where they belong. Harper tried to ignore her own longing to reach out and take one, to feel the warm weight of a baby in her arms again. At the same time she knew it couldn't ever be the same, to hold someone else's child.

"Did you recognise the person you saw?" asked Harper.

"There wasn't a person," said Patrick. "She just told you. She didn't actually see anyone. It wasn't there, there wasn't anyone there."

Harper stared at Patrick for a split second before returning her attention to Lauren. "But on the phone, Mrs Tranter, you said it was the same woman you'd seen in the hospital."

"Yes," said Lauren, "I —"

Patrick said, "This is quite a delicate subject, Detective. Do you think we need to explore this right now? Do you think my wife needs to discuss her mental-health issues with you, right now?"

Lauren was staring at Harper. Harper was convinced that, yes, Lauren did in fact want to talk about it. But her husband, clearly, did not want her to. Harper's instinct, and her training, told her to ignore Patrick.

"Mrs Tranter — Lauren? Is there anything

else you'd like to tell me?"

Lauren looked away. Her mouth turned down at the corners and she shook her head, no.

Hiding her frustration, Harper turned to Patrick. "So, Mr Tranter," she said, "tell me what you saw."

Irritation crossed his face. "I didn't see anything, or anyone. I went outside and had a look around, more for my wife's sake than anything. She was worried, and I wanted to make sure there was no one there."

"But you didn't think there was anyone there, before you went outside?" said Harper.

"No."

"So why did you go running up the road without your shoes?"

"I told you. I wanted to make sure."

Harper gave Patrick a long look. Why would a man rush outside barefoot if he was truly convinced there was nothing to chase? Shoes would only take a moment to find and put on. She narrowed her eyes. Patrick became uncomfortable under her scrutiny, crossing and recrossing his arms and frowning. He reached down to scratch his foot where a bandage had been applied. Was this the story of a dedicated husband, making a sacrifice in the moment to appease his

159

anxious wife? Or was this a man with something to hide? There was a veil over Patrick. She could smell his lies. In contrast, looking at Lauren was like looking at a glass of water. If she was trying to conceal anything, it was only her confusion, her shame.

Harper stood up. "If you don't mind, Lauren, I'd like to see the exact spot where you saw the woman."

"I thought I just told you," said Patrick. "There was no woman."

Harper smiled tightly. "You did tell me that, Mr Tranter, repeatedly in fact. I simply would like to make a routine check of the area, to put my own mind at rest. I trust you have no objections?"

"Well, I don't see why you would bother yourself."

"Nevertheless," said Harper, "could you please show me, Lauren?"

Lauren stood in the doorway, clutching the babies. "A bit to the left," she called, and Harper directed her torch towards the place she'd indicated. The undergrowth was flattened there, just as if a person had trampled it. Something had been here, quite recently, considering the freshness of the broken foliage. Patrick said he hadn't entered the bushes himself, only checked from the pavement to see if anyone was there. But there was no evidence it had been done by a woman; it could have been a fox, or a dog, or some children making a den, but the fact of it supported the general theory that someone or something had been there; Lauren had seen something, even if it wasn't what she thought. Apart from a few pieces of litter and a couple of scraps of dirty black fabric, there was nothing else to see. Harper climbed out of the ditch and walked back towards the house where Patrick waited on the doorstep. Lauren had gone back inside.

Patrick spoke quietly, as if he didn't want his wife to hear. "I contacted the out-of-hours GP about tonight. They've told me to make sure Lauren gets a good night's sleep. If she's still anxious in the morning I'm to make an appointment. I'm sorry you've wasted your time coming all the way out here. I would have stopped her from calling you, if I'd known she was going to."

Harper glanced back towards the bushes before she spoke. "Has it ever occurred to you, Mr Tranter, that your wife might be telling the truth about seeing this woman?"

He made a little explosive huff. "Don't be ridiculous, Detective. I was here too and I didn't see anyone. And that first time, in the hospital, no one saw anything then

161

either. The psychiatrist — and surely he should know — said it was a hallucination. The fact she's had another one is quite worrying."

"More, or less worrying than there being a real person outside your house, staring in through the windows?"

"Well, that's a stupid thing to say. Who would do that, anyway?"

"I don't know, Mr Tranter," said Harper. "But perhaps you do."

"I don't know what you mean," said Patrick, and stepped backwards into the house before shutting the door with a firm click.

CHAPTER FOURTEEN

July 22nd
Lunchtime

When her phone pinged with the message alert, Harper almost didn't bother to check it. It wouldn't be Amy, it never was. A week had passed now, and she'd stopped kidding herself it was ever going to happen, which was totally fine with her. Best to keep things simple. She raised her binoculars to her eyes, made a note of the time and took a sip of water. She unwrapped an energy bar, then glanced at her phone and immediately lost her appetite.

How about a cuppa? I'm free now xx

At first, Harper wondered if Amy had made a mistake, if she'd meant to send the message to someone else. Then she thought, don't be stupid, of course she sent it to the right person. That was just Amy's style —

163

she wouldn't have even noticed that a week had passed, or for a moment suspected that Jo had been waiting pathetically for this text. Harper debated with herself how long she ought to leave it before sending a response. She lasted about thirty seconds.

Great. I'm on a job, but it must be time for a break.

Ooo anything good?

Surveillance. Nothing doing though. Where shall we meet?

Tell me where you are, I'll come to you. Exciting!

Before she could think about it properly she fired off the street name in reply — but as soon as she pressed Send she wanted to take the message back. She had parked on a side street in town, in a spot within sight of the office of a company called Strategy Outsource Marketing. Patrick Tranter's car had been in the car park there for the past fifteen minutes. She really wasn't sure if she wanted to explain to Amy how she'd come to be there, or exactly what job she was on. Ah, maybe she won't ask, thought Harper.

Ten minutes later, Amy knocked on the passenger-side window.

"Darling," she said, and when she'd settled herself inside and handed Harper a hot cup of coffee, "what's happening? Who are we looking for?"

The perfume Amy wore was sweet and floral, something like lily of the valley. Harper thanked her for the coffee, a feeble effort at stalling.

"Well?" said Amy, not acknowledging the thanks.

"I'm just keeping an eye on, um, someone. Someone's car, anyway. He's gone inside that building."

"A suspect?" said Amy, blowing into the hole in the top of the takeaway cup. She rummaged in her bag, brought out a packet of walnuts and offered one to Harper, which she took.

"Not really a suspect, more a person of interest."

Amy lowered her coffee and gave Harper a hard stare. "What are you doing, Joanna? You absolutely have to tell me. I won't leave until you do."

There was a pause. "It's not that I don't want to tell you . . ."

"So tell me."

Harper thought about it. It was so pleasur-

165

able to give Amy new gossip; Harper could picture the way her face would be lit from within as she leaned in to listen. But, from twenty years of service Harper was hardwired to keep police business to herself. As Amy waited, she tapped her shiny blue nails on the gearstick. Harper's professional reluctance to share fell away. This wasn't actually, after all, official police business anymore.

"You have to promise not to say anything," said Harper.

Amy mimed zipping her mouth shut.

"I mean it, Amy. If anyone finds out about this, I won't just be slapped on the wrist. I could be in real trouble."

"I completely promise. You can trust me. It's off the record, entirely."

All playfulness gone, Harper could see that she was sincere.

So, Harper told Amy about the visit to the Tranters' house two days before. Amy listened, her eyes gleaming as Harper recounted how she'd become convinced that the husband was lying about something, but also that Lauren was scared and vulnerable and quite possibly mentally unstable. She added that the bushes had been trampled, and although that in itself didn't prove anything, it bothered her.

166

Like the shadows on the tape bothered her.

Amy sat up, remembering. "This is the abduction case from the hospital, isn't it? The false alarm?"

Harper nodded.

"But you just said there *was* someone hanging around outside their house, which would indicate somcone *is* out to get them. So was it a false alarm or not?"

"In the hospital they told me the mother was having a psychotic episode. But when I spoke to her at the time, I don't know. I believed that something had happened."

"I remember. You were upset. Because of the babies thing."

Harper lookcd at Amy. "Yeah. I told you that I . . ."

"Have a weird thing about babies, I know. It's a sensitive subject for you."

Maybe she'll ask me now, thought Harper. For a few seconds neither of them said anything.

"Anyway," said Harper, "I've been told by my boss to leave the case alone. Which is why I'm here on my lunch hour, and not on work time."

"You don't have a lunch hour." Amy cast her eyes about the car. "And, I don't see any lunch."

It was true, there was no such thing as a lunch hour at the station. You ate at your desk. All of the computer keyboards had a film of supermarket mayo and a dusting of crisp crumbs. "Well, I'm on my way to the shop, if you must know. We are allowed to do that."

Amy considered this information for a while. "None of this actually explains why you're here. Precisely here, right now, watching that car, which I am assuming from what you've said, belongs to Tranter. How did that come about?"

"Oh, that. Well, I was going to check the trampled bushes again, in the daylight, just to see if there was anything I'd missed. As I pulled up near the house I happened to see Patrick getting into his car. So, I followed."

"Makes sense. Nothing better to do. On your way to the shop."

"Right."

"And, it's a lovely day for it."

"Yes," said Harper, with less confidence.

"For a bit of freelance snooping."

"Well, I don't see it quite like that —"

"Not that I'm judging. Lord knows, that's my entire existence. Oh wait, who's this?"

A thin woman with dark hair approached the entrance to the office car park. She removed a mobile phone from a small red handbag and pressed on its screen, then held it to her ear. After a short conversation, she put the phone back in her bag and leaned on the bonnet of Patrick Tranter's car with her arms folded.

Harper looked through her binoculars at the woman, who was very pale and dressed in a long black T-shirt dress and flip-flops. Probably in her early twenties, the woman seemed as if she'd been crying, and her dark hair was greasy and limp. But, it was clear she was a naturally beautiful girl, even with puffy eyes and without make-up.

"I think this must be a friend of Mr Tranter's."

"She doesn't look too friendly to me," said Amy, before popping a walnut into her mouth and crunching down on it. Patrick appeared at the office door and pushed it open. He walked across the car park towards the woman and stopped several metres away from her, his fists shoved deep in his pockets. "She looks as if she might scratch his eyes out."

"Who do you think she is?" said Harper, lowering the binoculars.

"Why don't we find out? Let's do a stroll-by."

"Oh, I can't. He knows me."

"I'll go," said Amy, and hopped out of the

car before Harper could protest. She skipped jauntily down the road in her huge sunglasses, curls bouncing, and for a long moment Harper took her eyes off the couple and watched the journalist. By the time Harper returned her attention to Patrick and the mystery woman, they were on the move too: he had her by the arm, and was escorting her along the road, towards where Harper was sitting in her car. They passed Amy without so much as a glance, but a split second later Patrick's head snapped up sharply as he recognised Harper's car. She turned her face away but it was too late; she'd been seen.

She closed her eyes for a second and swore under her breath, hoping that Patrick wasn't the kind of man who would report her to the boss.

"He says you were harassing him," said Thrupp.

"That's a bit strong," said Harper. "I was just sitting in my car. What evidence does he have?"

"He says he saw you drive by his house yesterday, and then today you were watching him at his place of work. Is it true?"

"No. Well, yes. I did drive by, yesterday and today. But I wouldn't call it harassment.

It doesn't meet the criteria. I was doing police work, general investigation, information gathering. He's a person of interest."

"A person of interest? To a case I have already told you is not a case?"

"He was behaving suspiciously."

"Fortunately for you, Mr Tranter isn't interested in pressing charges or making a formal complaint."

Harper pulled a face. Of course he wouldn't press charges — there wasn't nearly enough to make a case that would stand up in court.

"But I think, for you, an internal disciplinary is now in order. You were warned."

Harper was silent, awaiting her fate. She felt surly, like a kid in the headmaster's office.

"You're desk bound, Joanna. No going out, not even to get lunch. You can go to the canteen like everyone else."

This was the perfect punishment for Harper, and he knew it. She tried to appear unbothered, but couldn't help but ask, "For how long?"

"Until I say so. From now on, if you're not in the office every day from eight until five, you better be at home with an impressive illness and a doctor's note. Now get on with those bloody reports."

After Thrupp left the office, Harper turned unwillingly to her task. She wasn't sure how long she'd be able to stay nice, no matter how much Thrupp wanted her to be sorry about her past mistakes, and to be grateful for the risks he'd taken on her behalf.

CHAPTER FIFTEEN

A branch of mountain ash tied over the cradle protects girls against fairy abduction, as according to ancient superstition the first woman was created from the mountain ash. A branch of the alder tree protects boys, as the first man was created from the alder tree.

Irish traditional

August 7th
Three Weeks and Four Days Old
Early Morning

The front door slammed and for a few seconds there was no sound. Then, the distant beeping of the car being unlocked, the car door opening and shutting, engine igniting in a low growl, gravel and grit twisted under tyres as Patrick drove away. The clock on Lauren's phone told her it was seven thirty-nine, and those numbers meant only that it would probably be almost twelve hours until he returned. In the brief absence of noise, a particularly egregious phrase he'd used in a recent conversation occurred to her, rudely by itself: "Marketing requires networking, darling." Going to a bar after work, in his world, was essential for business. She was too tired to argue.

A few nights before his return to work, he'd moved into the spare room. He hadn't wanted to, he said, but he couldn't sleep with the windows shut. She couldn't sleep without them being firmly locked.

"If you insist on leaving the windows open, anywhere in this house, at night," she said, "we're going to need a lock on the inside of the bedroom door so that I know we're safe in there, at least."

He'd got in the car, driven directly to the DIY shop and brought her three to choose from. She chose them all.

"Three locks?" he said.

"Yes."

Although he looked at her then in a way she couldn't fully interpret, he fitted them without complaint.

The locks made her feel safe enough to nap when it was dark outside, but the physical barrier it created between her and Patrick underlined their separateness: they were no longer a team. There was no point trying to wake him in the night, to watch over the babies or to help; it was easier just to get on with it herself, to stay awake when she needed to, and to sleep only when she and the boys were secure. For Patrick's part, he'd dropped off his caring cliff: I care, I care, I care, I would care but I simply do not have the time or energy to care anymore, mostly because of all that caring you just made me do. He implied, in both his speech and his actions, that baby-rearing was exclusively Lauren's department, and always would have been, obviously: the roles were pre-determined; man/woman, breadwinner/homemaker. The gut-punch of dismay was unexpected. Why hadn't she realised before now that he was so old-fashioned? Would she have married him, if she'd known? It seemed too much to try to argue, to wriggle out from under the weight of it all.

So, she would cope, because it wasn't a choice. Patrick was encouraging, even if he wasn't there very much. He sent regular "Love you' texts. And he always said, when he eventually did come home, what a great job she was doing, even as he let his eyes wander to the piles of unwashed clothes, the half-empty tin of beans with a spoon sticking out, the unopened mail on the doormat. Even as he whispered urgently into the phone to his sister so that the moment he hung up, Lauren's phone pinged with a message from Ruthie, breezily asking after her and the boys, promising to drop by as soon as she could.

When someone knocked on the front door, she thought about leaving it. It wouldn't be Ruthie, not at this time; she'd be at work. Lauren stood in the arch between the kitchen and the sitting room, as still as she could, so that whoever it was might just think she wasn't in and go away. But then, one of the boys made a loud sound, and the letter-box flapped open. A set of manicured fingers waggled at her through the gap.

"You going to let me in, babe?"

It was Cindy. Lauren crossed the room and opened the front door to her friend.

"I wasn't expecting anyone," she said, turning and quickly picking up several dirty cups from the carpet. "But come on in."

Cindy waited for Lauren to stop fussing and gave her a hug. Lauren, aware she might not smell that great, broke away quickly and stepped back. Now that she looked properly at Cindy she was stunned at the sight of her; Cindy was neatly dressed, her post-baby bump only just visible beneath a floaty vest. She was wearing full make-up and strappy sandals with heels.

"Wow," said Lauren, combing her hair with her fingers, "you look amazing. It's really good to see you." She glanced down at the baby. "Both of you. Isn't she adorable?"

Cindy's baby was sleeping soundly in the car seat, which she placed next to the Moses basket holding the twins, on the floor.

"Sorry to drop round like this," said Cindy, "but me and Rosa were getting a bit worried about you."

"Worried about me?" Lauren tried an offhand laugh that fell rather flat. She knew how it must look, how unwashed she was, how the house was a complete tip.

"Yes. Rosa set up that message group called Baby News, but you never put anything on it. You did see that she had the baby, the day after we came to see you?"

The time had all been sucked away. While she was in them, those hours that she fed to her babies went slower than they ought to, but then the days, the precious days flicked by as quick as streetlights on the motorway.

"I did see that, I think. Such good news. Have you visited them?" The other women's babies were vague to Lauren, conceptual. She knew of them, but there was no space in her heart to wonder, or to care. About this she felt guilty. Her capacity to feel guilt was apparently unimpaired, possibly infinite.

"Don't you read the posts? We've met up twice already. You were invited, both times."

She'd read the posts. They both knew it; the ticks, that went blue automatically when the message was read, would have given her away.

"Yeah, I know. I couldn't come. I meant to say one way or the other, sorry about that."

"You didn't even say anything in the group when I put on that I'd had Lucy."

Guilt again, prodding at her.

"Oh, Cindy, how awful of me. I meant to. How long has it been?"

"Lucy's two weeks and one day old now."

"Cindy, I'm so sorry. I was going to get you a gift, but I couldn't get out —"

Cindy waved away the apology. "Don't worry about that, we've got baby stuff coming out of our ears. I just wanted to make sure you were OK, and ask if you needed any help. Your fella must have gone back to work now, right?"

Lauren nodded.

"My partner went back yesterday, too. It's different, isn't it, once it's just you."

"Yes," said Lauren. "Kind of lonely. Even

though you're not technically alone."

Cindy said, "I don't know if it's the same for you, but it's as if he's left me with this little person who I don't really know very well, that I have complete responsibility for. He says he'll ring me every lunchtime, but still. If I feel like this after one day, with just one baby, you must be tonnes worse than me. I was OK yesterday, because I went out to meet Rosa. I thought — I hoped — you'd be there too."

There was an awkward pause.

"Is it something we've said or done?" said Cindy.

"No, it's not you. The truth is, I haven't been out yet."

"At all?"

"No."

"Not even to the registry office?"

Patrick had started bringing this up, too. They had six weeks, didn't they, to register the birth? There was no hurry. He'd said, *I just want them to be legal. At the moment, they don't exist properly in the eyes of the law. They're in limbo.* Lauren had said nothing, thinking, that is such bullshit. They're more real than you are.

"No," said Lauren, attempting breezy, "not yet. We've time. I'm not quite ready to face the world, I suppose." She indicated

179

her stained joggers, fiddled with a strand of her drooping hair.

"Babe," said Cindy, "that's nothing a nice bath wouldn't fix." She looked at Lauren from under her mascaraed lashes.

"I don't know how you do it, how you look so great after only two weeks."

"The make-up doesn't take long. You should see me without it, it's a horror show."

In the car seat, Lucy woke up with a small cry. Cindy rummaged in her bag, pulled out a bottle and a milk dispenser. "Can I use your kettle?"

"I'll do it," said Lauren, jumping up. Lucy's cries were getting louder, and Cindy bent to pick her up. It took a few minutes for the bottle, once made, to cool enough to give it but once it had, the room exhaled in calm as the hungry baby fed. Both the women smiled down at Lucy, dressed in a pink baby vest and matching socks.

"How are the nights?" said Cindy. "Are you getting enough sleep?"

Lauren realised after a few seconds that she hadn't responded, that she'd been thinking about sleep, how she craved it. How much was enough sleep? Occasionally she totted it up and all the little bits made up five, sometimes six hours. That was enough, wasn't it? She shook her head, forced a laugh. To keep from crying. "Well, I do all right, I think. Does anyone get to sleep with newborn babies? How about you? Please don't tell me she's sleeping through the night already."

Morgan had woken up and started to ask for milk by chewing his hand and moving his head from side to side, saying *ung-ung-ung*.

Cindy laughed. "No, nothing like. But Ryan and I take it in turns, so I do sometimes manage a longer stretch."

"I wish Patrick could do that."

"You mean he doesn't? Why can't he? Don't you express, so he can use a bottle?"

"I do, sometimes." It wasn't true, she never did. She didn't even know where the breast pump was. "But Patrick's not good at being woken up. He can't function properly at work. So, I suppose I said I would do the nights, and then it just, went on like that." As she said it she heard how pathetic it sounded, making excuses for him. Lauren raised her eyes and met Cindy's, where the kindness broke the weakened dam holding back her tears. Cindy gently patted her knee as she cried. When she could speak she said, "I keep crying. I can't stop it, I'm so sorry."

"You're doing the best you can do, and you're a great mum. Believe me. Look how happy and well-fed these two are."

The two women looked at the boys. Chubby wrists, cheeks as fat as plums. Lauren gently stopped Morgan's arm from whirring, stroked his fingers with her thumb which she then pressed into his little palm for him to squeeze.

"They should be well-fed," said Lauren, "they never stop feeding."

"Is there anyone else you can ask for help?"

"Not really. I don't know if I told you, my mum . . ."

"Oh, of course. I'm so sorry. It must be so hard without her."

More tears came, crowding her throat in great heaving sobs that she couldn't stifle. Cindy made soothing noises. She passed over a tissue from the box.

"I mean," said Lauren, "I don't know why I'm so upset. She's been dead for years. I'm sorry."

"Nothing to be sorry for. Nothing at all." She folded Lauren into a hug.

Lauren leaned into Cindy and cried like a little girl.

Later, Lauren was calm. The crying had been the good kind, the sort you feel so much better for. The two women sipped tea and watched the babies, who were falling asleep where they lay.

"Identical twins are funny, aren't they?"

Lauren was shocked. "No," she said. The offence hung between them as Lauren's frown deepened.

"Oh," said Cindy, "I don't mean funny. I mean . . . interesting. Part of it is the mystery. How can there be two people the same, but different? Something about their interchangeableness, maybe."

Lauren wanted her to stop talking. They weren't interchangeable, they were two different people. Two different personalities. Riley was serious, he wanted things his own way and was finding ways of making himself heard. He was determined, intelligent. Morgan was more laid back; he would be the artist. Totally different, unmistakably so. And, they looked different, the same but also so obviously different. To her, at least. It didn't matter what anyone else saw.

Cindy, oblivious, did not stop talking.

"There are stories about twins, you know. It came up in my English A-level. Lots of different cultures have different stories — they used to think magic was involved. You can see why, can't you?"

"No."

"Some African tribes thought they

brought a curse upon the village. They would just throw them into the bushes to die, the moment they were born."

The idea of baby twins, dying in the bushes; a painful stab in her heart. "Why are you telling me this, exactly?"

Cindy caught the warning tone in Lauren's voice. She took a sip of her tea. "Oh, well, that's just an example. I'm sure they're not all as gory as that. Look, I'm sorry I started this. Let's talk about something else."

Lauren remembered the storybook, the one she hadn't read, because she was frightened of what might be inside. Perhaps she ought to face it head on, the way her mother had done when she'd pretended to like spiders even though she was terrified of them, so as not to make her small daughter afraid too. Didn't she have a duty now, to try not to pass on her own fears to Morgan and Riley? Why was she scared of a few fairy stories anyway?

"Is that why you gave me that book?" said Lauren. "I haven't read it yet."

Cindy frowned. "What book? I gave you a fish and an octopus. Those ones." She pointed to the soft toys, dumped in a pile in the corner and still half in the wrapping.

Lauren rummaged in the pile and found

184

the book. The spine was coming away slightly, the binding soft to the touch. As she turned it over in her hands, a smell of ancient libraries rose from the dun-coloured cover.

She handed it to Cindy, who took it with her fingertips, as if she didn't really want to. "I would never have given you this," she said. "What makes you think it was from me?"

"It was in the gift bag, with the toys. You said there was a little something for me in there, didn't you?"

"Yes, it was soap. Hand-made lavender soap, from the craft market."

"Soap? I didn't find any soap."

Cindy's eyes were wide with disbelief. "That is so weird."

The crumbling hardback nearly fell apart as Cindy flipped it open to read the contents page.

"It's fairy tales."

"I know."

"They're all about babies. And, there's a section on twins. Oh, look. One of the stories is local."

Before she could be stopped, Cindy found the page and started reading aloud.

Once there was a man and his wife who

lived together in a hut on the side of a mountain. They had baby twins, both of whom the wife nursed tenderly. One day, while the husband was far away with the flock, the wife was called to the house of a neighbour who was dying. She did not want to leave her two babes, as she had heard tell that faeries were roaming the land. Still, the neighbour was in dire need and so she went.

Lauren's pulse started racing. Goose-bumps all over. The woman's face, her matted hair.

Choose one, that's what she'd said. *Choose one or I'll take them both.*

Don't leave them alone. Ever.

Cindy didn't look up. She kept reading.

On the way back she was dismayed to see a pair of old Elves of the Blue Petticoat crossing her path. She ran all the way home but when she got there saw that the twins were still in the cradle, and all was the same as when she had left.

But all was not the same. From that day forward, the twins did not grow at all, and the man and his wife began to suspect that something was wrong.

"These are not our children," said the man.

"Whose children can they be?" asked the wife.

You'll never know the difference. I can make sure they look just the same.

She picked up Riley, who'd started to fuss. She'd know him anywhere. She held him close and breathed him in. My baby.

They were both very sad for a long time, until the wife decided to seek the help of the wise man, who lived in a cave in the place they called the God's Graveyard a few miles hence.

It was the time of year for reaping, and not long until the oats and rye would be harvested. The wise man, hearing of the woman's woe, told her this: "You must clean out an old hen's egg and boil up some potage in it, then go to the door as if to give it to the reapers for supper. Then, listen for what the babies say."

"But they are too young yet to speak," said the woman.

"If the elves have changed them, they are as old as the hills, and more," said the wise man.

"And what of my own two babes?" she asked.

"If the babies speak, you will know that they are changed. But also that your own are close by, with the elf-mother."

"And if they speak, and they are changed, what am I to do?"

"You must change them back," said the wise man. "You must throw them into the river."

"Stop," said Lauren, too loudly. All three babies jumped.

Cindy closed the book. She examined the front cover, running her thumb over the gold embossed title.

"Who sent you this?" said Cindy.

"I told you, I thought it was you."

"I can't imagine what you must have thought about me, then. I promise you, I would never gift someone something so . . . ugh. A book of scary stories about twins, for a woman who's just had twins? How inappropriate can you get?"

Lauren couldn't stop thinking about the mother in the story. She wanted to know whether she went ahead and threw her own babies in the river, and if they drowned. At the same time, she didn't want to know, ever.

Cindy stood up and pushed the little book deep into the bookcase by the fireplace. "I wouldn't read it if I were you. Give it to a charity shop, maybe. I'll put the kettle on again, shall I?"

Lauren carefully arranged her face in a semblance of nonchalance. Underneath it she was a boiling ocean of mixed-up feelings. She wanted to be alone, to calm herself down, to try not to think too much about what she'd just heard. Also, more than anything, she wanted to get the book down and finish reading the story. Not knowing the end was somehow worse. Cindy wouldn't understand — especially after she'd shouted at her to stop reading; Lauren wasn't sure she understood it herself. She stood up, Riley still latched to her breast. She found her voice, small and careful. "Cindy, can you just pass Morgan over?" Cindy picked up Morgan from the carpet and tucked him into Lauren's other arm.

"Thanks, lovely," said Lauren. "I won't have that tea just now, actually. I think I might go for a lie down."

"You OK, Lauren?" said Cindy.

"Fine. A bit tired, that's all. I'm sorry. Do you mind?"

"No, not at all."

Cindy fastened Lucy into the car seat and stood up to leave. She opened the front door, letting the heat roll in.

"Shall I come again next week, or . . ."

"I'll come out next week," said Lauren, "to the park for a coffee. I promise. I'll be less of a state then. I'll even have a shower, how about that?"

"We'll be honoured. I'll tell Rosa."

They kissed on both cheeks and Lauren shut the door with a foot, hearing the Yale lock click into place as she did. She looked down at the babies in her arms, sighing, smiling, for a moment feeling almost normal before the tiredness descended on her once more. She sank down into a chair and closed her eyes. She'd just sit for a second. Then she'd get the book down.

When she opened her eyes, the light in the room was different. An unknown amount of time had passed, and the nap had somehow made her even more tired than she was before. She stood up, still holding the babies, thinking to go upstairs to bed. Taking a few steps towards the kitchen, the air shifted slightly, a chill touched the back of her neck. There was a faint scratching, tapping sound, and her head snapped around to find the source. Something was darkening the window at the back of the house. The woman's filthy face, her matted hair, her glittering eyes. Grinning, pressed against the window she pointed at Lauren, one fingernail scraping slowly down the glass.

Lauren screamed, screwed her eyes tight shut, threw herself backwards so that she was flat against the wall. The boys began to cry but it barely registered. When she dared to look again, the woman was gone. She forced herself to step closer, to peer a little further, and there was still nothing. Had it been a shadow — a bird? The light playing tricks? Cindy's visit had tired her out. It was so exhausting having guests. The colours in the kitchen were unreal, vivid and blurred at the edges, saturated by the terror. She ought to check the garden, see if anyone was there. No, there won't be, better to rest, to go where it's safe, quickly. Lauren, gripping her precious boys against her body, climbed the stairs to the bedroom and shut the door, before sliding the bolts across and squeezing closed the padlock.

She curled up on the bed, encircling Morgan and Riley, trying not to think of the horrible woman, or of the pictures her mind had made out of those awful stories from Cindy. But no matter how hard she tried, she couldn't banish the faces of any of them: not the dark mouth and flashing eyes of the woman at the window; not those poor, nameless babies, crying alone in the African bush, or the ones in the river, sinking.

CHAPTER SIXTEEN

When his first child was a few weeks old they found it on three different nights lying crossways and uncovered in its cradle, even though the cradle stood immediately next to the mother's bed. The father therefore resolved to stay awake during the third night and to pay close attention to his child. He persisted a long while, staying awake until after midnight. Nothing happened to the child, because he had been keeping a watchful eye on it. But then his eyes began to close a little.

Jacob and Wilhelm Grimm

August 13th
Four Weeks and Three Days Old
6 P.M.

"Have you been up here all day?" said Patrick. He was standing in the doorway surveying the scene in the bedroom, the messy little nest Lauren had made for herself. Wrinkling his nose and frowning, arms folded.

"I went down. To get food," said Lauren. She was cross-legged in the middle of the bed, feeding Morgan while Riley kicked his legs in the Moses basket. "Why do you ask?"

She felt defensive, but even Lauren could see that the situation was extreme. She'd buried herself like a worm at the centre of this vortex of items: dirty nappies in bags, baby clothes, wipes, food packets, mugs, bedding, DVDs, toys. Strewn didn't cover it adequately; it was as if a small tornado had passed through. But, the babies were clean, fed, happy. Wasn't that the only important thing?

"You can't stay in bed all day, Lauren. It's not healthy." Patrick uncrossed his arms and put his fists on his hips.

"It's comfier in here," she said, trying not to whine. "I can feed them both at once, without worrying if someone will look in the window and see me naked."

Patrick looked sceptical. "You could still do that downstairs. Just draw the curtains."

"I could," said Lauren, "but I like them open. I like the light."

Baby Morgan dropped off the breast, exposing Lauren's large nipple. It pointed downwards, a long pink teat, wet and sucked out of shape. Patrick shifted his eyes away, to Riley, lying in the Moses basket, curling his fingers into balls and shrieking intermittently. The shrieks were alarmingly loud, but it was a happy sound.

"Why is he doing that?" said Patrick. He came further into the room and knelt next to the basket, drawing his face close to the baby's. As she watched, they took each other in, father and son inspecting each other slowly and carefully. The two had matching frowns. Then Riley screwed his eyes shut and shrieked again, flapping his hands onto Patrick's head and grabbing a handful of hair.

Patrick shouted, "Ow, get off me," and tried to dig his great finger into the baby's fist to make it release. "Why won't he let go?"

Laughter bubbled up in Lauren and she tried not to let it out. The extrication took a while, but Patrick finally pulled his head away, leaving long strands of gold behind in Riley's hand.

"The little blighter," said Patrick. "That really hurt."

Lauren thought of the labour pains. Her smile died on her face.

"Did it."

She watched Patrick rubbing at his head

through his curls, throwing aggrieved glances in the direction of the tiny baby, who shrieked, happily. She said, "You know, he wasn't doing it on purpose."

"Hmm," said Patrick. "I guess."

"They can make fists at this age, but they can't release them at will. It's a developmental thing."

He didn't seem convinced, just grimaced doubtfully, as if he thought she was making it up.

"You could try reading one of those books I bought," she said, nodding to the pile of jauntily titled baby bibles placed on the recessed shelf, Post-it notes sticking out marking particularly good bits she wanted him to read. *The Truly Happy Baby, Why Love Matters, The Baby Owner's Manual.* She'd even bought *The Expectant Dad's Handbook,* but she'd never even seen him pick it up.

"Ha, yeah," said Patrick, rolling his eyes. Lauren felt something opening up between them. Something unfixable, like cracking glass. He sat on the edge of the bed and took one of Morgan's feet in his palm.

"This one likes me, though. Don't you?" He lifted Morgan from Lauren's arms and held him close, wrapping him in his own. For a brief moment she felt something like pride. He would be a good daddy. He just needed a bit of guidance. "What's for tea?" said Patrick. He was still looking at Morgan, so it took Lauren a second to register that he was talking to her.

"Oh, I don't know," said Lauren. "What do you fancy? Chinese?"

His dissatisfied face made her think again of Riley's. "We can't live on take-out, Lauren."

Riley shrieked, loud enough to make them both wince and turn towards him. Then Patrick turned back towards Lauren and shook his head. "Chinese," he said, and, "Jesus," under his breath. He stood up and went downstairs, taking Morgan with him. From within her nest she heard him cross the kitchen, open the fridge, whisper an expletive.

He marched back to the foot of the stairs and shouted up, "There's absolutely nothing in, Lauren."

Lauren did not move, or speak. She lay on the bed, face towards the window. The sky was purplish in places, streaked with clouds. The decimated ski village was in shadow. Riley had fallen asleep. The house thrummed with Patrick's rage, which had whipped up from nothing when he realised how pathetic she was; how she had failed.

She ought to be able to shop, to go downstairs, to make the dinner. Other people managed; Cindy managed. Tears slipped down Lauren's cheek, wetting the pillow.

Patrick came thundering upstairs. The baby, a startled expression on his face, was still gripped in his left arm. "You should have called me, I would have dropped in to the shops on my way home."

"I would have called," she said, not looking at him, "but I thought you'd be cross with me."

"I wouldn't, why would you think that?"

He was almost yelling now.

"I think it because you keep saying I need to get out, get to the shops. I didn't do it. I'm sorry."

"Don't be silly, darling."

That phrase again. She no longer felt sorry, only annoyed.

"I know you're having a tough time," he said, "but the only reason I keep on at you to go out is because it will make things easier for you, in the long run. You need to get back to normal. Stop hiding inside — it's not healthy for you, or for the boys."

"The food delivery is due tomorrow afternoon. I must have ordered badly last time, we don't usually run out so soon. I've made sure there's enough to see us through."

"It's not the shopping; that's not the point. You need to get yourself out of the house. What are you doing all day, anyway?"

Morgan, as if to demonstrate, opened his mouth and began to cry. Such a sad, mournful sound, almost enough to make everyone around him cry as well, in empathy. *I hurt, Mummy, I'm frightened, help me.*

That's your fault, Patrick, thought Lauren. It was the harsh, unfamiliar deep voice, and the tense atmosphere. She held her arms out to take him from his father.

Patrick passed the baby to her. He must have noticed that Lauren's eyes were red, her face wet with tears.

"You're upset again," he said, matter-of-fact.

She nodded, sniffed. He passed a tissue from the box. She wiped the baby's face, and then her own.

"You really need to go outside," said Patrick.

I need to stay here, thought Lauren, where we are safe.

"When was the last time you went out?"

"I don't know."

She did know. She hadn't left the house since she was pregnant. She'd told him once or twice that she'd been out for a walk while he was at work, but she'd been lying. She hadn't dared put the boys in the car yet. Pregnant Lauren had forced herself to watch an online video of a crash-test baby dummy being slammed against a windscreen in slow-motion and the image would not leave her.

"You used to walk, every day," said Patrick, apparently struggling not to sound accusatory, failing. "You said it kept you sane."

Before Lauren went freelance, she'd worked as a product designer at a manufacturing firm. The long hours and stress of the office environment meant that, for a long time, she wasn't looking after herself properly. Then her mother died suddenly, and instead of taking a break, she worked even harder to keep her mind occupied. The depression, when it finally hit, floored her completely. Some days she hadn't been able to lift her head from the pillow, and just the thought of having to get out of bed made her cry herself back into an exhausted sleep. It had taken a lot to drag herself out of that pit. A lot of antidepressants, a lot of therapy. She'd left the medication behind, now, despite everyone telling her she shouldn't, and she self-medicated with fresh air, good food and exercise. It worked, for her. Each time she stepped out of the door and started to walk, she could feel the darkness lift, as if a layer of it were being physically removed from her body.

After her recovery, she didn't want to return to the office that had made her so ill. It was three years now, since she'd decided to go it alone with her garden fountain business. Patrick had been worried that she might get lonely, working on her own all day. Lauren hadn't shared his concern for a single moment; the flexibility and the solitude suited her. She'd loved working from home out of her little studio, building up her client base of garden centres and private projects. Being her own boss meant that she had total artistic freedom, but it also meant she could take off into the countryside whenever she wished, which was almost every single day. It wasn't only about the exercise; the valleys, woods and rivers often provided inspiration for her flow-form fountain sculptures. She would take her sketchbook just in case she saw a useful natural shape or a leaf formation that she might copy in clay, cast and reproduce in concrete. Patrick was completely right about the daily walks. Her old life had been punctuated by them, enhanced by them, restored by them. But things were different now. All the things were different. For thirty-one days, her boots had stood unused on the shoe rack by the back door.

"I think I might wait a week or two more, before I take them out. They're so little, and they might get too hot in this weather."

Patrick sighed.

The worst of the heat had passed, leaving scorched, parched earth and an indefinite hosepipe ban. There'd been no rain yet, but the last few days a fresh breeze had been blowing up the valleys. Really, the weather was perfect, like living in the Mediterranean. So inviting. But no, she shouldn't go out. Just in case.

"Tomorrow," said Patrick, decisive. "Promise me. You just need to take them for a stroll, somewhere where there's shade. Breathe a bit of fresh air. It'll do you the world of good."

And despite his irritatingly parental tone, she found herself considering it. It *would* be lovely to walk under the sky again, breathe the air, see what the birds were up to. There was an ache in her, a need to surround herself with nature, bigger in this moment than the fear that kept her inside the house.

"The girls from antenatal, they keep asking me to meet them in the Bishop Valley Park. They're going there tomorrow, actually."

"Perfect, then that's settled."

Later they ate Chinese food in bed, and she thought perhaps she did love him, that it could be just as good as before. But when the meal was finished he yawned, kissed her on the head, picked up his earplugs and went through to the spare room, leaving her to a night of snatched half-hours of sleep.

The babies were still more active at night than in the day. Six weeks, she had read, was the magic time when they could tell night from day, developmentally. Sometimes babies slept through the night from six weeks; perhaps hers would do it. She envisaged an unbroken night of sleep, but far from craving it, the idea made her anxious. Those precious hours were hers alone, safe in the locked box of the bedroom, just Lauren and the two miraculous boys she'd created from within her body, who belonged to her, who were part of her and through whose veins her own blood flowed. When the time came for them to sleep through the night, something would be given: the gift of rejuvenating sleep, essential to life. But like every bargain, something would also be taken: it would be another of those inevitable steps away from her and into themselves. Let it go on, she thought, this beautiful torture, the time of the sleepless nights. For as long as it will.

CHAPTER SEVENTEEN

The Nickert is a small grey person that lives in the water and has a great desire for human children. If they have not yet been baptised, he will steal them, leaving his own children in their place.

Kuhn/Schwartz

August 14th
Four Weeks and Four Days Old
Morning
Lauren and the babies fell asleep for the third or fourth time (she lost count) at about 6:30 a.m., just as Patrick was getting in the shower. She woke again at 8 a.m. to find a note pushed under the bedroom door.

Don't forget to go outside today

There was a smiley face and a couple of little hearts, which made her roll her eyes, but she found that she liked it. And, there

205

was a PS:

Can you pick up some tagliatelle? It wasn't on the order. I'll cook later.

She felt sour about the pasta. He was only asking her to get it to make sure she went out, if only to the shop at the top of the road. Lauren opened the bedroom window and the soft late-summer air filled the room. Already the sun was hot, and the day had only just got started. She *would* go outside. But not because he said so. She would go, to prove to herself that there was nothing to be afraid of.

As she gathered up the things she would need in order to leave the house, she kept changing her mind. A feeling of dread descended and she decided she couldn't do it. Then, she stepped into the garden in her bare feet and was overcome. The light and the warmth gave her strength. Patrick was right — going outside was the answer; staying inside made her mad.

Shower — quickly because Riley was crying. Get dry, get moisturised, dressed in shorts and T-shirt. Sun cream. Change babies' wet nappies. Feed babies. Change babies' dirty nappies and clothes, since the stuff had gone everywhere. Two car seats, get them strapped in. Double stroller, folded. Changing bag, nappies, nappy bags, wipes, four changes of clothes. Pacifier for Riley, just in case. Mobile phone, handbag, purse, boots, car keys. Bottle of water. Muslins for mopping up sick.

She managed to pick everything up and hefted the boys and the luggage down the road to where her car was parked, so that her arms ached by the time she got there. She battled with the seat belts in the back of the old three-door Ford, heaved the stroller into the boot, slammed it. Got in, shut the door, put the keys in the ignition and realised she was hungry. Starving. She'd missed breakfast, and now it was lunchtime. The front door was probably sixty yards away. She could just nip back and grab something quickly. She opened the car door to step out.

A jolt, a flash of black something in the bushes. She stared at the spot, feeling adrenaline rushing through her, thinking of the woman hiding, watching her, waiting for her to make a mistake. No one there, just a blackbird. Her eyes searched the undergrowth, every shadow morphing into clumps of hair, black rags, then back again to branches, leaves, nettles and shadows.

I can't leave them, even for a second.

Lauren struggled to unbuckle both car seats and lugged them back up the street to the house, listing in her head the reasons she need not be afraid. I need not be afraid because: there's nothing to be scared of; I'm jumping at shadows; it's always worse when I haven't slept well; everything is fine; I'm just nervous because it's the first time I've been out; I'm fretting about the driving, but I need to get it done, get back on the road, or I'll be stuck forever, a prisoner in my own house.

Keys mined from the handbag where she had sunk them, she went into the house and put the babies, both sleeping, on the couch in their car seats. In the kitchen there wasn't much to be had in the way of sustenance: an elderly banana, alone in the fruit bowl. An almost empty pack of rye crackers from the cupboard. When she found herself deliberating over a can of tuna, she shook her head, *Ridiculous.* Anyway, it didn't matter: she was going to a cafe, so she could get something there.

As she struggled back towards the car with a heavy car seat hooked over each arm she hesitated, then stopped opposite the place she'd thought the woman had stood. Another flicker of black made her jump. But no, nothing, it was that blackbird.

■ ■ ■ ■

Down in the valley she parked the car by
the old millpond and clipped the brightly
coloured car seats into the stroller frame.
She positioned Morgan above, facing her
and Riley below, facing forward. She briefly
worried that Riley might feel snubbed
somehow but he was asleep, after all, and
she could swap them round on the way back
so that it was fair. Changing bag, handbag,
phone, wallet, keys. She laced up her boots
and set off along the river, feeling immediately better. She thought of it as her
river, she'd walked the path so many times.
In the old life she would regularly go all the
way to the New Riverby reservoir, five miles
out — she'd even driven over there and
hiked the circumference of the lake on the
morning of the day she went into labour.
Hugely pregnant and sweating in the heat,
halfway around Lauren had stopped to rest
on a bench. The view was so familiar to her
that she almost didn't notice the triangular
thing, sticking up in the middle of the lake
like a skeletal hand, pointing. What was it?
At first, she thought it might have been the
mast of a sunken boat. As she stared, shading her eyes with one hand, another walker

approached.

"That's the old Selverton Church spire," said the man, "from the drowned village." He'd nodded and smiled, pleased to be able to pass on a bit of local knowledge. Then he'd gone on his way, leaving Lauren to wonder about what he'd said, about what remnants of village life had been preserved under the water, what else might be revealed should the drought go on much longer.

She'd stared at the tip of the spire, at what she could now see was a rusted weathervane, for long minutes before pushing on to where she'd parked the car, driving back home and feeling the first trickle of her own water seeping down her leg as she bent to unlace her boots at the door.

With the stroller it was different, but the ground felt the same beneath her feet. She had to go slowly, manoeuvring the three chunky wheels over the roots, awkwardly around narrow paths of packed mud she'd never noticed were narrow. The leafy canopy spread camouflage patterns onto the babies, flashing sunlight through the gaps so that she worried they might wake up. She stopped to drape a muslin square over the handle of each car seat, shading the sleeping boys, and then pushed on, filling her lungs again and again with delicious warm air. There was the slow return of a sense of freedom, for the first time in a month, her limbs loose and her head full of the wonderful natural perfume of water, rocks, soil. So familiar, so glorious, she was healed by it. The way summer trees smelled when they were heated by the sun.

Half a mile up the river path was the scrubby box of a cafe, and seated on the picnic benches outside on the veranda, Cindy and Rosa. There was a compact black stroller next to Rosa, and Cindy was wearing her baby in a bright purple wrap over her belly. They hugged each other, and Lauren settled the twins' stroller in a shady spot before sitting down.

"How are you feeling?" said Cindy, directing a knowing look towards Lauren. "Less . . . stressed?"

Lauren laughed. "Yeah, I'm fine, thanks. I think everyone was right — I just needed to get out of the house. I should have done it sooner. It's lovely here, isn't it?"

"You look good," said Rosa, "especially after having twins. What's your secret?"

"Never have time to eat?" She remembered the banana in her handbag. It was probably crushed now, inedible. She thought of the pastries inside the cafe and her mouth began to water.

Rosa did the head-tilt in sympathy. "I know what it's like with one, honey, you must be wrung out."

Lauren nodded, sighed, and glanced at Cindy who pretended not to see the meaning in it. The other two had obviously been talking about her, but she didn't mind. It only meant they cared. She looked back at Rosa. "How was your birth, in the end?"

"Oh," said Rosa, throwing up her hands, "it was amazing. I feel for you ladies, I really do. The stories I've heard. I would totally recommend a C-section."

"What about the recovery, though?" said Cindy. "Is it all healing up OK?"

Rosa grimaced, placed a hand tentatively on her belly. "It's not too bad. I'll get there."

"My birth was bloody awful," said Cindy. "What was all that bollocks they told us about at antenatal? Breathe the baby out? Try to avoid drugs?"

"I know," said Lauren, beginning to enjoy herself.

"Breathe it out, for fuck's sake," said Cindy, "as if it's a little cloud of oxygen, or something. Well, might work for some people but not me, I had to push it out and it was bloody painful."

"Oh, so no interventions, or anything?" said Lauren.

"No. They were going to transfer me to the hospital but at the last minute she decided to make an appearance. Didn't you?" Cindy reached into the sling on her front and squeezed her baby's chubby cheek between thumb and forefinger. The baby stayed asleep. Must be used to the cheek-pinching by now.

"You were lucky," said Lauren, "forceps are not much fun, I'm afraid."

Rosa sucked air through her teeth.

"You know what, though?" said Cindy, "We're all OK, aren't we? We should be grateful. There are no bad births, when the result is a healthy mum and baby."

There was a moment, then, as Lauren thought about the endless alternative lives they could be living, having been through this, had the outcome been different. Rosa's baby sighed in her sleep.

"She's so beautiful," said Lauren. "It's Stevie, isn't it? Like the singer."

"Yes. She's Stevie Matilda."

"Brilliant. Such a cool name. She looks like a bonny one — what was her birth weight?" The baby had three chins, and rippling rolls of fat on her arms. Fattest baby ever — one of those people who needed a crane to winch them to hospital for a gastric bypass, but in miniature. And cute.

"Ten pounds two."

Lauren was impressed. "That's a big baby. Mine were five-seven and five-nine."

"That's good, for twins, right?" said Cindy.

And it went on. Weights, names, nappies per day. Who else in their group had given birth, when and how. Bottle feeding, breast-feeding, night-time routines. Where to find the best organic cotton baby clothes. *Are you reading bedtime stories yet? Apparently, it's good for them — we used to read to my bump. Us too, how strange.* The talk went on, and Lauren found that she needed this. People with some of the same concerns that she had. Details that almost nobody else would have found interesting in the slight-est, the mundane, tedious minutiae, given a new significance in their post-birth world, where each choice they made, however small, seemed life-alteringly crucial.

They ate cake and drank coffee and laughed, until eventually it was time to go. Rosa left first, and Cindy soon after. Lauren checked the boys' nappies (no need to change — a welcome blessing) and packed up her stuff, wheeled the stroller to the river path and found to her surprise that she didn't want to go back just yet, to her safe place, her fortress. Now that she was out in the world she wanted to stay out a little longer. She turned upstream and began walking. I'll just go a little way, she thought. It's such a lovely day.

There was a clearing a short distance upriver, where the path followed the water around the edge but the grass was criss-crossed with desire lines. Lauren followed the meandering path, and halfway around she was overcome with the need to sit down and rest. She felt weary, her legs heavy, the caffeine and sugar she'd consumed burning up and crashing, leaving her headachy and weak. Just into the woods on the other side of the clearing she knew there was a secluded bench and she headed for it, parking the twins to one side, sinking down gratefully, closing her eyes.

Her mouth was furred, tongue dry. A chill drew itself up her arms. Her eyes flew open. She was alone. The stroller was nowhere.

Lauren stood and looked both ways. Nothing but trees, and the river. Where was the stroller? Where were her babies? Gone. They'd been taken. While she was asleep.

She shouted out, a guttural mashing of vowels, sprinted one way, tripped on a root and fell, a crunching of bone or cartilage in her wrist as her hands shot out to break the fall. No matter; she couldn't feel her body, only a terrible absence, the babies like limbs ripped from her, missing parts, a wrongness so intense she wanted to hurt herself, to tear at her hair and skin. She ran back the other way to the clearing and screamed her children's names. Startled birds took off in a grey cloud of squawks and flapping wings from the giant silver pine that stood by the water.

Chapter Eighteen

The car park at the Fresh Ground Cafe was crammed with haphazardly parked police vehicles, stopped where they'd screeched to a halt at odd angles. On the journey from the station, the dashboard readout told Harper it was thirty-one degrees in the sun. It was marginally cooler under the trees but when she stepped out of the car, the humidity made it feel like she was breathing through a hot wet sock. The trees formed a dense tunnel to a distant bend up ahead, and beyond. This road was one she knew well, that she had driven many times — it got narrower as it curled into the peaks, and went all the way to Manchester.

The cafe stood in the full beating sun, with brown sandy grass all around. Its own shadow, a rhombus of black, lay like a carpet at its feet, and in the contrast of the glare Harper couldn't see the interior. Behind it, a little playground, and on the path, two

217

officers were taking statements from members of the public. There was a straggling of gawpers, attracted by the commotion and being turned back or moved along quickly, asked politely by a pair of fresh-faced PCSOs to clear the area.

Harper crossed the bridge and walked the short distance to the wooden cafe, which was little more than an upmarket shed, erected on a concrete platform above the path. She passed the separate breeze-block toilet building, watched by two huge spray-painted cartoon eyes. It felt good to be off desk duty. When the call came in, Thrupp had assigned the case to her immediately, so he can't have lost all faith in her abilities. Mind you, it was true that he hadn't had much choice: she'd been the only DS available.

As she got close to the cafe one of the uniformed constables turned to her and was about to speak, ask her who she was, when she flashed her warrant card and introduced herself. The officer, a squat man with close-cropped hair and a nose warped by historical breakages, said his name was PC Atkinson.

"Where's Mrs Tranter?" she said.

"Who?"

"The mother."

For a moment the officer seemed surprised at the question, but then he moved aside. "This way, Sarge."

Inside the cafe there was a strong smell of ground coffee and sunbaked wood preserver. It took a second for her eyes to adjust to the light.

Atkinson leaned in close. "How did you know?"

"How did I know what?"

"The name. She won't tell us anything. She's just been ranting."

"Dispatch had it," said Harper, realising that in fact, they hadn't. No one had told her the name of the mother. But she'd known it, none the less. From the moment the first communication came into the office, blaring out of the police radio she kept on her desk.

All units, please assist, this is a code ten-ten.

Code ten-ten, in their district, was the highest-priority incident. A call to arms, that only the most urgent incidents were assigned. Was it a murder? A terrorist attack? The whole building held its breath for the next part: *Two infants, twins, four weeks of age, male, last seen by the mother in the Bishop Valley Park. Missing, suspected abducted. All units respond.*

How could it have been anyone else? Harper's eyes rested on Lauren, who hadn't noticed her enter the cafe. She wore dark brown shorts and a black vest, walking boots and a pair of sunglasses on her head that were half lost in the large pillow of barely tamed brown curls. Sweat patches, face drained of blood, and those haunted, terrified eyes.

"Besides, she would have said her name when she called 999."

The constable gave a small frown and a shrug, apologetic, assuming he must have been wrong, or that he'd missed something.

"Look, if you didn't get it, maybe others have missed it, too. Radio through to HQ. The mother's Lauren Tranter, husband is Patrick Tranter. And the babies are Morgan and Riley."

"We know the babies' names. She's said them a lot."

"Get them to run a background check on Mr and Mrs Tranter, would you? See if there's any information on the system. Now, go." This was something she'd been dying to do ever since she followed Patrick, but it was too risky. Every background search request was traceable. Thrupp would have found out for sure.

In the back of the cafe Lauren was struggling, being made to sit at a table, a police community support officer encircling her shoulders with a restraining arm. There was another officer standing, palms forward, in a posture of *Please stay where you are, madam.*

"Look," Lauren was saying, "just let me go and help. I can't stay here. I can't."

"Please, madam, you need to leave it to us now. We'll find the boys, don't worry. It's really better for everyone if you stay here and wait for news."

"How can I stay here?" She was shouting now. "When someone's out there and they've taken my babies? Some mad bitch has gone off with my boys. Would you stay here if it was you? Could you?"

She shook off the arm at her back, managed to stand up and started to push against the two officers, both of whom were taller and broader than she was, and well trained in passive restraint techniques. Harper approached cautiously, just as Lauren was starting to kick out with her legs against the other women, teeth bared.

"Mrs Tranter? Lauren."

She stopped in her struggle to be free, stopped trying to run out of the door. She glared at Harper, her strained face settling into recognition before becoming hard, accusatory.

"You," she said, raising a finger, "I told you this would happen. I told your people, I told the doctors. That woman in the hospital threatened me, she followed me home. Everyone thought I was crazy. Now look."

"Not me," said Harper, "I didn't think you were crazy. I believed you."

Lauren's face twitched with surprise. She searched Harper's. "You did?"

"It was the same person?" said Harper. "The one in the hospital, the one you saw outside the house? Are you sure?"

She nodded. "Detective. Please, help me. Tell them to let me go. I need to . . . Morgan and Riley, they need me . . ."

Without warning the fight went out of Lauren and she was limp, her head flopping to her chest. The PCSO pulled gently downwards on Lauren's arm so that she sank, deflated, into the chair and started to sob.

Harper knelt beside her. She could smell the sweat and the fear. The other officers waited to see what the DS would do, and she knew that, right now, she needed to play it strictly by the book.

"Lauren. I have to ask you this. Where are Morgan and Riley?"

The question shocked the sobs to a stop.

She drew in an angry breath, wiped her wet nose with the back of a hand.

"How can you . . . ? I don't know. If I knew that, I wouldn't be here — why do you all keep asking me that?"

She was telling the truth, Harper was completely sure of that.

"I'm sorry. It's procedure. We're trained to start at the beginning, with you, the last person to see them."

"You're just wasting time. You should be searching, not asking me stupid questions."

"Tell me where they were, when you last saw them."

"I fell asleep. I didn't mean to. So stupid, it's my fault." Lauren pounded on her head with the heel of one hand. Harper gently prevented her, holding each of Lauren's hands in her own.

"So, you didn't see the person who took them away?"

"No, but who else could it have been? She warned me, she said she would take them, if I ever left them alone. I left them alone, I didn't mean to but I did. I sat down on that bench, shut my eyes, and that was it. My brain just shut off. I don't even know for how long I was out. When I woke up, they'd gone. My babies." Lauren hid her face in her hands.

The babies were gone. Harper felt as if a void had opened up within her chest, that too much air was trapped in her lungs and she couldn't push it out. They had to be found. The alternative was unthinkable.

Light-headed, Harper stood up and went outside to find Atkinson. Once they were out of earshot, she said, "Did you check the parents' names against the records?"

"Yes, there was nothing apart from a filed 999 call, marked as —"

"Picked up by MHS, I know about that one. I thought maybe the husband, Mr Tranter, anything on him?"

"Nothing."

"Where is he now?"

"He's on his way. He was at work, in an office in the centre of town."

She'd been sure Patrick was involved somehow. Perhaps she'd allowed her feelings about him to cloud her judgement. Careful, Harper, she told herself. Keep it professional. For the sake of those babies.

"Where are the search teams?"

"Everywhere, Sarge, but no one's co-ordinating things strategically yet so it's a scratch search, everywhere in the vicinity, everyone we can find. Major Crimes are on the way but it might be up to an hour before the search advisor is able to assist."

"And, what have you found?"

"Nothing yet. We've got eighteen officers on the ground but there's no sign of the missing infants. More uniform personnel are on the way; dispatch is directing resources from all over."

Several sirens wheeled in the air, some close and some from further along the valley. Blue lights flashed in the road.

"What about cars?" said Harper. "Are you looking for suspicious vehicles?"

Atkinson nodded.

"We've got witnesses with descriptions of cars seen in the area at the time. We've started calling up data from road traffic cameras —"

"There aren't any cameras for miles on this road," said Harper.

"I know that," said the constable, slightly tetchily, "but we can check which cars turned off the main road, because there's CCTV that covers that junction. We'll get the information soon and start to run background on them."

That would take too much time. Each minute that passed meant that the chance of finding the twins alive diminished further.

"How long has it been, since they were taken?" said Harper.

Atkinson checked his watch, and his PDA.

"Twenty-seven minutes from the 999 call."

And, thought Harper, Lauren doesn't even know how long she was asleep for, which added an unknown number of minutes to that total. "Shit. Could be absolutely miles away by now, if they're in a car."

The bench was a short walk upstream. Atkinson led the way. The area had been checked over already; nothing had been found but some scraps of litter.

"She was sitting here?" said Harper.

Atkinson nodded.

"Let's get it cordoned off. It's a crime scene."

It was impossible to tell in which direction the stroller might have been taken, but from here there were three possible routes — upstream into the peaks, downstream towards the cafe or away from the water along an overgrown footpath leading to the road, and from there, with a vehicle, the possibilities started to spool in all directions.

She walked down to the edge of the river, careful not to step on any visible prints, taking photos of the ground as she went. Here the river was wide and shallow, running over large stones, sparkling in the bright sun. A popular paddling spot, partly shaded as the river ran deeper under the trees a little further down. Beyond that, it passed the cafe and continued on to the disused mill-pond before entering the city's vast network of channels. Upriver, it wound its way through a good stretch of dense woodland. You could follow the path alongside the river, all the way through the woods, passing deeper through the valley as the peaks rose higher and wilder, right to the New Riverby reservoir, probably five or six miles out. That immense stretch of lake hadn't always been there. The New Riverby was built before the first war, but before that, for centuries, the valley had been home to a thriving community, the drowned village of Selverton.

"We've got officers on the river path, haven't we?"

"Yes, boss. Several, in both directions."

Harper's eyes were drawn to the water. On the other side of the river, the high brambles would have been impossible to breach. There were areas further up where a person could get through. Perhaps they needed to search the other bank, too.

Behind her, Atkinson approached and lowered his voice. "Sarge. The mother, she's very distressed."

"Well, yes. She would be."

Harper returned her attention to the water, the large rocks and shadowed areas to her left and right.

"I mean, health and safety, and all that. I think she's a risk."

"To who?"

"Herself. Us. Just a risk. You saw what she was like in there. I think we might need help with her."

"Help how?"

"I mean medical help. Just in case. I mean, if the last call she made was dealt with by Mental Health . . ."

Harper remembered the hospital, how Lauren had had to be sedated after what happened to her there. Atkinson was right — they couldn't predict what she might do. She nodded.

"You do what you think, Constable. Get an ambulance on standby if it's appropriate."

"Yes, boss."

The constable turned and began walking back towards the cafe, lifting his radio to summon the medics. Harper was about to follow him, when she spotted something at the water's edge. She called the officer back.

"Give me an evidence bag. Quickly."

There, leading into the shallows, in the mud that had been exposed by the lowered water level, were the imprints from three wheels — two large ones with a smaller one

228

in the middle. Three tyres, possibly a three-wheeled stroller, exactly like the one they were searching for. There was a scrap of dirty black fabric caught in one of the tyre tracks. She took out her phone and snapped several pictures of its position, then bent towards it, poked the scrap out with a pen and bagged it. Then, she searched the surrounding area for matching tracks. There were none. The stroller had gone into the water. But Harper couldn't see any immediate evidence of where, or if, it had come out again.

"Constable, we need to search the river. I mean, in it, not just the path."

"But boss, it's so shallow, we'd have seen it."

"Just get a diver down here, now. It's not all shallow. Look."

He followed her gaze up the river, to where a bend formed a dark pool under the trees. In that small section, you couldn't see the bottom. The water could have been two metres deep. It could have hidden a stroller, easily. There would be pools like this all the way up and down the twisting Bishop. And of course, the river joined the deep and murky millpond further down, where whole cars had sunk without trace. Harper banished a vision of the sinking stroller, the helpless babies strapped in, sucking water into their little lungs. It hadn't happened, it couldn't have. Somewhere in her mind she just knew that it hadn't, but she couldn't trust it. The knowledge was mixed with both hope and uncertainty.

"You go and look at the millpond, see if there's anything to be found there, tracks or footprints," said Harper. "I'll go that way."

The constable set off immediately in the downstream direction, while Harper went the other way, intending to note where the deeper parts of the river were, all the possible places where a person might submerge a baby's pushchair. She wanted some useful information to direct the divers when they arrived to start searching in the water. Trying to remain detached, she pushed away the queasy feeling that came in waves when she thought of the babies under the water, or the fact that she might be too late to save them.

She walked swiftly upstream along the path, hopping over tree roots and rocks, searching left and right. She swept the thickets with her eyes, alert for any trace of the lime-green car seat covers clipped to the stroller. In the woods, there seemed to be flashes of lime-green everywhere, so that her eyes kept alighting on patches of new leaves, bright bushes, thinking, there it is, and realising a second later that she was mistaken. Even an old plastic bag caught her attention, before she thought, if it were that easy, they'd have been found already — after all, she was going over old ground, places that had already been searched before she arrived. Every so often she stopped dead, listened for the cries of babies, but heard only birdsong, and her own slightly quickened breathing.

The light dimmed rapidly under the canopy as the clouds knitted together above it. She pressed on, nodding at three uniformed officers waist-deep in undergrowth, all of them scouring the ground for evidence of the abduction, for anything that might help the search.

She passed a wide, deep section of river where the path was low, only just above the level of the water. The edge here curved around, creating a little shore. It would have been easy to push a stroller in at this point, but there were dozens of places up and down the river that were similar. She had a quick search for tyre tracks, saw none. Up ahead, the tunnel created by the river and the woods turned a corner that she couldn't see around. Just a bit further, she thought, then I'll go back the other way and get a good look at the millpond myself.

She heard the rain before she felt it. Loud and heavy as stones falling on the leaves above. I'll just go as far as the corner, she thought, but then drops of water big enough to hurt began to land on her arms and head, soaking her in moments. She jogged to the bend in the river; she'd come this far after all.

And there they were.

A female dressed in dark clothing was knee-deep in water, struggling with the double stroller, which was at an angle, tipping into the sluggish murk. The lower seat was almost underwater. Any further in and it would fill up.

Harper sprinted towards the scene, the woman, the water all around them full of tiny explosions of raindrops battering down, the noise of it almost but not quite drowning out Harper's cry of "Stop, police," but the figure turned, saw her, shouted out and let go of the stroller. She turned her back on the pushchair, the lightning flashed, and she pulled her sodden form onto the bank. She tried to run, but even before the thunder could answer, she flew straight into a uniformed officer who'd come from further upriver.

"Arrest her," Harper managed to shout

while wading as fast as possible towards the slowly sinking stroller. Mud pulled at her ankles, slowing her, slowing time itself.

There was no crying. Her heart dropped — what if the stroller was empty, what if she had found evidence that the babies were no more? She rushed to look inside the top seat and the baby in yellow looked steadily at her, and she said, "Oh thank fuck," but the fear remained. One baby safe, what about the other? She looked into the bottom seat, the water gathering at its lip and there was the baby in green, with a matching watchful gaze. She seized the handle of the stroller and pulled it towards the shallows, the wheels sticking just as her feet had done but she was strong, and soon they were safely ashore.

The rain-wet male officer, a tall young rugby fan called Wright, held the upper arm of the handcuffed woman who'd been in the river with the babies. The woman was young, with smooth skin and long dark hair, mascara running down her face and dripping off her chin. Harper knew her. She'd been in the car park with Patrick, on the day she'd followed him — the day she'd been complained about, and benched as a result. The rain kept falling in curtains on their heads, so that they hunched up their shoulders and wiped at the water running down their faces.

"What's your name?" said Harper.

"This is not what you think," said the woman. "I was bringing them back."

Harper shook her head, "Sorry madam, that doesn't make it any better, I'm afraid. Abduction is a serious offence."

"No, you don't understand. I found them. I didn't take them."

"State your name, please."

The woman said nothing.

Harper addressed PC Wright. "Get her to the station, get her processed. I can easily find out who she is. She knows the father."

Mention of Patrick seemed to cause the woman physical pain. She made a small moaning sound and tried to crumple but her thin frame was held up by the officer.

Wright said, "The babies OK?"

"They're here. They're alive. We did good." The two officers grinned at each other.

"You want me to call it in?" asked Wright. "Or do you want the pleasure?"

"What do you think?" she said, still grinning.

Wright pulled the woman in the other direction, back the way he'd come. He must have parked his patrol car further up the road, not at the cafe with the others. Harper set off with the boys towards the cafe. They still weren't crying. She stopped and checked them again. The babies stared back, each with an identical unwavering gaze.

As she hurried along in the rain she reached for her radio and depressed the button, shouting, "This is DS Harper, I've got them, copy, both boys safe," but the radio was dead. Water must have got into it somehow, though the devices were supposed to be impervious to weather of all types. Maybe the battery was flat. Too late now to call Wright back, he wouldn't hear her over the sound of the rain anyway. Quicker to keep going. The most important thing was to get these two baby boys back to their mother.

CHAPTER NINETEEN

Lauren scanned the river, the woods, the road. The babies were nowhere. That's what it felt like. Her heart drummed painfully in her chest, someone punching her in the thorax over and over. Each time the police radio crackled a message, she searched the officer's faces for signs that they had been found. Nothing, nothing, nothing.

When the first dark cloud rolled over the valley, Lauren thought there was something dirtying the ground. A large dark pool of something. Then another, larger cloud passed in front of the sun and it occurred to her that she hadn't seen a proper cloud for weeks, and that the strange dark shape covering the playground was simply a shadow, not an ominous sign of something unexplainable. The patchy shadows fused together and became an immense low roof of dense grey. Electricity charged the air. Lauren's skin was prickling as she stood outside the cafe, tensed, waiting.

The police officer had let her get up after she'd promised repeatedly that she would not run away. Patrick was coming, he'd be here soon. He'd sounded devastated on the phone. Was it the worst thing imaginable, to tell your husband that you had made a mistake and allowed someone to take his children, that you had no idea where they were, who with, and why? Not the worst thing, not even close. But it was bad. During their short conversation, they'd both failed to say anything even remotely comforting to each other.

She felt weak, and fierce, and angry and guilty. Ready to fight, light on her heels, yet holding such a heavy weight in her chest that she could have been crushed by it, had she let it pull her down. Powerless, and at the same time full of potential for something. With a jolt, she realised that it was violence. Lauren was ready to beat someone pulpy if they'd harmed her precious ones. She was looking forward to it, in a sick sort of way. Fists bunched, in readiness. *Come on, then.*

The gathering storm pressing down from above made her eyes hurt. Beside her in the doorway, the officer assigned to "look after" Lauren kept gripping at her own temples as if she were in pain, puffing out sighs. The air pressure was a boot on everyone's head, adding to the atmosphere, the feeling, unbearable, that something had to happen soon or the consequences would be terrible. Out of all the police officers only Jo Harper seemed to have come dressed for the heat. Come to think of it, where the hell was Harper? Lauren hadn't had a chance to speak to her properly before she'd disappeared again. Harper would understand, not like these uniformed monkeys. She'd let her join the search for her own children, for pity's sake.

Something shifted in the air, loosening. A few fat spheres of rain smashed into the hot concrete of the path, throwing up dust from the gritted car park like angry gobfuls of phlegm, banging down on the tops of the police vehicles and the flat felted roof of the cafe. More fell, hard and sparse, but then the pressure escaped and the clouds burst and the rain poured out of the sky. Lauren felt the sharp missiles of water hitting her bare arms and the top of her head, painful, stinging. She did not move, even as a surge of people rushed past her into the shelter of the building.

Hair plastered to her face by the force of it, Lauren watched as the storm disrupted the surface of the Bishop, which turned brown and started to swell.

"Mrs Tranter, come inside, you'll get cold," said someone from behind her, one of the police. She ignored the suggestion. She liked being cold, it made a change. And she wanted to hurt, even in this small way. Physical pain was a distraction from the crushing dread and the rising panic.

On the other side of the river, Patrick's car was pulling into the car park, windscreen wipers madly slashing, just as the first flash of lightning made her jump. The thunder followed, quick and loud as an explosion.

Thunder, lightning, rain smashing down. A crowd of eyes behind her, looking past her, widened, the thrill of the storm. Then she hears Jo Harper's voice, and sees a scream of lime-green, fluorescent under the trees. The stroller. Harper has the stroller, she's running towards her with it and Lauren sets off sprinting. Jo is shouting, but the storm is louder, and Lauren's steel-toed walking boots on the path crack out an urgent staccato that drowns out her own words, "Are they there? Do you have them?" until they meet on the bridge, Patrick too, and they are there, her babies, they're alive and she reaches inside the top car seat and unclips one baby and Patrick unclips the other and holds him but she wants them both so she pulls Patrick close with the two babies between them and the rain is pounding down upon them and they're all drenched but the babies, the babies are alive and they're here in her arms, her precious boys. Lauren is saying their names, over and over, "Riley, Morgan, are you OK? Did she hurt you?"

Then Lauren straightens up and looks at Harper, who is watching her in a strange way, and she looks at Patrick, who is crying and shaking, then turning his face up to the sky in anger as if someone up there were responsible, his white shirt translucent on his skin, tie hanging wet and limp so that suddenly he is vulnerable, pitiable, the sight of him tearing at her. She kisses him then, the smell and the taste of him tugging at something low in her belly, a memory of a time, the base chemistry that all this came out of.

"Thank God," Patrick said, and though he kept glowering at the sky as if he really meant, *fuck you God,* when he spoke to the babies his voice was tender. "We thought we'd lost you, little buddies. Where did you get to?"

Lauren and Patrick turned towards Harper, the question in the air and in their faces.

"They were with a woman," said Harper, "in the river. Don't worry, we got her, she's in custody."

"Who was it?" The question roared out of him, and he stepped towards the police officer, the baby in his arms protected, but his hands curled into fists. Lauren shifted the baby she held so she could put a hand on Patrick's shoulder, feeling the taut sinew and coiled muscle beneath the thin cotton. It's not Harper you want, Patrick. Save it for the woman, the child thief, the witch.

"I don't have that information yet. She didn't identify herself. She's being taken to the station as we speak; we'll know very soon."

Lauren turned her face skywards, feeling spatters of raindrops in her eyes. She drew the baby closer. Thank all the gods, she thought, that horrible woman has been caught. She won't be after me anymore.

"Did she have the basket with her?" said Lauren.

"The what?" said Harper.

Patrick turned sharply in Lauren's direction. She was about to explain about the creepy woman's babies, but something in his expression stopped her. Instead she said, "So she was alone? There was no one else with her?"

"That's right," said Harper.

Lauren wondered what the woman had done with her own babies, if she didn't have them with her. She wouldn't have been surprised if they'd been taken into care, the filthy state they were in when she saw them in the hospital. She pressed her cheek to the top of her baby's head. The feeling of the downy skin was exquisite, more so now that she'd feared she might never feel it again. Looking at the baby Patrick held, she felt greedy for him, too, upset that she didn't have him in her arms. She wanted them both, and she wanted everyone else to go away.

"Where exactly were they found?" asked Patrick.

"Not far away. Only half a mile or so. That way." Harper pointed upstream.

"So how come no one found them sooner?" said Lauren, wondering with growing horror what might have happened to the boys in the time they were gone.

"I don't know, Lauren," said Harper. The DS was starting to shiver, her jaw clenched against the chattering. "They must have been hidden. We'll know more very soon. But the important thing is, they're safe. They're here. We found them."

"Come on," said Patrick, "let's get inside.

I'm freezing. The boys must be, too. We have to put them back in the seats, they're getting soaked. Lauren? We need to get them warm and dry. Come on."

He put the baby he held back in the top seat and prised the other one as gently as he could from Lauren's arms. He put the blankets over them. The hoods of the seats stopped the worst of the rain.

Lauren moved to take the stroller from Harper, to push it towards the cafe, where the small crowd was waiting to be allowed to cheer, to send up thanks for the safe return of the twins. As she walked, she gazed down at her babies, grateful and elated but not quite able to shake off the fear, telling herself, they're safe, they're here, it's over.

Then, she stopped dead. Patrick and Harper kept on towards the cafe, but after a second they stopped too and turned back.

"What are you doing?" said Patrick.

She stood in the drenching downpour and looked at the two babies, so nearly lost forever to unknowable horrors. The two best things in her life, whom she lived for, and loved more than any others. Who were watching her from under the bright hoods of the car seats. The one dressed as Morgan was looking at her, and smiling strangely.

243

She knew the clothes, a yellow stripy all-in-one that she had picked out herself from the nice little shop on Division Street. The whorl of hair at the front of his head. The curve of his nose and the shape of his earlobes. Riley gazed at her in the same strangely intense way as his brother, clasping his hands together in an identical position. For the first time, she questioned if she'd know which one was which without the green and yellow colour coding that was only for Patrick's sake anyway. Had they been changed around, dressed in each other's colours? Both had the same blue-grey eyes they'd had before they were taken. But Morgan didn't look like Morgan, not exactly. Riley didn't either, something about the way his lip curled.

And then she knew, with a terrible certainty. It wasn't Morgan and Riley, not anymore. Something else was looking at her, out of the eyes of her babies. That creepy, evil woman — she'd done it, somehow, exactly as she'd threatened she would. She'd taken the boys and put her own in their place.

I can make sure they look just the same.

She stared at the babies, and as she did, a smell of rotting river-weed filled her nostrils. The twins had been changed. She knew it in her soul. It was just like in the story, the horrible story in the *Twin Tales* book.

If they are changed, what am I to do?

You must throw them into the river.

These creatures had come from the river. That must be where the woman had hidden Morgan and Riley. There could be no hesitation. She turned the stroller towards the rising water and started to run.

CHAPTER TWENTY

By the time they'd loaded Lauren into the ambulance and shut the doors, the rain had stopped completely and the hot sun was back. White light reflected off the wet pavement and the surface of the river into Harper's eyes, making her squint.

Patrick stood on the steaming asphalt with one hand on the handle of the stroller, watching as the emergency vehicle drove across the bridge and turned onto the Bishop Valley Road, heading away from the city. In the stroller, Riley and Morgan were awake, alert but silent, taking everything in. Their matching postures, hands clasped together in front of them, serious faces, made them look like tiny vicars. Patrick gave them each a squeeze, saying *don't worry lads,* but they were serene, as still as dolls. Perhaps they're in shock, thought Harper.

Beyond where Patrick stood, the crowd of onlookers were all still there, not even pretending not to stare at the man, waiting to see what he would do next. Patrick turned and scanned their faces, locking eyes with a flat-headed grunt who was probably a head taller than he was and twice as heavy. Harper stepped forward, sensing the bristling of male anger, turning to violence.

She kept her voice low. "Now, Mr Tranter . . ."

He shouted past her as if she hadn't spoken, "Why don't you all just go the fuck home, hey? The show's over."

The flathead in the crowd looked backwards over his own shoulder, incredulous, and finding no one behind him turned back to Patrick and narrowed his eyes. "You talking to me?"

Patrick balled up two fists by his sides.

The man kept staring right at him. "You looking at me?"

One hand poised at his radio, Atkinson said, "Please, Mr Tranter . . ." and placed a hand on Patrick's shoulder that he shook off, forcefully.

Taking a step towards the crowd, Patrick said, "What are you all staring at, anyway, you losers? This is my life. These are my children . . ." and he might have said *that was my wife* but suddenly he bent over and sobbed into his knees, curling pitifully into

247

a ball on the ground next to the stroller.

Harper spoke to the crowd. "If you could go about your day, please, ladies and gentlemen, I think we need to give this man a bit of privacy. Thank you, thank you," and the onlookers began to grumble and disperse. Some of them had the grace to look shamefaced as they shuffled off. Evidently the sight of a grown man crying on the pavement was not as enthralling as the earlier sight of a woman ripping clumps of her own hair out and screaming *where are my babies,* over and over when they were there, right there in front of her. "They're here, my love," Patrick had said, and when Lauren had met her husband's eye she'd been unrecognisable, her face an animal snarl, the whites of her eyes turned pink with bloodshot as she tried to get away from him with the stroller and roll the twins into the river, her own children. There was blood on Patrick's face from where she'd scratched him in the struggle, but between he and Harper, they had somehow managed to hold on to the stroller, stop it from tipping, prevent Lauren from doing whatever she was trying to do. Thwarted, Lauren went for Harper's face but Patrick got his arms around her, pulled her backwards away from the babies, towards the river.

"Just hold her," she'd said to Patrick, and he'd tried. Lauren stomped viciously on his toe and he let go, then she flailed, shrieked, threw herself forward and fell badly on the concrete, everything slippery on the river-bank under the rainstorm, before being restrained by a team of police, a horrific mud-wrestle, the tragedy made lurid as the sun came out and threw rainbows onto the rippled, swollen surface of the Bishop.

Harper wrote an address on a page in her notebook and tore it out.

"Patrick?" He was still curled on the wet ground, hugging his knees. "You OK?"

For a while he just stared at her shoes. He took a breath. "Yeah. No." Then he stood up, brushing grit from his damp behind, and took the note from her hand. "What's this?"

"It's the address of the psychiatric unit where they've taken your wife."

He held it out in front of him, but he didn't read it. "Has she been arrested?"

Patrick's hair was stuck down by the rain — he rubbed at it now and shook his head like a dog, spraying droplets over Harper, whose sodden outfit was dry on the shoulders but still soaked everywhere else. The sun was strong; she felt it burning her face.

Water evaporated in tendrils from her sleeves.

"No," she said, "not at all. She's been detained under the Mental Health Act. She's not a criminal. She's unwell. It's a hospital."

"But a secure unit?"

"For her own protection."

"Oh." Patrick looked down at the baby in the top car seat. Yellow vest. Morgan. The baby looked back at his father, unblinking. "So, what about the babies?"

"They'll need to be checked by a doctor as soon as possible. I'll escort you."

A sweet, familiar fragrance drifted by. Amy, in an orange linen tunic, appeared at Harper's elbow and smiled demurely at Patrick.

"Excuse me, Mr Tranter?"

"Just leave it a few minutes, Amy," said Harper, "Mr Tranter is busy and doesn't want to talk to journalists at the moment."

"I'm sure Mr Tranter can make up his own mind, Sergeant." Amy flashed her smile at Patrick again, but he just frowned slightly. "I'm from the *Mail*, Mr Tranter. I wonder if you'd like to have a chat? Maybe get a coffee? You must be parched, after everything that's happened. Don't you need a sit down?"

"Oh," said Patrick, his eyes flicking to Amy's cleavage and back to her face, before he blinked and gathered himself. "No, sorry. I need to sort my kids out."

"I could just buy you a take-out? No pressure."

Patrick, unbelievably, hesitated, appearing to consider the offer.

Harper stepped between the man and the journalist, and lowered her voice to speak to Patrick. "We need to get the babies checked by a doctor as soon as possible. We need to make sure they are unharmed, and also it's going to help our investigation. Depending on what the doctor finds, we may need to collect physical evidence."

Patrick looked sickened at the idea of physical evidence. Good, thought Harper, keep your mind on what's important.

"So Patrick, coffee?" said Amy.

"I'm sorry," said Patrick, "I can't, not now."

Amy dropped a hip, stuck out her full, lipsticked lower lip and handed Patrick a business card. Big, faux-sad eyes, followed by a little smile. "If you ever want to tell your story, Patrick. I'll be waiting."

The two women exchanged a not entirely friendly glance before Amy turned on her heels and walked towards the cafe. The journalist leaned towards a loitering nosy bastard near the door, taking him by the arm. Harper heard her say, "Excuse me, can I have a word? I'm from the *Mail*," before they disappeared inside.

The uppermost baby was looking at Harper. The other one, in green, made a noise like a sea-bird. The baby's voice must have jolted Patrick into remembering, so that he blurted, "They'll be hungry soon, what shall I do? They're exclusively breastfed."

"We can stop on the way to the hospital for some formula," said Harper. "They'll be fine with that until you can get them over to the unit and back to their mother."

"We're taking them to the psychiatric unit? Is that allowed?" Patrick's face betrayed his horror at this idea.

Harper smiled reassuringly. "Yes, it's encouraged. In fact it's mandatory — the place she's gone to is especially for mothers and babies."

He seemed doubtful. "Right."

"They're really lovely over at Hope — your wife is in safe hands."

His eyes were on the babies. She knew he was thinking: *but what about the babies? Would they be safe in their mother's hands?* She'd been about to push them into the river, after all.

The Bishop was a good deal higher than it had been before the storm — the water must have been running off the hills further upstream, collecting in the bottom of the valley. It had swelled and flooded over the grass, almost to the edge of the pavement they stood on. Patrick locked eyes with Harper.

"Do you think she'll be OK?" he asked.

"Of course. She just needs some rest. She's a strong person, I can tell."

"You're right, she is strong. Or, she used to be. Before the birth."

Harper patted him on the shoulder, twice, and bent to inspect the babies. "They're very calm, aren't they?"

"Are they?" said Patrick. He glanced down at them distractedly. "I suppose."

As Patrick swivelled the stroller to push it towards the car, both babies kept their eyes on Harper until the last possible moment.

CHAPTER TWENTY-ONE

They strapped her down. Like a mad-woman. They injected her with something, and now she was floppy, her head swimming. They loaded her into the ambulance, and she was relieved that she couldn't see the green of the stroller anymore, her husband's distraught face or the terrible vision of whatever was behind the eyes of either of those babies, where her sweet little boys should have been, and were not.

Bang bang went the doors and she thought they would drive off immediately but someone was talking to her. The words were indistinct. Maybe they weren't talking to her at all. She kept saying the boy's names, *Morgan, Riley, where are you?*

One of the paramedics was shining a light in her eyes. "Don't you worry, love," she heard. "You're safe now. Can you take a deep breath for me?"

Pretending to be nice, she thought. A

minute ago you were gripping me so hard it hurt. I could hurt you, too. I could bite you. I might do it.

"Where are my babies?" asked Lauren. Maybe she knew. Someone knew.

"They'll be following on soon, petal. Your husband's got them."

"No, no, no," said Lauren, shaking her head, "you don't understand. That wasn't them. Not my boys. They've been taken."

Someone else spoke. A man's voice, from somewhere above her head.

"Yes, love, that's right, but we got them back. They were taken, but then they were found. And we got the woman who took them, too."

Lauren turned her head slightly. She couldn't see his face but she could read the word POLICE in white writing on the shoulder of his uniform.

"I told you, that wasn't them," said Lauren, "whatever was in that stroller. They've been swapped. They're evil, those things, they're not my babies."

The paramedic and the police officer said nothing.

"Did you see them?" said Lauren, "did you look at them? They weren't human."

"You've had a bad experience, Lauren," said the paramedic. "We've given you something to calm you down."

"No," said Lauren, "no." Her head was the only part of her that she could move and she shook it, *no no no*. The repetitive motion was soothing, so she kept doing it. "Why am I strapped down?" she asked. "Are you taking me to prison?" She thought of the bad thing she had done, trying to get rid of the evil babies into the river. No one seemed to understand why she'd done that, even though she kept telling them. *I need to put them back in the river, where they came from, so that I can get my own boys back. She's got them under the water, that woman. That's where she lives, that's where she's taken my boys.*

The policeman sat next to her. "I'm just going to explain what's happening, Lauren. You've not been arrested."

"No?"

"No, love."

"So why have I been tied up? Let me go if I'm not under arrest."

"It's to protect you. We're detaining you under Section 136 of the Mental Health Act. That means we're taking you to a place of safety as we deem you to be a danger to yourself and others at this time."

"Oh, no," she said, "you really don't understand. I wasn't harming them. They live there, don't you see? They came from there, I was just taking them back. They don't belong here, and my boys don't belong down there." Her voice cracked and broke as she thought of her lost little boys, under the water, needing her but not being able to find her. "You'll see," she begged in a whisper, "just let me out. I know what I have to do."

The police officer said, "The detention lasts for seventy-two hours, during which time you'll be assessed by a doctor who will decide if you need to be detained under Section 2, which lasts for a little while longer."

Three days. How long until Morgan and Riley forgot about her altogether? She needed to find them right now.

"They won't drown, not those two in the stroller. They can swim. I've seen them before, in their normal bodies — they look like eels, not like babies at all. I saw them in the hospital, in the basket she had. But Morgan and Riley, they've never even been to a pool, they're too little. They won't know what to do. Something's gone wrong, don't you see? I need to put it right. Just please, let me go, please."

"You're a lucky lady, actually. Usually we'd have to take you to the station tempo-

257

rarily but we've called the Hope Park unit and they have a spare bed, so we're taking you straight there. You'll be nice and comfy. Not like in the cells." The man gave a small chuckle.

She was sure she was speaking aloud, but no one seemed to be able to hear what she was saying. Maybe she ought to stop speaking.

"Do you understand what I've just told you, love?" asked the policeman.

She turned her face towards the white wall of the ambulance. The policeman must have moved away, because the next voice she heard near to her head was the female paramedic.

"Do you have any pain at all? You took quite a tumble."

Tumble, thought Lauren. You pinned me down on my front, strapped my arms to my sides, ground my head into the mud. I have pain. It's mine. I'm keeping it. She shut her eyes as the ambulance started to move away.

After a while the vehicle stopped. The doors opened. They rolled her out of the ambulance and she felt a soft breeze and the sun on her face. She kept her eyes shut. She saw bright red, and the veins in her eyelids streaked blackly across her vision in the shape of lightning.

They wheeled her roughly up a ramp. The light dimmed and she smelled bleach and bad food. She heard babies crying and screwed her eyes tighter.

"Lauren?"

No.

Then, more gently, "Lauren? Are you awake?"

She turned her head towards the voice. She opened her eyes a crack and found herself looking into the face of a woman with kind, crinkly eyes and a mean, thin-lipped mouth. Whose enormous ears poked sideways through delicate curtains of extremely fine, carefully combed white hair. Lauren's voice creaked as it came out. "Where am I?" she asked the woman. She remembered where the rawness in her throat came from, how she'd screamed her babies' names into the storm.

"You're at the Hope Park Estate, Lauren. It's a mother and baby psychiatric unit."

"Oh." Her brain was treacly. The words seemed to gather into several separate concepts. Hope. Baby. Psychiatric. She couldn't quite put it together.

"This is a place of safety. You're safe."

"Who are you?" asked Lauren.

"I'm Doctor Summer. I'm a psychiatrist."

"I'm not mad," said Lauren. "Someone took my babies."

"I know. Don't worry. Your husband will bring them along later. I spoke to him just now. He's waiting for a doctor to check them over, but I don't want you to worry. He says your boys are very calm, not at all distressed."

They are not my boys. They are not my boys. They are not my boys. Will the doctor see what I saw, or will she be fooled, like Patrick, like everyone? Lauren cried softly, while the psychiatrist wrote on a clipboard.

"Do you have any pain, Lauren?"

Lauren nodded her head, yes.

There was another injection, and the heat of it took the treacliness away, replaced it with a feeling like candy-floss in her head. She slept, heavy, as if under a weighted blanket.

A sharpness in her arm pulled her up, awake. She found she could move her limbs. When she opened her eyes there was a pink face very close to hers. With short black hair and small eyes, the woman was dressed in a white tunic, and she smiled at Lauren as she withdrew, a syringe in her hand.

"Hello, love. Do you think you can sit up?"

Lauren was in a small room, not unlike a

260

room in a hostel, which was freshly painted white. She lay on a single bed against the wall. There was an empty baby's cot against the other wall. For a second she didn't understand what was happening, what had happened, but then everything rushed in at once. The woman squeezed Lauren's hand as she trembled, as the wave of fear crashed, receded, left her beached on the bed, struggling to remember to breathe.

"You're all right," said the nurse, whose name badge said *Pauline*. And it was strangely comforting, hearing that, even though it wasn't true in the slightest.

"Where am I?" asked Lauren, remembering hope, psychiatric, baby.

"Hospital. Sort of. We're much nicer than your average hospital though, don't worry."

"Psychiatric unit," said Lauren. They think I'm insane. She looked sideways at the nurse. Does she think that, too? The window was ajar, but had white-painted bars over it. No escape that way.

"That's right," said Pauline. "We're going to get you better."

Better from what? she thought. The only thing that's wrong with me is that someone's got my children. She glanced at the door, which was reinforced in a metal frame. The nurse had a thick leather belt with a chain

261

looping from a pouch. Keys to the doors. She's not a nurse, she's a guard.

"What about the babies?" asked Lauren, "Are they here, too?"

"Not yet. They're on the way. They'll be here soon — your husband's going to bring them. In the meantime, I brought you a breast pump."

Lauren looked down at herself. There were two large wet patches on the front of her vest. She felt the throbbing then. Both breasts were full, and hard, and leaking. There was an urgent need to release the pressure. She said, "My boys. They haven't fed. They'll be starving."

"Don't worry, they'll have had a bottle by now."

Who gave them the bottle? Patrick? He'd never get the mix right. What if he gave it to them when it was too hot? What if he burned their delicate mouths? But then, they weren't talking about her boys, not really. The ones Patrick had weren't hers. Wherever hers were —

And her breath caught before she could complete the thought.

"Let's get you plugged in," said the nurse, who had bad teeth and sewage breath. She brandished two plastic funnels attached to lengths of tubing, with collection bottles underneath.

The breast pump began to hum as it sucked, and the let-down was quick; the pressure was released. In no time she'd filled up the bottles.

"We'll need to chuck this," said the nurse. "Hang on."

"Why are we chucking it?" asked Lauren. "It'll be fine for a couple of hours."

"It's the drugs they gave you, flower. It comes out in the milk."

Drugs. Her eyelids were still drooping. How long until she could feed them again? That was supposed to be her job now, to feed those boys. It was the whole of her. Her body cried out for them. But then she thought of the babies that had come back. The idea of letting those changelings suckle her was repugnant.

"The babies," said Lauren, experimentally, "the ones Patrick's bringing. Do you know if they're the same ones they found at the river?" The moment the words were out, she regretted it: Don't say that, Lauren. It sounds insane.

There was a pause before the answer came. "Of course. Your babies, Lauren. Riley and Morgan, right? There aren't any other ones."

Two new bottles were soon attached to

the machine, which carried on pumping, *whoosh-whoosh, suck, suck.* The nurse reached into a pocket for a notebook and pen. What were they for?

"Oh, yes," said Lauren, "I know that. Sorry. I'm really tired, and all the drugs and everything. I don't know what I'm saying." She tried to laugh but it sounded forced.

Pauline flipped the notebook open. She's not just a guard. She's a spy.

"You don't have to write that down, do you? What I said, I mean."

Pauline turned her vulpine eyes on the prisoner.

"Sorry, petal. You're under observation. I have to write everything down."

"Yeah, but, not that. I know they're mine. Morgan and Riley. I can't wait to see them. I don't know why I said that before, it wasn't what I meant."

"Sorry," said Pauline, pen to paper.

"Please," said Lauren, begging. But it was no use. Every stroke of the pen was further evidence against her. The doctor would read it, and decide she was mad.

The nurse finished writing and put her notebook away. She smiled at Lauren with a closed face, reaching over to rub Lauren's shoulders as she sat there being milked. Lauren's back was rigid and wouldn't be loosened. She couldn't tell what Pauline was thinking, this gaoler, this enemy dressed up as a care worker.

Another two bottles were half full before the milk flow slowed to a trickle. Pauline took the bottles of thin white fluid into the bathroom, from where there was the sound of splashing in the sink. The tap was turned on for a second before the nurse came out and started to bag up the machine and its tubing. She looked at Lauren and smiled again in that flat, unsympathetic way.

"The psychiatrist will be along for a chat soon."

"Everyone thinks I'm nuts, don't they?"

Pauline sat down next to Lauren on the bed. "Whatever you do, don't say the word *nuts* to Doctor Summer. She hates that kind of thing."

"What do you think I am then? Loopy?"

A laugh escaped from Pauline, but she clapped a hand over it and frowned with forced concern. "You've been under pressure, flower. It's affected you badly, that's all. We're going to help you."

"I need to go home. How long do you think they'll keep me here?"

"Doctor Summer knows what she's doing. You'll feel better after you've chatted to her."

"I feel fine," said Lauren, thinking that she definitely sounded very reasonable, very sane. So why wasn't she writing that down?

"Don't worry, my lovely," said Pauline. "Let me get you a nice cup of tea. Doctor Summer will probably be ready to see you after that."

CHAPTER TWENTY-TWO

At the Infirmary, the doctor explained what she was going to do before she did it. She would check the boys over, inspect all their "nooks and folds", then weigh them.

"Nothing invasive. They've been through enough today already, from what I hear."

Patrick didn't respond to that. He glanced at Harper, who smiled her reassuring smile again. It was a dumb thing for the doctor to say, under the circumstances. Nobody knew what the babies had been through — what the suspect had or hadn't done to them in that hour in which they were missing. Patrick's imagination would be coming up with infinite excruciating possibilities, if it was anything like hers. The difference between them, the father and the police officer, was that she didn't need to imagine the depths that humans could sink to; she knew it first-hand. His fear that something terrible might have happened to his sons was matched and beaten by her certainty that the outcome could easily have been much worse.

The doctor asked for the boys to be undressed, and Harper watched Patrick fumble with the babies' clothing, pulling the yellow vest over Morgan's head with unpractised fingers. As he removed each item from the baby he passed it to Harper, who placed it in a labelled evidence bag. Morgan woke up when his father started to undress him, but he didn't cry. He kicked his legs and looked amused when the doctor made a face. Riley, still strapped into the car seat, made the sea-bird sound, and Morgan copied it precisely. The doctor smiled at Patrick.

"Cute," she said. "They'll have their own language soon."

"Yeah," said Patrick, rather dismissively, as if he didn't believe it.

Harper had also heard that twins sometimes developed a language no one else could understand. The idea of it fascinated her and creeped her out in equal measure.

Soon the boys were side by side on the hospital trolley, vests successfully removed.

"I'm just going to get them out of their nappies, if that's OK with you, Dad," said the doctor.

"Sure."

The doctor raised her eyebrows at Harper, who nodded, go ahead. She pulled off the nappy tabs, then picked up the naked baby and turned him onto his front, shining a pen light all over the skin, her gloved hand gently parting folds where the chub met itself. She turned the boy back over and shone the light into his mouth. Patrick looked sickened, his lips twisted. His hand rose slowly to cover them, and Harper could see that the man's eyes were filling up.

The doctor repeated the procedure with the other baby, placing them both on their backs, naked on the trolley before she spoke.

"I can't see anything notable."

"OK," said Patrick, his voice thick, "what does that mean?"

"It means there arc no signs of any maltreatment, in my opinion. No injuries," she looked at Harper, "no, um, visible evidence of foreign objects, fluids, or matter of any kind."

Patrick groaned, a pitiful sound of disgust and relief. He covered his eyes with his hands. When he took them away, white finger marks at his temples slowly faded. The doctor put the nappies back on the babies before she turned towards the computer and began to make notes.

"You can get them dressed now, Dad," she said, over her shoulder.

And Patrick looked at them both, lying there, gurgling, and then he pulled from the changing bag two clean vests, one yellow and one green. He held one in each hand, for a moment stood motionless then slowly raised his eyes to meet Harper's, who saw the panic in his face. He looked from vest to vest, from baby to baby. Which was which?

"Did you see which way round they were?" Patrick's voice was high and quiet.

Harper couldn't say. She mirrored his panicked eyes, shrugged helplessly. Morgan had been the one on the left, she thought. But did the doctor put them back in the same places? She hadn't been paying attention.

Patrick scrutinised them both, picked one up in his hand, turned him over. The baby's arms and legs stuck out like a parachutist. He put the boy back down, picked up the other. No way to tell. They looked exactly the same.

Harper said, "Don't they have moles, or something?"

"No," said Patrick, "Yellow for Morgan. Green for Riley. Lauren wanted to paint their nails but I wouldn't let her. Stupid, stupid."

"You weren't to know," said Harper, thinking, yes, that was stupid, why wouldn't you do that?

Patrick slid his eyes over to the scale, just to the right of the trolley. Of course, one would be bigger. They could check the notes, find out which one was which. Harper allowed herself to relax.

To the doctor, Patrick said, "Um, could you tell me their weights again, please, by any chance?"

The doctor tapped at her keyboard, scrolled down the screen.

"Oh, yes, funnily enough they both weighed the same. Four point six-two kilos. Amazing. You'd think one would be bigger and one smaller, even by point zero one of a kilo. Huh." The doctor laughed, but when she caught sight of Patrick's face she stopped laughing and stood up.

"Oh, no," said the doctor, "can't you tell —"

"Of course I can," snapped Patrick, "I just, wanted to make sure. I think I know my own children, thank you very much."

He picked up the one on the left. Decisively he began to dress the baby boy in the yellow vest. The doctor turned back to the

271

screen and started typing again. Her cheeks had turned a shade of dark pink.

Well, thought Harper, even if that one isn't Morgan, he is now.

Both babies were gazing coolly at her as their father struggled with the fastenings on now-Morgan's vest. It was as if they knew what he'd done, and they wanted her to know that they knew.

CHAPTER TWENTY-THREE

The therapy room at the secure unit had been decorated with babies in mind. There were black and white patterned posters on the ceiling. Contrast stripes were supposed to be good for little babies to focus on. On one wall was a painted mural of a yellow bear, holding on to a red balloon. Lauren looked at the thick rug between the two chairs, and the crossed feet of the doctor in her low-heeled powder-blue pumps. Next to Doctor Summer's chair, there was a small table with a clipboard and a pen. Next to her own, a bright red plastic box of board books and a yellow one of rattles and crinkly fabric leaves.

"What are you thinking, Lauren?" asked Doctor Summer.

Lauren ceased her inspection of the room. She looked at her hands in her lap. "I was thinking about my babies," she said.

"Can you tell me what the thought was,

precisely?"

"I miss them."

Doctor Summer uncrossed her feet, and re-crossed them the other way. The shiny skin on her legs looked as if it might be naturally hairless. It sagged slightly at the calves, shot through with spider veins.

"Do you know why you're here?"

Lauren noticed a smear of dried mud on the back of her thumb and rubbed at it.

"I think so," she said. "I got upset."

"You were upset," said Doctor Summer, making a note.

"Yes. The boys were gone, I didn't know where they were, I was going crazy waiting for them to be found. It was the worst thing imaginable."

"You didn't know where they were."

"No. And I didn't know if they would ever come back. You don't know what it was like."

"Tell me, Lauren. I want to understand."

Lauren didn't say anything for a long time. She kept thinking that the rug on the floor between them should have had her two kicking, smiling boys on it, and it was odd being here in this room without any babies at all. Morgan would have loved the black and white posters. Riley would have loved the crinkly fabric leaves.

"Tell me about what happened when they found the babies," said the doctor. "When they brought them back to you. How did you feel?"

It seemed a loaded question. Surely she already knew what happened. Lauren tried to work out what the doctor wanted her to say.

"At first I was happy. They'd been gone for . . . I don't know how long. It felt like forever."

The doctor waited for her to go on. After a time, Lauren said, "So, when they were returned, it was the best feeling in the world."

The doctor waited again for Lauren to continue, but she did not.

"And then what happened?"

Lauren looked past doctor's head at the sky through the window. There were several enormous trees in the distance. She could hear laughter, from somewhere outside. A toddler's laughter. She tried to imagine what the boys would be like as toddlers, but could only conjure those unnerving, unknowable faces from the riverside. The doctor moved her head into Lauren's eye line. The woman really had an alarmingly unusual face. Wouldn't her parents have been given the option, as a child, to have those

275

ears pinned back?

"Lauren," she said, "you told me you got upset. Why do you think you felt that way?"

"I don't know." She did know.

"Was there something about the babies that upset you? You just told me how much you missed them. Why would seeing them upset you so much?"

Lauren looked directly into the doctor's eyes. She opened her mouth slightly, but didn't speak.

Doctor Summer waited patiently for a very long time. Then she said, "The police officer who brought you in said you tried to push the stroller into the river. Why would you do that, Lauren?"

Lauren dropped her eyes.

"I don't know." But again, she did know. The answer ran through her mind: I wanted to put them back where they came from. I hoped that, if I put them back in the river straight away, maybe my boys would be returned to me.

"I'm on your side, Lauren."

Lauren thought, she thinks I'm mad. Am I mad? I can't tell her the truth, I know that. She said, "I just . . . for a second I thought . . . it sounds ridiculous, actually."

"Nothing you say will sound ridiculous to me. Believe me. You can trust me."

No, she thought, I can't trust you, writing things down. Who's going to read it? How long do they keep the notes for, before they throw them away, wipe the record clean? Lauren wanted to say nothing, but at the same time had a strong urge to explain herself. Perhaps if she explained it in the right way they would let her go. Give the doctor something, half of the truth, or the old bat wouldn't give up trying to find it out.

She cleared her throat. "Well, I just thought for a second that they weren't my babies. But I was wrong, I know they were. Are. I know they are."

Silently, while she lied to the doctor, her brain kept supplying the truth: I know they *aren't.* I have never been surer of a thing. The thoughts were so loud in her head she was scared she would speak them and not even realise. Am I mad? she thought. I might be. What if I am? What if I've got it wrong and the boys are my boys and I did all of that for nothing? I feel like I know. But what if I can't trust that feeling?

Doctor Summer wrote something down. "Is there anything else you can tell me about that?"

Lauren swallowed. "Only that I know it sounds insane. I know it. That counts for something, doesn't it? I don't think it was normal, to think that. I think it's crazy. Crazy people think they're sane, don't they? I understand how it looked, I do."

"We don't like to use that term here, Lauren. No one is crazy. Within these walls, we won't have any of those stigmatised insults. I want you to know that you won't be judged. Nothing is too unusual for you to talk about. It's simply words, feelings, brought out here into this safe space so they can be dealt with. Don't feel you have to hide things from me. I'm going to help you, and being truthful is the first step to recovery."

Is she being truthful with me, though? she thought. Can I really say whatever I feel and still be safe? How can that be true? Here in my darkest heart, there are things I won't even tell myself.

"It's all my fault."

"Do you think you're to blame?"

"Yes. If I hadn't left them, fallen asleep, she wouldn't have taken them in the first place, would she?"

"Did you see the person who took them?"

"No. But I thought they said they'd caught her." Did they say that? She was suddenly unsure. If they caught her, did she have the basket with the other babies with her? The memory was slipping away; she grasped at it. There they were by the river, and the stroller was there, returned like a miracle and she felt such joy in that moment before she looked into their eyes and knew the truth of it. There on the bridge, in the rain, it was Jo Harper, she said, *we got her.* And for a blissful second, she thought she was whole again. But it was already too late, the boys had already been changed.

The doctor made several long notes on her piece of paper. What is it, she thought, what did I say wrong? Lauren leaned forward to see what she was writing but the doctor tipped the clipboard so she couldn't.

"What did you see when you looked at Morgan and Riley after they were found?"

Lauren shuddered at the memory. She'd looked into the stroller. What did she see?

"I saw the babies. Morgan and Riley." It wasn't them.

"Was there anything different about them, that made you think they weren't your babies?"

Yes, she thought.

"No," she said. "They looked the same; it was just that first second. I was wrong. I was mistaken." Whatever's inside them now, she thought, it's not Morgan and Riley.

The doctor was writing, writing. What was

she writing? Was Lauren saying the wrong thing?

"After what happened to you, and how it affected you, the police decided to refer you to us. Do you know why they would do that?"

Ah, she thought, now this is because I tried to push them into the river. They could have put me in prison for that, but they didn't, because they think I'm mad. Instead, they've sent me here. So perhaps I still have a chance.

"I didn't want to harm them. I know it was wrong to try to put them back in the water."

"I hear that you didn't want to harm them."

"They're still somebody's babies. I shouldn't have done that."

"Somebody's babies?"

Shit

"My babies. I meant, they're my babies. I thought they were the wrong ones for a minute, so I suppose I just . . . I don't know. But I do know it was wrong to do that."

They are not my babies, she thought. They are that woman's, that horrible woman from the hospital, from the dream. Who wasn't there. Was she? She must have been there, all along, because now she's with the police.

What is happening to me?

Doctor Summer bent forward to write on the paper on her clipboard. Eventually the pen stopped moving and she smiled at Lauren. Lauren felt very tired.

"We're going to bring the babies here so that you can be with them."

"OK. Good," she said, thinking, no, don't bring them here.

In trying to control her facial expression, to hide the panic she felt expanding in her chest, her eye began to twitch involuntarily and she pressed her fingertips to it to make it stop. I don't want to see them, she thought. We need to find the real babies, my Morgan and my Riley. She's put them inside the bodies of the other ones, the ones from the river. They won't like being eels, being those fishy creatures. They won't know how to swim, how to breathe underwater. And, if the woman who took them is with the police, they'll be all alone. Lost, calling out for their mother.

The doctor was frowning at her. Lauren was sure she hadn't spoken out loud. Almost completely sure.

I think she lives in the river, that woman.

Don't say that. Did I say that?

The doctor put down her clipboard and leaned towards Lauren, her hands clasped

281

together. "Let's keep an open mind," she said. "We'll give you all the support you need — the staff here are very experienced with mums and babies. When the boys arrive we'll make sure you're all happy and we'll go from there."

Lauren swallowed. Her throat felt tight. She needed to keep it together, because she needed to get out of here as quickly as possible and put things right. There might be a deal to be made, with the woman, but she'd do anything. Anything except let it go on — anything except let her keep them. She intended to force the woman to change them back, and she would do whatever it took.

"Relax, Lauren. You're safe here with us."

The doctor placed a hand on top of both of hers, where she was gripping them tightly together in her lap. She tried to take long, slow breaths. The doctor spoke softly, and Lauren held her gaze, attempting to seem calm.

"I know that at the moment it's difficult for you to tell the difference between what is real and what is a symptom of your illness."

Lauren shook her head. Whatever they thought her illness was, she had to make the doctor think that there'd been a mistake, that she was well. Begging wouldn't help. Healthy people didn't beg. "No, I'm fine, I understand now." Doctor Summer sat back, glanced at Lauren's twitching leg. Lauren swiped a hand across her sweating forehead, then pressed down on her knee to stop it bouncing.

"That's good. It sounds like we're making progress." As she got up she said, "You can go and wait in your room for a while. I'll let you know when Patrick gets here with Morgan and Riley."

"How long do I have to stay here?" said Lauren, thinking, how long until I can start looking for my boys?

The doctor sat down again, perched on the edge of the seat. "Let's not think in terms of definite timescales at this point."

"Can I leave? I mean, am I allowed to leave?"

"We're going to help you, Lauren. We're going to make sure you can be the best mother to those boys that you can be."

On some level Lauren understood that this was a turning point. A threat was implied somehow, but she didn't know the consequences one way or another. She had to play the game, even before she knew what the rules were. She managed to smile at the doctor, when she wanted to scream at her, *let me go, let me go, before it's too late.*

"I understand," she said.

"Good," said the doctor, and she got up again and pulled out her keys to unlock the heavy door. Lauren would never get used to that sound, the deep clunk of the cylinder turning, the rattle of the key chains. The doctor left the door open, and Lauren thought for a moment she might be able to walk out on her own, unchaperoned, but Pauline came in after a second to take her back to her cell. The slow walk down the corridor felt like she was on her way to the gallows, a blank-faced attendant at her side. Lauren watched her own feet, trudging in the ugly black plastic clogs, but looked up when she heard the squeak of someone else's clogs coming the other way. A woman was shuffling towards them, pushing a stroller containing a baby that was crying weakly. She too had a guard at her side, and kept her dulled eyes down until the very last moment. When she looked up at Lauren, the woman's gaze in her sunken face was confused, and devoid of hope. Lauren wondered if that was how she looked, too.

Back in the bedroom, with its view of the grounds and the high fence in the distance, the guard and the prisoner sat in the armchairs.

"Shall I put the telly on?" asked Pauline.

Lauren nodded. Then, "Do you know how long Patrick will be with the babies?"

"Sorry, flower. I don't. Shouldn't be too long a wait, though. You must be looking forward to seeing them."

Lauren pointed her face at *Escape to the Country,* and told herself to be calm, normal, like nothing was different. She felt a twitch in her cheek and rubbed at it, tried to control her breathing. She was afraid she couldn't do it. She couldn't have those things near to her, and pretend they were her own. She missed her boys so much.

CHAPTER TWENTY-FOUR

The Hope Park Estate had ancient stone pillars on each side of the entrance, but the blank metal security gate was an incongruous modern addition. Harper had driven Patrick and the twins from the hospital; his car was still at the riverside where he'd left it earlier. She drove up close to the intercom, reached out and pressed the buzzer under the blue and white NHS logo.

"Hello?" said a nasal voice, emitted from a grille.

"Detective Sergeant Joanna Harper, and Patrick Tranter. We're here to see Lauren Tranter. The twins are with us. We're expected."

"Look at the camera, please," said the unseen doorkeeper. Patrick leaned over so that the security procedure could be completed. The camera swivelled on its little stalk, pointing itself at their faces and making a digital shutter-sound to indicate that it had recorded their image. The gate juddered open at an agonising rate, revealing the leafy surrounds within, one centimetre at a time.

Three or four huge old oak trees stuck out of a lawn the size of a farmer's field. The richly landscaped setting gave an illusion of easy affluence, but the electric gates and high perimeter fence, barely masked by low shrubs, told the real story. This was a place of refuge, for those in crisis, but it was also, effectively, a prison. As Harper drove towards the car park she could see people in twos and threes dotted about the grounds, pushing buggies or playing with babies in the shade. Each patient, without exception, was accompanied by a nurse in a white tunic.

The unit itself was a low, modern building — what Harper's mother would have described as a monstrosity of concrete and glass. Nearby, what must once have been a grand country house made the new structure even uglier by comparison. The older building stood a short distance away, handsome but neglected, the paint on the double front door peeling, one or two panes in the leaded windows cracked or missing and replaced with sheets of ply. Encircling the old house was a metal fence, the type they used to fence off building sites, each panel held in place at the bottom by two concrete blocks. On the gabled roof, dark windows stood out like eyes.

Patrick crouched in the car park, struggling to reassemble the stroller. He wrestled the car seats away from the seatbelts in the back of the car and slotted them in place on the frame. As he worked, the boys regarded their hassled father with the same uncanny calmness they had possessed since the disappearance, though their hands occasionally waved in the air. They both made the sea-bird sound a few times, tossing it back and forth between them, copying each other.

When both boys were clipped in, Patrick leaned over the top twin, dressed in yellow.

"Where's your smiles, Morgie?" He tickled the baby under the chin, rather self-consciously. "You got any smiles for Daddy? No?"

Briefly he bent to examine Riley, who lifted his eyes to meet his father's with an expression as sombre as his brother's.

"You too, huh? Well, I guess we've all had a long day."

Wearily he pushed the stroller towards a big sign that said VISITORS THIS WAY. Harper followed on.

At the external door, another buzzer, and the same woman who had spoken through the intercom at the gate asked for their names again. They were let through the first door, which clicked itself locked behind them. Another locked glass door led through to the corridor, but for now they were trapped in the vestibule. A woman with grey hair and huge glasses appeared at a hatch, behind thick glass. She moved her lips but there was no sound.

"Can't hear you," said Patrick, tapping his ear to demonstrate.

A speaker crackled into life, the same voice they'd heard outside, with the same grating nasal squeak, slightly fuzzy and not quite in synch with the woman's mouth. "Forgot the button," she said, smiling. "Sorry. Here are your badges."

Under the hatch, a tray popped open and Harper peered inside. There were two name badges that said VISITOR. She handed one to Patrick.

"Are either of you carrying any weapons?" asked the woman, looking at Harper.

"No," said Harper and Patrick together.

"Any drugs, prescription or otherwise?"

"Um, paracetamol," said Harper. "Does that count?"

"Yes. Are they in the bag?"

"Yes."

"Can you put them in the tray, please. What about in the stroller?"

"Only the changing bag," said Patrick. "Nappies, you know. That kind of thing."

The woman grimaced, as if nappies and that kind of thing could easily constitute contraband.

"Can you leave the bag, please, sir? I need to check it. Just pop it in the tray. And both of you, your phones, wallets and keys if you don't mind. You can collect them on the way out."

After everything was loaded into the tray the inner door buzzed and clicked to indicate it was unlocked.

In the corridor, the receptionist said, "I've a note here from Doctor Summer. She wants to see you, Mr Tranter, before you take the boys to see Lauren."

Harper waited while Patrick spoke to the psychiatrist. She'd offered to watch the boys but was secretly glad when he said he'd take them in with him — the way they stared was beginning to unnerve her. She was on the verge of asking if they'd always done that or if it was a new thing, but the question seemed inappropriate, under the circumstances.

After a few minutes, a buzzer sounded

somewhere further down the corridor and a nurse, a woman in her forties with lots of thick dark hair piled above a pleasing face, emerged from behind a heavy door. Big eyes and high cheekbones, she could have been a model in her youth. She marched smartly past where Harper sat and knocked on the door of the counselling room into which the doctor had taken Patrick and the twins.

"I'll take you down," she said, holding the door open for Patrick to come out with the stroller. He got its wide wheels stuck a few times before succeeding.

Doctor Summer followed Patrick into the corridor. As the door to the therapy room was closed and locked behind them by the nurse, the doctor peered at each boy in turn, giving them a little squeeze.

"They're so chilled, aren't they?" she said. "Such good boys."

Then she smiled and started to walk away.

"Aren't you coming, too?" said Patrick to the doctor.

"No, but I'll be watching." She nodded towards the CCTV camera mounted next to the smoke alarm in the ceiling, "and there will be two nurses there with you, for support if it's needed."

Patrick watched her walk away, his wide-eyed expression that of a lost little boy.

"Do you want me there?" asked Harper, and he nodded.

As she followed the nurse, the father and the stroller down the long, wide corridor Harper noticed the art — huge canvases, each of them covered with rectangles of primary colours in different formations. The white walls and the large paintings made it feel a bit like a gallery. There was a stillness here, too, a sense that etiquette required a certain kind of reverence, and that all behaviour was being judged and examined, and found wanting.

A little further on something in one of the rooms hit the wall with a force that made the frames of the screwed-on art rattle.

"Jesus," said Patrick, "is that . . ." He looked in desperation at Harper, seeming to ask, *it's not Lauren, is it?*

"No, no, nothing to worry about," said the nurse, lifting her radio handset from her belt and holding it to her lips. "Room seven, assistance please," she said brightly, and smiled at Harper as she caught her eye. Something slammed against the wall again, harder this time, and two nurses appeared, running up the corridor, keys jangling, shouldering their way into the cell.

"What was that?" asked Patrick.

"Here we are," said the nurse, as they arrived at a door marked Room Eleven. She knocked on it, then opened the hatch and peered through. The sound of keys in the lock from inside, and the door swung inwards, to reveal another nurse, not nearly as friendly. "Lauren?" called the nurse. "There's someone here to see you, sweet-heart."

Lauren sat in a chair next to the window. She looked small, wary, hunched up. Her legs were splattered with dried mud from the riverbank. The nurse who had got up to open the door sat down next to Lauren, but lightly, as if ready to leap up again. Lauren raised her eyes.

"Oh," she said, pointing at the stroller, "oh, no. I thought I could do it, but it's too soon."

She stood up out of her seat and tried to back away, pressing herself into the bars on the window, crossing her arms over her body, eyes large and scared. Patrick took a step inside the room.

"Honey," he said, "what's wrong?"

"No, Patrick, please, take them away," she said, "I'm sorry. I can't."

"But Lauren," said Patrick, as she started to shake her head and repeat "no, no, no," getting louder, and the nurse in the room formed a human barrier, taking up all the space between him and his wife.

"Let's try again later, shall we?" said Lauren's nurse to Patrick's, as together they walked him backwards out of the door and the nurse inside shut it, hard. The locks turned loudly in the silence of the corridor.

In the stroller, the babies seemed startled, but then their little faces screwed up and they started to cry.

"Oh, don't cry, shh," he said to them, and wiggled the stroller back and forth. They didn't stop. It was almost mechanical; insistent and relentless. Each of them filled the gaps where the other breathed, creating a continuous, ululating shriek at the frequency of a band saw going through metal.

Under the noise, behind the door to Room Eleven, there was the muffled sound of Lauren crying and the low murmur of the nurse trying to comfort her, persuade her to stop.

Patrick's eyes were filling up, too. Harper reached out and patted him on the shoulder. She felt for him then, witnessing his total powerlessness, his palpable sense of impotence. The noise of the twins' crying went on and on.

"Right then," said the nurse, taking the stroller by the handle and pointing it back the way they'd come, "I think these boys are a tad tired. Shall we all go for a little stroll?"

In the car on the way back, neither of them spoke until they reached the New Riverby reservoir, where the valley was filled with glittering silver to the horizon. The water level was low, after the month-long heat-wave. Harper could see the stubby outlines of the remains of walls at the exposed edge of the lake, and in the centre the tip of the old Selverton Church tower, black and pointed like a blade pushing up through the surface.

To Harper, the inside of the car seemed a much calmer place without the twins. She relished the silence, the sense of peace. As the car travelled over the viaduct, Patrick lifted his head from where it rested on the passenger window. For a few moments he watched the landscape slip by.

"I should never have left the babies with her. They're not safe."

"I don't think you need to worry," said Harper. "They have procedures. Didn't the doctor say that Morgan and Riley wouldn't be left alone with Lauren, even for a moment, until they could be sure everything would be fine?"

"You saw what she was like."

"Yes," said Harper. "But they're going to help her."

"She's not fit to look after them. I should have brought them home."

"If you'd done that, they wouldn't be able to treat her at Hope. She has to have the babies with her for that. Believe me," said Harper, "you don't want her to be transferred to the general ward. Hope Park might be a bit like a prison but the alternative is . . . well. You don't want to know."

"Why?" said Patrick. "What's it like?"

She'd only had to go into the Selver General unit once, for an interview. There'd been a confession by an inmate to a historic murder case. *Inmate,* she chided herself. She meant patient, of course, though the unit was worse than any prison she'd been inside. For Harper it was always the small details that held the most power: the porcelain-and-meat sound of teeth knocked askew on metal bed rails; the pop of ligaments stretched to breaking as arms were expertly twisted back in restraint; the moment, hours later in her own bathroom, when she reached forward to rub at the mirror, thinking it was dirty, but no, there on her face and over her white shirt a light splattering of pink, a man's saliva mixed with his blood, which must have sprayed over her as he was carried past, choking.

"Don't think about that now," said Harper, wondering, if it came to it, what favours she could pull in to keep Lauren away from that place. "It won't happen. She'll come around. She loves those boys."

"Yeah," said Patrick, sounding lost, "I thought she did, too."

Patrick directed Harper to drop him off at his sister's house. She pulled up outside and turned off the engine.

He smiled weakly as he thanked her and opened the car door. "You're all right, Harper. I know we've had our differences. But I couldn't have got through today without you."

Harper nodded in acknowledgement. "I'll be in touch, about your interview."

"My interview? Why do you need to question me?"

"Because I think you know the suspect. A young woman, with long dark hair. Very slim. Rather uncooperative. Sound like a friend of yours?"

"No."

But the shock of realisation on his face told a different story. In that moment, Harper knew that they were both thinking of the same thing: the day that Harper had followed him, seen him — caught him — in the car park with the young woman with the red-rimmed eyes, the very same young woman who turned up again today in the river with his babies. The way that, before he knew he was being watched, he'd taken that woman by the elbow as if he wanted to be rid of her.

CHAPTER TWENTY-FIVE

The interview room was hot despite the noisy buzz and flap of the fan unit, which must have had something caught in it to be making that much racket. James Crace, the duty solicitor, a young man with thick lenses in his fashionably geeky spectacles, held a tissue over his mouth and nose like a Victorian dandy. The reason he was doing this became clear before Harper had even sat down — there was a strong smell of body odour and river mud coming from the suspect, who slumped in the chair, eyes half closed, hair lank and drooping. Someone had placed a white plastic cup of tea on the table in front of her. The camera in the corner displayed a steady red light to show that it was recording.

"First things first," said Harper. "We ran your fingerprints through our system, and it seems that you are a citizen of previously good conduct. The computer didn't recognise you."

The suspect said nothing.

"We also ran your number plates. The DVLA knows who you are. For the tape, please. Can you confirm your name?"

When she still said nothing, Harper said, "If you want to keep that clean record, then I suggest you confirm your identity. I'm perfectly happy to charge you with obstructing an investigation, if that's how you want to play it."

Harper waited for a minute, then made to get up. The solicitor sat forward. "Wait," he said. "She'll cooperate. Won't you, Natasha?"

The woman mumbled something incomprehensible.

"Speak up," said Harper.

"I'm Natasha Dowling."

"Excellent," said Harper. "Not too difficult, was it? Now then, Ms Dowling. Can you tell me what you were doing when we met earlier today, please?"

It seemed the suspect had clammed up once more. She remained silent.

"Natasha," said Harper, more softly, "it's in your interest to talk to me. At the moment it looks very bad for you. You've been arrested on suspicion of abduction, but the charges could be much worse, in a case like this, involving babies."

The voice, when it came, was deeper and louder than before. "You were there," she said, "why don't you tell me what I was doing."

"I only know what I saw. I want you to tell me what happened, from your side."

"It won't make a difference," said Natasha, reaching for the drink in front of her. "You've already made up your mind about me. Haven't you?" She sipped the liquid, spat it back. "That's disgusting," she said, dropping the cup back on the table between them so that some of it spilled, a pale pool on the grey plastic laminate. The whitish film of cold milk that had formed on the surface of the beverage slipped up the side of the cup and hung there, dead sagging skin made of lactose, proving her point. Harper frowned at it for a second.

"I'll tell you my theory, if you like," she said.

"I can't wait," said Natasha, crossing her arms.

"I think you've got a grudge against Patrick. I think you took his kids to get back at him."

"Who's Patrick?"

"You know who he is. I saw you together, at his office, a couple of weeks ago."

Natasha said nothing for a long time. The solicitor blew his nose repeatedly, coughing, apologising, coughing again. Harper sighed, looked at her watch. She was about to get up and leave when the suspect spoke. The voice was suddenly small and girlish.

"I told you at the time. I knew you wouldn't believe me. Nothing I say makes any difference."

"I need you to tell me again. For the record."

Natasha's voice was so quiet then that Harper had to lean in to hear the words.

"I was saving them."

"Saving them."

Natasha nodded. One dark eyebrow twitched. "That's the truth. I thought I'd be thanked for it, not arrested."

"What do you mean, you were saving them?"

"I mean, I didn't take them. I found them in the stroller in the woods, hidden out of sight. I was trying to bring them back to where the police were and I took a short cut across the river, only, I got stuck. And then you came."

"Did anyone see you? See you find them, I mean. Can anyone corroborate your story?"

She shook her head. "No. I was alone. And

302

that's why it doesn't matter what I say. Does it?"

Harper thought about it. Could that have been the truth? Could it have been someone else who took the stroller? She tried to look at it objectively. There'd been no other suspects identified as yet, and no witnesses, apart from herself, unless there were any yet to come forward. All she had to go on was what she'd seen in those few seconds immediately after she'd come around that corner, spotted this woman in the river with the stroller, shouted *stop, police,* and ran towards her. Natasha had let go of the stroller and scrambled out, trying to get away, almost as quick as the lightning that flashed in that moment, just as if she were guilty.

"So why did you run, if you were trying to bring them to safety? You left them there and tried to leg it. Doesn't make you look like much of a hero."

Natasha dropped her eyes. "It's true, I panicked. I knew you were police, and I knew what it would look like, me with the pushchair, in the water, when everyone had been searching for those babies all over." She looked back up into Harper's eyes. "And I wasn't wrong, was I?"

"Why were you even in the valley? What

303

were you doing there, in the first place?"

"Walking. It's a nice place for a walk."

One of the most obvious of the lies. But to show disbelief in an interview was a powerful weapon that needed to be withheld, so she simply said, "Where did you walk from?"

"I drove from town. I parked nearby."

"But you didn't park by the millpond, or at the cafe."

"So?"

"So, that's where most people park, when they're walking. We found your car at the edge of the woods, further out towards the peaks. Just past where you were arrested, in fact."

The two women stared at each other. Natasha said nothing.

"Did you follow Lauren to the valley today?"

"No. I told you. I was walking. I would never follow her. I had no idea she'd be there."

"So," said Harper, "you don't know who Patrick is, but you know who Lauren is?"

Crace rolled his eyes, blew his nose and began to make frantic notes on his pad.

Natasha looked over at him and the lawyer made a chopping motion with his hand, *stop talking*. She looked back at Harper.

"I . . . no comment."

"On the subject of not knowing who Patrick Tranter is, for the tape, I am showing the suspect a transcript of a text-message conversation."

Harper placed the tablet on the table so that it faced Natasha.

"Also for the tape, I'm going to read out the transcript. Tell me if I get any of it wrong."

From her printed copy, Harper started to read out the relevant section. Natasha stared at the screen in front of her.

Natasha Dowling's phone
TO PATRICK TRANTER (PT), FROM NATASHA DOWLING (ND)
July 21st, 1:45 a.m.
How would you feel if I killed myself? Would you even care?

7:51 a.m.
I'm really sorry about that last text. I promise I won't send any more. I'm just feeling really down

12:03 p.m.
I know you might say no to this but would you meet me for coffee? Just for a chat. I really need to see you

11:34 p.m.
I don't know how you can just switch off your feelings like this Patrick. I can't do it. I need to see you

July 22nd, 12:09 a.m.
You're a fucking bastard and I hate you I hope you die

TO ND, FROM PT:
July 22nd, 12:10 a.m.
This is the last message I'm going to send. My wife is ill. I have newborn twins. I'm sorry if I hurt you but I don't have time for this. Please leave me alone now. I hope you get the help you need

TO PT, FROM ND:
July 22nd, 12:39 a.m.
You're going to be sorry you said that. Really, really sorry.

1:44 a.m.
Why should you be happy when you've destroyed my life? Why should you get to keep what you have?

7:48 a.m.
I'm sorry. I didn't mean it. I really miss you. Call me anytime. Or I could meet you from

Harper put the papers down on the table. "In light of this evidence, would you like to tell me how you know Patrick Tranter?"

Natasha glanced at the solicitor, who nodded. Wearily, she looked back at Harper, then dropped her eyes.

"He was my boyfriend. Or, I thought he was. We met in a bar, around four months ago."

"And he tried to end it recently?"

"Yes."

"But you didn't want it to end."

"I suppose."

"If you threaten to hurt a man's family, do you think that will make him love you back?"

"I didn't threaten him."

"Look," said Harper, pointing at the words on the screen, "you said, among other things, *why should you get to keep what you have.* Looks like a legitimate threat to me. It could easily be construed, in hindsight, as a threat to take Patrick's children. To hurt him, the way he hurt you."

Natasha pushed the tablet away with one finger. "I did say that. I also said, *I'm sorry, I didn't mean it.* I didn't do what you say."

"Patrick's a married man. You must have

known that when you got involved with him. What did you think would happen?"

"He said he was separated, and that his wife had serious mental problems. He said he still lived with her because he was basically her carer, and he needed time to get her sorted out with someone to look after her. I didn't know about the babies until they were almost born." She was tense, her lips puckered into a mean little *o*.

"You didn't know about the fact that his wife was pregnant?"

"No. Not until she was almost ready to pop."

"Anyone would be angry."

"Yes."

"It's understandable to want to try to get at him."

"Well, yes, but not like this."

"Lauren's an easy target. And she's the one who gets to keep him. I can see why you might lash out at her, at the babies. They're all that's standing between you and a happy life with Patrick."

Natasha laughed mirthlessly. "This is stupid. Anyway, I don't know her. I've never met her. I don't even know what she looks like."

"You've never seen a photo of her and Patrick together? You've never searched her name on social media? These are things I can easily check, on your phone and your laptop."

Natasha stuck her lip out, a petulant child. "Fine. I know what she looks like."

"So you saw her in the valley today? You recognised her?"

Natasha didn't respond. Crace whispered something in her ear. "No comment," she mumbled.

"You followed her in your car, didn't you?"

"No comment."

"Where were you on the thirteenth of July?"

"No . . . July? Why are you asking me about July?"

"The date means nothing to you?"

"I don't know. It was ages ago."

"According to the messages on your phone, Patrick dumped you that night. It was also the day his twins were born."

"Well, you know already then. I was being dumped. Drowning my sorrows, if I remember rightly."

"In the text messages there's a conversation where you threaten to go to his house. He says he's at the hospital. You say, and I quote, *well maybe I'll come there then.*"

"I didn't go there, of course I didn't. Is that what you think?"

"Patrick's wife thinks someone came on to the maternity ward that night and threatened her. I've heard evidence that backs up that claim, and I'll be getting it analysed very soon. Whose voice do you think I'll find on that tape, Natasha?"

"From what Patrick's told me about his nutjob of a wife," said Natasha, "I couldn't say. I expect you'll find that it's a figment of her crazy imagination."

CHAPTER TWENTY-SIX

In the moments before the door opened she'd been ready, she thought, but the sight of the stroller winded her. That fluorescent green she'd chosen, suddenly the colour of river-weed. And there was Patrick, usually so confident, seeming hesitant and uncertain; his frightened eyes tore away her mask. She thought she could feel them, the things in the stroller, wanting her, wanting something and she couldn't stop herself trying to get away from them; the reflex was too strong to fight. But, a split second later, when the door closed and she felt the shards of paint under her fingernails from where she'd been scrabbling at the window bars, she knew she'd made a huge mistake.

She heard the babies crying outside in the corridor and the sound was not Morgan and Riley. When her own babies cried, the frequency of it was so hard-wired into her brain that it tugged her from her thoughts, and milk would immediately begin to leak from her nipples. This new sound was high and hard, the same sound twice where Morgan and Riley were each distinctive. It sharpened her thoughts instead of muddying them. Her breasts remained indifferent. It was confirmation: they are not my boys. My mind knows, and so does my body. But both had betrayed her in the moment, as she'd panicked and screamed and clawed at the barred and bolted window, trying to flee when she should have been pretending all was fine, smoothing things over, allowing the staff to believe she ought to be released.

The crying sound faded as it got further away. Then Pauline was telling her, in a very parental tone, to calm down because everything was all right. Lauren stopped crying very quickly and sat back down in the chair. I've blown it, she thought, desperate to collapse inwardly with despair. But no. She had no time for that. Morgan and Riley were still missing. And she was not mad, no matter what they thought.

"What was all that about?" asked Pauline.

"I don't know," said Lauren, "I'm sorry."

"Don't you want to see your babies, Lauren?"

"Yes," she said, "I do. More than anything." It was true. She thought of how

312

much she wanted to see Morgan and Riley, and she started to cry again, hopeless, helpless tears, before stopping herself abruptly. To see them again, she would first need to see the imposters, to appear to accept them as her own. She had to make this woman believe, so that she could convince the doctor. "I don't know why I did that. Will Patrick bring them back? I really want to see them. I do."

"Let's give it a few minutes, shall we? They'll go up to the nursery, and when you're ready we can have them brought down again. OK?"

"OK. But not too long?"

"You need to be calm, petal. Babies can pick up on emotions."

"I'm calm. I'll be calm." But the way she said it, far too quickly, and the way Pauline looked at her with eyebrows slightly raised, cast doubt on her words.

The nurse put the telly on, that big rectangular pacifier. The notebook came out a moment later, the pen scratching away at the paper for what seemed like forever, recording all of the things Lauren had said and done, all of the things she didn't want the doctor to know about. Lauren's hand twitched. She wanted to get hold of that book and rip the pages away from the spine.

There had to be a way to get it off her.

A knock-knocking, a cry of "dinner," and Pauline tucked the notebook out of sight. She got up and unlocked the door.

"Lovely, thanks," she said to someone outside and the door gave a squeak as it closed. She came back with the tray and placed it on Lauren's lap. Horrors. On the tacky wood-effect surface were two plastic bowls and a plate piled with matter; all of it emitting a thick odour of meat, fat and over-boiled vegetation, none of it Lauren would have chosen to put in her mouth and chew. Next to the bowls and the plate, plastic cutlery. Patients weren't trusted with metal. I could still fashion something pointy from those, she thought.

The nurse was watching her. Lauren needed to get this right. She was on the back foot now. There needed to be a plan if she was going to get out of this place before it was too late.

Staying focused was crucial — she couldn't afford any more mistakes. Morgan and Riley were somewhere out there, waiting for her to rescue them, and she was the only one who understood the truth about what was happening. The creatures inside the bodies of Morgan and Riley had fooled everyone but her. She could see why; she wouldn't have believed it herself if it hadn't been happening to her. And why was it happening to her? Maybe she deserved all of this, for being a bad mother. And perhaps she deserved it because, when they were born, she didn't love them immediately, the way you're supposed to do, the way she expected she would.

She hadn't loved them immediately, but she loved them after a spell. It seeped into her. Slowly. Like the love was something she'd been sipping at. Intoxicating. Accumulating. Snowballing. Slowly, quietly but unstoppably until she was quite drunk with it, and it was all she did. She loved them, it was her calling. Every instant was devoted to it, every thought, every action, every reaction. All her plans, all her dreams were about them, through them, for them, because of them, because of this love, that had not been there immediately but came upon her slowly, inexorably, irreversibly. That was why it was such a shock when it disappeared, the love: just like that, click your fingers, gone. She'd looked at those creatures in the stroller and the love was not there, not for them. It existed in her as a painful yearning, a missing part, reaching out to her real babies, wherever they were now, wherever that revolting woman had taken them. Under the water, somewhere. It didn't matter, she'd find them. Because she was their mother, and that was her job.

Nurse Pauline watched Lauren inspecting the tray of food, and without taking her eyes from the patient she slipped her notebook and pen out of her tunic pocket and rested them on her knee. If I don't eat this, thought Lauren, what is that nurse going to write? She needed to stop the treacherous note-taking, starting right now. All of the evidence needed to be in her favour. Lauren cleared her throat and reached for a piece of cutlery. She forked up a lump of the sloppy beige and brown mess and held her breath as she swallowed it down. Pauline nodded, smiled and wrote a short note, but what did it say? *Lauren ate her meal nicely? Lauren pretended to like her meal? Lauren hesitated before attempting to eat her meal? Lauren ate the food even though she clearly didn't want to?*

The smell of the food was outrageous. She took a gulp of lukewarm water from the plastic beaker, but the taste of the gelatinous yuck stayed on her tongue. Yes, she thought, placing the flimsy vessel down again, if I had a real glass perhaps I would think about slashing my way out of here. She glanced up at Pauline, who was openly staring. Did she have to do that? The whole situation

316

was inhuman. Don't they know, can't they see that this kind of close scrutiny would drive anyone mad? The way she was being inspected made Lauren wonder if her face might be giving too much away. She flattened her expression, and then, suddenly overcome with fatigue, turned towards the window to see sparrows kicking up dust in the brownish remains of the lawn outside.

"You not hungry, love?" asked Pauline. The woman seemed suspicious. Was Lauren allowed to not be hungry?

"Oh, not really, I'm afraid," said Lauren, worrying about how the words were coming out. She sounded like she was lying, but it was true. Her stomach felt like it was full of stones. She forced another wet globule into her mouth. Swallowed. Smiled. "It's nice, though." Weirdly, the lie sounded more convincing than the truth had. Don't gag, don't gag. More water, but the goo had stuck on her teeth, coating them in starch.

"What about your pudding?" said Pauline, "Don't you like steamed sponge and custard?"

In this heat? Who ate custard in summer?

"Not much of a sweet tooth," said Lauren. The nurse was still looking at the bowl of yellow-and-red, which reminded Lauren of a film she'd seen once in which a zombie

317

ate its own ear during a dinner party. After a moment, the nurse was still looking; she licked her lips. "Do you want it?" said Lauren. "Help yourself."

Without further hesitation, Nurse Pauline reached over and picked up the bowl and the plastic spoon. She sliced off a huge chunk of the sponge with the side of the spoon and shovelled it in, custard dripping from her lower lip. Don't gag, don't gag.

"Yum," said Pauline, before she'd even swallowed. Lauren turned away. The sparrows had gone.

Nurse Pauline finished the dessert in four or five spoonfuls, then replaced the bowl on the tray in front of Lauren, who stared at the smeary yellow streaks and the spit-slick surface of the plastic spoon.

"That filled a hole," said Nurse Pauline, patting the front of her uniform.

It wasn't too late. It couldn't be. She had seventy-two hours to convince them she was fine before they committed her to any more treatment. The clock would have started at lunchtime, when she'd been admitted. Time was ticking. She turned to the nurse.

"I think I'm ready now."

Pauline said, "Ready?"

"Yes," said Lauren, "to see the boys. They

must be hungry; they usually feed at this time."

"Are you sure? We don't want another performance like last time. It will only upset the little poppets."

"I know, I think I was just . . . over-whelmed. I'm ready now. I'd love to see them."

Pauline considered for a while. Then she made a quick note.

"Right," she said, "OK. I'll get Susan to bring them up from the nursery." She stood up and unlocked the door to lean out, but kept a foot in it to stop it closing completely. Lauren could hear her exchanging muttered remarks with another nurse over the two-way radio. Why couldn't she do that in front of Lauren? What was she saying, exactly?

Nurse Pauline re-entered after a minute, replacing her handset on her belt. She said to Lauren, "They'll just be a few minutes — you're lucky, the babies haven't woken up for a feed just yet but they will soon. They'll be happy to be fed by their mummy. Though, you do know you won't be able to breastfeed them yet, don't you — because of your medication?"

Lauren managed a disappointed smile, but she was sickened at the idea of breastfeed-ing those things, and desperately grateful to the drugs that had contaminated her supply.

"I'll just be happy to see them again," said Lauren.

"Shouldn't be too long though, until you can."

"Can what?"

"Breastfeed them. Depending on what they keep you dosed up with, of course. There are some anti-anxiety medications you can take and still feed."

A jolt of fear. *No.*

"Great," said Lauren, keeping her eyes on the smiling face of the man on the screen, who was gesticulating in a yellow hard hat at a half-built concrete house. Lauren felt her blood pulsating in her head. She concentrated on breathing slowly.

Knuckles rapped on the door.

"Here they are," said Nurse Pauline, flicking the mute button on the TV.

Don't panic, Lauren told herself. Whatever else they are, they are two small, helpless things. They can't hurt me. There is nothing to be afraid of.

The door opened and two more nurses came in, each holding a baby-shaped bundle.

"Aw," said Nurse Pauline, "they're asleep, little angels. Just pop them in the cot, ladies, if you don't mind."

"They've not had a bottle yet," said the smaller nurse, "not since Dad fed them earlier. They've just been sleeping, bless them."

"Lovely," said Nurse Pauline.

"Are you planning to keep them overnight?" asked the smaller nurse. "Or should we pop back and get them in a couple of hours?" Lauren was thinking about the answer when she realised the nurse wasn't asking her, she was asking Pauline. The patient didn't get a say, of course.

Pauline glanced at Lauren and frowned doubtfully. "We'll see how we get on."

"Right. We'll leave you to it, then." The two nurses turned to leave.

"Is Patrick still here?" asked Lauren.

"Sorry, love," said the small nurse, "he went home about an hour ago. He'll be back tomorrow."

Night was falling fast. The taller nurse flicked the lights on as she left.

With their eyes shut they could easily have been normal babies. But even with their eyes shut, she could see it, the wrongness. Lauren and Nurse Pauline stood, looking down at the small figures, the pair of babies breathing in tandem, stomachs rising and falling together. Pauline was taking careful notice of her charge.

"Right then, Mum," she asked, "which one's which?"

I don't know, she thought, I can't tell. They look exactly the same, apart from the colour of the vests. She knew now how other people had felt when looking at the twins before they were swapped. It was eerie, how alike they were.

"Green for Riley," said Lauren, feeling her pulse quicken but keeping her voice steady, "Yellow for Morgan."

Lauren glanced at Pauline. When she looked back at the babies their eyes were open. She gulped back a gasp and grabbed one hand with the other to stop them flying to her mouth. Both of the creatures were fully awake and concentrating on her with a steady gaze. Baby lips pressed together, miniature hands clasped.

"Hello, there, Morgan and Riley," said Pauline in a sugary voice. "Mummy's been missing you. Haven't you, Mummy?"

Three pairs of eyes upon Lauren, waiting for her response. The nurse *wanted* her to be insane, that much was clear. It probably made her job more interesting. But those two babies, what did they want from her? The eyes were old, full of knowledge. Her boys had crystal-blue eyes, with grey at the edges, just like Patrick. But these two pairs were starting to turn green. River-weed green.

"Yes, I've missed you," said Lauren, aware not only of the eyes, but of the unit's CCTV camera mounted in the ceiling, making her self-conscious, so that she felt forced to put on a show. She could do this. She told herself, pretend you love them, Lauren, you know what that looks like. "I don't ever want to be parted from you again. My precious boys."

The tears that came were real. Pauline patted her shoulder. The babies watched Lauren crying for a minute, fascinated, then turned their faces towards each other. Lauren saw something pass between them before they both inhaled and started to cry too. It was the same sound she was making. They were copying her. Lauren's throat closed, her sobs strangled. The twins continued. That same unnatural tone.

"Hungry, are we?" said Pauline, apparently not noticing that the boys were doing an exact impression of Lauren's soft sob, her adult cry. They didn't sound like babies at all.

Lauren tried not to stare at them as Pauline went over to the little table by the cot where the formula and the baby bottles

323

stood. She picked up an empty bottle. "Oh, fiddlesticks," she said, "I need boiling water. Hang on, love."

At the click of the closing door the two creatures stopped their bizarre mimicking of Lauren's cry and were suddenly calm, absorbed in watching her. Did they want acknowledgement? *Hear that? Didn't we sound like you? Aren't we clever?* She shivered, and would have moved away to the other side of the room. But for the camera at her back. She kept her eyes on the facsimiles of her children. What do you want? she wondered. She tipped her head to the side, and both the boys did, too. A whisper, then. One in each of her ears. Plaintive and distant, she could have imagined it: *Mother.*

The door opened and Pauline came barrelling back in, holding two steaming bottles of water.

"Sorry, love. You OK?" She seemed nervous. The nurse checked the babies, coochy-cooing them under the chin. She glanced up at the camera in the corner. Then Lauren realised what it was that was making her nervous. *She's not supposed to leave me alone with them.*

"That CCTV," said Lauren, holding Pauline's gaze, "is it recorded?"

Pauline looked away, arranging bottles, teats, the big tub of formula.

"It's a monitoring system," said Pauline. "It's to help us make sure you're getting better."

"But is it recorded?"

"I'm not supposed to discuss it with patients."

"Oh," said Lauren, "I see. Well, I suppose there are things I could keep to myself, too. If I wanted to. Or I could tell people. Depending." She could feel her heart beating. This wasn't her, she wasn't a bully. But she had reason, and she had to grab every little chance she was given. "Like just now," she glared straight at the nurse, "when you left me alone with these two."

Pauline wiped her sweaty hands on her tunic. She took a step back, to just behind the corner created by the ensuite, the only place in the room not covered by the camera. "I was only gone for a second," she hissed, her face turning red.

"How long do you think it takes to smother a baby?" whispered Lauren, without turning her head. Both twins were paying attention, their eyes travelling between the two women.

"You didn't do it, though."

"No. Because I'm not insane. Whatever

you might think."

"Huh," said Pauline. "You all say that. The ones who deny it the loudest are the most insane, in my experience."

Lauren took a small step towards Pauline, making it look like she was bending to examine the babies more closely. "You could lose your job for that, couldn't you?"

Pauline's whole head had gone beetroot. "Nothing happened. They're fine."

"Do they record it?" she asked again.

"OK," said Pauline, "what does it matter? Yes, they record it. But they don't watch it all. Only if something happens that's significant. The footage is stored for a week and then wiped."

"They don't watch it? Why do they bother, then?"

"There are twelve beds here, all full. That's twelve days' worth of footage, every day. Plus, the hallways, the entry doors, the grounds. You couldn't watch it all if you tried."

"Aha," said Lauren. "So you might get away with it then? Leaving a patient alone with babies, when you've been told not to."

"I might, yes," said Pauline, swallowing nervously.

"If I keep my mouth shut."

Pauline just looked at her.

"So, barring the unlikely possibility someone was watching the screen at that exact moment, no one will ever know. Unless I tell them, within the next week, before they scrub the footage."

Pauline's face screwed up in anger, then went slack in defeat. She shrugged and went about the business of scooping powdered formula into the bottles of hot water. The twins started making soft mewling noises and flapped their hands by their sides. The one in green chewed his right hand, while the one in yellow chewed his left.

"Which one do you want?" asked Pauline, swirling the milk in the bottles to mix it up and cool it down.

"You choose," said Lauren.

They sat in the chairs to feed the babies, who both kept a fixed gaze on Lauren. The one dressed as Riley showed no interest in Pauline, turning his head determinedly in the arms of the nurse so that she had to shift her position to get the bottle in. Lauren smiled down at the one she held, feeling cold. The small body was holding itself in a strange way. Morgan would have curled into her arm. This baby didn't know how to do that. In a way, she almost felt sorry for it. But her revulsion for the things, and her longing for her boys were hard to keep in check with pity alone.

Without moving her lips very much, she nodded towards the camera and whispered, "Does it have sound?"

Pretending not to respond, Pauline breathed out, "Yes, but it's not very good quality."

Lauren saw her opportunity and grabbed it. She could make things right, before the doctor saw the things Pauline was writing about her.

"I need your notes from earlier," whispered Lauren.

"What?" said Pauline, much too loudly.

Lauren stood up with her back to the camera, still feeding the baby. "Give me the notes," she said, "or I'll tell the doctor to check the footage."

Pauline's expression was sour. But she knew she had no choice if she wanted to keep her job. Within twenty minutes, Lauren was in the bathroom, waiting for the shredded pages from the notebook to soften enough that she could flush them and they wouldn't come back up.

CHAPTER TWENTY-SEVEN

August 15th
11 A.M.

It was falsely pleasant inside the Hope Park unit. Yesterday, when she'd come with Patrick and the boys, the fresh paint and clean floors had masked it, but now Harper could feel the constrictive undercurrent, the echoes of the Selver General psychiatric ward: the clanging metal doors; the jangling of key chains; the smell and the occasional moan or shriek from within a locked room. However, even taking all that into account it was still vastly superior to the Selver in many ways. The staff she'd met in the Hope were upbeat, friendly and professional. The setting was beautiful, too, which made a real difference to the feel of the place.

After the routine of the secure entry procedure, Harper had been shown into a bright, clean day room and given a cup of terrible vending-machine coffee as she waited to speak to Lauren and Patrick. Over by the window, a young mother fed her baby. The woman ignored Harper, or was at least only vaguely aware of her presence. Harper smiled at her but she continued to stare at a point on the wall near a bookshelf. Harper cleared her throat, and wished there was a radio or a TV on to fill the silence.

Presently the door was opened by a uniformed nurse, who held it for Lauren and Patrick to enter, each of them pushing a single stroller in front of them containing one of the twins. Lauren's skin was dull, her face impassive. The babies were still and silent, but when Harper glanced into the buggies they were looking directly at her.

"Hey, Morgan," she said to the one in yellow. The baby continued to stare at her. She transferred her gaze to the one in green. "Hey, Riley." She always ran out of things to say to babies.

"Thanks for meeting me," said Harper, reaching out to shake Patrick's large hand, then Lauren's cold and bony one.

The nurse who had held open the door took a seat a short distance away, picked up a magazine and flicked through it, pausing to look up at them every few moments. Nurse, or guard, thought Harper.

"Shall we sit?" said Patrick.

Lauren lowered herself warily. Her gaze flitted around the room and landed briefly on Harper.

"Why are you here?" she asked.

Patrick sat next to Lauren on a long settee, while Harper was opposite the couple on a chair, next to the two babies in their buggies angled towards their parents. In the far corner of the room the young mother had stopped feeding her baby and was staring into space, rocking backwards and forwards, humming something tuneless. The baby had fallen asleep in her arms.

Harper looked at her hands. She knew that what she was about to do was risky, considering the information she had about Patrick and Natasha's relationship. She suspected that Lauren wouldn't know a thing about it, and she wasn't planning to be the one to tell her. She could question Patrick later, at the station, regarding that. But, it was crucial to discover if Lauren knew Natasha from previous sightings. If Natasha had been spotted by Lauren in any context — even if Lauren wasn't aware of who Natasha was — it would help to build the case against her. Also, it would be interesting to see what Patrick was willing to admit in front of his wife.

"I'm gathering information about our

suspect. I've reason to believe that one or both of you know her. Anything you can tell me will help the investigation. I'm trying to establish why she might do something like this. We only have a right to hold her for twenty-four hours, then either charge her or let her go."

"Why does it matter if we know her or not?" said Patrick. "Didn't you catch her in the act?"

"The evidence is rather inconclusive, I'm afraid."

"How can it be? You said you saw it with your own eyes."

"She claims that what I saw, was her trying to return them to you."

"So what? She's lying, obviously. She took them, then changed her mind, decided it was a stupid idea. I mean, you can see why, she wasn't going to get very far with them. But how does that absolve her of the crime, the fact that she took them in the first place?"

At that moment, a nurse entered the room backwards, pulling a metal drugs trolley. She had red-framed glasses and short black spiky hair, and wore a white tunic and green uniform trousers.

"Medication, ladies," she called, in the same sort of upbeat voice you might say *ice-*

cream all round. She handed the woman in the corner a small white cup, followed by another, and a beaker of water. After the woman had tipped both cups of medication into her mouth and taken a swig from the beaker, she automatically opened her mouth wide so the nurse could check inside it to see that she'd swallowed.

"Here's yours, petal," said the nurse to Lauren, checking a clipboard before handing over the paper cup. Lauren looked at the pills before she took them. She had trouble swallowing, asked for extra water and was given it, gulped it down with effort.

"Open up," said the nurse, and Lauren paused for so long that Harper thought she would refuse. Then, she tilted her head back and opened her mouth while the nurse shined a small torch inside.

"Thank you," said the nurse. She wheeled across to the door and exited backside first, pulling the trolley with her.

When the door had shut, Lauren started to cough, covering her mouth with her hand. The nurse in the room glanced up without interest, slowly turning a page. Patrick slapped Lauren on the back gently, asked if she'd like some water.

"Not water," she said, "tea or something.

From the cafeteria."

After he'd gone, the two women faced each other. Again, the nurse flicked her eyes towards Lauren, then yawned extravagantly.

"This woman," said Lauren, "you're right, I think I know who it is. And why she'd do it."

Harper leaned in to catch Lauren's words, which were spilling out quickly and quietly as she tried not to be heard by the nurse or the young woman across the room.

"Did you see anything?" said Harper. "Did you remember something important?"

"She's not normal. She's evil. And everyone told me she wasn't real. But this proves it, right?"

Harper gave an encouraging smile, but she had a feeling she was losing the thread of what Lauren was saying. Were they still talking about Natasha?

"I never told you what happened," said Lauren. "I didn't think you would believe me."

"Try me," said Harper. She glanced at the nurse, who seemed to have fallen asleep. Her head was on her chest, eyes closed, magazine slowly edging from her hand towards the floor.

"In the hospital, when I had them, this woman was there — I mean she was really there, I don't think I was imagining it. Well, sometimes I do. It's complicated. Anyway, she frightened me. And then later on, when she was outside the house, and I called you — I was right about that, Harper, I knew it, I saw her so clearly." Lauren's eyes drifted away and she shuddered. "She's from the water, that woman. Where the two rivers meet. Just like these two." She nodded towards the babies, both of whom seemed to be smiling faintly as they gazed at Lauren.

"The babies?"

Lauren nodded. "You saw them before. Do they seem different to you?"

Harper didn't know. All babies looked similar. They were a bit bigger than they had been in the hospital when she first saw them, definitely. But different? Different how? She shrugged. "Not really."

"Look closely," said Lauren. "Look in their eyes. She changed them."

"In the water?" said Harper. "You mean she changed them . . . in the water?" What was she talking about? Natasha was from the water? And the babies, too? Did she think that, while they were with her, Natasha had performed some strange baptism on them and that they were somehow altered by it?

"Yes," said Lauren, "yes, yes, you do understand. Thank God."

A voice from the corner, then. "I've heard them singing."

Harper turned to where the vacant young woman had suddenly come to focus.

Lauren's head snapped round. "What did you say?"

"Those boys, they sing at night. In the nursery. It's beautiful."

In the stroller, the boys tipped their heads towards the woman's voice. Just as if they knew they were being talked about.

"I heard them talking, too. You know what they call each other?"

Lauren's voice was barely a whisper. "What?"

Patrick gave the door a kick to open it, and the nurse woke with a snort. "Tea's up," he said. Across the room Harper saw the young woman's focus drift away as she faded into her thoughts again. The babies started flapping their arms and making baby noises. Harper realised her mouth was hanging open and she shut it.

Lauren reached for the tea that Patrick offered, blew on it. She swilled the hot liquid round a few times and placed it on the table, rather too close to the edge.

"Thanks, love."

"Aren't you going to drink it?" said Patrick.

"Of course. It's just a bit hot."

"Sorry, Detective Sergeant, I didn't get you anything. Did you want —"

"Oh, no, don't worry. I just had one." She felt a little light-headed. The twins, when she turned towards them, did not return her gaze. To look at them now, they seemed like normal babies. But just a minute before, they'd been eyeing her as if they understood everything she was saying.

Harper became serious, remembering why she'd come. "I'm going to show you both a photograph now, of the person we caught. If you could first tell me whether or not you recognise the person, that would be helpful."

She slid the print on to the table. In it, Natasha was as pale and drawn as Lauren. Her dark hair stood out in unattractive contrast to the skin, white and dry as paper.

Lauren's face fell. "That's who you think it is?" she said.

"Yes," said Harper. "This is the person we arrested at the scene."

"You're wrong," said Lauren, shrinking back against her husband. "That's not her. I've never seen that person before." Tears began to spill.

337

"A moment ago, the woman you were talking about, who threatened you, and that you saw outside the house," said Harper, "this isn't her?"

Lauren pressed her face against Patrick, shaking her head, no.

"You don't recognise her at all?"

"No. I just told you, no."

"What about you, Mr Tranter," said Harper, "do you recognise this woman?" she didn't bother to hide the knowing tone, the fact that she already knew the answer.

"That's Natasha," said Patrick, without expression.

Lauren drew her breath in and grew still. She raised her face. "Natasha from your work," she said, "who gave us that weird present?"

"Yes," said Patrick, looking at Harper, who knew that Natasha had never worked at Strategy Outsource Marketing, because she'd visited the office on the way to the unit and discovered that none of them knew who this person was. The receptionist identified her as someone who "sometimes hangs around outside waiting for Patrick," but wouldn't be drawn on what she made of the arrangement.

"I knew it," said Patrick. "She's out to get me. Of course she'd deny it, if it means there'll be a trial and I'll have to face her in court."

"Why would she be out to get you?" said Lauren.

"She's mad. You saw that rat thing she sent, not even knocking on the door, just leaving it on the doorstep. The girl's a nut."

The nurse in the corner cleared her throat pointedly. "Sorry," said Patrick. "She's mentally . . . challenged."

Harper said, "What's this rat thing? Do you still have it?"

"No," said Patrick, "it was a really tasteless little ornament. I threw it in the bin. I don't know what she meant by sending it, but it wasn't funny."

"But Patrick," said Lauren, "what did you do to her?"

An infinitesimal pause, then, "Nothing. She's just obsessed with me."

"Why?" said Lauren. "Why is she obsessed with you?"

He looked at Harper then, and back at his wife.

"I . . . sacked her. I had no choice; she was useless, not at all right for the job. But since then, she won't leave me alone."

The most convincing lies, thought Harper, are the ones that are almost true; for sacked, read: dumped.

Harper said, "Did she send you any text messages, or emails?"

"Yes. Hundreds. I deleted them."

Harper said, "That's another reason I came. I'm afraid I need to seize your phone. Don't worry, you'll get it back once it's been analysed."

"My phone?" said Patrick. "I don't have it. It's with reception."

"I know. I can get it on the way out."

"But I just told you, I deleted everything anyway."

"We have people who can recover all sorts of things from phones, Mr Tranter." She watched as his face paled by a couple of shades.

"Oh," he said, and then swallowed hard. "Good."

"You never said anything," said Lauren to Patrick. "If you were being stalked, you should have told me."

"I didn't want to worry you. I thought if I ignored her, she might eventually go away. I'm so sorry. I feel like this whole thing's my fault. For having her sacked. For hiring her in the first place."

"You shouldn't blame yourself," said Lauren. "I believe her."

There was a silence. Harper watched the couple with interest.

340

"You what?" said Patrick.

"I don't think she took them." Lauren turned to face Harper. "You've got the wrong one. You need to keep on looking. This girl," she indicated the print, still on the table between them, "she's innocent."

Patrick stared at his wife, his face full of pity.

"The woman you want is young, she's got dark hair, bad teeth, piercing eyes. She stinks. She's got a basket. She took my babies, she took them. Not this one."

Patrick put his hands on top of Lauren's to stop them flitting in the air. He said, "Shh, honey, you're babbling."

Harper cleared her throat. She didn't know what to make of Lauren's certainty that they had the wrong person in custody. She could have been describing Natasha, apart from the basket, and maybe the teeth. Perhaps, in her heightened state of agitation in the hospital, she simply hadn't taken in what the person looked like, and had constructed something from her own imagination that didn't match reality. "Natasha Dowling is our only suspect at this time. So far, the evidence isn't conclusive, but I think we'll soon be able to prove that she's the one who took them. Hopefully she'll be charged soon, but I'll keep you informed as much as possible. And Mr Tranter, you may also have to come in to give a statement."

Patrick didn't look too happy about that prospect, but he nodded that he understood.

Lauren kept her eyes averted as Harper got up and said her good-byes. As she walked over to the door she heard the splash of liquid spilling and turned back to see Lauren's tea had fallen to the floor, was streaked across the carpet at her feet.

"Oh, I'm so clumsy. I don't know how that happened. I'm so sorry. Let me clear it up . . ."

"Don't worry, it's fine, I'll do it," said Patrick, reaching for some paper towels and dabbing at the floor.

Harper stopped and stared. There on the darkened patch of carpet, dissolving rapidly in the hot liquid, were fragments of what she thought were medication capsule cases. Almost immediately, the fragments were gone, melted entirely away, leaving no evidence that they had ever been there.

"You didn't even drink any of it," said Patrick. "I'll get you another one."

Patrick went past Harper and out of the room towards the cafeteria, disappearing around a corner. Harper stepped into the corridor, wondering what she ought to do about what she'd just seen. Should she report Lauren for avoiding her meds? Should she go after Patrick and tell him? The more she thought about it, the less sure she was about what she'd seen. Hadn't the nurse checked Lauren's mouth, to make sure she'd swallowed? As the door started to close, she heard the dreamy young woman start to sing. The tune was ancient, sad, and heavy with feeling.

I'm a four-loom weaver as many a one
    knows
I've nowt to eat, and I've worn out me
    clo'es
Me clogs are both broken and stockings
    I've none
They'd scarce give me tuppence for all
    I've got on

Harper listened. And then she thought she heard more voices, a high harmony. She put her hand on the door to stop it closing completely, and through the gap she looked at Lauren to see if the sound came from her, but her mouth was shut. It was the babies; she could see the twins in profile, their mouths taut and open as if they were crying, but the sound, in that split second, was like singing. The police officer's eyes raced between the young woman and the two babies, an impossible trio. Impossible. She pushed the door wider and looked in desperation over at the nurse, who'd fallen asleep again, the magazine on her chest.

Lauren gazed at Harper, shining eyes triumphant. "You see, now, don't you?"

Then the nurse snorted awake and the young woman stopped singing and the babies were crying, long, sorrowful screaming cries of the kind that cannot be ignored.

CHAPTER TWENTY-EIGHT

The visit to the unit was very troubling. Harper had been hoping that Lauren would identify Natasha as the woman who had been harassing her, so that she could build the case against Natasha, but it seemed Lauren didn't know her at all. After the conversation, Harper's conviction that Lauren wasn't as mad as everyone thought was disappearing fast. But, just imagine if your babies had a cry that sounded like singing. That would be enough to make anyone question their grasp on reality. Such an eerie moment, she shuddered to think of it.

When Harper returned to the office, her phone showed a missed call from Amy, so she rang back. The journalist picked up immediately.

"You weren't as friendly as usual yesterday, Joanna," said Amy, by way of hello.

So much had happened yesterday, Harper had almost forgotten she'd even seen Amy at the riverside. Of course she hadn't been friendly — she'd been dealing with the aftermath of the abduction, sorting Patrick out, thinking about what the doctor might find in terms of evidence, trying not to imagine what had happened to the babies. Since then she'd been up to Hope Park and back, then interviewed Natasha. All in all, a really long day, after which she'd collapsed at home for a few hours, unable to sleep properly because she hadn't done her usual two hours' training. So yeah, it was possible she hadn't been all that friendly.

"I wasn't?" said Harper. "I suppose not. I was working. Sorry, I didn't mean anything —"

"Did you see the television news yet? You looked great. If you like that kind of thing."

Harper had caught a glimpse of herself on the monitor in the big office. The footage, captured on a bystander's phone, showed Harper emerging from the woods with the stroller as the rain battered down. A moment later, the parents rushed towards the babies, arms outstretched, a happy ending from a Hollywood movie, as the family was reunited. Footage of the aftermath was more difficult to watch, and Harper was irritated that they'd decided to put it out. Lauren's breakdown, the messy restraint

346

that could easily have looked like an assault to the untrained eye. People didn't need to see that. Though this was a point on which she and Amy would have disagreed entirely.

"I do an excellent drowned rat, right?"

"You found those babies. You did well."

"Huh. I did OK. I was lucky really, right place right time. But, thanks to that, I've still got a pile of stuff to finish."

"How long do you think it will take you?"

"It might be a late one."

"But you'll have time for a drink, right?"

"A drink?" Harper's face flushed red. This woman had terrible timing. "Well, I . . ."

"Look, I found a witness you might be interested in talking to. A cyclist. He says he rode by just before the rainstorm, saw a woman pushing a stroller and nearly knocked her into the river."

"This is great, Amy, really excellent. Do you have a name, a number?"

"Of course, sweet pea. But it might cost you."

"Cost me what?"

"That drink, for starters."

"It's a deal."

"OK, where and when?"

"I'll deal with the suspect first. Then I'll call you, OK? I'll just get a pen. What's the name?"

When Harper ended the call, she still had no firm idea what kind of "drink" Amy was talking about, but she did know that she was going to go through with it this time, if only to find out. She sometimes wished she wasn't attracted to women at all; they were so confusing. Men were a lot easier to deal with, and usually a lot easier to forget about. Forgetting about Amy was proving quite a challenge.

Work always helped with that, and right now she had a new lead to follow. She lifted the internal phone and arranged for the witness to be brought in immediately.

Jimmy Durrell was small, his face rodentish. He worked shifts at the petrol station near the big supermarket, lived on a housing estate about a mile up the Bishop Valley, and he liked to cycle to work along the river. Amy had tracked him down at work, goodness knows how — it was more than Harper's own officers had managed. Durrell remembered the bright green stroller, the woman pushing it, and how, now that he thought about it, it hadn't seemed right at the time.

"I was cycling along the river, going to work. I had to swerve around this woman pushing this big green double stroller, and I

348

said, 'Sorry love,' but she didn't even look at me. I thought she was very rude."

"Which direction was she going?"

"Upriver, away from town. And she was in a hurry, which I thought was odd, because there's nothing to hurry up there for. Makes sense now, of course. Bitch were taking them."

"All right, Mr Durrell. I'm going to read out your description of the woman, as given to my constable when you came in, and you can tell me if you have anything to add." Harper looked at the paper in front of her. "Dark clothes, dark hair, ugly face."

"Yes."

"Is that all?"

"Short. She looked like a gyppo. But your officer said she couldn't write that down."

"Quite right," said Harper. "It's not terribly specific, for a start."

"Well, I know what I mean."

"Did she have trousers? A dress? What kind of dark clothing?"

"Beyond that she was wearing black, I don't know — I was looking at the ground, trying not to run the stupid trout into the river. I only saw her for a second."

"Right. Well, that's useful. We can rule out anyone in light-coloured clothing."

"Ugly, too, and filthy. Child stealing

349

gyppo, that's what she were."

Harper flinched at the repeat of the racist term. It was a double disappointment: apart from her personal distaste for such attitudes, someone so prejudiced rarely made a reliable witness.

"Can you be more specific? Ugly isn't very descriptive. Can you describe the shape of her nose, eyes, ears perhaps?"

"Not exactly. She smelled terrible, that I do remember. I got a right whiff as I went by."

Harper tried not to sigh. "Did you see anyone on a bench, a bit further down?"

"On the bench? Not that I recall."

Harper brought out a laptop and opened it, turning the screen to face the witness. "I'm going to show you a video of nine people, one of whom is a person of interest. I want you to look at each one carefully, and tell me if any one of them is the woman you saw pushing the stroller."

The Video Identification Parade Electronic Recording, obtained from the national bureau, showed a head-and-shoulder shot of a dark-haired woman on a grey background, who turned her head from left to right. This was followed by eight more women of a similar age and appearance, who all turned their heads in the same way.

Natasha was number seven, her dark hair in oily ropes, cheeks streaked by the ghosts of mascara lines. Durrell stared at her in the same blank way that he stared at the others, showing no sign that he recognised her.

When the tape ended he shook his head.

"I can't be sure. You know, I thought three and eight were the same person. Were they all supposed to be different?"

Brilliant, thought Harper. She closed the VIPER window and clicked an image open.

"What about this one. Did you see this woman at all?"

He pulled the laptop closer, squinted at the screen.

"Oh, yes, I think that's her. She looks the type to steal babies, I reckon. She was number four, right?"

Harper took back the laptop. The close-up of Lauren's face, taken from her driver's license, stared out at her, unsmiling.

The twenty-four hours she could hold the suspect without charge were almost up. The first interview hadn't given them much to go on that wasn't circumstantial. If nothing came out of this second interview, Harper was going to have to let Dowling go. She called down to the custody sergeant to have the suspect brought up from the cells once more.

Natasha and the solicitor, Crace, were already seated when Harper entered the room, carrying a jug of cold water and a stack of plastic cups. It was, if anything, hotter than it had been the last time the three of them had gathered here. Crace plucked at his shirt and fanned himself with a piece of A4.

Harper made the official introductions for the sake of the recording, then turned to Natasha.

"So. We've talked about the fact that you and Patrick were in a relationship that ended recently, and that you were angry with him because he didn't tell you his wife was pregnant. You've admitted that you followed Lauren to the valley —"

"I never admitted that. I said I was going for a walk."

"Watch your step, Sergeant," said the solicitor.

Harper looked up at them both and gave a friendly smile. "Sorry. My mistake. Let's go through what happened on the day the twins were taken. You decided to go for a stroll in the woods. Yes?"

"Yes."

"Then what?"

"I heard someone screaming about their babies being taken. Then a few minutes later I heard the sirens, and I saw some police officers. I knew what had happened, from what she was yelling. I knew someone had snatched those babies."

"None of my officers said they saw you in the woods."

"I was on the other side of the river. There's not really a footpath there. And anyway, I hid from them."

"Why would you do that?"

"I saw that it was Patrick's wife there, and I thought people would think the worst. I didn't want to be seen."

"Well, of course you wouldn't, if you'd taken the stroller."

"I didn't take it. Do you want to hear this, or not?"

"Sure. Carry on."

"I hid for a while, behind a fallen tree, and then when things seemed to calm down and the screaming had stopped, I walked on. I thought I saw another officer, so I went to hide in the old mill wheel tower, and that's where I found them. They were pushed all the way in, out of sight. You wouldn't have seen them unless you went right inside. At first I thought the stroller must have been empty, but there they were.

It was weird, they weren't crying or anything. They just stared at me."

"What did you do then?"

"Well, I couldn't leave them there, could I? I'm not a monster. I hauled the stroller out and pushed it towards the river, the shallow part that I thought I could get across, because it would have been much quicker than going all the way up to the bridge and back. But by then, the water had started rising, and it wasn't as easy as I'd thought it would be. It must have started raining in the peaks just before, so the river had already swelled before the storm came. I got stuck. The rest, you already know."

"What I still don't know is why you followed Lauren to the valley in the first place."

"For crying out loud, Harper," said Crace. He turned to Natasha. "Don't answer that."

"I didn't follow her. I just went there. It was a coincidence."

Harper flipped the cover from the tablet in front of her, swiped it a few times, placed it back on the table.

"For the tape, I am reading the suspect a transcript of a text-message conversation, the recorded date of which is the day in question, the time around two hours before the abduction. This message was sent from Natasha Dowling's phone to the phone of

354

Patrick Tranter, and reads: 'I'm outside your house. Maybe I'll knock on the door, tell her everything. How would you like that?' Do you have anything to say about that, Ms Dowling?"

Natasha stared at the table. Harper let the silence continue until it was uncomfortable. Then she leaned in close. "You must see the problem we have here."

Natasha pressed her lips together.

"This clearly places you at the house, just before Lauren set off for the valley, on the day the twins were taken. I suggest it might be a good idea to start telling the truth. Especially if you want people to believe that you didn't take them."

"I could have sent that message from anywhere."

"Sure," said Harper, "you don't think we can pinpoint precisely where it was sent from? The GPS on your phone will prove it, either way. Forensics are analysing it as we speak."

Natasha sat up. "You can do that? You can tell the precise location the phone was in when text messages were sent?"

"Of course."

"Well, there you go. I sent loads of messages to Patrick that morning, while I was in the woods. If you can tell exactly where I was when each one was sent, you'll see that I wasn't even on the right side of the river; that I couldn't possibly have taken the twins."

The solicitor looked up. He grinned at Natasha like she'd done him proud, and started to pack his things away. "I think that's enough for now, don't you?" he said. "When do you expect the results from the phone analysis?"

"Tomorrow, at the earliest," said Harper.

"Well, Ms Dowling, I think it's safe to say that by tomorrow all suspicions will be eradicated." He turned towards Harper. "And seeing as you don't have nearly enough evidence to charge my client now, she'll be glad to leave immediately."

CHAPTER TWENTY-NINE

Pink light from the setting sun reflected off the glass in the door as Harper pushed it open, her bike balanced on one shoulder. Inside the building, perching on the communal stairs in her pencil skirt and heels, was Amy.

"I texted you," she said, a greeting and a reproach all rolled together.

"How did you get in here?" said Harper, thinking, and how do you know where I live?

Amy shrugged. "Someone from the flat upstairs let me into the building. I rang the station and they said you'd gone home, so I thought I'd pop round. Actually, I thought we said we were going for a drink."

Harper lowered the bike and leaned it against the wall, unclipped her helmet.

"Ah," she said, "sorry. I didn't take my phone out. I needed to clear my head." She found herself slightly irritated by Amy's presence, by the way she was acting hurt

357

that Harper had ignored her, when really it was nothing to do with Amy at all. She'd just needed to ride. Her mind had been spinning with the events of the last day and a half, and the Peak District always cured her of that. Two hours out there on her bike, and she knew she would sleep. It was her medicine. This, she thought, is why these things never work out. No one ever seems to get that I need to be alone sometimes.

Amy said, "Was my witness of any use?"

"Um, kind of."

"Oh," said Amy, "you sound like you didn't find it that helpful."

"No, it's not your fault. What he said didn't really give us much to go on, that's all."

"What did he say?"

"That the woman was wearing dark clothing. Which could have been the mother, or the suspect, as they were both in black."

"I see. Didn't you show him a line-up?"

Harper nodded. "He couldn't make a positive ID."

"Huh. That's a shame. I hope I haven't complicated things. I didn't mean to."

"Not a bit. I'm really grateful for your help. My own people didn't manage to find any witnesses at all. But I had to let my only suspect walk today. Not enough evidence."

"Oh shit, I'm sorry."

"There'll be other evidence. We'll get her eventually." As she spoke, Harper rolled and stretched a stiff shoulder. She was starting to get itchy in her sweat-soaked Lycra.

Amy took a large white envelope from her bag. "I found something else you might be interested in."

"What is it?"

"A newspaper article. From 1976. I was doing some research for a comparison piece about the heatwave, and this caught my eye."

Inside the envelope were several photo-copied pages from the *Sheffield Mail,* dated July 3rd, 1976. Harper could see why a comparison piece would be of interest; every time they talked about the current temperature on the news they would say it was the "hottest summer since 1976". Harper hadn't been born then, but from what she could gather, 1976 held the record for the longest, hottest summer in living memory — until this year. The copied pages from the newspaper she held contained mainly different angles on reports about the weather; the unprecedented numbers of heat-exhaustion cases in the hospitals, the devastating effect that the water shortage was having on crops. There was an article that described how four of the rivers in Sheffield had dried up completely, and the level of the reservoir had dropped low enough to reveal parts of the ruined village for the first time since it was filled in the 1890s.

Amy took the sheets and shuffled them. She handed them back, pointing at one particular story.

"Here," she said.

The main story on the page reported on the swarms of seven-spotted ladybirds terrorising the city, but halfway down, there was a smaller article:

Suspected Kidnapper at Large in Maternity Hospital

Police have received reports of an attempted kidnap that was perpetrated in the early hours of yesterday morning. The attempt, which involved a pair of newly born identical twins, took place at the city's maternity hospital. The mother of the twin boys was able to alert the nurses and prevent the person from making off with the babies, but as the suspect has not yet been apprehended police are warning all mothers of infants to be vigilant. The suspected kidnapper is described as being female, of unkempt appearance, rather thin, of average height with long black hair. If anyone has any information, they are asked to contact the police immediately.

Harper said, "Wow."

"Creepy, right?"

"Yes." She read the article again. "This is from 1976?"

"Do you think it might be related?"

Harper shook her head slowly. "I don't see how. Our suspect wouldn't even have been born then."

Amy said, "Well, I thought you'd want to see it. I got the shivers when I read it the first time."

Harper put the copies back in the envelope and tucked it under an arm. She could smell herself now, and it wasn't good. She glanced up at the door to her flat, thinking, hot shower, then bed. But the confidence she'd had that she would fall asleep immediately was fading away as her mind started to work on this new information, calculating, extrapolating, creating new working theories. Say it was the same person in both cases — if they were at least twenty when they did it in 1976, then they'd be at least sixty now, so therefore . . . Leave it, she told herself, concentrate on Natasha. Natasha was there.

She had a motive.

"Thanks," said Harper, "I really appreciate it. And thanks for bringing it over, too. You didn't have to do that."

Amy stood, placed a hand on her hip. She had that forties movie-star thing right down. "Aren't you going to invite me in?"

The flat was in no state to be seen by guests. No one had been into it for months except Harper, not since her little sister visited at Christmas and pointed out to her with a measure of disgust that she lived like a teenage boy. She couldn't let Amy see it, not yet. Harper frowned, looked at her watch, said, "Hey, I'd love to, but I'm exhausted and I have to get up early because of the case, and —"

"Don't worry," said Amy, all flirtatiousness completely erased from her voice and manner. "I get it."

Before Harper could think of the right thing to say, Amy had gone. She stood for a moment at the foot of the stairs, inhaling Amy's perfume, wondering what it was that had just happened. Had she blown it, whatever "it" was, or might have been? Oh well, thought Harper, trying not to feel the sting of disappointment, it's probably for the best.

CHAPTER THIRTY

Is it said that River Mumma lives in the cool depths of water. She sometimes comes up to sit on a rock and comb her long black hair. If you see her, do not look at her. If you catch her eye, she may draw you down with her, where she may live but you may not. If she catches hold of you, all manner of terrible things will happen. No one knows exactly what, because no one she's got hold of has ever come back to tell the tale.

Traditional Jamaican

August 16th
Four Weeks and Six Days Old
9 :30 A.M.

"This is cosy, isn't it?" said Ruthie, who'd come for a visit.

The hospital seemed to think that one extra visitor meant that there needed to be two nurses on duty, one for each twin. The room, designed for one person to sleep in with a baby, held five adults plus the two infants. Pauline leaned on the windowsill while the other nurse stood by the door like a sentry.

Patrick breathed out through his nose. The babies, held by Patrick and Ruthie, were intent on Lauren. They never seemed to blink. Every now and then, they raised up their arms and made that sea-bird sound, almost in synch, puppets on the same string. Patrick frowned, and she studied him. Could he see it, too? How different they were from before, and how strange?

Lauren turned towards him, her smile fixed in place. Her eyes flicked towards the nurses. *Get rid of them,* she tried to say with her eyes.

Patrick cleared his throat, turned to the nurses. "Do you both have to be here?"

The two women looked at each other. The shorter one said, "Well, I could wait outside, I suppose. Unless you want to?"

"I'll go," said Pauline, launching herself towards the door, which she flung open in her hurry to leave. It closed slowly and clicked shut after a minute, cutting off the sound of her quick retreating feet in the corridor. Lauren breathed out.

Patrick raised an eyebrow. "Are you two,

um, getting on OK?"

No, thought Lauren, I hate that nosy bitch. "Yes," she said, "it's fine. It's odd, being watched all the time, that's all."

Leaning against the wall, the remaining nurse's eyes followed the birds out of the window but she was listening, assessing, judging. Lauren could tell.

Ruthie said, "I was so worried about you. Both of you. What a nightmare. I can't tell you how glad I am that you got them back so quickly, but still. Lauren, I would have been a complete mess, if it were me. I would have been even worse —" She halted abruptly, with a little sound that indicated she thought she'd gone too far. "Not that you were . . ."

"Don't worry, Ruthie, she knows what you meant."

Patrick tucked a springy coil of Lauren's hair back into the puffball of her ponytail. She complained about the hair but it had excellent qualities. You could mould it into a shape and it stayed. Plaits needed no binding on the ends. She liked it that Patrick loved playing with it as they watched films together, or he used to, before there was no time in their lives to watch films. He would divide the hair into two and twist it until it became two large horns that curled up and met above her head. She'd thought it was funny, when she looked in the mirror afterwards. The memory saddened her.

"You look better today though," said Patrick, "not so pale."

"I got loads of sleep, that's what it is," said Lauren. "They've been looking after the babies in the nursery overnight. It's the first time I've had more than two hours straight since they were born. I feel like a new woman."

"Was it hard being away from them?" said Ruthie. "After what happened, I mean."

No, she thought, it was sweet relief to have the things in a separate room. But yes, it was hard being away from Morgan and Riley. She felt like something had been ripped from her heart, and that her life was draining away through the open wound with every passing second.

"Yes," said Lauren, "being away from them is torture. But they gave me something to help, you know, a little pill."

Patrick said, "The doctor says you've made progress. She says there's a chance you won't need to stay much beyond the three days, if you carry on the same way."

"She said that to you? That they would let me go?"

"She didn't promise. She just said it was

366

possible. If you seemed like you were coping with the boys, taking your medication, all that."

"Good," said Ruthie. "That's good. Three days? Not long then, only another day and a half."

Ruthie looked at her lap, where the one in green was propped with his fat legs splayed. She gently took hold of the baby's foot.

Lauren thought, a day and a half. My boys might not be able to hang on that long. In two days, they could be anywhere. That woman could take them anywhere. She sank down and away, until she was curled on the bed facing the wall.

She heard Patrick saying, "Can you take the baby?"

And the nurse said, "Of course," as if she'd love to, as if it was a privilege. "They're such little darlings, aren't they?"

Little darlings. Lauren wished she was back in that life where the babies were her precious boys, the ones she'd given birth to, who were adored without condition. These ones, had the building been on fire, she would have happily stepped across to get away.

Patrick lay down behind Lauren. He drew her towards him, forks in a drawer. She was tensing all of her muscles, twitching with the effort but when he curved himself against her there she let it go. She cried with her whole self. He absorbed the waves of it. She shook and bucked and shuddered and reached back to grab at him, curled up fists of his jeans so hard that he sucked his teeth in pain. It finally peaked and gradually ebbed, while he stroked her gently, telling her, "It's all right, you're safe, I've got you." She turned to him, under the gaze of his sister and the nurse, who both quickly averted their eyes, and the two babies who did not. Lauren hid in the dip between Patrick's body and the wall. The blank eye of the camera observed everything but he made her a shadow to hide in, and she was glad in that moment of his large size, and that he served a purpose: he was a barrier, protecting her. She held her hands up by her face the small pink paws of a defenceless creature.

She was breathing quickly, susurrations that turned into words. He leaned in closer, frowned that he didn't understand.

"Get me out of here," she said.

He kissed her so that she felt the hot blood rushing. In that kiss she could feel only him. Not the babies' eyes on her, nor the numerous ears that witnessed the gentle suck and smack of it. They were alone, together, in this place where they would never be alone.

A baby's cry tore through her, hooking her out of the kiss, quick as a caught fish. Patrick's body tensed. She gave an anguished groan and lifted her hands again to cover her face.

"Which one is it?" she asked, thinking, I used to be able to tell.

Patrick shifted to see which baby was screeching, but by the time he turned his body it was both of them. She glanced up; they were throwing out their arms and legs, wriggling to be free, shrieking. Ruthie and the nurse jiggled and cooed, but the sound filled the room like water might, panicking her, make it stop.

"They're hungry," said Lauren. "They need milk."

When Lauren remained on the bed, Patrick said, "I'll go," and went to the little cupboard where the formula tub and other equipment was kept. He opened it up but there were no bottles. He looked to the nurse, gesturing helplessly, screwing his face up against the sound.

"Down the corridor," said the nurse, smiling, singing the words gaily over the crying, "the sterilisation room. You'll find bottles, kettles. Off you go."

"Right." He swung the door open and

strode away from the sound, which was like being inside a small speaker with a pair of police sirens. No one could stand it; she hoped he'd be quick.

Ruthie, struggling to contain the screaming thing in her arms, gaped at Lauren, who had made no move to take the baby from her, to comfort him or his brother as a mother ought. Lauren saw a glance pass between Ruthie and the nurse, and forced herself to go near, placing herself in a position where she could reach out and stroke the heads of the babies but avoid taking either of them.

The screams seemed to enter her head from the front and sides, from above and below. She stood still and let it saw through her, shutting her eyes and imagining that the pain of the sound was happening to someone else, that she was wrapping it up in cloth and holding it apart in her mind. Eventually she could bear it. She opened her eyes, watched the unlocked door, calculating how far she might get if she went to it now, opened it and ran. Not far. there'd be sentries out there, and more doors, with more locks.

The moment the door opened a crack Lauren sprang forward and pulled it open. She took the bottles from Patrick's hands and held them up to eye level. Seeing there was too much water in them she went into the bathroom to tip out what wasn't needed, her hands shaking slightly. The two boys, who had turned almost purple with fury, continued to shriek and kick and slap in the arms of Ruthie and the nurse, who were bobbing up and down on the balls of their feet, to no effect. The nurse was trying to distract Riley, singing something that couldn't be heard over the crying, but Ruthie looked stricken, bouncing with a sense of defeat. After a second she just stopped still and looked in horrified wonder at the small, impossibly loud and angry thing in her arms.

Lauren tipped the measured powder into the hot water and handed Patrick a bottle. "Keep shaking it," she said. "It's too hot."

As if they could tell that milk was within reach, the crying got louder, the shrieks more insistent, more demanding. And then she heard the words they were saying, and she stopped. These nearly five-week-old babies. They were forming words.

"Is it OK now?" said Patrick, still shaking the milk.

But she'd frozen, in disbelief, and didn't respond.

"Lauren." He squeezed her arm, and she

blinked.

"Can you hear that?"

"The milk, Lauren. What do you think? Can they have it now?"

"Test it," she said, "on your wrist." She listened again, desperate for it not to be real. But the words were there.

Patrick squirted a bit of the milk on the inside of his wrist. He shook his head, too hot. Then, his face lit with an idea.

"Get some cold water in the sink."

She ran the tap until the small basin was half full. They plunged both bottles in.

"Try them now," he said. Still much too hot.

She covered her ears with her hands. It couldn't be. But the plea got in, the creatures' plaintive, desperate message. In the mirror, in the harsh light of the windowless bathroom, her eyes were bloodshot. She looked away towards the bottles, floating slightly and steaming in their bath of cold. Come on, cool down, she thought. Once they're feeding, they'll stop.

Surely Patrick could hear it too, but he showed no sign, he hadn't noticed. She took hold of his arm. "Listen," she hissed.

He tried to take his arm away saying, "Ow, that hurts," so she squeezed it tighter. He shook her off and she grabbed for him.

"No, really listen."

The boys were screaming, screaming. He shook his head.

"What? All I can hear is screaming."

"They're saying *words.*"

He frowned, searched her face, almost laughed but stopped himself. If he just listened, it was clear, revealed in what one moment before was just a jumble of long purposeless sounds. She mouthed the words to him as they screamed them, and his face changed. He heard it then, she knew he did. The screams, and Lauren's mouth, formed the long, drawn-out shape of the words *help us,* over and over, sad and panicked and pitiful.

"You hear it?" she breathed.

Patrick stared at her, his lips tight.

He checked the milk again. "It's fine," he said, and he whisked the two bottles out of the basin and charged into the room, handed one to the nurse, one to Ruthie. The babies' mouths were plugged. Sweet silence relieved them all. Lauren's ears whined in the sudden quiet, and she went to the bed and sat down. Ruthie and the nurse settled themselves in the two chairs.

"Thank heavens for that," said Ruthie. "They've got impressive power, those little lungs, haven't they?"

"That's better, isn't it, Morgan?" said the nurse. She glanced up at Lauren. "You OK, love?"

Lauren drew a long breath and nodded, smiled at the nurse. She held her hands together so they wouldn't shake. "I'm fine, yes, thanks."

"Do you want to feed him?"

"Me?" She stared at the baby in yellow held by the nurse. "Oh, yes," she said, attempting a smile, "of course. If you don't mind."

Patrick said, "You don't have to, babe, if you don't want to."

"I do," she said quickly, "I do want to. I do."

She cradled the baby in her arms and crossed her legs underneath. Morgan watched her from above the bottle as he suckled. The milk was disappearing fast.

"His eyes," said Patrick, "are they changing colour? They used to be blue, didn't they?"

"You see it too?" she said.

"Well, sure. They look kind of green at the edges."

Ruthie said, "Riley too, actually, when you look closely. How odd."

"It's odd, isn't it?" said Lauren. "Really odd, right?" So it wasn't just her, she wasn't

374

imagining it. "They're changing, right in front of us. And you can see it too. Can't you?"

She knew she'd said something, or done something strange, by the way they all looked at her then, sort of sideways.

Ruthie said, "Yes, but honey, I don't think it's *that* odd, not really."

"No?"

"Babies' eyes do change colour," said the nurse.

"They do?" said Lauren, feeling the tremor in her voice.

"Yes, often. Especially if they start off blue. It's nothing to worry about."

"But no one in our family has green eyes. No one."

When she looked again at Morgan's eyes they were closed. In Ruthie's arms, Riley had finished his milk and was also asleep.

"Peace at last," said the nurse.

CHAPTER THIRTY-ONE

August 16th
11 A.M.
Harper's email pinged with a message from Forensics. The subject line read: GPS analysis results. When she opened it, she saw that it contained a map showing the location of Natasha's phone at several critical points. There was the phone, right by the cafe at the exact time the cafe staff confirmed that Lauren had left with the stroller, after her coffee with Cindy and Rosa: the GPS signal was nearby, but on the other side of the river. So, Natasha had been watching Lauren from the far bank, perhaps concealed behind the bushes that grew there.

The text message that corresponded to the coordinates read: *Why can't you love me the way you love her? She's nothing special.*

Further points on the map showed that Natasha had followed Lauren upriver for a while, but then gone past the bench where Lauren had been sitting and back towards her own car. At the approximate time the babies were taken, Natasha was at least half a mile further on, sending Patrick a long apology for everything she'd said and done, and begging him to reply.

Harper studied the timecodes between the messages carefully. She soon realised that there was no credible case against Natasha: there wasn't enough time between any of the texts for Natasha to have taken the babies; in fact, nothing indicated that she'd even crossed over to Lauren's side of the river, not until Harper had seen her upriver struggling to cross with the stroller. The last text Natasha had sent was ten minutes before Harper had caught her. By then she would have known from what was happening around her — the screams from Lauren, the police cars converging on the area — that Patrick's babies had been taken, and that they hadn't yet been found. And yet, the message read: *I'll be here for you always. Whatever happens xx*

Harper found the message puzzling in its ambiguity considering the circumstances, until she realised the position the woman was in: Natasha couldn't let on to Patrick that she was already in the valley herself, spying on Lauren. To do so would have pushed him further away. When she found the hidden babies a moment later, then, she must have considered leaving them, running back to her car and pretending she'd never been there. But she hadn't. She'd tried to help, despite knowing what the consequences of that might be. Perhaps she thought, at least she could do something good, and maybe Patrick would be grateful for that instead of focusing on the stalking. She certainly couldn't have realised how badly it would backfire.

Harper felt defeated. Admitting that Natasha was innocent meant the abductor was still out there somewhere, and she had absolutely no clue how to find them.

Harper parked her car next to the millpond in the Bishop Valley Park. Lauren Tranter's blue Fiesta was still there, now covered in a film of brown dirt and sticky leaves, abandoned since the day of the abduction. This was where it had all started. The weather was the same, hot and muggy. She hoped there wouldn't be another storm.

She made her way towards the cafe, feeling the peace of the place, hearing the gentle sound of the river running through. She stopped briefly by the water, noticing a dark place under a big tree. There was something moving under there, flashing silver as it turned — three or four big fish, sheltering from the sun, trapped there by the low water level. She shivered, despite the heat.

Outside the cafe, she studied the far bank, where a person could easily be concealed in the thick bushes. She imagined the pitiful form of Natasha crouching there, watching Lauren laughing with her friends. Someone else had been watching Lauren too, but who? And where from? There were dozens of places to hide nearby; behind the cafe, among the people in the playground, in the woods.

She walked on, along the river path and up to the bench where the stroller was taken. GPS showed that Natasha had been walking along on the other side. What then? At some point, Jimmy Durrell had ridden past on his bike; Lauren had sat down on the bench, and fallen asleep; Natasha had gone back in the direction of her parked car. If only she'd not done that, and kept watching instead; she would have seen whoever did it.

Harper tried to put herself in the mind of the perpetrator. He or she was waiting nearby, somewhere within sight of the bench. Then, when Lauren fell asleep, they'd seized their opportunity, snatched the stroller, and made off. The path was narrow here, the roots snaking thickly across it. It wouldn't have been easy to get the stroller away — the person must have been strong, determined, both.

When she reached the place where Natasha had been found with the babies she saw that it would just be possible to push a stroller across without it getting too wet, if you lifted it over the rocks. Natasha wasn't strong enough to do that, from what Harper had seen; she'd got it stuck. But then, in the time between the taking and the returning, the sudden downpour had swelled the river, made it dangerous to cross.

On both banks, Harper could still see faint tyre tracks and footprints at the water's edge. She pulled out her phone and studied the crime-scene photographs from the day of the abduction. In the images, on the far bank there were more than one set of tracks: one going in, one coming out. But, on the near side she could only identify tracks coming out, and those were probably made when Harper herself had hauled the stroller out of the water. In the photos from back at the bench, there were tyre tracks only on the bench bank, as if a stroller had been pushed in there, too. So, they knew that Natasha had pushed the stroller in from the opposite side, and Harper had pulled it out on the path side. The other tracks went in at the bench, and out at the river bend on the opposite bank. Harper considered it, and almost laughed. Swimming upstream with a stroller? Impossible. Perhaps it was impossible to know the truth. The rain and the swelling river had no doubt washed some tracks away before the photos were taken.

Harper used the rocks sticking out of the river as stepping-stones to get to the other side. She tried to form an image of the perpetrator but Natasha's face kept popping into her head. Lauren had known it wasn't Natasha, long before the evidence proved it. But the trouble was, you couldn't put much trust in what Lauren said, because of her condition. For example, her insistence that being in the water had changed the babies: pure fantasy. And yet, it was understandable, because of how frightened she must have been, and probably how guilty that she didn't do enough to protect them, even though it wasn't her fault. Harper knew all too well how that kind of guilt worked; how it tapped you on the shoulder at night, telling you that you should have

381

tried harder, known better, fought back. That you, rendered powerless in the moment, were also somehow to blame for that lack of power.

The path on the other side of the river was overgrown, but she could see where the stroller had been forced through. Branches were broken, nettles trodden underfoot. A large log lay across the path at one point. Harper stepped over it. Just beyond were the derelict remains of the mill wheel tower.

The mossy shell of the tower was no higher than a large garden shed, the stone from the upper floors long since fallen into the pit on one side that once housed the wooden water-wheel. There was the opening in the wall, where the stroller must have been pushed through, where Natasha went in to hide from the police and instead found the twins. Harper put her head inside. Spent needles and empty plastic bottles littered the floor of the space, which was partially open to the elements. Imprints of the stroller's wheels showed in the dust between the flagstones.

So much of this felt wrong, but the meaning of the wrongness eluded her. Truth to Harper was like a blade sometimes, she could see it so clearly, the right and the wrong, the real and the false. This case had a murky cloud surrounding it, the shape of it, obscured. ABC, she thought, get back to the basics: assume nothing; believe no one; check everything. An itch of something at the back of her mind, then. What was it she'd forgotten to check?

Harper took out her phone, flicked open her email and searched her inbox for the mp3 file of the 999 call Lauren had made from the maternity unit just after she had the babies. She pressed the play icon and held it to her ear. As she listened, she started to walk back the way she had come.

The operator was a young man, calm and professional.

"Nine-nine-nine, which service do you require?"

"There's a woman and she's trying to take my babies. Help me."

Lauren's voice was almost unrecognisable. Shrill and panicked.

"What's your name, please?"

"She's trying to get in, I've locked the door but she's trying to get in go away you bitch get away from us —"

"Madam? Can you confirm your location, please?"

"I'm in the hospital, the Infirmary, the maternity ward, please send someone to make her go away."

"You're in the maternity ward at the Royal Infirmary Hospital? Is that right?" The sound of the operator's fingers on the keyboard, inputting information to the system.

"Yes, yes, I'm locked in the bathroom, but she's trying to get in."

"Is there someone there with you?"

"My twins, my babies, they're safe in here with me but she's trying to unlock the door from the outside, she's trying to take my babies don't you understand? Help me."

"Try to stay calm. I've already let the hospital know and someone will be there very shortly. I'm going to stay on the phone until someone is there with you. Can you tell me your name please?"

"Lauren Tranter."

"Lauren, don't worry, I've alerted the hospital security, and help will be with you soon. Very soon, OK?"

"Make them hurry up, I can't hold it for long, she's too strong. She's turning the lock from the outside, it's turning —"

"Are you hurt in any way, Lauren?"

"My arm, she . . ."

There was a sound then, a hissing sound, and Harper couldn't make any sense of it. She played the section several times. It sounded like someone was putting on a funny voice and saying something, but it

384

was impossible to make it out. Then Lauren shouted, *"No, no —"* and the call was cut off.

Harper crossed the river, and made her way back towards the cafe. She replayed the hissing section once more, and this time she heard a few words among the jumble of incomprehensible sounds. The voice seemed to say, *"What's fair? You had everything . . ."* She had to play it again, and even then she wasn't sure she'd heard correctly. The sound was too fuzzy, a radio between two stations. Immediately she clicked to forward the message to Forensics, who could have it cleaned up and analysed within a couple of days, sooner if she pushed for it, before remembering Thrupp's warning: she had to go through him now, for every bit of Forensics budget, no matter for what or how small a job. That meant waiting until she was back at the office, going begging to Thrupp, standing there while he scrutinised the evidence and decided if it was worth their while. Cursing, she pocketed the phone and jogged past the cafe, towards the car.

In Thrupp's office, Harper stood in front of the desk. She hated having to ask. But she had to try. She had to check everything.

"There's a recording that I'd like to have

analysed. I need you to authorise it for Forensics."

"Is this for the Tranter twins abduction case?"

"Yes. It's from the 999 call Lauren Tranter made from the hospital. Despite the doctors' reports asserting that there was no intruder, the tape suggests that there was one."

Thrupp rolled his eyes. "Oh, that. Haven't we wasted enough time on that? The doors were locked, the nurse said there was no one there. Is the tape conclusive evidence? Good enough to contradict the statements of a senior midwife and a consultant psychiatrist?"

She couldn't lie, not directly into his face. "Not exactly. But if we have it analysed —"

"OK. Do you have a suspect in mind?"

No, she did not. But she couldn't say that. "Maybe it was Natasha Dowling."

"Aha. Didn't we just eliminate Natasha Dowling?"

"Yes, but I think there's more to it. Perhaps she had an accomplice, we've not considered that. I came across this article, which may be of interest." She handed over the photocopy from the *Mail*.

When Thrupp had read it, he snorted and

handed it back. "Where did you get this from?"

"A journalist, if you must know."

"Well," said Thrupp, "let's not start letting the hacks do our jobs for us, shall we? It never turns out well. That's a coincidence. Nothing more. It was more than forty years ago."

"Yes," said Harper, folding the piece of paper and putting it back in her bag, "I thought that, too, at first. But perhaps it's linked somehow. Perhaps the perp from that case is pulling the strings, getting Natasha to do her dirty work." It sounded ridiculous, even to Harper.

"Seriously?"

"Well, it's a theory."

"It's a stretch, is what it is."

Harper tried again. "If it is Dowling on the tape then we can still charge her, with harassment. She followed Mrs Tranter, after all, we can prove that much. She's been stalking Patrick for weeks. And, even if it's not her voice, then we'll have something on file to compare when we do find the perpetrator. The point is, it's worth having it analysed, don't you think?"

Thrupp gave her a long look. "What does the voice say, exactly?"

"It's not entirely clear, but the voice

makes threats of some kind. It needs cleaning up and investigating, firstly to see what the words actually are, then to see if the vocal patterns match."

Thrupp made a sceptical face. "This case is about to be dropped, Jo, so the evidence trail needs to be truly rock solid. I mean, like, granite. If it's just a fuzzy recording of nothing, and there's no suspect in the frame, then I can't justify it."

"The case is being dropped? Why?"

Thrupp started counting on his fingers. "One. The babies are, in fact, no longer missing."

"Yes, but they were still abducted. There's still a crime to investigate."

Thrupp ignored her. "Two. The timeline is vague. Three. The witnesses are unreliable. Four. There's no evidence to charge anyone with intention to harm. Five. GPS has just proved that Dowling's phone was nowhere near the babies at the time of the abduction. If we carry on, we're chucking money after nothing."

"But, sir —"

"I think we need to consider the mother herself for it. Have you looked into that?"

Harper closed her eyes briefly. Stay calm, she thought, make your case.

"I understand all of your points, sir, but

you haven't heard this recording. I think if we have it analysed, then we'll at least have all the facts to work with."

He steely-eyed her. "What I think is, that if we have it analysed, we'll be wasting money and time."

"Not at all. If we can identify the voice on the tape we'll at least have ticked all the boxes. We wouldn't want to drop a case without making sure we'd done all we can, right sir?"

"There's no reason whatsoever for us to analyse that recording. It is absolutely clear to me that Lauren Tranter saw no one that night but the ghosts in her own head. She was hallucinating. And, if I didn't know better, I'd say you are, too."

"But, sir."

Thrupp drew a long breath. "Mrs Tranter is the only one in the frame for this now. We have to admit that it's not a criminal investigation. What we're dealing with is a mental-health event."

Later, Harper slouched in her office chair, staring glumly at the blinking cursor on a staff-development review, telling herself to let the case go. But she couldn't do it, not with all the evidence she had; she knew her mind would keep working on it until she'd got some kind of answer — or at least investigated every possibility. From her bag she took out the *Mail* article from 1976 and read it again. Maybe there was something in it — maybe it was the same perpetrator. It wasn't unheard of for criminals to have big gaps in their offending history. Forty years was a long time, sure, but maybe whoever it was had been in prison for something else, got out recently and decided to try abducting babies one last time. Harper spent an hour searching the archives for the police report that corresponded to the newspaper report. Frustratingly, there didn't seem to be anything at all recorded in relation to the incident in question. Perhaps it had been filed incorrectly; the digitization of the archive had been done on the cheap, of course. There might still be a paper copy somewhere that had been over-looked, but if that was the case, it could take weeks to lay hands on what was probably a single thin sheet of A4, tucked behind a box file, somewhere among the towering shelves and stacks of crates in the vast basement storage facility. She gave up looking for the report and spent a while searching for similar incidences of twin-abduction cases with female perpetrators, but also found nothing.

Research was not one of Harper's best skills; if only Amy were there to help. She checked her phone for messages, but there was still no reply to Harper's lame apology she'd sent first thing about the way she'd behaved the night before. Then all at once, she knew exactly what to say to get a response.

I need your help on this case. Totally OFF THE RECORD. Are you in?

Within two minutes, the screen lit up with Amy's reply:

YES. Where shall we meet!?

CHAPTER THIRTY-TWO

Harper pulled up to the kerb outside the *Mail* offices so that Amy could jump in.

"I found them," she said, pushing a piece of paper into Harper's hands. It contained the contact details for the victims from the 1976 case.

"You're a bloody genius," said Harper.

"I wasn't going to be the first to say it," said Amy, "but I suppose you're right."

The mother's name was Victoria Rose Settle, and the twin boys were Robert and Vincent, born at 0141 and 0147 respectively on 2nd July 1976. Amy found the family easily — a search of Sheffield's public birth records from that year showed only two sets of identical twins born at the right time, and the other set were female. But, when Harper tried the current listed phone number for Mrs Settle while Amy listened, a man told her that his mother no longer lived there.

"Perhaps you'd be able to pass on a message," said Harper. "I'd really like to talk to her if possible."

"Why on earth would the police want to talk to her?"

"She may have some information that could help us in a current case."

"I doubt that, Sergeant."

"If you don't mind, I'd like to ask her anyway."

"You say this is a current case?"

"That's right."

"Then I don't see how she could help you. She hasn't even been outside on her own for nearly nine years."

"This relates to a crime recently committed, but the questions I have are to do with something that happened to your mother during July of 1976. There appear to be some similarities to our case that we'd like to investigate."

"Nothing happened to my mother in July 1976. Unless you mean having me and Vinny. I expect that kept her pretty busy. But nothing involving any crime, as far as I know. Surely I would know if that was the case?"

Harper felt she wasn't getting anywhere. Perhaps she should try a different tack.

"Mr Settle. Robert?"

"That's right."

"Is it possible she might not have told you about it? That maybe she might not have wanted you to know?"

"Oh," said Robert, drawing out the sound as he considered. "Well. I suppose. If she . . . did she commit a crime? She'd probably have kept that to herself."

Harper left a small pause, enough to cast doubt, but not sufficient to confirm or deny.

"I would rather talk to her about this, if you don't mind. I can call her directly, if you'll just give me the number."

"I'm afraid you won't be able to. She's got dementia. Early onset Alzheimer's. She barely knows who I am anymore." A small sob escaped from Robert Settle then.

Harper hesitated. She felt bad for him. She could imagine that dementia was a particularly cruel way to lose a loved one. "I'm sorry to hear that. It must be very difficult for you. I'm so sorry to have called out of the blue like this."

There was a silence. Then Robert said, "Mind you, if it's something from forty-odd years ago, then I don't know. Maybe you'll get something out of her."

"Really?"

"She can't remember what she had for breakfast. She doesn't recognise her own

394

children most of the time, but sometimes things come back to her, from when she was younger. Actually she was telling me about the birth only the other day — a bit too much information, to be honest. Maybe it's the weather, triggering something in her mind. She thought it was still the seventies."

"So, I can talk to her?"

"I suppose it's worth a try. I can't promise she'll give you the answers you want. Some days she doesn't say a word."

High-backed armchairs lined the room, most of them empty but one or two occupied by an elderly person. A care assistant was helping one of the residents to drink through a straw. Amy and Harper waited in a corner, smiling at orderlies, refusing offers of tea. When Robert arrived, late and hassled, he greeted the staff by name, then introduced himself to Harper and Amy before leading them through to the far side of the sitting room and down a corridor to his mother's room. The man was tall and rangy, physically similar to DI Thrupp but with none of the self-confidence. He wore brown leather sandals and a slightly defeated expression that stayed in place even when he tried to hide it behind a smile.

Outside the room he placed one hand on the door handle and turned towards them.

"Just, don't expect miracles, OK?"

They nodded and he led them inside.

Victoria sat in a chair by the bed, her unfocussed eyes staring at a spot not quite near enough to the TV screen for her to be seeing the images flashing there, soundlessly.

"Hello, Mum," said Robert, taking a seat next to her and gently lifting one of her hands into his own. "I've brought you some visitors."

The woman's head swivelled slowly towards him. Her faint smile faded as she took him in. "Who are you?"

"It's me, Mum. Robert."

She pulled her hand away, frowning. "Robert who?"

"Your son, Robert."

"I don't know you."

While the men and women in the sitting room were curled and ancient, the woman in front of them was young in comparison. Only sixty-eight years old, her hair still mostly brown, her skin mostly unlined. She turned her body away from Robert's and Harper saw his shoulders droop slightly with the rejection.

"I come here every day," he said to them.

"Sometimes she knows me straight away, and we have a nice chat. Other days, she thinks I'm my brother Vinny, or my father. And then sometimes she's like this, and she won't even speak to me. It's a cruel disease, Alzheimer's."

Victoria had resumed the position she'd had when they entered the room, staring at the wall near the TV screen, her expression tranquil.

Amy said, "It must be terribly frightening for her."

"I meant for me. She'll have forgotten it in five minutes. I'm the one who has to bear it."

Harper pulled up a chair near to Victoria's.

"Excuse me, Mrs Settle? I'm a police officer. I wanted to ask you some questions about something that happened in 1976."

The woman didn't move or look at the DS. Harper glanced over at Robert, who shrugged.

"Go on," he said, "you might as well try."

"It's about the twins," said Harper, "your little babies. Robert and Vincent."

"Where are the twins?" said Victoria, turning her head to look around the room. "Where are my boys?"

"I'm right here, Mum," said Robert. "Vin-

397

ny's in Australia, remember?"

Victoria stared at her son, clutching the arm of her chair until it creaked. Harper saw a flicker of recognition. "Robert?" She reached a hand towards him and he took it.

"Mum?" he said, a wobble in his voice.

She gazed into his eyes. "Where are my boys?" she asked, desperate now. Robert kept hold of his mother's hand, and she let him.

"Victoria," said Amy, "we found a newspaper article that said there was a kidnapper in the maternity ward, who tried to take your babies."

"Yes," she said, taking her hand from her son's and glaring suspiciously at him before turning towards Amy. "Yes. Horrible woman. I stopped her. She was going to take my boys. But I stopped her."

"I didn't know anything about this," said Robert. "Who was it, Mum? Who tried to take us?"

"Where are they?" said Victoria, glancing around despondently, but she was drifting off once more. "Did I lose them? I keep on losing things."

"Can you tell us anything about what happened, please?" said Harper. "What was she like, this woman? Can you describe her at all?"

But Victoria stared at that spot on the wall, and didn't speak.

Robert turned to Harper and Amy. "I don't think you'll get much more out of her today."

Harper said, "It was worth a shot. Thanks for letting us try."

As they turned for the door Harper heard Victoria gasp and turned back. The older woman's hand flew to her mouth and she said, "That woman. I remember now. She had her own babies, horrid little things they were too. She wanted to swap them for mine — for my perfect bonnie lads. Ha. I remember now. 'No,' I said, 'no no no, get away with you.' I had to kick her. Good and hard. I'd do it again."

With the word *kick* she kicked a leg out and nearly caught a slippered foot on the bed frame. Her hands fluttered by her sides and she glanced frantically from left to right. "Are they here? Where are the twins? Have you seen them? She's not having them. She's not."

"Calm down, Mum, you're safe now. I'm here, I'm right here. We're all grown up now, there's no danger."

Victoria seemed to take some comfort from her son's words. She let him pat her knee and grew gradually calmer.

"You should probably go," he said to Harper and Amy. Harper nodded and took a step towards the door.

"They were named for the rivers," murmured Victoria.

"What was that, Mum?"

"Their names are Bishop and Selver," she said.

"The rivers?" said Robert, shrugging at Harper, *see, this is what it's like.* "That's right, Mum, the rivers are called the Bishop and the Selver. That's right. Then there's the Don, and the Loxley . . ."

Victoria pushed her son's hands off her lap. "I'm not talking about rivers," she said, "I mean the twins. That horrid woman's twins. 'Remember their names,' she said to me. Their names are Bishop and Selver. I've never forgotten. I kicked her. I'd do it again."

Harper and Amy waited for a long time, but Victoria didn't say anything more.

Back in the car, Amy said, "What do you think?"

"I felt for her," said Harper, "but I've no idea what she was saying. The Bishop and the Selver? Some kind of sordid forced child exchange?"

"Yes. Very weird."

"Funny names for kids. Who'd call their babies those names?"

"I can look them up if you like, see how many Bishops and Selvers are on the electoral register. Maybe we can find the perpetrator that way."

"No," said Harper, "don't worry. I think it's pretty clear she was confused. Maybe she was remembering that the rivers all dried up in that heat wave, when she had her babies, and the words got mixed up somehow."

Amy said, "Well, sorry about that, Joanna. Another dead end."

"There's still the CCTV from the hospital. And the recording from the 999 call. I just need to find a way to get them analysed. Then we'll have the full picture, and perhaps a new lead on a suspect. If only Thrupp wasn't such a tight arse."

Amy got out her phone and began to search through her contacts.

"Leave it with me," she said. "I think I know someone who can help us."

CHAPTER THIRTY-THREE

In the daytime, most of the rooms were unlocked for freedom of movement within the unit. Lauren's room was not one of them, but she knew that the other patients had more liberty than she did. She'd seen them coming and going, unchaperoned, when she herself was being led as if in shackles to the day room, or up to the therapy room.

"You're category A, love," Pauline had said, when pressed. Apparently Lauren was among the very few in the unit assigned such close observation, never to be left alone even for a moment. There was a hierarchy of madness, here.

In the little, hot room, the babies were asleep and swaddled, and Lauren and Patrick sat in limp silence with the nurse a short distance away in a chair, twirling the end of her leather belt over and under her fingers, endlessly. The bedroom was oppressive, and it had become uncomfortable. The wide open space visible just the other side of the barred window was tantalising, and yet unreachable without special permission, and a chaperone. It was a strange kind of gratitude Lauren felt towards Nurse Pauline then, when she said, "Shall we go for a walk outside?" and led the way, through the security doors and into the grounds.

The Tranters became one of the slow-moving knots of people pacing the nuthouse lawn from end to end in the sun, each group harbouring a baby stroller or two, and among their number, always, a white-coated figure acting as guide, spy, and protector.

At first, being outdoors diminished Lauren further; beneath the sky she felt small, an ant under a glass. The skin on her hands seemed semi-opaque in the sun, veins standing out. She found herself jumping at the unexpected movement of birds, gripping Patrick's arm when a squirrel ran along the branch of one of the huge old oaks. But after a short time she started to breathe easier, and her muscles relaxed slightly. Her gait went from shuffle to meander. She hooked her arm through Patrick's and laid her head on his shoulder. She hung back, allowing their unit to split into two, allowing a distance to open up between them and the listening ears of the nurse, who had volunteered to push the twins. Up ahead, she could hear the babbling of the babies, and the silences in between, when they themselves were listening.

"What did you do with our double stroller?" said Lauren.

"I took it to the tip, of course," said Patrick, slightly defensive. She suspected, from his tone, that he might not have done it yet.

"That's good," said Lauren, "I didn't want you to sell it. It's bad luck."

"Bad luck to sell it?"

"No, I mean the thing itself. It's got bad energy, luck, whatever you want to call it. Best not to pass it on to anyone else."

Lauren thought, I don't believe in luck. Neither does Patrick. But nevertheless I don't want anyone else having that stroller, and I never want to see it again.

Patrick cleared his throat. "Well, it was covered in mud round the bottom, anyway. It stained the fabric. No one would have paid money for it."

They walked along in the shadow of the old stately home. The nurse was out of earshot: perhaps now they could talk about what they were going to do to get the boys back.

"Patrick, I —"

"Listen, darling. I need to say something first. Earlier, when Ruthie was here, and the boys were crying," said Patrick, "I know it sounded like they were making words —"

"Yes."

"Well, you don't really think they were, do you? It sounded like words, sure, but they weren't actually speaking. You know that, right?"

Lauren didn't say anything. She stopped walking, and looked him in the eye. Smiled a little, looked away. For a moment she thought she might cry. But then she took a breath and smiled again, with more certainty. So, she was alone in this, as in everything.

"Of course I know that, silly. They're only four and a half weeks old. They can't speak yet."

He drew her towards him, held her pressed against his body. After a while he pulled back and smiled at her, brushed a springy strand of hair from her face and tucked it behind her ear. "Nearly five weeks now," he said. "Seems like a really long time. Almost like we've always had them."

"Time feels like a completely different thing now. To what it was before."

"Yeah," said Patrick, though he sounded unsure.

They walked in silence for a while, across the soft grass towards the chain-link fence where you could look out over the valley.

They both watched the back of the nurse up ahead, pushing the stroller in the sun.

"What do you think will happen to that girl, Natasha?"

"I don't know," said Patrick, his voice clipped. "I suppose she'll be charged with abduction."

"That's if it was her. I'm still not sure how it can be . . ."

"Huh," said Patrick, "if you knew her, you'd know this is just the kind of thing she'd do. She's vicious."

"In a way it doesn't matter what she's like. I'm supposed to look after them, protect them from danger. None of this would have happened if I hadn't fallen asleep in the first place."

"You can't blame yourself, my love. You were having a hard time. I should never have insisted you go out. I'm so sorry."

He turned towards her and she saw that tears stood in his eyes, waiting to fall.

"I'm sorry too," she said.

"You've nothing to feel sorry for."

"I do though, for what I did when they

406

were given back, trying to push them into the river. But I couldn't help it, I thought they'd been swapped over — which is nonsense, of course. Then, when you brought them to the unit, I don't know why I reacted the way I did. I was missing them so much. I must be going mad."

"You're not mad, honey. At least, we're not supposed to call it that, according to the doctor. You just need a bit of a rest."

She slipped her hand in his, squeezed.

"It's good, don't worry. It's all good, don't you see? I can see it was all in my head, and the solution's simple. I can get better. I feel better already."

"The important thing is, we have them. They came back to us. That stupid girl took them, but she brought them back."

Lauren thought, if only that were true. But I'll find them again, even if I have to do it alone. Even if it kills me.

"When they were gone," said Patrick, "in that short time when we didn't know where they were or who had them, I felt like I'd died and gone to hell. We'd lost our babies, and the life I took for granted had been lost along with them. I got a taste of what it must be like to lose them for good. It was devastating. It changed me."

"Yes. I know," said Lauren, thinking, it

changed me too, but not because they came back; because they didn't.

They stood on the edge of the estate, a little way from where the nurse was standing looking through the wire mesh of the security fence towards the valley. Pauline must have decided they'd had enough couple time. She started to wheel the stroller in their direction.

Lauren could feel the creatures getting closer. She began to tense up.

"I'm so glad you're feeling better," said Patrick, kissing her on the top of her head. "For a moment there, I thought I'd lost you as well."

Lauren let her eyes drift down across the valley, where the sunset bloomed on the surface of the reservoir. "Hopefully I'll come home soon, and we can get back to normal. Those boys need a mother, not a mental patient."

"It's not for long," said Patrick, wrapping her in his arms, forming that barrier between his wife and the rest of the world. "It's going to be alright, I think. We're all going to be all right."

Chapter Thirty-Four

"Is this right?" said Harper, hoping there'd been some mistake. Amy had directed her to an address she knew already from her days as a uniformed constable. The man who lived in this house was a known drug dealer, and was also on the "watch" list at the station for having links to extremist eco-anarchist groups.

Amy turned towards her from the passenger seat and looked up through her eyelashes. "Now, Jo. Gideon is an old friend, like I explained. He's an absolute genius with technology, and I guarantee he's trustworthy."

"I wouldn't have come if I'd known who you meant. When you said you had a friend with specialist knowledge in ICT I was imagining, I don't know, an office? Maybe a web designer, a computer engineer. I know Gideon Jones — and he knows me. I arrested him last year for a public order offence, along with a few other crusties who were staging a protest in the centre of town that got out of hand."

"Oh, did you?" said Amy, brightly. "Well, never mind. He's very forgiving. I'm sure he'll have forgotten all about it."

"I doubt that very much. I haven't. He wasn't terribly happy with me at the time. What makes you think he's going to help us? Or anyway help me — a police officer? I'm pretty sure he was wearing a T-shirt that read *Pigs are Scum.*"

"He and I go back years. I've known him since university — I even lived here for a while in my second year."

"I'm not sure, Amy. He tried to kick me in the face when we were putting him in the cells. I don't think he's my biggest fan."

She leaned her head to one side, considering. "No, perhaps he's not." She opened the car door to step out. "But, he'd do anything for me, darling."

As she got out of the car, a dark part of Harper thought, oh really, why? What is it that you do for him, or did do for him once? Her mind concocted a montage of beautiful Amy and wrinkled, crusty old Gideon, laughing together, kissing, worse. But then even as she thought it she knew the scenario was unlikely, or at any rate irrelevant: Har-

410

per herself would have done anything for Amy, and there'd never been anything more between them than a bit of light arm-linking.

The building was a once-proud Edwardian semi at the dead end of a wide street lined with mighty limes, the roots pushing up the pavement in ripening humps that swelled and cracked gently with each passing year. The trees were reclaiming the street: *we are stronger,* they said. *Given time, we shall prevail.* The trees and the high wall at the end of the road together blocked most of the light and formed a lush green cave, carpeted with a mulch of fallen vegetation, old and new. Houses here were well spaced, large and set back from the road with their own private driveways, but Gideon's was not a drive you could pull into, crowded as it was with high grasses and wild shrubs that spilled from the borders, untamed.

Harper followed Amy along the narrow path of trodden grass that led across the drive and round to the back door — there was no way through to the front door. It seemed that no one had used it for years. As she got closer to the house she could hear a repeated bass line, the unmistakable fuzzy groove of trance music.

"Good," said Amy, "at least he's up."

Harper checked her watch — it was gone 1 p.m. Amy knocked on the peeling wooden door.

After a while, there was the shuffling of feet and the tell-tale darkening of the spyhole which showed Harper that they were being observed from within. Then, the door opened a crack. Half of a bearded face, one lens of a pair of spectacles. A section of a tricksy smile. All accompanied by a waft of sickly smoke. The man coughed productively into his fist before he said anything.

"Amy, babe. It's good to see you."

He seemed about to open the door wider when he caught sight of Harper. A frown, then a flash of recognition, of fury.

"Hello, Mr Jones," said Harper.

"What is this?" said Gideon, pushing the door further shut so that he was peering through a gap no more than a centimetre wide. "Amy?" His voice was high-pitched, like a child's. *How could you,* he seemed to ask.

"Darling," said Amy, "it's OK. She's a friend."

"You're friends with a copper? You never said."

Harper stepped away in the direction they'd come. "Look, Amy, I don't think this is going to work. Why don't we just go?"

Amy said, "No, it's fine, honestly. Hang on a second."

She leaned towards Gideon and mumbled something Harper couldn't hear.

"Well, if you're sure," he said, throwing a suspicious glance towards Harper. "I suppose I could. Not for her, though. For you I will."

"That would be marvellous. We'd be so grateful. Wouldn't we, Joanna?" Amy gave Harper a hard nudge with an elbow.

"I'm sure you're a very busy man, Mr Jones. Don't put yourself out on our account."

"He doesn't mind one bit, do you, Gideon?"

There was some hesitation, but then after another phlegmy cough, "That's right," he said, "I'd be happy to help. There is one thing, though — could you both come back in half an hour? I have some friends here."

"I don't mind," said Amy.

"No, I'm sure you don't, but let's just say that my friends might not want to meet your friend, if you know what I mean."

"It's just a social visit," said Harper, "I'm not on duty. I don't want to know about whatever it is you're all doing in there. As long as I don't see it, I don't care."

"Fine," said Gideon, "shut your eyes then.

I'll get rid of them."

Harper turned her back on the doorway. The back garden was as wild as the front, apart from a roughly circular section of undergrowth that had been cleared. In the centre of the clearing was the blackened remains of a campfire, surrounded by a ring of logs to sit on. Just over the hedge could be seen the top of the neighbour's children's trampoline net. On the other side, creepers climbed the high wall. Vehicles could be heard beyond it, rushing down the hill towards the city centre.

Harper pretended not to listen as three sets of feet scuffled past her out of Gideon's house and around to the front. She turned her head and caught a glimpse of the back of them: black-hoodied, fat-trainered types in the kind of voluminous trousers that never seemed to go out of fashion with a certain set of students. Once they'd gone, she turned back towards the house, where Gideon had swung wide the kitchen door and was standing back to let them in.

"Sorry about the state of the place," he said to Amy.

Gideon was bald on top, and what hair he had left was gathered into straggly dread-locks of varying lengths at the nape of his neck. He wore a collarless shirt of rough

414

yellow cotton and loose black trousers with pockets and elasticated cuffs. Barefoot on the sticky vinyl floor, he gave off that oily, herbal smell that Harper associated with those shops that sold silver skull jewellery and joss sticks.

"Do you guys want some tea?" He rummaged around near the window and unearthed a once-white plastic kettle, then held it dangling from a hand as if he'd never seen it before.

"No, thanks," said Amy.

"I'm sure there's some milk here somewhere."

When he opened the fridge a bad, cheesy stench wafted out and the two women exchanged a glance. Amy gently closed the fridge, assuring Gideon they weren't in the mood for tea. Harper couldn't believe these two knew each other, that Amy had once lived here. The man's surly, generally unwashed appearance made Amy's neat, charming, carefully made-up self shine even more brightly. She stood in that large, grimy kitchen like a rose growing in a landfill site.

Harper followed Gideon and Amy through to the front room, where she immediately put a hand over her eyes.

"Whatever you have in that plastic box, Gideon, get it out of here now."

415

"Oh, Jesus, sorry."

Harper waited while Gideon hastily removed the container in which there was something that resembled a bright green brain, to somewhere Harper did not have to see it, think about it, or arrest him for it. That amount of marijuana would put him away for a year or more, and right now Gideon was far more useful to Harper if he remained a free man. Though she was perfectly willing to reassess this opinion at any time, should the need arise.

"So, Amy my Amy, what's up?" said Gideon, folding his thin frame into one of his huge armchairs. The couch on which Harper sat had once been blue, but the arms were now brown and tacky to the touch. She perched, unable to relax. Amy stood a short distance away.

"Well, Joanna and I, we're having a little problem, and neither of us have the specific skills required to sort it out," said Amy. "I immediately thought of you, but of course at the time I had no idea that you two had any history together."

"It's fine," said Gideon, his eyes on Amy, "I don't hold grudges."

"I knew you'd say that," said Amy. "I told her you were a good sort." She turned to Harper. "Perhaps you can explain to Gideon what it's about?"

"I have a CCTV tape, and an audio recording. I need someone with technical expertise to analyse them for me."

"From a criminal case? Why don't the police nerds look into it?"

"The boss doesn't know I'm here. This is kind of a side project," said Harper. "Off the books, so to speak. Can I really trust you not to tell anyone?"

"Sounds like exactly my kind of thing," said Gideon, "a police officer coming to me with some secret bits of evidence they want me to take a look at, that the rest of them don't know about. Of course I won't tell anyone. This is what I live for, the mainstream going underground, undermining their own, seeking out what's hidden. Ha. Show me."

Gideon opened his laptop and pushed the flash drive that Harper handed him into the USB port. Very soon the screen opened on the maternity ward, the nurse intent on the keyboard, the picture green and slightly fuzzy.

"There," said Harper, "those shadows. That's what I'm interested in."

"OK," said Gideon, "what do you want to know?"

"Are they real — as in, did the camera

417

capture them happening in the room, or are they a mistake, some sort of damage on the file?"

Gideon watched the section again. The three shadows swam across the floor at the corner of the screen. He zoomed in, played it again.

"It looks like it might be both."

"What do you mean?"

"Look," said Gideon, "see how the shadows follow each other? And just there," he paused the tape, "you can make out the shape of a foot."

He zoomed in further. The image was pixelated on one side, but the other was the rough shape of a bare human foot. Harper's pulse began to race.

Gideon went on, "The cameras jump at the slightest vibration, causing the images to skip a few seconds, or add trails to the images they capture. That's what's happened here."

"But there are no figures here, just shadows. And a disembodied foot. Jeepers."

"It's ghastly," said Amy, rubbing her bare arms as if she were cold.

Gideon watched the section again, frowned. "I can't be sure of course, but the shadows there look like glitch trails. As if someone, or more than one person, walked through the screen, and at that exact moment the tape jumped, then cut back in and just caught the trails. I love it. It's so creepy. Can I have a copy?"

"No," said Harper. "How can you check if that's what happened?"

"It's tricky. The lost section is impossible to recover, because the tape hasn't recorded it. But if there was something else in the picture that was moving, you would see a jump there too, proving that a second or two is missing. This is so great. It's brilliant when this kind of thing happens. I've used CCTV glitches as visuals at parties."

"What if there's nothing else moving in the image? How can we check?"

"How about we zoom in on the nurse's fingers?"

And there it was. On the screen Anthea Mallison lifted a hand from the keyboard to take a sip of tea. Then the tape jumped, her hand was back on the keyboard and the shadows drifted by. A second or two was missing. Now she'd seen it, it was obvious. But it wasn't evidence, not if the lost moment was unrecoverable.

"What are you looking for, anyway?" said Gideon.

"An intruder. Someone that a patient said was there, but no one else saw."

"Awesome."

"Not for her."

"*The Matrix* did this, you know that, right? There's something they don't want you to know." Gideon pulled out his tobacco tin and started rolling a few pinches into a liquorice paper. "Can I get a copy if it's just for the collection? I wouldn't share it around."

Harper gave him a look that he understood meant he ought to give up asking for a copy. What was he gibbering about, *The Matrix*? Wasn't that a film? These people were full of conspiracy theories. It was the drugs that did it.

"What did the nurse say?" said Gideon, tapping her image on the screen. "She was there."

"She said she didn't see anything."

"Huh." Gideon placed the cigarette between his lips and flicked open his lighter. He touched the flame to the tip of the chocolate-brown cylinder and inhaled.

Amy went over to the window and opened it. "Sorry, darling, I can't bear it these days. No, don't put it out, I'll just stay over here."

If Gideon was right about the glitch trails, it meant there was someone on the ward that night. So why didn't anyone see anything? Why didn't the nurse see it, if the someone was right there? Harper thought about the trampled nettles in the bushes opposite Lauren's window. That time, Patrick hadn't seen it either. There was a darkness to this, something unknown, the tang of evil.

"What about the intruder?" said Gideon. "I mean, what happened to the patient?"

"I'm not sure I should discuss it with you. I'm sorry."

Gideon shrugged, turned to Amy. "She's no fun, is she?"

From the window, Amy said, "How about the other thing, Jo-Jo?"

"There is another thing," said Harper, "an audio recording. It's fuzzy, I can't make out the words on it. Do you think you could sharpen it up?"

"Of course," said Gideon, "my speciality. If you'll go through to the lab."

They climbed the stairs, long since stripped of their carpet and showing several generations of paintwork where many feet had worn through the layers. Gideon led them into one of the four bedrooms, which had been transformed into a music technology suite. It was lined with sound-insulating foam and filled with all manner of gadgetry: keyboards, a huge mixing desk, electronic drum pads, black boxes and racks of hi-fi type equipment, all of it a mystery to Harper. Right in the centre were two computer screens. Gideon took a seat in the swivel chair and pressed four or five buttons to boot the system up.

"Won't be a moment," he said as the studio came alive around them, with blinking coloured lights and the hum of several tiny electronic fans. Above the desk there was a square hole in the wall fitted with a thick glass panel through which the neighbouring bedroom could be seen — or what would have been a bedroom, had it contained a bed. Instead there was a drum kit in there, a set of record decks and a selection of guitars hanging on the wall.

"This is also, of course, highly confidential," she said to him. "I really don't want you talking to anyone about this."

"You can trust me," said Gideon, and in that moment she was surprised to find that she believed him.

She sent the mp3 file of the 999 call to Gideon's email account and he played it through the huge speakers mounted in the upper corners of the room. Lauren's terrified voice exploded at them, cutting through Harper painfully in the split second before Gideon reached for the fader to bring the volume down. Even at a low level, the recording was chilling.

"My twins, my babies, they're safe in here with me but she's trying to unlock the door from the outside. She's trying to take my babies, don't you understand? Help me."

Gideon caught Harper's eye, shocked, sickened. He paused the recording.

"That poor woman," he said. "She sounds terrified. But what needs cleaning up? It seems clear enough to me."

"It's not this bit. It's towards the end. You'll know when you hear it."

They reached the hissing section and Gideon started to work. He cut and copied it into his computer so that the screen showed a fat waveform with jagged peaks where the louder parts were. Still the words were incomprehensible, but Gideon was undeterred, in his element. He twiddled knobs, applied filters and processed the audio so that the fuzz was reduced. Eventually, words emerged. The three of them listened in silence.

"Play it again," said Harper, the blood draining from her face. Gideon pressed the space bar on his keyboard and the voice came through once more.

"Did you hear that?" said Amy, reaching for Harper. "Did you?"

"What did you hear?" said Harper to Gideon, needing to check, to make sure, that it wasn't just because of what they thought they knew already.

"I'm not sure I know," said Gideon. "Part of it sounded like, 'Remember their names.' "

"What then?" said Harper. "What did the voice say the names were?"

"Well, it doesn't make any sense."

"Just say what you think you heard," said Amy. "Please."

Gideon said, "Did it say, 'Their names are Bishop and Selver'? Like, the rivers?"

Harper tried to swallow the lump that had risen in her throat. "Yes, that's what I heard too."

Those unlikely names that Victoria had told them at the nursing home: Bishop and Selver, the two rivers that fed the New Riverby reservoir, the man-made lake that rose up a hundred years ago to drown the village of Selverton. The River Bishop that ran along the length of the valley, passing through the park, by the place the twins were taken. And the Selver that swirled into the reservoir, its new mouth since the walls went up, never again emerging to reach the sea.

In Harper's head, Lauren spoke quietly. *She's from the water, that woman. Where the two rivers meet.*

"What does it mean?" said Gideon.

"I don't know yet," said Harper, her voice reduced to a whisper.

"You have to go back to see Victoria," said Amy.

CHAPTER THIRTY-FIVE

On the journey across the city, Harper had too much time to think about why Amy had declined to come with her to talk to Victoria again. The two of them had walked back to the car together, Harper assuming they would both be heading to the nursing home. But when they'd got in and shut the doors, Amy asked to be dropped off at the *Mail* offices.

"What, you're not coming?"

"I have an appointment with an interviewee tonight. I can't miss it. Deadlines, you know."

Harper had sensed something dishonest in the exchange. Not lies, exactly, but Amy was holding something back. The two of them had travelled in silence until Harper pulled up outside the huge grey building in the centre of town. Then, Amy leaned over and kissed her on the cheek. Harper felt a small thrill, but it seemed conciliatory somehow. She wasn't being kissed for the sake of it; Amy was making up for something. Something she'd done, or something she was about to do?

Amy said, "You have to promise you'll tell me what you find out, the very moment you do. Send me a message, don't ring — I might have my phone on silent."

"Who are you meeting?"

"It's no one you know." And there was the lie, shining like silver. A squeeze of the knee, and she was gone, leaving a cloud of perfume in her wake. Harper could taste it, bitter at the back of her throat. She opened the windows wide to let it out.

It seemed that Victoria hadn't moved at all. Harper knocked lightly on the open door but the woman didn't turn around. Then she said, "Hello, Mrs Settle," but there was no response.

She moved across the room and positioned her chair so that she could sit right in front of the older woman, blocking her view of the TV. Victoria didn't flinch; she looked right through Harper, that faint smile on her lips.

"My mum's about your age," she said, thinking, it must be so sad for the children, to be forgotten by their mum. The woman's eyes were blank; she didn't appear to know that Harper was there.

"Tell me about the woman who tried to take your babies."

Something flickered in Victoria's eyes, and the smile faded. Still she didn't speak.

Harper said, "The thing is, I think whoever did it has come back. There's a woman with baby twins, and someone took them and hid them in the woods. The mother's very sick, and everyone thinks she did it herself. No one believes what she says, that there was someone else involved. But I do. I think it was the same person who tried to take your babies. You have to help me find them."

Victoria's eyes widened, and her fingers clutched at the arms of her chair. "Where are the boys? Where's Robert, and Vinny?"

"They're safe now. You stopped her, remember?"

"I stopped her. Yes." Victoria smiled, satisfied, a thing done well. She raised a finger. "She was trying to take my boys. But I stopped her."

"You kicked her."

"Yes," said Victoria, "I kicked her. Horrible woman. I'd do it again."

"Where did she come from? What did she look like?"

"Do you know, she tried to get me to swap

for her horrid pair? Nasty little things they were. Named for the rivers."

"Bishop and Selver."

"Yes."

"What does that mean? She also had twins? Why would she want to swap them for Robert and Vincent? What happened, Victoria?"

The woman seemed to focus on Harper for a moment, but then she frowned in confusion. "Where are the boys?" She searched the room with her eyes for a moment, then seemed to forget and resumed staring at the wall.

Harper felt she was losing control of the interview. "Mrs Settle, I think you might be able to help me find this person. If you can remember anything else about her, anything at all."

"I didn't go out, after that. In case she came back. Not for eight weeks. I read in a book that staying inside would keep them safe."

"Did she have long hair, or short? What sort of age was she, do you think?"

"Once I found the book, I kept it under the bed always. Instructions, just in case, you see. Just in case she came back and got inside and somehow managed to swap them."

"What book was this?" Why was she talking about a book?

"It's a brewery of eggshells, you need, to trick them. That's what you need. That's what the book said. Then she'll know for sure."

"A brewery of what?" The phrase was meaningless. If she could somehow steer Victoria back to what she was saying about the woman, she felt she had a good chance of getting some useful information. "Was the woman tall, perhaps? Or not? Shorter than average?"

"If you don't trick them, you see, you'll never be sure, because they're very good at pretending. You don't want to throw the wrong ones away, do you? Got to be sure. Brew the eggshells. That'll trick them."

At that moment, Robert appeared in the doorway.

"What are you doing here?"

"I needed to ask a few more questions. I thought she might remember something this time that could be useful."

"You should have called first. What have you said to her? She's all worked up. Look at her."

Victoria was sitting bolt upright, her neck straining. She stared at something in front of her that neither of them could see.

"I stopped her, that nasty woman. I kicked her. I didn't need no eggshells, not me. She's not having my babies. She's not. And I'm not having hers."

Robert stepped between Harper and his mother. "You're frightening her. She doesn't know what she's saying."

"I'm sorry," said Harper, "but I have reason to believe that your mother might know something important."

"Whether she knows anything or not, you'll have to come back another time. She's upset, can't you see?"

Victoria started moaning, clutching her hands together in her lap. Robert put his arm around her shoulders.

"It's OK, Mum, the lady's going now. We'll have a nice cup of tea." He turned to Harper and hissed, "You can let yourself out."

"I went to see the wise man," said Victoria, "and he told me I had to trick them first, to make sure. Then, if they speak, throw them in the river."

"Do you have any idea what she's talking about?" said Harper.

Robert appeared to think about it. "It sounds like a story. She's remembering a story from an old book we had as children, and she's confusing it with real life. She thinks it happened to her. It happens with TV programmes too, She thinks she's one of the characters."

"What book?"

"There was one that she sometimes read to us. Folk tales about twins. It had a whole section on changeling babies. We hated it. Can you imagine? It still haunts me, that book." He turned to his mother. "It haunts you too, doesn't it, Mum?"

"Do you remember what it was called?"

"I think it was something like *Twin Tales*. I don't have it anymore. Vinny didn't want it either so I gave it to a charity shop."

As Harper moved towards the door, Victoria said, "Once she knows for sure, she'll have to put them in the water, if she wants her own back. That's what the wise man said. Right under the water."

"The babies?"

Victoria nodded repeatedly, and rocked back in her chair. "It's the only way. Tell her. Tell her to do it. Quickly, as quick as she can. Hold 'em down. Faeries'll come running."

"But they'll just drown, won't they?"

Victoria turned to Harper, looked her straight in the eye, lucid and intense.

"Only if she's wrong."

CHAPTER THIRTY-SIX

Fairies, however, when bent upon mischief, are not always baulked so easily. They effect the exchange, sometimes in the house, and sometimes when the parent is at work in the fields and incautiously puts her offspring down the while. In these circumstances, grievous as may be the suspicion arising from the changed conduct of the nursling, it is not always easy to be sure of what has taken place.

Edwin Sidney Hartland

August 17th
Five Weeks Old
1 P.M.

Waiting in the therapy room for Doctor Summer, Lauren felt quietly confident that this would be her final consultation before they discharged her. She knew from Nurse Pauline that the whole system was under pressure to move people on, as beds in the

433

unit were expensive, and scarce. Doctor Summer wouldn't want a healthy, sane person taking up a space that someone more obviously in crisis could make use of. The police section she'd been detained under only allowed them to keep her for three days. After that they were required to make a full assessment and decide whether more medical intervention was required. If not, she was free to go. Today was day three, decision day.

Lauren had been carefully, patiently normal for more than two whole days. She'd made sure Nurse Pauline had noted down many positive things in her book, to replace the pages Lauren had removed containing less flattering comments about how she'd behaved during Patrick's first aborted visit with the accursed stroller. She'd torn those notes into small pieces, wrapped them in loo roll and flushed them, along with the first several doses of whatever medication they were trying to make her take. Her mind was crystal clear; she was completely in control; the picture of a model patient.

Yesterday the doctor had decided she was well enough to have the babies back with her full time. Under the supervision of a nurse, of course. They'd been with her the whole night, and her eyelids stung from lack

434

of sleep. It was amazing that the babies themselves were still awake, as they hadn't appeared to close their eyes at all the entire time. They'd been playing games with her — pretending to be Morgan and Riley when the nurse was awake, then each time the nurse had dropped off Lauren heard them speaking to her, hissing at her. She knew their names now, which one called himself Bishop and which one Selver. She knew they wanted the same thing she did — for them to be returned to their rightful place under the water, for Morgan and Riley to come home. And in those moments, when the nurse was asleep, they told her exactly what she had to do to make it happen. They would lead her there, to where the exchange would take place. But first, she had to get them out of this prison.

The babies were lying on their backs on the rug, singing as they watched Lauren. Their eyes were almost completely transformed into a bright shade of green, so different from the blue her real boys had. They were goading her, with this song, with their staring. She gritted her teeth and did not react. With exaggerated nonchalance, she leaned forward to pick up a plastic cup of water and their twin gazes followed her, the movements of their heads synchronised, like

435

all their movements when they weren't pretending to be Morgan and Riley. Staring back at them, she said nothing, pressed her lips together in a thin line. She wanted to plug her ears so she couldn't hear the terrible, gurgling, high-pitched hum of it. The tune was the same as the one their mother sang in the hospital when the boys were only hours old, before the swap, before the nightmare started. They sang it wordlessly, yet the tune lit up the words in her mind, as they probably knew it would, and she couldn't help but think of the story it told, two poor illegitimate babes, bloody and abandoned. "The Cruel Mother", that was the name of it. The choice of song seemed accusatory. In it, a mother threw her babies away. I'm not abandoning you, she silently told the creatures, because I'm not your mother. She abandoned you. I'm just putting things right. She did it all, blame her. Sing the fucking song to *her*.

In the past three days she'd used up all her fear, and what was left was a kind of ground-up weariness and a whole lot of disgust. Lauren could have alerted the hospital to what the twins were doing. It had been in front of the camera, after all — she could have made them watch the footage and that in itself would have proved that she was sane. Or she could have suggested that they question her fellow patient Felicity, who'd heard them singing, who'd first told Lauren the names they called each other when they thought no one else was listening. But nothing had convinced Lauren that, even with the evidence in front of them, anyone would see the truth. It was too risky to try it now — suppose the CCTV hadn't worked, and they dismissed her story as crazed ranting? Felicity had psychosis: she wasn't a reliable witness. Best to stay with the plan, now that there was only this small, crucial hurdle to get past. No one was going to help her. Certainly not Patrick — he couldn't even begin to understand it. And not even Jo Harper, who'd seen the creatures unmask themselves, and still walked away.

The door opened and the twins immediately stopped humming and started pretending to be Morgan and Riley. Doctor Summer stepped cautiously around the two small bodies and sat down opposite Lauren, smiling, placing a clipboard on the side table.

"How are you feeling?" she said, the classic opener for any conversation with a psychiatric patient.

"Fine," said Lauren. Despite the lack of

rest, she felt focused, determined and strong. She smiled faintly at the doctor, hoping to strike the right balance: sane but tired, grateful for all the help but ultimately, better off at home.

"Did you manage to get any sleep?"

"Oh, not really," said Lauren, laughing weakly. "They were up quite a bit. But it's good, to get back in the swing of things. Yesterday and the night before, I had the whole night off — not many new mums can claim that, can they?"

Lauren felt her cheek start to twitch, rubbed at her face to stop it.

Doctor Summer regarded Lauren with interest. "The time limit for the temporary detention order is up very soon. But you know that, don't you?"

"I can't deny it's been on my mind." She swallowed. Careful, now. "Everyone has been so kind, and the support has been excellent but I sort of feel guilty, now that I'm better. There must be people who need the bed much more than I do."

The doctor nodded, and then she said, "Your case has been a very unusual one, Lauren. I've not come across anything like it before."

Lauren raised her eyebrows. "Oh?"

"When you came in, I thought you were

definitely suffering from puerperal psychosis. When I see a patient with the level of paranoia you initially presented, we usually expect to keep them for a while. It takes weeks to recover from a crisis like that, in normal circumstances. But here you are, apparently better, in less than three days."

"I do feel well. I'm glad you think so too."

The doctor frowned. She lifted her pen and looked as if she was about to sign the paper in front of her, but then she lowered it again. Was that the release form?

"What do you think happened, the day you were brought in?"

This was a test; she must answer correctly in order to pass. She took a controlled breath before she began. "I believe I was in a sort of waking dream," said Lauren. "I don't know much about shock or anything, but the idea that the boys had been changed seemed to come upon me, I'm not sure why. When they were returned after they were taken I looked at them and my eyes saw something else. I was definitely hallucinating. But then, it went away. Very quickly I started feeling normal again."

The creatures had forgotten themselves, and were watching her, listening to her attempt to lie her way to freedom. She glanced at them and the one on the right, who

439

looked like Morgan in his yellow vest but who she knew was really named Selver, squeaked and struggled, baby-like, to fit his fist in his mouth. His arm hit out at the other one, the one she now knew was called Bishop, and he started to cry, an absurd facsimile of a baby's cry. She picked him up, cuddling him close as her skin crawled, as the doctor watched. She laid him on her knees and tickled his tummy, and the thing smiled at her with only his mouth, making a poor imitation of a giggle.

"May I?" asked the doctor, indicating the baby in yellow on the rug.

"Of course," said Lauren, smiling pleasantly, ensuring she made her eyes smile, too.

Reaching for the baby, not looking at Lauren, the doctor threw out another loaded question disguised as idle conversation. "I'm curious," she said, "on the day you were brought in, you say that you quickly realised the babies weren't changelings, and were in fact your children. But later you also reacted badly to seeing the babies when your husband brought them to your room. Do you remember?"

"Yes," said Lauren, still regretting her inability to control herself at that crucial early stage.

"So perhaps you still thought, at that

point, that they'd been switched?"

"I don't know. Perhaps. But it was over very quickly. And since then, I've been absolutely fine." Haven't I been fine? she thought. Won't you just admit that I have, so we can get this over with and I can go home?

The doctor sat heavily back in the chair, the baby in her hands, dangling there. It had gone stiff again; she could stand it up on her tendeniered knees. "Nurse Pauline gave you a glowing report," said Doctor Summer, grunting with the effort of trying to make the creature sit. The thing was board-stiff, unyielding. "Even on that night, she said you made excellent progress."

"She did?" Lauren managed to sound surprised, even though she'd dictated the notes herself, forcing Pauline to add bad grammar, just like the notes she'd flushed, to make it seem authentic.

"She said you very soon recovered, and within an hour were able and willing to feed the boys yourself."

"Yes, that's right. I think the stroller had a lot of negative associations for me. I reacted badly when I saw it because it reminded me of the abduction. The fear of losing them again overwhelmed me."

"That's completely understandable, in

441

your position."

"I'm still so grateful they were returned so soon," said Lauren, her eyes spilling tears as she thought of her lost boys, the terrible possibility that they were forever lost, and that after these two aberrations had gone back she would have nothing at all.

No. Don't think like that. There's hope, she thought, if I can just get to the water.

Lauren watched the doctor struggle to cradle the baby in her arms. Soon she was forced to place it back on the floor, where it seemed happier and began to behave like a baby again. Lauren put the one in green back down, too. Bishop and Selver were not like Morgan and Riley in any way, apart from their appearance; they hated being held and couldn't tolerate it for very long at all. Morgan and Riley, in contrast, were the cuddliest babies in the world. Her arms ached for them. When all this was put right, when she found them and switched them back, she silently promised she would hold her boys in her arms and never let them go.

The doctor put her pen and clipboard on one side.

"I spoke to the Senior Investigating Officer on your case today. He said there have been some developments."

"Oh?"

"He said that due to a lack of evidence they've decided to drop the case."

"What does that mean? They don't think that woman Natasha did it, after all? I did tell them that it wasn't her, that they needed to keep looking."

"They say they're no longer looking for anyone else in relation to the abduction."

Lauren stared. She couldn't work out what was being implied. But then, suddenly she could. "Oh, they don't think I did it myself? Is that what they're saying? That's not even possible, I was asleep. How could it have been me? I was asleep, on a bench, and someone took my children. I know I have to take some of the blame, but —"

"When deciding on the best care plan, I have to take many things into account. Sometimes, with puerperal psychosis, it's difficult to tell precisely when it's medically safe to discharge. Sometimes, symptoms can be masked temporarily, only to return very rapidly, and indeed much more acutely."

Why has she put the pen down —

"I'm afraid what I'm about to tell you might be disappointing . . ."

No —

"We won't be letting you go home tomorrow . . ."

"NO!"

"I have applied for detention under Section —"

"YOU HAVE TO LET ME GO!"

The doctor reached for the emergency button. A few seconds later, two security guards entered and relieved Doctor Summer, who in the process of restraining Lauren from throwing herself at the window, had bruised a finger quite badly.

The guards placed Lauren back in the chair just as Nurse Pauline entered with a cup of medication.

"There's no danger to the boys," said Doctor Summer. "She's just had a bit of a shock, that's all. Haven't you, dear?"

No one but Lauren saw the twins watching the drama, motionless and focused, unnatural. No one but Lauren saw their quiet smiles, the sadness they held.

"I'm sorry," said Lauren, relaxing her muscles completely. "I'm fine now. I'm fine." The guards released their firm grip slightly but they didn't let her go. The twins were taken away to the nursery.

Lauren took the pills into her mouth and allowed herself to be led back to her room. As the nurse fumbled with the keys, Lauren coughed discreetly and transferred the unswallowed drugs to her palm.

Later, she thought she might die of de-

444

spair. But then, sitting in front of mindless TV, side by side with Nurse Pauline, the plan appeared in her mind like a gift, fully formed.

445

CHAPTER THIRTY-SEVEN

Harper dreamed of crushed eggshells in a cup, and awoke with a gritty taste in her mouth.

She dressed and drove to the swimming pool where she powered out forty lengths, running the last conversation she'd had with Amy over and again, searching for clues. After she'd left the nursing home the previous night she'd texted, as requested, and then called even though she'd been told not to, but there was no response to either. Who was Amy meeting? Why wasn't she interested in what Victoria had said? Unable to discuss it with anyone, the encounter had churned all night in Harper's mind. Now, she wasn't sure if she'd tell Amy about it even if she asked.

It was impossible to make sense of what Victoria had said. The woman seemed to be confusing what had actually happened to her and something from a story in a chil-

446

dren's book. Nevertheless there was still that maddening phrase, which Victoria had known and the person had said on tape to Lauren in the hospital: *their names are Bishop and Selver.* The perpetrator said the same thing to both women, in identical crimes. They had to be linked. Maybe it would be worth trawling the electoral roll for people with those names, like Amy had suggested. If Bishop and Selver were indeed actual people who had been babies in 1976, then they'd be in their forties now. Could be a lead.

Maybe, she thought grimly, it would be worth trawling the death-certificate records for baby twins with those names. The desire to take other people's babies could have been the action of a mother driven mad with grief. And that would explain why the perpetrator might be using that same phrase: *remember their names.* But why the forty-year gap between offences? Something must have triggered a second attempt at the crime. She had to look for more similarities, the links that might not be immediately obvious. It was the weather that had led to Amy discovering Victoria Settle's story. But why would the heatwave have any relevance?

Harper pulled herself from the pool in one graceful movement. The water puddled at her feet as she removed her goggles. She remembered Victoria's voice, then. *She needs to put them in the water. Right under the water.* Harper shook the drops from her face and went to get changed.

Retrieving her bag from the locker, she couldn't help but check her phone, again, and there was nothing from Amy, of course there was not.

Harper drove up to the Tranters' house, stood on the doorstep and knocked. The door swung open and Patrick stood there, sleep-ruffled and beautiful, his face wary.

She spoke first. "Mr Tranter."

"Detective Sergeant."

"I've brought your phone back."

"Oh."

He held out his hand for the plastic-bagged device.

"The police have ceased investigations on the case; I don't know if anyone has been in touch . . ."

He nodded. "Your boss called me. He said it was on the cards. He implied that you thought there was no one else involved, that it was all Lauren."

"That's the official line. Are you OK?"

He nodded. "I didn't want to think that it was her, but in a way it's a relief."

448

"It's not her fault. You know that, don't you?"

"Of course. She never meant to hurt them, but she's ill. That's why you're not pressing charges against her for attempting to . . . I don't know. Whatever it was she tried to do."

Harper left a pause, looked at her feet for a few moments. "I want you to know, off the record, that I don't agree with my boss, entirely. I've got some evidence that he doesn't believe is significant, but I do. I still think it's possible there was someone else involved. You see, it's happened before, a long time ago, and I think the two cases might be linked."

When she met his eyes, she was surprised to see that he looked angry. "Why can't you just leave it alone?"

"Mr Tranter, I —"

"Look. Natasha was a mistake. A small, insignificant mistake that anyone might have made. It was over before it began. Now I'll probably have to explain it to Lauren, and she'll think the worst, obviously. As if that's not enough, here you are insisting that her paranoia is real. Do you think that's going to help her?"

"I'm sorry, I'm just trying to find the person who did this."

"It was obvious from the start that it was my wife. Anyone could see that, looking at her medical history, and what happened just after the boys were born."

"What medical history?"

"She's been medicated, in the past, for depression. When her mother died she went into a slump for a while. Apart from her father, who she's never been close to, and a grandmother in Scotland, I'm the only person she has left in the world. So it's important that she trusts me, especially when she's unwell. Those hallucinations she had in the hospital, she was confusing dreams with reality. Then you come along and start taking her at her word — well, it only made her think that her delusion was real when really, she should have been accepting that it was not, and concentrating on getting better."

Harper was confused. "Why are you so angry? Is it because your affair was almost revealed to your wife? Because, not that it's any of my business, I was careful to make sure it wasn't."

"It wasn't an affair, I told you, it was a . . . friendship gone wrong. The girl got the wrong idea. She's got all these issues that I didn't know about, that I couldn't deal with then and that I certainly do not want to have to deal with now. It's complicated, and I don't want to have to try to explain that to Lauren while she is in the midst of a psychotic breakdown. Surely you can understand that?"

"Look, it's up to you what you tell your wife, I —"

Harper looked down and drew in a shocked breath. There, inside the house to the side of the doorway were a pair of green high heels that she'd seen before, many times. She thought, no, of course not, that's ridiculous, but then she inhaled a trace of a familiar scent and she couldn't prevent herself; she pushed Patrick out of the way and went into the house.

"Hey, what do you think you're doing?"

Two steps inside and there was Amy, perching in the kitchen, her bare feet wrapped like vines around one leg of the high stool, her hands encircling a coffee mug. No lipstick. Damp hair scraped into a high bun.

"Hello, Joanna," said Amy, a languid smile developing. "What on earth are you doing here?"

Harper couldn't speak. She shut her eyes, hoping to dispel the image but no, it was all too real. She shook her head and went back out of the door, avoiding looking at Patrick,

451

slamming the Tranters' front door after she went through it and breaking into a run when she hit the pavement.

Back in the car, Harper rubbed at her temples and tried to forget she'd ever thought about Amy in any way other than professionally. The humiliation burned. She'd got it wrong, misread the situation, made herself look a fool. Amy was the flirty journalist she'd always been, but it was a shock to discover that she would go to such lengths for a story. She must have slept there. While the wife and children were locked safely away. She probably did this sort of thing all the time, made people think she was interested in them, when really it was all about the copy. That's why she's stringing me along, too, she thought, because I'm a bloody good source. And I fell for it.

Stupid to have let her guard down. To have let her professionalism be compromised. All those things she'd told her, that she thought were in confidence. Amy was probably planning to publish all of it. *Stupid, stupid, stupid.*

CHAPTER THIRTY-EIGHT

Dinner arrived, brown and glutinous, with the standard revolting dessert. Nurse Pauline didn't need to be persuaded to slurp it all up, too quick to notice that the gritty powder added to the top was not all sugar: it also contained Lauren's combined allocation of meds from the past four doses. Pauline placed the bowl back on the tray with a long *mmmmm*.

So far, so good. The next part of the plan was trickier: Lauren knew she had only about twenty minutes before the drugs started to work. She was afraid that because of her outburst with the doctor, she wouldn't be allowed her usual supervised stroll in the grounds with the boys.

Thankfully, the routine of the post-dinner walk outdoors was considered too therapeutically important to miss. Pauline led the way, unlocking doors to the nursery, watching as Lauren strapped the babies into a double stroller. By the time they got outside, the nurse was slurring her words. They set off in a direction that led them away from the other patients walking the grounds, and towards the gate.

"Why are we going this way?" said Pauline, her eyes starting to droop shut and her gait weaving from left to right, like a drunkard.

"You said we should, remember?" said Lauren.

"I did?"

"That's right." She pulled the nurse with one arm, pushed the stroller with her other. Hopefully it looked to any onlookers as if they'd linked arms in a friendly way, that perhaps they were having a heart-to-heart.

After a few more shaky steps, Pauline stopped. She wiped the back of her hand across her brow. "I need to sit down," she said, and collapsed at the foot of a tree. Lauren managed to shove her behind the trunk as she went down, so that once she was on the ground the parts that stuck out were partially obscured by some flowers. But Lauren knew that she couldn't hesitate; it wouldn't take long for someone on the staff to see that she was out here alone.

She walked quickly towards the gate without looking back, pushing the babies in front of her. Halfway there she slowed, not sure how to proceed: the gate was shut, and wouldn't be opened unless and until a car tried to get in from the other side.

Frantic, she scanned the wall and the high chain-link fence, knowing it was impossible to climb, even without two babies to carry. But the shrubs on either side of the shut gate held a possible answer. She picked up the pace again, praying she wouldn't be seen in the moments before she was able to conceal herself and the stroller against the wall. She had to be quick; there was only a small window of opportunity.

In the pushchair, Selver and Bishop were gleeful. They wanted her to succeed, too. The three of them had a common purpose, and this knowledge caused the revulsion she felt for the pair to lessen slightly. The imposters had almost as much to lose as she did: if she was caught, they'd never get back to their home, to their strange river-mother. Lauren, this psychiatric patient whom the authorities thought mad enough to incarcerate indefinitely, was the only person in the world who could help them. If she was caught, she wouldn't be treated in a mental hospital, either, she'd more likely be sent to prison. But, much worse than that: if anyone stopped her, she might never see her real babies again.

She reached the bushes and found a place to hide, gathering the babies in her arms and pushing the stroller further under the branches; she needed to be able to run without being held back by that unwieldy trolley. Holding them was a grim necessity that none of them were entirely happy about. The stiff little bodies relaxed against her a little, but the movement was self-conscious. She tried not to meet their gaze.

Before too long, there was the sound of a car's engine slowing and stopping on the other side of the gate, the beep of the intercom, a metallic voice asking for identification. The driver made a cheery response to the receptionist that Lauren couldn't quite make out. She held her breath in the short pause that followed, praying that whoever it was had official business, that their ID was all in order and that they would be let through. Then, there was a crunching of gears and a high electric whine as the gate drew slowly back. Lauren let her breath out carefully in a long stream, flattened herself against the wall and hoped the driver wouldn't turn their head in her direction. They didn't. After the car drove by into the grounds, there was easily enough time to

slip through unseen before the gate clanged
shut again.

CHAPTER THIRTY-NINE

Harper's phone started to ring, and she prayed it wasn't Amy, calling to apologise or explain. She had no wish to hear any kind of explanation, not that she was owed one. Harper was so cross that she almost didn't look at the screen, but when she did she felt a little stab of disappointment. It wasn't Amy, whom she was hoping to enjoy ignoring. It was Thrupp.

"What is it, sir?"

"Your girl, Lauren Tranter. She's abducted her babies. She's missing. I'm on the way to the unit now but she's got a head start on us."

"She's escaped from the secure unit? How on earth —"

"Apparently, she drugged a nurse. She was hoarding her medication. They don't know how much of this tranquilliser the woman was spiked with, but she's out cold. Maybe a few days' worth."

458

Harper swallowed hard. The spilled tea, the medication not taken but disposed of. Lauren must have saved some of the capsules up, then used them to drug the nurse. She should have said something. But how could she have known that Lauren was planning something like this? Avoiding your meds was one thing. Hoarding them to be used against someone else was quite another.

"When did it happen, sir?"

"About thirty minutes ago."

"Surely she can't have gone far? She won't be moving very fast with a stroller in tow. We should start small, search the unit first."

"No stroller," said Thrupp. "They found the pushchair abandoned in a bush. She must be carrying the babies in her arms."

"She'll have to rest, then. To put them down. Is she definitely on foot?"

"As far as we know. She had no phone, no way of arranging to be picked up in a vehicle. I've authorised a helicopter. They should be operational within the hour. What's she thinking, Jo?"

"I don't know, sir. How should I know?" But she did know, at least the essence of it; the desperation, the protective instinct that would be driving her on, twisted though it might be.

"Well, you saw her a couple of days ago, didn't you? What was she like? Would she harm the babies, in your opinion?"

"I don't think so."

"OK. Maybe she's not planning anything sinister. Let's hope."

"She might simply be hiding somewhere nearby. Should I head for the unit, to help the search?"

"Yes, do that. I think you're right, we should go through the building and the grounds thoroughly before widening the search area."

"You should put the helicopter on standby until we've completed. No point wasting resources if we think we might find her in a cupboard or something."

"Good point." Thrupp sounded very approving of her cost-saving suggestion. "One more thing. I can't get hold of the husband — could you try him? I've left messages on his landline."

"I'm at the Tranters' now, actually, returning his mobile phone. I think I know why he hasn't picked up his landline messages. I'll make sure he does. And I'll meet you at the unit as soon as possible."

Harper typed one last message to Amy before she started the engine: *Tell your boyfriend to listen to his messages.*

She'd been driving for only a few minutes when her phone rang again. She hoped it was Thrupp, calling to say they'd found Lauren and the babies safe and well.

It was Gideon. She put him on speakerphone and continued to drive.

"What is it?"

"I did the analysis you asked for, on the phone call. I thought you'd like to know the results."

She'd forgotten all about it. Yesterday she'd asked Gideon if he could compare the voices on the 999 call, to see if the intruder's voice matched with a sample of Natasha's that she'd retrieved from Patrick's phone. It didn't seem to matter now.

"Thanks, but we've had to drop that line of enquiry. I'll still pay you for your time, of course."

"I still think you'll be interested."

"Oh?"

"Firstly, there was no match with the suspect, the sample voice you provided."

"Ah. Well, I would have been surprised if there was, at this point. I think we're looking for someone older, maybe in their sixties . . ."

"In fact," said Gideon, "there were only two distinct voice patterns on the whole recording."

461

"Two?" said Harper. "What do you mean? There's the operator, Lauren Tranter, and the suspect. That's three."

"Definitely only two," said Gideon. "I checked again and again. There was one unique vocal pattern for the operator, and the only other one was . . ."

". . . Lauren Tranter." She remembered then, her first fleeting thought about the hissing threats, that it sounded like someone putting on a voice. It was Lauren's voice, hissing the threats, to herself.

"Are you still there?" said Gideon.

She thanked him and ended the call.

For a while her mind wouldn't focus and she concentrated on the road. The car climbed the next hill, into the woods, and then slowed as she rounded a bend and the valley was revealed. Scorched by the sun, the late-summer landscape seemed prematurely autumnal. Burnt yellow and brown heather across the flats, huge majestic rocks of grey. The land fell away behind a wall made of newly cut stone, car-sized patches of different colours along its length, evidence that it had been rebuilt one too many times. Harper thought, imagine if I hadn't slowed down enough. Imagine driving the car off the edge. The way the road swerved, it would be all too easy on a dark night, to

462

lose concentration, to tip over here, into oblivion.

At once it was like someone flipping tarot cards in a row, revealing the truth:

The wounds on Lauren's arms, that the doctor had said she'd done to herself.

The sightings of the woman, whom no one but Lauren could see.

The missing babies, found by Natasha in the mill wheel tower in the woods, and no one else seen with them except the mother.

Even the glitch trails on the CCTV: the bare foot. Of course the nurse wouldn't have flinched, if it was a patient who had wandered by in the middle of the night. And now, the analysis of the 999 call had revealed that Lauren had been alone on the ward all along.

Finally Harper forced herself to consider that what everyone else was saying might be true: that Lauren had done it all herself. Whether she knew it or not.

When Harper had spoken to Lauren about the woman who took the babies, she'd talked about her being from the water. She'd said that the woman had taken them into the water, and changed them. Harper realised that Lauren didn't mean that they'd been altered, or baptised in some way. She meant it literally: she thought the boys were changelings.

She's from the water, that woman. Where the two rivers meet. Just like these two.

What if Lauren also thought she knew what Victoria did, about the solution.

She'll have to put them in the water, if she wants her own back. Right under the water.

Harper pulled the car to the side of the road and dialled Thrupp. There was still time. There had to be.

"Sir, I've had a rethink. I don't think we're going to find her at the unit."

"No?"

"No. There's something she said to me, that I've only just remembered. She'll be heading for the place where the two rivers meet. The Bishop and the Selver."

"Where's that?"

"The only place it can be is at the reservoir. That's where we'll find her, the New Riverby."

"The reservoir? Can't you pin it down any more than that? The bloody thing is miles wide. I'm at the unit now, and there are two routes to the reservoir, to opposite sides. If we go to the wrong one it can take up to ten minutes to get to the other on those tiny roads."

"Sorry sir, that's all I know. We'll have to split personnel to different search areas. And

464

forget what I said about putting the 'copter on standby. I think we'll need it as soon as possible."

"Oh really. Anything else?"

"Yes. I'll have Patrick picked up, and get him sent to the east side. If she's there, maybe he can be a good influence. I'll head west to the viaduct, so we've got two sides covered at least, with someone that she trusts. It's closer from here to the east side, so the husband's ETA will be about the same as mine to the west if we get him blue-lighted. Also, let's notify the dive team, though I pray we won't need them: I think we need to consider the possibility that she might intend to drown those babies."

CHAPTER FORTY

Long deep cracks had formed in the mud
at the edge of the lake, green algae stretched
across the gaps in places, dried-out clumps
of weed poking through, dead-looking.
Perhaps the rain, when it came, would
rejuvenate the plants after the long, dry
summer; or perhaps it was already too late.
Lauren looked out across the still water and
for a moment there was peace. She took a
breath, a lungful of the warm fresh air, a
short respite before the next part. Her arms
were burning inside and out, from the sun,
from carrying the boys all this way. It had
to be more than an hour since she'd ducked
out of the gate with them. The babies
hummed and chewed their fists, looking
across to each other, and up at her with
something like anticipation. As she approached the reservoir they started wriggling, the humming sound getting louder.
They knew where they were, how close they

466

were to the end of all this madness. This realisation gave her strength. But the doubts were still there, and growing. She'd been so sure that this was the right thing to do, that she'd ignored a small voice within her that told her she was wrong. What if the voice was her sanity, trying to talk sense to her? What was it the nurse had said? *The ones who deny it the loudest are the most insane, in my experience.*

The small doubting voice spoke to her now. *Look at the babies,* it said, *they're your boys. They're not changelings; it's just your mind playing tricks. Think about it. If you put them under the water, they will drown.*

She heard the helicopter before she saw it, a faint disturbance in the air that became an oppressive pressure in her ears as it drew closer. The arrival of the police didn't come as a surprise, as she knew that once they realised she'd escaped they would be searching. She resented the helicopter for pushing her on, for reminding her that the authorities were doing everything they could to stop her. The creatures gazed up at her, and she did her best to dismiss the doubting voice. They looked a lot like her boys, sure, but they didn't behave like Morgan and Riley. Besides, she'd come too far to stop now, to consider fully whether she was, in fact, as mad as the doctors seemed to think. There was little time and absolutely no choice.

Across the water there were figures on the viaduct, waving their arms. They'd seen her, and the people in the helicopter would soon if they hadn't already, but for those on the ground it wouldn't be a simple thing to locate her. She was well hidden, in a small cove that could only be accessed by wading through brambles and stingers, scrambling over uneven ground. She'd twisted an ankle, stubbed her toe, gone on regardless. Her legs were torn to shreds, and she'd lost a shoe. She kicked the other off and it landed toe-down, sticking out of a crack in the mud.

She still had time, but only if she hurried. Bishop and Selver didn't seem concerned, only eager. *Go,* they seemed to say, *now.* They had led her to this place, working together like divining rods, and all she had to do was complete the last part. Under the water, they would see their mother again, and Morgan and Riley would be returned to her. If she could bear it. If she believed it. And yet, the doubts persisted.

The search teams were drawing closer. Given time, she knew that the officers on the ground would eventually find her, maybe arrest her. She heard a shout from someone searching, the crackle of police radios not too far away in the woodland on her side of the bank. Meanwhile the helicopter hung overhead, pressing down with relentless noise and thudding blades. They started bellowing at her through a loudspeaker, to wait, to stay where she was. She stepped forward into the water and the helicopter seemed to retreat, circling back and away. She heard her name, then. It was Patrick. From somewhere close by he begged her to wait. He sounded desperate. She stepped back from the water, her legs gave way underneath her and she sat down hard onto a ledge of dried mud. Perhaps she couldn't do it, perhaps she ought not to, perhaps she was wrong after all.

In her arms the creatures started to sing, and the doubts receded. Then those doubts were replaced with certainty as a third voice joined in, rich and low. It was her, the woman, from under the water. The time was here. She scanned the water for signs, for the exact place she ought to enter, but the surface of the reservoir was opaque with ripples from the helicopter, a broken mirror.

There was no time for further hesitation. Lifting the creatures in the perfect shape of

469

her sons, Lauren stood and walked into the water.

CHAPTER FORTY-ONE

Harper left her car and sprinted past the roadblock to the top of the great brick arches, the structure of the viaduct spanning the width of the valley. Spotting Thrupp, she pushed through to the front of the helpless collection of officers standing near the railing.

"There," he said, pointing across the valley. The reservoir was a kilometre wide, the bridge on which they stood, about halfway across it. Directly opposite them at the furthest point, Lauren Tranter could be seen, ankle deep in the water, looking down. To Harper she looked almost childlike in that moment, her shoulders hunched against the noise from the helicopter hovering above them. Harper shouted above the din, pointing up, "Can't you get them to pull back? It's frightening her."

Thrupp nodded and spoke into his radio briefly. The craft flew over their heads, back

471

towards the city, not leaving entirely but holding position in a big circle as if trying to land. They wouldn't find anywhere near — everything in the valley was either reservoir or densely wooded slopes.

After the helicopter had retreated, Lauren stepped back from the edge of the water and seemed to collapse to a sitting position.

"She's not going in. Thank goodness," said Thrupp, and breathed out heavily. One of the uniformed officers clapped Harper on the shoulder but she shook the hand away, concentrating on Lauren, who was staring out at the water, still clutching the two bundles. Thrupp handed her a pair of binoculars. Through them she could see the waving arms of the infants, and Lauren's unreadable face. There was no way of telling what she might do next, and until an officer reached Lauren on the shore, the babies were still in danger. Harper calculated the distance across. She could swim that in six minutes, if she had to. She'd done it in training, but not from this side of the reservoir, where the water had dropped so low that yellow Danger signs, usually flush with the surface, stuck out on the ends of their long poles.

Thrupp raised his radio to listen to a transmission. "The ground team have got eyes on her," he said, "but they can't see a way through. It's dense brambles all the way up that part of the valley."

"Where's Patrick?" said Harper, trying not to spit the name out.

"He went round the other way. He's already over there with the search team."

"I'll go, too." She started to move towards the car, but Thrupp called her back.

"Don't bother, it's a ten-minute drive, at the very least. Listen, Jo —"

But Harper cut him off by thrusting the binoculars back at him. She kicked off her shoes and climbed to the top of the railing.

"Hey, what are you doing?" he said, before he swung round and saw what she'd already seen — Lauren Tranter was no longer sitting on the far shore. She had stood up and was walking towards the water.

Thrupp held Harper's upper arm and said, "Don't even think about it," but she shoved him out of the way and dived off the high wall, bracing herself because the water was low and she had no idea how deep it might be, or what obstacles she might encounter. The church tower could be plainly seen, but there could have been other buildings under there for all she knew, or unrecovered vehicles that had fallen in, or high levels of silt in which she might become stuck. As she dived she caught sight of a sign sticking out of the water on her right, black lettering on a yellow background: *Danger of death: do not jump from the bridge.*

Half-expecting to hit something, she entered the water cleanly and was relieved to encounter only a few streaming weeds which caught on her head and arms. The arc of the dive took her under and up again to the surface, where without losing pace she began a front-crawl sprint towards Lauren.

Every third stroke she breathed and checked where Lauren was, whether there was anyone on the shore, ready to stop her. Every third stroke, Lauren was further into the water, and alone. The distance between them closed agonisingly slowly.

More than halfway across the reservoir, she couldn't hear Thrupp shouting at her anymore because the approaching helicopter had drowned him out. The noise became deafening and she realised it was hovering over her, dipping dangerously low, the pressure from the blades slowing her progress, pushing her under. A rope ladder dropped down in front of her and she swam right past it, but they followed. Glancing towards the shore, she saw that Lauren was waist-deep now.

"Get on the ladder," commanded the loudspeaker.

"No," she shouted, though there was no way they would hear her. "Get back. Get away. I'm fine." She gestured with jabbing hands. When they finally got the message and it lifted, she started out again, but her arms were beginning to tire.

Up ahead, only Lauren's head was visible. The babies were under.

"No, Lauren, don't," she shouted, but then she couldn't see her anymore, only ripples where she'd gone down and disappeared, concentric circles gradually growing and fading away.

Time itself seemed to slow as she made the last few strokes to reach the point where she'd seen Lauren disappear. Taking a deep breath, she dived down and searched with her hands, pulling up clumps of mud and slimy matter that felt like old rotting fabric, disintegrating as she swiped at it. Opening her eyes under the water didn't help — all she could see was the silt she had dislodged, that had turned the water into clouds of murky brown. No sign of Lauren, or the babies. Soon she started to run out of oxygen; her lungs began to burn and her ears were pulsating painfully. With no choice but to surface for air, she swam up, stuck her head above the water and breathed hard. There on the shore was the dark figure of a uniformed officer.

"Sarge," he shouted, "don't put yourself in danger. You don't know what's under there."

Harper drew a deep breath and dived again. I know what's under here, she thought. One woman and two little babies. And they only have a few minutes.

Her hands met rocks, and soft mud. Her feet became entangled in something, but she shook them free. Beyond the dullness that filled her ears she heard someone, probably the young officer on the shore, shouting her name, but it seemed very far away. Much closer, she heard a musical sound, thin and high, like singing but not quite like any singing she had ever heard before; somewhere between a cello and a whale song. Soft but getting louder, the music entered her and she relaxed into it. It was so beautiful. For a moment she forgot about the pain in her lungs. She wanted to stay there, to listen to that song for a few minutes more. Stars appeared in her vision, and distantly she knew that this was not the sparkling display of ethereal lights that she took it for, that it actually signalled oxygen deprivation and imminent unconsciousness, and even though she knew that, she didn't mind. What am I here for? she thought, before she remembered with a small jolt. I'm here to save lives, that's right.

The urgency she felt before had all but gone. She carried on the search for Lauren and the boys with sweeping, dancing motions. If she found them, then great. But if not, what did it really matter, in the great scheme of things? She floated gently in the dark, enchanted by the sound and the twinkling lights. Just as it all began to dim, as she almost gave herself to the drifting, her hand clasped itself around something bony. A cold, round thing. Then, her fingers found a mouth-sized hole, with the unmistakable feel of the surface of human teeth on the pad of her thumb as she grasped it.

Suddenly, her other arm was pulled violently upwards, and the skull slipped from her hand. The dimming stars and the beautiful song were replaced with scaring pain in her chest and eyes as she was pulled out of the lake by two sopping, fully uniformed officers who dumped her onto her knees, where she began vomiting water onto the dried mud at the side of the reservoir.

She'd failed. She'd been distracted and forgotten what she was doing when she needed to find Lauren and the boys. They needed her to save them, to get them out, before it was too late. Thrupp's voice stopped her as she tried to crawl back towards the edge of the water.

"You stupid bloody idiot," said Thrupp. "Why do you never listen to me?"

Harper rested on her side, just for a moment, just to get her breath. The air in her lungs seemed to be made of knives. She tried to answer, but at first she could do nothing but cough. When the spasms in her lungs ceased she croaked out, "How did you get here so quick?"

"I got a lift," said Thrupp, gesturing at the helicopter. "You could have done that, too. There was no need for you to swim. That was what I was trying to tell you."

"I didn't find them," she said. "I need to go back in."

"No, you don't."

"But sir, what about the babies?" Harper could barely see, but she squinted up at Thrupp from her curled position on the ground. She pushed herself to her knees. "They'll drown, if someone doesn't get them out."

"Don't worry, we got them. Look."

Harper looked to where he was pointing. There on the shore, a little further away, was Lauren Tranter, wrapped in a blanket. She was crying, and hugging two small bundles to her. Patrick was there too, crouching next to his wife. He tried to take one of the bundles from her but she shouted *no,* turning away from him. Harper couldn't see what was in the bundles. She couldn't see their faces, whether they moved or breathed.

"Did you get to them in time?" said Harper, steeling herself for the answer. But before Thrupp could respond she heard a baby crying and another one joined in. Tears burst from Harper's eyes and she sank down onto her knees in silent thanks.

The sun was low, the water reflecting the spread of reds and pinks as it set behind the hill. The helicopter had gone away, leaving a kind of peace broken only by Lauren's voice in the shadows, over and over,

"Morgan, Riley, you came back to me, you came back."

CHAPTER FORTY-TWO

The water had never dropped as low as it did that summer, not since the reservoir was built and filled more than a century before. Even the record-breaking drought of 1976 hadn't drained it quite to that extent, though it was close, according to Amy, who'd checked the Met Office data. When the police returned to search the lake for the body that no one but Harper was convinced was under there, they could still see the tip of the old church sticking up above the surface. It was only the second time it had been seen since the water covered it up in 1896, its weathervane, amazingly, still standing almost straight on a sliver of rusty metal. Of all the buildings that survived in the lake, it was the last thing to disappear, the first thing to be revealed.

Harper led the search, and it wasn't long before they pulled the human skull from the water and laid it carefully on black plastic sheeting. She looked at the skull for a long time before she turned and addressed her team of divers in a hushed voice.

"This is a crime scene, people. Let's give it everything we can."

On the first day, they surveyed the vast search area, using a diving camera to photograph everything that lay under the surface of the reservoir, where the drowned village of Selverton once thrived. The images showed mostly piles of rubble, but also several buildings that were untouched, preserved, with furniture floating around as if in a broken snow globe.

Thrupp put the brakes on the investigation when he learned how extensive the search would have to be.

"It's a historic case," he said. "We can't afford to direct resources to it, not when there's so much else happening right now that we need to cover."

Harper remained calm, though she wanted to scream with frustration. "This is a new murder investigation, historic or not," she said. "We should prioritise it for that reason."

"Do you have evidence to prove it was murder, not an accident?"

Harper had to admit that she did not. The body was unidentified, and didn't immediately appear to relate to any missing-persons case they could find in any police archive. Damage to the bones would need to be assessed by a specialist, to determine whether injuries occurred before or after death. Harper felt that she didn't need to wait to read the forensic pathologist's report. She just knew it was a bad death, preventable, and unjust. The bones them-selves seemed angry to her.

"You've got a week," he said, "and that's it. Unless we find something to identify the body, or something that points to foul play."

A week wasn't anywhere near long enough, especially with the scratch team she'd been assigned. She needed someone who would be able to research the history, maybe find some people with connections to Selverton. Amy was the obvious person to ask, but the thought of contacting her again after how they'd left things at Patrick Tranter's house didn't appeal. Harper had already ignored two of the journalist's text messages, and quite liked the feeling of be-ing the one in control. But, the case needed a researcher, and there was no denying that Amy was good at her job. Great, actually. And Harper didn't have a lot of time to play with.

"Leave it with me," she'd said to Thrupp.

"If there's anything to be found, I'll make sure it is." Even if I have to swallow my pride to get it done, she thought. Later she stared at her phone for a long time before she finally called the journalist and laid out what she needed her to do. Amy said yes, of course she would help, and after the call Harper felt OK, surprisingly. They'd both kept things very professional. And she had to admit, despite everything, that it was good to hear Amy's voice again.

Three days later, Harper was standing on the shore when she looked up from examining the objects her divers had recovered to see Amy, tottering across the mud and stones towards her in her heels, clutching a plastic binder filled with papers.

"Where did you find all this?" asked Harper, when they'd spread the findings on the table in the police operations vehicle they were using as a base.

"Easy," said Amy. "There's a museum dedicated to Selverton and the New Riverby reservoir. It's tiny, and it only opens for half a day on a Tuesday. Otherwise I'd have got it sooner."

Tony Fisher, who ran the museum, was the great-great-nephew of the Mr Fisher who had owned the Selverton mill, which was the main employer for the village before it was drowned. The Fishers owned the mill for generations, but when the news came that the valley was to be flooded they shut the business down and moved to Manchester.

"Makes sense," said Harper. "The man's got a business to run."

"True, but the Water Board gave the villagers four years to clear out. He could have kept the mill running for at least some of that time. It ripped the heart right out of Selverton, at the exact time when the families about to be displaced needed more than anything to keep earning for as long as possible. Selverton was a sinking ship, and Fisher was the proverbial rat. Tony says his great-great-uncle wasn't too popular after that."

Amy slid a glossy volume over to Harper. The title of the book was *Diaries of a Mill Owner: The Truth About Selverton Village and the New Riverby Reservoir.* It ran to four hundred and seventy-five pages.

"Did you read the whole of this?" said Harper.

Amy shook her head. "Don't be silly. I just asked Tony if there was any mention of a missing girl, and he led me straight to the relevant parts."

She indicated the first bookmark, and

Harper opened the book and began to read.

Fourteenth of May, 1895.
I hear from Cook at Bishopton Hall that Betty Fairweather, who worked the looms at the Selverton mill with her father (God rest his soul), is missing. No one has seen her these three weeks last. She asks if the girl has been to me, to seek work at the mill, as by all accounts she did not find the Hall an agreeable place to work, though I can't think why. She was more fortunate than many of the Selverton mill girls in finding employment so quickly. I admitted that I hadn't seen her or heard tell of her. I cannot shake a feeling that no good has come to the child.

"Did Fisher try to find her?" said Harper.
Amy shook her head, and opened the pages at another bookmark, a later entry.

Twenty-third of July, 1895.
Today I was visited by Billy Rowles, one of the boys from Selverton village. He asked for work and I was able to oblige. I enquired as to whether he had heard any news of young Betty, since they were at school together. Without a trace of shame he told me a filthy rumour, some nonsense

about Lord Pincher getting her in trouble before she went missing. For that I almost sent him on his way, but at the last minute I thought better of it. The boy was only repeating what he'd overheard in some dirty backroom of a public house. Still, it set my mind at rest about the poor girl's fate. The truth is no doubt far more prosaic: Betty probably got into trouble with a stable boy or some such, then ran away to hide her disgrace. Girls are so wayward these days.

Neither of the women spoke as they took this in. Harper's opinion of Fisher took a sharp nosedive.

"Is there any more?"

"No," said Amy, "that's the last mention of Betty."

"Did you manage to find her in the city records?"

"I did. There's a birth certificate, but no death certificate, which means it's possible that the bones you found belong to her. But I'm afraid the trail stops there. Betty was an only child of two only children."

"So there's no way to compare our skeleton with Betty's relatives, to check for familial DNA."

"Not unless you dig up the parents."

Harper knew that Thrupp wouldn't authorise that. The case had hit a dead end, with nothing to go on but a fourth-hand account of a girl who might or might not have gone missing, more than a hundred years ago. The lack of a death certificate wasn't evidence, either: the fact was that Betty Fairweather could have simply left the area, got married and had a happy life, and her death would have been registered under another name in a different county. Without a budget for serious amounts of expensive research, they would never know. Harper went back to the edge of the reservoir, deflated about her chances of solving the case.

From Amy she'd learned a bit about the history of the reservoir itself. "Drowned village" was an emotive term, but really the village would already have been evacuated, half-derelict when the flooding began. The Water Board dropped the dam gates sometime in 1895, trapping the river Selver, but it took a year to fill. The New Riverby crept higher every day, eventually subsuming the remains of the buildings. What was a post office, now a lakebed. Where once the schoolhouse stood, fish began to make their home. A slow drowning. This woman, trapped and buried in the lake, most probably wasn't killed by the lake itself. She must have been lying dead somewhere in the village before the water rose over her.

Harper approached the black box of remains and took out the skull. Small and delicate, there was a hole at the base which could have been caused by a blow to the head, or as easily by a falling rock at any time in the century it had been under water. She held the skull carefully in her hands, trying to visualise the person to whom it belonged.

The tip of the church caught her eye then, piercing the surface. The only other time that weathervane had been seen since the drowning, another pair of twins had been threatened, those of Victoria Settle. It was almost as if there was something in the lake, that could only get out when the old village was revealed. That something was angry, and it wanted justice. Perhaps it also wanted to be taken care of; to be laid to rest.

"Hello, Betty," said Harper, and immediately she swore she felt something shift in the air, a release of tension. Soon, it began to rain.

That evening, Harper walked into the pub half-expecting to be stood up, but Amy was already there, immaculately dressed in a fifties-style dress with a full skirt and bodice.

"You look nice," said Amy, raising half an eyebrow at the box-fresh creases in the black T-shirt Harper had chosen.

"So do you," said Harper, sitting down and inhaling that floral perfume, telling herself it was too cloying anyway. "Shall I get drinks? I'm buying. I've got to thank you for all your help with the research."

"It's a pleasure," said Amy. "Research is one of my skills. Though I have many." She gave a slow, flirtatious blink that Harper pretended not to see.

"Many skills," said Harper, "hmm. You've certainly got a way with interviewees. From what I saw at Patrick Tranter's house, anyway."

A puzzled expression crossed Amy's face. "I'm not sure what you're thinking, but you've got it completely wrong."

"I don't know, Amy. What could I possibly be thinking, finding you at a man's house looking like you'd just got out of the shower?"

"I had just got out of the shower. The one at the gym, where I'd just come from. Why, what did you think was going on?"

Harper paused, suddenly unsure. But she'd started now.

"Look, it's nothing to do with me, what

489

you need to do to get the job done. Even if sleeping with interviewees is not entirely ethical."

Amy's mouth dropped open. "You're joking, right?"

There was a silence in which both women sipped from their drinks and looked in opposite directions. Harper tried to relax her shoulders; she could feel herself tensing up.

"If you must know," said Amy, "he invited me round, so I thought he might have something useful to tell me about our case. He didn't, though. In the end he just kept trying to sell me a marketing package for my freelance work."

"But why were you still there the next day?"

Amy nearly choked on a mouthful of drink. "The next day? You think I'd been there all night?"

Harper studied Amy's face. She wanted to believe her, so badly.

"But you said you couldn't come with me to the old people's home to see Victoria because you had an interview. I thought — I had a feeling — that you weren't telling the truth. You never answered your phone, or sent me a message. And then the next day, there you were, in his kitchen. It was a complete shock. I just thought —"

"That is *quite* a leap."

Now that she'd said it out loud, it did seem ridiculous to Harper. Amy and Patrick? She just couldn't picture it. She started to feel rather silly.

"Oh, Amy, I'm such an idiot. I don't know what to say . . ."

"He is *so* not my type," said Amy, twirling her straw and licking a grain of salt from her margarita.

"So where were you? The night before, I mean."

Amy dropped her eyes. Harper said, "You don't have to tell me. I'm sorry, I'm being a dick."

Concentrating on her fingers as they picked at the edge of her beer-mat, Amy said, "No, it's fine. You were right, I wasn't seeing an interviewee. I was moving my stuff out of my partner's place. My ex-partner's place."

Harper felt her cheeks glow red-hot, and lifted her glass to her face to cool it.

At the end of the evening, Harper had drawn close to Amy, who had gazed amusedly into her eyes. But at the last second, she'd panicked, swerved, kissed Amy's cheek and practically ran away. She'd completely blown it. No, she wouldn't be calling Amy for a few weeks yet. Not until the sting of the shame of that pathetic encounter had faded. But even so, there was hope there, and a sense of possibility: Amy had sent her a text message afterwards, a red lipstick kiss emoticon, followed by a single *x*.

As the sun set on the final day of evidence gathering, Harper stood on the shore where Lauren had stood a few weeks previously, looking out at the water. Harper had done all she could for this poor dead woman with only her bones surviving. The black box containing the remains was a few metres away, waiting to be taken by the undertakers and laid to rest elsewhere. The case itself would stay open, filed as unsolved until evidence emerged to prove beyond a doubt who this woman was, and how she came to lie in the New Riverby reservoir for all this time, undiscovered. Harper would move on to the next case, but she felt this would be one of those she'd find it hard to forget; partly because it was linked in her mind with that other tragic case, Lauren Tranter's.

During drinks, Amy had asked her about it. "You really had a thing for that case, didn't you?"

Harper nodded mutely.

"Why do you think that was?"

A first date was not the time to bring up heavy subjects, so Harper had made a few vague noises about feeling sorry for Lauren, and the fact that Victoria Settle's case seemed to suggest a link, that it had happened before. Then, knowing she hadn't really answered the question, she'd gone to the bar and bought them both another drink. When she got back to the table, although Amy's journalistic instinct must have been urging her to dig deeper, she'd allowed Harper to move the conversation on. One day, I'll tell you, thought Harper. But perhaps the right occasion would never come. She would leave it, for now, anyway. Let Amy think there was some history there, a painful past involving a pregnancy, because that was certainly part of the truth. The rest would come out, in time. She was pretty sure there would be time.

In a way, Harper felt fraudulent in feeling that her baby was lost: she knew exactly where Ruby was. She spoke to her at least twice a month. The story of Harper's lost baby was one of transformation, just like Lauren's. Lauren Tranter had looked at her babies and seen something no one else could. No matter how hard she tried to trick herself not to, every time Harper looked at the person the world insisted was her sister, she saw only her own child.

The divers were about to come in when one of them signalled that he had found something else, buried in the clay. He waded towards the shore, cradling two small bundles in his arms. The bundles were grey with river mud and wrapped in dark rags. Rags, she thought, exactly like those she had found at the riverside when the twins were taken. Exactly like the scraps in the bushes outside Lauren's window.

On the grid Harper had created, showing the exact location of each bone, the diver with the bundles indicated that he had found them in the same square where they had found the mystery woman's pelvis and the lower half of her spine. Harper watched as the pathologist carefully picked up the two small bodies so lovingly wrapped and buried, mummified in the silt, each no bigger than her two cupped hands. She placed them in the box and closed the lid.

CHAPTER FORTY-THREE

A woman, as she heard tell, had a child changed, and one, a poor thing, left in his place, but she was very kind to it, and every morning on getting up she found a small piece of money in her pocket. My informant firmly believes in their existence, and wonders how it is that of late years no such things have been seen.

Hollingworth

October 10th
Twelve Weeks and Five Days Old
3:30 P.M.

The Selver General psychiatric ward was a modern addition, an annexe to a much larger hospital within the city. Ten patients were housed in rooms built on one side of a wide corridor. Opposite the rooms were observation points, desks behind which members of staff could watch several patients at one time. Lauren's room, like the other nine, had a large window taking up the entire top half of the front wall. This window was made of toughened safety glass, and she knew this for certain because, very early in her incarceration, she had pounded on it with her fists repeatedly as hard as she could, and it hadn't even vibrated.

At one end of this corridor was the secure entry system opening onto the rest of the hospital, and at the other was a small dining room which doubled as a visitors' room. The tables were in rows, all of a piece with a bench on either side, and the whole lot screwed to the floor. Patrick and Lauren sat close together on a bench. There were four orderlies stationed around the room, paying close attention to the patients, but she only noticed because Patrick kept glancing anxiously at them. She was used to it now, and most of the time she almost didn't see them.

The room smelled strongly of bleach, and was too hot, as usual. Light through the high windows cast grids on the far walls, shadow cages for the shadow birds that perched there. Some of the other patients had visitors, but not many. Those that did were sitting opposite each other, talking quietly or playing card games. Unvisited souls sat alone, and those patients on Amber or Red lay placidly in bed, or paced behind the glass walls of their rooms, lost in a haze of medication.

At the next table along, a filthy, skeletal old man sat alone playing a game of patience. Every few seconds he forced out a cough.

"Do you mind sharing with males?" said Patrick, in a low voice.

Lauren turned towards him. Her mouth hung open wetly; increased salivation was a side effect of the anti-psychotics she was taking. They also made her bloated, and dopey.

"It's fine," said Lauren, trying not to drawl. "We have our own rooms. We only mix at mealtimes, and that's only the people on Green."

The traffic light system was rather primitive, but it seemed to work. Follow the rules, take your pills, don't throw anything at the glass or bite anyone, you could stay on Green for weeks. Only when on Green could you be considered for release. Lauren, like all patients, started out on Red. It had taken some adjustment of her meds before she was calm enough for Amber, and a lot of hard work and concentration to get on Green, but she'd done it. She'd been on Green now for five weeks. The doctors would shortly be meeting to discuss a visit home.

Lauren's problem, according to the psychiatrist, was that she was very good at appearing outwardly to be mentally well, while maintaining a dysfunctional inner monologue. Her face had remained entirely placid as she'd thought, well, how the fuck would you know the first thing about my inner monologue? The thought that followed was one of hopelessness: If that's what the doctors think, then there's not an awful lot I can do about it, is there?

As if she'd spoken aloud, the psychiatrist had said, "Obviously, the only way we can understand what's happening with you is if you tell us. It's an issue of trust. Trust takes a long time to build, I'm afraid."

Of course, he couldn't say how long. She'd wanted to pound the window again when she returned to her room after that session, but she hadn't. She sat rigidly on the bed, her hands clasped. Eventually an orderly entered the room and took hold of her shoulders, manoeuvred her body into bed and turned off the lights. She lay there in the semi-dark, waiting for the sleeping pills to work.

"Ruthie sends her love," said Patrick. "And Sonny and Daisy, too. They miss you."

"What about the boys?"

"The boys are doing well," he said. "Riley rolled over the other day."

"Did you bring them with you? Are they nearby?" She turned her face to the high window, as if she could sense them somewhere just outside, maybe hear their voices, call to them and have them answer.

"Oh, honey," he said, "no, I didn't. I left them at home with the nanny."

Lauren slumped down on the bench, her chin falling to her chest. Her grey sweatshirt was soon dotted with dark teardrops.

Patrick placed his arms around her as she cried. He smelled of unfamiliar shampoo, and sweet pastry.

"Patrick, I can't stay here any longer," she said. "You have to get me out."

"I want you to come out. I do. We all want you home with us. But there's a court order, you know that. We have to convince them that it's OK now, that you won't . . ."

"What?"

"Well. They're just thinking of the boys. When you come home you'll need help with them, and the nanny says she'll be willing to stay on, at least at first. But at times you'll be left alone."

"They're my babies, Patrick."

"Yes."

"I wouldn't harm them."

"No." The denial sounded too emphatic to be authentic.

"You don't believe me."

At the next table they heard the old man cough three times, four.

"He does that all night long, you know," said Lauren. "I can hear him through the walls." She turned around to look at the man. "Hey, Rod." Rod swivelled his hooded eyes in their direction. "Can you give it a break, please? You don't even *have* a cough."

The man didn't blink. He snaked out a shocking pink tongue at Lauren, opened his mouth and coughed, spittle flecking their table and one foul bubble landing on Patrick's hand, which he wiped with a measure of disgust on his nice clean trousers. They were glared at for a few more pointed seconds, and then the man turned away. After a moment, he coughed, louder than before.

From the door, a nurse pushed a trolley towards them. "Medication." The solidly built green-uniformed man gave a flat stare that wasn't quite directed at either of them.

Lauren was handed a small paper cup that held two yellow capsules, dangerous-looking things. She eyed the nurse, and the paper cup, with a barbed resentment, but she tipped the pills into her mouth, swallowed a slug of water and leaned forward for inspection. The nurse shone a light inside Lauren's open mouth. "Tongue," he said, and Lauren lifted it. Without a word, he clicked the torch off and moved the squeaking trolley in the direction of Rod.

"They let me bring my phone in today," said Patrick. "I took some films for you, of Riley and Morgan."

She clapped her hands together and sat up, illuminated with anticipation, as much as she could be; her movements were slow now, even when she was upbeat. He held out the phone for her to see, but he didn't allow her to take it from him. "They said not to," he explained, in response to her questioning frown.

There was Riley, rolling over from his front, pushing against the floor with great effort until he tipped sideways. He lay on his side, legs curved stiffly backwards preventing him rolling all the way over, eyes and mouth wide with surprise that the world had flipped so suddenly. Soon though, his neck got tired and he lay his heavy head on the carpet, one arm stuck out to the front and the other waving desperately in the air. Behind the camera, Patrick was chuckling, calling his son's name. Then Riley looked up again and his expression had changed, he was crying, he was stuck — why was no one helping him? The film ended.

"Oh, bless him," said Lauren. "Love him."

In the next one there were the two of them, smiling and flapping their arms, each in a different coloured bouncy chair.

"New bouncers?" she said.

"Yes. Look," said Patrick, pointing. "Green for Riley, yellow for Morgan."

Lauren didn't react. That was another side effect of the drugs: her usually nimble mind was slow on the smaller nuances. But then, incredulous, she said, "You don't mean you still can't . . ."

"I'm joking," said Patrick, laughing. "That was a joke. I know they're in the wrong bouncers — the nanny did it. Of course I can tell them apart. They're so different. It's obvious."

She laughed, but it turned into a sob and he caught her before she sank down towards the floor.

"I knew it," she said quietly into his ear. "I keep doubting it. But it's true, it worked. What I did was worth it; those boys are mine, Patrick. My babies."

"Of course they're yours, sweet thing. Of course they are. Mine and yours. They always were."

He meant, *not because of what you did, but in spite of it.* She knew he'd never understand, but it didn't matter if he did or didn't. She knew the truth of what had happened underneath the water, when they were switched back: Bishop and Selver had slithered away, and her arms were immediately filled with her own boys, warm and familiar. When she'd looked fleetingly into the river woman's eyes as the exchange was made and expected to see anger, what she saw was gratitude. In the end, the river woman had wanted the best for her babies, just like Lauren. And in the end the river woman knew she'd been wrong; that the best place for Bishop and Selver was under the water, with their loving mother.

Lauren moved her head to look into Patrick's eyes. "Do you think they'll keep me here much longer?"

He assured her that it wouldn't be much longer. She smiled at him.

One of the stationed orderlies stepped forward. He planted his feet and crossed his arms like a doorman. "Visiting's over now," he said loudly to everyone, and the three other visitors in the room started to make their way to the dining room doors.

Lauren allowed Patrick to kiss her on the

cheek, but held onto his arm as he tried to straighten up. "Did you bring that book I asked for?"

He patted his pockets and pulled out a small, light brown volume. "This it?"

She reached for it, ran her thumb over the faint shadow of the old-fashioned gold lettering.

"Yes."

"Where's it from?"

"It was a gift," said Lauren, inhaling the fragrance from the antique paper. Perhaps she would never know who it was that left the book in Cindy's gift bag. In her heart, she wanted to believe it was somehow arranged by her mother, who knew that what was printed within those dusty pages provided the key to everything that followed. The frightening truth that she had to face, that she had faced, and lived through. And it had saved her babies, if not quite herself. Her mum would have known that that was the only thing that mattered to Lauren.

"I had a flick through," said Patrick. "Some of those stories are pretty gory. You're absolutely sure this is what you want to be reading?"

The orderly appeared, standing very close to them. "Excuse me, you need to leave now." It wasn't exactly threatening, but the tone he used wasn't to be argued with. Patrick took hold of Lauren's hand and squeezed. "I'll see you next week."

He turned and held up a hand in farewell before stepping through the door. When he was out of sight, Lauren's smile soured and her finger-wave curled into a fist. She knew he wouldn't leave the building immediately; first he would slink into the consultation room and pour poison into her Observation Log. The therapeutic regime at the Selver required each visitor to add comments to the log after a visit, under headings that were supposed to function as guides or prompts, but which Lauren thought encouraged exaggeration and misinterpretation. At least, they did in Patrick. Headings included: *Comments by the Patient Indicating Continued Unwanted or Inappropriate Thoughts; Behaviours Deemed to be Out of Character; Signs of Anxiety or Withholding of True Feelings.* She'd seen what he'd put in there, describing her perfectly reasonable responses as emotional outbursts, or her unguarded comments as proof that she was deluded. When she'd first read the Observation Log, two things had occurred to Lauren: firstly, her husband was a traitor and couldn't be trusted; secondly, for him to diligently record such flagrant half-truths, he must have had hidden reasons of his own for wanting to keep her locked up.

One recent entry read:

Lauren is still referring to her paranoid delusions as if they were real. She's very emotional. I wouldn't trust her alone with the babies. Perhaps look at extra medication?

Aware of the psychiatrist's scrutiny while she read, she'd kept her face neutral as her inner monologue let go a stream of swears.

"What are you thinking?" the doctor had said.

I'm thinking, my husband is a liar and a bastard.

She said, with deliberate mildness, "I don't like it. But I suppose I think he has a point."

The doctor smiled and noted something down. Baby steps, she thought.

When all the visitors had checked out of the ward, the patients were escorted back to their glass-walled rooms. Lauren sat on the bed, holding the *Twin Tales* book in her hands. After a while she let it fall open at the beginning of the story that she had turned to so many times, and began to read, her eyes skimming quickly along the words she knew so well. Although it had frightened her when Cindy had first read it to her, now the story was a comfort. She'd done what was required, and her boys were back in the world, where they belonged, even if they weren't yet with her because she was stuck in here, for now. It was the ending she needed to see, to be reassured, to make sure it was exactly as she remembered.

A Brewery of Eggshells (Traditional, Peak District, England)

Once there was a man and his wife who lived together in a hut on the side of a mountain. They had baby twins, both of whom the wife nursed tenderly. One day, while the husband was far away with the flock, the wife was called to the house of a neighbour who was dying. She did not want to leave her two babes, as she had heard tell that faeries were roaming the land. Still, the neighbour was in dire need and so she went.

On the way back she was dismayed to see a pair of old Elves of the Blue Petticoat crossing her path. She ran all the way home but when she got there saw that the twins were still in the cradle, and all was the same as when she had left.

But all was not the same. From that day forward, the twins did not grow at all, and the man and his wife began to suspect that something was wrong.

"These are not our children," said the man.

"Whose children can they be?" asked the wife.

And so arose the great strife. The man and his wife were both very sad for a long time, until the wife decided to seek the help of the wise man, who lived in a cave in the place they called the God's Graveyard a few miles hence.

It was the time of year for reaping, and not long until the oats and rye would be harvested. The wise man, hearing of the woman's woe, told her this: "You must clean out an old hen's egg and boil up some potage in it, then go to the door as if to give it to the reapers for supper. Then, listen for what the babies say."

"But they are too young yet to speak," said the woman.

"If the elves have changed them, they are as old as the hills, and more," said the wise man.

"And what of my own two babes?" she asked.

"If the babies speak, you will know that they are changed. But also that your own are close by, with the elf-mother."

"And if they speak, and they are changed, what am I to do?"

"You must take hold of them both and throw them into the river."

So, on harvest day, the woman cleaned out an eggshell and did as the wise man had said. She cooked up the potage on the fire, saying, "Here is a feast for the reapers, more than enough for ten," and she took it to the door where she stood and listened. Immediately, the twins began to speak. One said to the other:

Stream before a river I knew
A rock before a hill
But how can she cook up an eggshell
    brew
With ten empty stomachs to fill?

Upon hearing this, the woman knew at once that the babes were not her own. She took hold of them and threw them into the river, just as the wise man had told her. Immediately the elves in their blue trousers appeared and jumped into the water to rescue their off-spring, and once they had done so off they scuttled, back to their homes, spitting, and cursing the woman for what she had done.

When the woman returned to the cottage, her own true babes lay in the cradle, and all was well.

Lauren read the final line again and again, tears streaming. She rocked back and forth on the bed, cradling the book, repeating it in a whisper, over and over. "All was well, all was well, all was well."

EPIGRAPH CITATIONS

Chapter 1

James Russell Lowell, *The Poetical Works* (Cambridge: Riverside, 1904), vol. 1 (*The Complete Writings of James Russell Lowell,* vol. 9)

Chapter 3

Yeats, William Butler, *The Wanderings of Oisin, and other poems,* (Paul, Trench & Co, 1889)

Chapter 7

John Greenleaf Whittier, *The Complete Poetical Works,* Cambridge edition (Boston and New York: Houghton Mifflin, 1894)

Chapter 10

W. B Yeats, *Fairy and Folk Tales of Ireland,* (A.L. Burt, 1900)

Chapter 12

Jacob Grimm, Stallybrass (tr.) *Deutsche Mythologie,* 4th ed. (George Bell & Sons, 1877), v. 3

Chapter 15

Oral retelling of Irish folklore

Chapter 16

Keeping Watch Over Children, Wilhelm and Jacob Grimm, *Das Schauen auf die Kinder, Deutsche Sagen,* (1816) no. 89

Chapter 17

A. Kuhn and W. Schwartz, *Norddeutsche Sagen, Märchen und Gebräuche* (Leipzig: F. A. Brockhaus, 1848)

Chapter 30

Oral retelling of Jamaican folklore

Chapter 36

Hartland, Edwin Sidney: *The Science of Fairy Tales: An Enquiry Into Fairy Mythology* (New York: Scribner & Welford, 1891)

Chapter 43

Hollingworth, Rev A. G, *The History of Stowmarket the Ancient County Town of Suffolk,* (1844)

ACKNOWLEDGMENTS

I would like to thank my brilliant agent, Madeleine Milburn, and the talented, dedicated team at the MM agency for all of their hard work and unwavering belief in my writing. To my editors and publishers, Manpreet Grewal and the team at HQ, Jennifer Lambert and all at HarperCollins Canada, Chelsey Emmelhainz and the Crooked Lane team, I thank you for your encouragement, expert editorial advice and enthusiastic championing of the book, without which there would not be a book at all.

Many good people contributed to this journey. Your support, early reading, comments and conversations have helped to improve the novel far more than I could possibly have done alone. Heartfelt thanks to Alison Dunne, Kitty Fordham, Mary Reddaway, Mel Sellors.

To my specialist advisors, Dr Laura Hole

and Rebecca Bradley, my humble thanks. Any mistakes or liberties taken with medical details and police procedure are entirely my own.

To all of my fellow students in the critique workshops on the MA in Creative Writing at Bath Spa 15-16, especially Daisy McNally, Tam Purkess, Emily Goodman, Mike Manson, Jay Millington, Ariel Dantona, Madeleine Streater. Your surprising, intelligent, and occasionally hilarious notes on this book in its very early stages helped to shape it and make it better.

Many thanks also to my inspirational tutors, Samantha Harvey, Fay Weldon, Celia Brayfield, Gerard Woodward, Gavin Cologne-Brookes. Your thoughts and insights were invaluable. Thanks also to Tessa Hadley, for a chance conversation over breakfast that planted the seed.

If you have helped me in writing this novel and I have forgotten you, feel free to curse my name, track me down and force me to give recompense. I'm good for a beer at least.

To Jonathan, who has enabled this entire thing. To Wilfred and Elspeth, who have put up with it stoically. To my mother, who has read every version, and never doubted me for a moment, even when I doubted myself. Thank you, thank you, thank you.

ABOUT THE AUTHOR

Melanie Golding is a graduate of the MA in creative writing program at Bath Spa University, with distinction. She has been employed in many occupations including farm hand, factory worker, childminder and music teacher. Throughout all this, because and in spite of it, there was always the writing. In recent years she has won and been shortlisted in several local and national short story competitions. *Little Darlings* is her first novel, and has been optioned for screen by Free Range Films, the team behind the adaptation of *My Cousin Rachel.*

The employees of Thorndike Press hope you have enjoyed this Large Print book. All our Thorndike, Wheeler, and Kennebec Large Print titles are designed for easy reading, and all our books are made to last. Other Thorndike Press Large Print books are available at your library, through selected bookstores, or directly from us.

For information about titles, please call:
  (800) 223-1244

or visit our website at:
  gale.com/thorndike

To share your comments, please write:
  Publisher
  Thorndike Press
  10 Water St., Suite 310
  Waterville, ME 04901